THE
TRIGGERMAN'S
DANCE

T. JEFFERSON PARKER

THE TRIGGERMAN'S DANCE

NEW YORK

Mys

Library of Congress Cataloging-in-Publication Data

Parker, T. Jefferson
    The triggerman's dance / T. Jefferson Parker.
        p.   cm.
    ISBN 0-7868-6142-8
    I. Title.
    PS3566.A6863T75   1996
    813'.54—dc20   95-50062
                            CIP

FIRST EDITION

10 9 8 7 6 5 4 3 2 1

FOR MARY ANN AND MAE,
SAM AND EMILY,
KATIE AND SUSAN

MAN GROWS WISE AGAINST HIS WILL.

AESCHYLUS

THE
TRIGGERMAN'S
DANCE

CHAPTER
ONE

In the most widely published of all photographs of the aftermath, Rebecca lies beside a raised brick planter, arms gracefully extended, her face to the camera, legs together but relaxed. Her shoes are visible beneath the pastel, rain-punished petals of the Iceland poppies that had bloomed two weeks earlier. Above her droops a eucalyptus tree with a thick white trunk and branches heavy with leaves that curve like scimitars. Rebecca seems to be leaning the small of her back against the bricks. There, her waist opens skyward and her torso makes a feminine turn that allows her shoulders to lie flat upon the asphalt while her face confronts the photographer and her arms rest above her head. Her left hand, cupped yet not quite closed, appears to be catching rain. She wears no ring. She is still wrapped in the raincoat she had worn into the gathering storm; a hat is still atop her head. In the photograph, her blond hair spills from beneath the hat and blends in wet waves with the pavement.

The picture was taken just moments after the incident, by a *Journal* staffer who had been in the darkroom pouring solution. A photo editor barged in and told him something had just "gone down" in the parking lot. As would any professional, the photographer grabbed his camera and ran from the eternal red twilight of the lab in search of a shot that might make his reputation.

This was his lucky day. Print 1B26 on the proof sheet turned out to be the best of his or anyone else's pictures. It appeared not only in the *Orange County Journal*, where Rebecca Harris was serving an internship, but also in papers across the globe—New York, London, Tokyo, Sidney, and many thousands of journals in between. It is one of those shots that just flat-out has it all: a worthy subject, perfect lighting and composition, and the loaded visual hush common to many great news photographs.

Adding to its greatness are the background characters. These are the five unnamed employees of the *Journal* who were the first to arrive and comprehend what had happened. These onlookers form a not-quite focused chorus beside the planter, and are caught in postures that might well have been arranged by Titian. A woman sobs into one hand while with the other she tries to cover her head from the downpour. Another runs back toward the *Journal* lobby but is caught mid-stride, as if she wants nothing more in the world than to escape from this image. A uniformed security guard speaks into a belt radio, his jaw histrionically agape. The center of the five, a young man in a long leather coat and a fedora, steps through the rain toward Rebecca, his expression indecipherable but the squared shoulders and alert angle of his head suggest that something can and will be done to correct this . . . mistake. The young man seems to speak for the millions of people who later saw the photograph. He is hope itself, deluded as he was. Of course, in the minds of some foreign observers his action was just one more example of the sadly skewed American concept that, with good intentions, anything can be fixed.

Costa Mesa Police arrived first, followed by the Orange County Sheriffs. The young police officers went about their work with an air of confidence far beyond their experience, which is part of their training. They began by interviewing briefly the two witnesses closest to Rebecca Harris when the first shot rang out, then they tried to seal off the crime scene. Wearing clear slickers to repel the rain, they dragged yellow-and-black folding sawhorses from the trunks of their patrol cars and began stringing up the yellow crime scene—do not enter tape.

But this procedure went inexactly. Because the reporters and photogs had so long endured the rigid protocols of police investigations while on assignment they felt that this event—in their own parking lot—entitled them to do pretty much what they pleased. So they did. The television side of the *Journal* operation used Rebecca's body—draped with a blanket—as a backdrop for their live, on-scene coverage. Photographers meandered within the taped perimeters, setting up lights and reflectors, snapping away. A dispute broke out regarding the best angles. Reporters took notes or spoke into tape recorders. Editors loitered, and the copy desk people rubbed their eyes. The young police officers were ignored. It was full access.

Through this rainsoaked tableau marched the *Journal's* most celebrated columnist, a tallish and solid woman named Susan Baum. She limped slightly, which gave her a kind of embattled dignity. She was wrapped in a tan Burberry, with the collars turned up around a hot violet scarf. From beneath her hat bobbed sand-colored curls of hair that framed a square face, deep brown eyes, furiously thick brows, and a mouth set in a perpetual frown. Behind her trailed the *Journal* publisher, who was apparently too flabbergasted by what had happened to even put on a coat. His white shirt, sleeves still rolled to his elbows, clung to his body like old skin. Next to him was head of plant security, and beside him, the executive editor. They approached Rebecca near the raised brick planter.

"M'am," said one of the officers. "Please remain behind the tape."

"Shut up, you fool," said Susan Baum, freezing him with a look of such hostility that the officer actually nodded and backed off.

Susan Baum barged past the TV crew, ruining the intro segment. The attractive on-air reporter, Ensley Moffett, shook her head, ducked under an assistant's umbrella and watched Susan with an air of respectful resignation.

Baum stood some ten feet away from Rebecca and looked down at the body. First she put her hands on her hips and leaned slightly forward, like someone measuring the depth of a hole. Then she stuffed her hands into the Burberry's side pockets and brought out a small notepad. She scribbled something. She gazed past the planter toward the massive *Journal* building, her eyes settling on the young man in the felt hat and leather coat soaked all the way past the knees. She hadn't even known he was there, just thirty feet away, stuck in the rain like a post. The "Sporting Life" writer, she thought—John? Jim? Mike?

She turned to her publisher and spoke in a quiet voice. "I

asked Rebecca to bring my car so I wouldn't have to go out in the storm. This was clearly intended for me."

She nodded to the new Lincoln Town Car the *Journal* supplied for her as a sign of her high status. It sat just to the right of the planter, behind a little sign that said, simply, "Baum." There was a small round hole near the top of the driver's side window, surrounded by an opaque aura of shatters and a spray of what could only be Rebecca Harris's blood. A bulky key chain dangled from the door lock.

With this, two large tears ran down her unquivering cheeks, and Susan Baum took one last look at her part-time assistant lying beside the planter. Then the columnist walked toward the TV crew, accurately assuming that they would want to interview her, limping due to chronically bad circulation in her left foot which today was aggravated by the cold wet weather.

Within an hour, the local police had assembled some apparent facts, scant as they were. Rebecca Harris was shot at least twice—once in the back as she unlocked the door of Susan Baum's Town Car, and once in the chest. The latter could have happened either as she turned when the first bullet hit her, or perhaps after she had fallen by the planter. Firearms and Toolmarks would determine the caliber of the gun. One of the crime scene investigators had already dislodged from the interior of the car next to the Lincoln a slug which had apparently passed through the young woman, through the Town Car and into the Acura Legend beside it. It had stopped in the burnished wood of the sedan's right-side dash. To the police it looked like a big-bore rifle slug, but that was only a guess.

It was likely fired from one of the two .30/06 cartridge casings that had been collected in the gutter of Fairway Boulevard, where the parking lot ended and the homes began. This corner was easily over three hundred yards from the Lincoln, suggesting a very good marksman using a very good firearm.

Something had been skillfully etched onto the shells: The script was flowing, as if handwritten. It looked like the engraving inside a wedding band, but larger.

One case read, "When in the course of human events—"

The other, "—it becomes necessary."

"Constitutional scholar," said a cop.

"That's the Declaration of Independence," said another.

One neighbor described seeing an older Chevrolet van, white, parked streetside before the shots were fired. There were two, three, four or five shots, she wasn't positive. Of course, they had sounded to her like firecrackers. Loud firecrackers. The van was there for "at least twenty minutes" before the shooting. It was gone, westbound on Fairway, just after the shots rang out. She hadn't gotten a look at the van's occupants because when the van was parked she didn't see anybody in it, and by the time she reached the window after hearing the shots, it was already blending into the traffic on Fairway, headed for the Interstate. It was quite possible that the shots had not even come from the van. No plate numbers, no distinguishing characteristics.

The entire crime scene took on a different personality when a newish Ford blazed into the parking lot at high speed and came to a fishtailing, tire-smoking stop just outside the yellow crime scene ribbon.

Two people jumped from the car, ducked the ribbon and walked directly toward the covered body. They took the long, assured strides of the indispensable. A Costa Mesa Police officer approached them and they badged him without missing a step or even slowing down. They both wore dark suits and the lightweight, nylon overcoats Southern Californians mistakenly believe will protect them from heavy weather. The woman was tall, early thirties, had very dark wavy hair, a clenched expression on her suntanned face, and the calves of a weightlifter. The man, roughly her height, was bespectacled, pale and thin, with black hair cropped short. He had a prominent Adam's apple, nose and ears, and he could have been twenty-five or thirty-five. He looked scholarly, except for the lean, pronounced muscles of his jaw and neck. He projected into the space around him the kind of calm with which a mountain lion might observe.

He approached the body, stopped and considered the photographers still milling about the scene.

"If you shoot any film of me, I'll confiscate that film and your cameras," he announced. For a thin pale man, his voice was quite clear and deep. His knot of a larynx rose and fell as if in emphasis. His partner put her hands on her hips and made a slow turning circle, locking eyes, briefly, with each person holding a camera. No one moved.

He went over to the blanketed form, knelt, looked up once at the ominous dusk, then lifted the material. He seemed to study Rebecca's face for a long time. He touched her lips, then her forehead, pressing a soaked blond curl back under the hat. He kissed his fingertips and touched them against her lips again.

After that he froze there, kneeling beside Rebecca for a long time. Then he slowly rose and stood over her, but to many of the observers—and they were trained, professional observers—the man who had kneeled beside Rebecca Harris was not the man who stood up a few minutes later. The new man had a different posture. He was stooped a little, whereas the original was erect. His face was no longer simply pale, but ivory colored and very hard, as if cast from a mold or sculpted. He was most definitely smaller. And certainly, the man who first approached the body did not have the very large black eyes that now challenged each of their faces—eyes so filled with fury and heartache that some of the journalists couldn't even meet them, let alone think of taking a picture.

Susan Baum, possessing the keenest instincts of all the *Journal* writers, felt in her pocket for the notepad and pen, and approached the bespectacled statue standing over Rebecca.

The young man in the leather coat and fedora had retreated from the throng outside the crime scene tape, and stood alone in the vague middle distance, studying this newly arrived official with the booming voice and the corded neck muscles. He thought: I wonder if that's *him*.

The pale man took a few steps away from the body, and considered the dozens of people—police, sheriff department, *Journal* staff, plant security—still meandering on either side of the crime scene ribbon. He held up his badge again, showing it around. His voice was resonant and did not seem to belong to his slender, almost ascetic body.

"My name is Joshua Weinstein, FBI, Orange County Office. This is my partner, Special Agent Sharon Dumars. Anyone . . . *anyone* not on the other side of that tape in the next ten seconds will be placed under arrest and face federal charges of tampering."

Astonishingly, he actually started counting.

There was a generalized grumble from the crowd, but everyone inside the tape migrated toward it, their movements accelerating noticeably when the count got to eight. Everyone except Susan Baum, who on the count of ten stood directly before Weinstein and gazed straight into his huge dark eyes.

"God, Joshua," she whispered. "She'd mentioned you to me."

"Get behind the tape, Ms. Baum."

"If I remember right, the wedding was planned for June."

"You remember right. Now get behind the tape."

"Can we talk later?"

"We have forever to talk."

"I want to tell you something right now. I won't die before I write the name of the man who did this in one of my columns. He'll be identified. I swear this, to every god that's ever slept a night in Heaven."

"Thank you. Now step back."

A tragedy creates waves, and waves can carry people away. For those involved, everything changed with those shots, at approximately 4:45 p.m. on Wednesday, March 22. Rebecca Harris, age 24, a bright, kind-hearted and lovely young woman in the prime of her young adulthood, died almost instantly. Her fiancé, Joshua Weinstein of the Orange County, California office of the Federal Bureau of Investigation, was swept by one wave into a journey of hatred so deep that, according to those who know him, he has yet to fully return. Rebecca's father was carried away by another wave, straight to heart failure three weeks later. The young man in the long leather coat and fedora, a talented if underproductive staff writer for the *Journal* named John Menden, rode yet another wave outward from Rebecca. He quit his job and floated around the South Pacific for three months until both his money and liver were close to giving out, then returned to move into a battered old trailer way out in the bleak Southern California desert. The security guard with the radio was fired. In fact, his entire company was released from its contract with the *Journal*—financial waves for financial concerns. The photographer who snapped the now famous picture of Rebecca won an award, then several more. The only living things proximate to the event that remained truly unrippled were the eucalyptus tree and the poppies in the planter near where Rebecca, heart-shot and staggering, then heart-shot again, fell and died in the pouring rain.

Six months came and went.

During this time, the lead agency responsible for the case was the FBI, taking its powers under recent Federal Hate Crimes provisions. They worked in concert with the police and sheriffs and, intermittently, with the Bureau of Alcohol, Tobacco and Firearms. Josh Weinstein took all his vacation time, then an unpaid leave of absence for nearly half a year. He said he was going to Israel, and vanished with hardly a good-bye for anyone.

Five months later he was back, his pallor gone to a ruddy tan, but his eyes still lugubrious and not a little haunted. His Bureau-mate, the dark-haired and strong bodied Sharon Dumars, noted that Josh spent a lot of his extra time with the Rebecca Harris files before him—a case from which his official participation was forbidden by Bureau policy. But since Joshua spent twelve-hour days on the job, he could easily take an hour here, a few hours there, to venture out into this sacred and unsanctioned ground. Dumars saw that Joshua's own private file—which he carefully locked away each night before he left—was growing in thickness.

Driven by curiosity, she glanced once at his time card to find that Joshua had officially charged no hours at all to his private investigation. The idea crossed her mind that she might be the only one who even knew about it. She certainly wasn't the only one who knew about his long telephone calls, since all Bureau calls were recorded and saved for an unrevealed period of time.

All she knew for sure was that he talked almost inaudibly during certain calls (the longer ones), with his thin shoulder blades hunched up like a vulture's wings, his neck down and his back to her. He would then hang up and swivel his chair around to look at her with a kind of fierce nonchalance before going back to his work. For all Sharon Dumars knew, Josh could have been talking to his mother back in Brooklyn.

Then, on a blazing September morning six months after the death of his betrothed, Joshua Weinstein rang off from one of his near silent telephone conversations, stared blankly for a moment at Dumars, then stood, locked his files and put on his suit coat.

"Come with me," he said.

Following Joshua's lead, Dumars left the building with him, failing to sign out or say a word to anyone. Never in her three years with the Bureau had she done anything so bold and so flagrantly against procedure.

CHAPTER
TWO

Sharon Dumars drove her white Bureau Ford because Weinstein asked her to. They headed in silence out toward Riverside on the 91, then picked up Interstate 15 south to Temecula, then branched southeast on State 79. The highway ran along a green valley rimmed with estates on the left, oaks and pastures to the right, fruit stands and white fences. The stables of a well known Arabian horse ranch passed by on the right.

"Where are we going, Josh?"

"We are going by context."

"What case do I bill this context to?"

"Personal Time."

"There's no case called Personal Time, last I checked."

"Just pay attention, and later, I'll ask you what you think."

Finally, they hit State 371, which took them east and higher in elevation. Dumars handled the car well on the curving, rising road, passing a cement mixer and a pickup filled with hay bales without taking her left hand from the armrest. In fact, her shoulder holster and 9mm were uncomfortable enough against the left side of her rib cage without moving around any more than she had to. There were just a few houses out here, set far back amidst the boulder-strewn hills. They looked planted. Occasionally, a dilapidated trailer peeked into view from a deep ravine or precipitous hilltop.

"I guess the people who move out here don't like anyone around them," Sharon offered. The landscape was quite pretty in an austere way.

"Or no one likes to be around *them*," said Josh absently.

They passed a sign that said "Cahuilla Indian Reservation", then, a few miles on, a sign for the city of Anza Valley, elevation 3,918 and population less than that.

The town appeared ahead of them. Dumars cut her speed to fifty. They passed a real estate office that was closed, a hardware store that was open, and a liquor store that had three pickup trucks parked in the dirt patch out front and windows filled with beer posters featuring beautiful women.

"We want Olie's Saloon—it's on the left," said Josh.

They drove past the market, the gas and propane station, a tire and brake center and the Feed Bin. Dumars slowed behind a faded gold Mercury four-door slung so low to the asphalt it looked like its trunk was filled with bowling balls. She could see through its dirty rear window a passel of dark-skinned children in the back seat, a huge female with raging black hair behind the wheel, and beside her a graying head lost in a cowboy hat. Dumars thought of the current battle back in Orange County between two tribes claiming rights to the land—the Gabrielenos and the Juanenos—and all the backbiting, corruption and betrayal in the name of federal funds and perhaps a bingo palace. Dignity is a hard thing to come by anymore, she thought.

"Is this reservation land?" she asked.

"Not the city. But all around it."

Olie's was a fragile-looking structure of dark wood, with a sagging roof and a hitching post out front. There were more pickup trucks in the dirt lot. It was either built to look like something from 1870, thought Dumars, or actually was. She pulled in and parked where Joshua pointed. The air outside the car was clear, dry and hot. An Indian in a white shirt watched them as they pushed through the saloon-style doors and into the late afternoon darkness of the bar.

They took a booth along one wall and studied the plastic-sheathed menus. The chili cheese omelet was being heavily discounted that day. The waitress was a thin, dry looking woman in her fifties who smiled tightly at them and talked about the omelet. They ordered soft drinks. Dumars thought that they couldn't have been more conspicuous if they had dressed in sequins, though it hardly mattered.

"So, you come here a lot?"

"I want you to listen, and corroborate when you can. What

I want, when we're finished, is a candid, honest, and hopefully helpful opinion."

"Joshua, does this have to do with Rebecca?"

"This has to do with everything. He'll be here in ten minutes."

In fact, he was there in less than ten minutes. He came through the saloon doors with a soft clunking of boots and, like the regular he was, walked straight for a row of bar stools that stood along one window, facing the street. He set his fedora on the counter beside him.

Joshua had covertly situated Dumars so that she would see his entrance. Joshua easily followed the reflection of John Menden, former *Journal* writer, in the bar mirror, as he arrived at his usual time, took his usual route to his usual stool, and put his hat down next to him. Joshua studied him, as those in law enforcement do, for some change, some new intelligence that might illuminate a subject. He found none. Menden looked as always, tall and on the slender side, with the easy, gliding gait of an athlete or, as Weinstein knew, a hunter. He wore the long denim duster he preferred for warm weather, the scuffed moccasin-style, flat-soled boots, the work shirt and brown cotton vest in the pockets of which he kept his cigarettes, lighter and pen. Weinstein quite frankly didn't know what to make of John Menden's style of dress. It was like something out of the past, part cowboy, part Indian and part gangster, maybe, what with the hat. The clothing seemed to suit him. Weinstein had observed John here, in his daily post-work lair, a total of five times, and the costume John wore had come to seem less foppish than simply eclectic and functional. As for Weinstein's own clothes, he had come in various guises—businessman, golfer, tourist, local—wanting neither Menden nor the regulars of Olie's to remember him. Joshua noted again that John's hair was the mix of brown and blond common to those who spend a lot of time outdoors, and it was kind of shaggy, falling onto a forehead from which he often had to push it back. His eyes were a pale gray. Like a lot of tall people, Menden stooped slightly, a habit developed early to help him fit into the pack, Josh decided. He smiled rarely and appeared relaxed. But Joshua had noted long ago that Menden's eyes were always alert and busy, whether he was choosing a bar stool, lighting a cigarette or taking a sip from the shots and beers he drank. Weinstein had learned from a routine medical history check that

Menden's uncorrected eyesight was 20/15, impressive for anyone, especially a thirty-four-year old who made a living reading
and writing. Yes, Weinstein had decided, John Menden's physical
nonchalance was good camouflage for his greedy, gathering eyes.
Weinstein was pleased to see the interest in Sharon Dumars's expression as she watched Menden sit down. He had expected no
less.

The waitress approached John with a hearty, "Hello, handsome."

"Hi, gorgeous," John said back, again as usual.

If anyone ever wanted to do a number on John Menden, it
would sure be easy, Weinstein thought for the hundredth time.
He's reliable as cement. Weinstein glanced through the smudged
window to Menden's pickup truck outside in the shade and the
brown Labrador retriever standing in the bed. The big dog was
diligently regarding the saloon doors through which he had
watched his master disappear. Menden called him Boomer. Beside Boomer was a yellow Labrador, smaller and female.
Weinstein, not a dog man, was pretty sure this one was Bonnie.
Not visible, but surely laying in the truck bed somewhere, would
be the old black lab that John called Belle. Weinstein had yet to
see Menden go anywhere without this herd. Yes, thought
Weinstein, Menden is predictable as a country song. We would
have to change that.

And this was certainly not the biggest of Weinstein's worries
about John Menden. What disturbed him most was his belief that
Menden's easy charm and rough good looks—so adroitly used
on women, no doubt—were the tools of a man who could take
no pressure. A coward. And his drinking. God, the fellow could
put the stuff away. But again, like so many times in the last six
months, Joshua was way ahead of himself.

During the time it took Weinstein and Dumars to drink one
cola each, the waitress brought John Menden two beers and a
shot of something. Weinstein and Dumars talked shop for a
while.

Then, abruptly, Weinstein got up and made his way across
the room to the window where John Menden sat.

Weinstein had been imagining this moment for almost two
months now. As he approached he could feel the slight speed-up
of his heartbeat, and the warmth that always came to his ears
when something was important, or dangerous, or much desired.

When he had been around Rebecca Harris, for example, his damned ears had been on fire all the time. But Weinstein was now better at divorcing himself from his own symptoms. He saw himself standing beside the stool with the hat on it, viewing up close for the first time the man he hoped might someday help accomplish the greatest mission of his—Joshua Weinstein's—life.

"I want to talk to you," he said.

Menden looked him straight in the face, then starting down at Joshua's black wingtips, gave him a longish assessment that ended with his eyes again on Weinstein's own.

"Then I guess you better get started. This is your fifth time in here if I'm counting right, which I am."

"I'm with the Federal Bureau of Investigation. My name is Weinstein, and I want to talk to you about Rebecca Harris."

"Good enough."

The tone rang false to Weinstein, and he wondered again what Rebecca had told John Menden, and what she had not. For his purposes now, it didn't matter.

"I've got a table over there, and someone I'd like you to meet. Please."

Menden took his hat and his half-full beer glass and followed Weinstein to the booth. Joshua introduced him to Sharon Dumars, who stood and offered her hand. He watched carefully as their eyes met, because how a man comes off first—at that very first moment of encounter—can set the stage for everything that will follow. Menden's light gray eyes betrayed little.

When the waitress came, Weinstein ordered another round of drinks for his guest, and beers for himself and Dumars. He disliked alcohol, but he was also aware of the irrational distrust that drinking people often reserve for those who aren't. After the waitress had delivered the drinks, he picked up his glass, touched its bottom lightly to the rim of Menden's, then Sharon's, and took a sip of the cold, bitter brew.

"That's good," he muttered without conviction.

John Menden sipped and nodded.

Joshua took off his glasses, pressed the two dents they had long ago engraved on either side of his nose, then set them on the table beside his glass. He looked again out to Menden's pickup truck, but it was just a blur with a bunch of dogs in it.

"I'd like to talk for a while, and for you to listen. Do you have, say, a couple of hours to give us?"

"I'll give you a minute at a time."
"That's how the hours pass, Mr. Menden."

Later, when Sharon Dumars thought about it and had finally realized the scope of Josh Weinstein's plans, she admitted that she had never seen him so impassioned about anything in his life. Focused, yes, Weinstein was always focused, his large dark eyes drinking you in from behind those glasses. Serious, certainly: the man actually seemed to possess no sense of humor whatsoever, and if possible, even less than that for the last six months. Convincing, totally, because no matter what Joshua Weinstein said it was difficult to believe it was anything other than the truth. But the passion was new to him, or at least to her. She wondered later that night, alone in her bed in her suburban Irvine condo, her big tabby Natalie purring on her chest, if passion was even the right word for it. She tried out other nouns: conviction, emotion, desire, hope. But none of these was what Joshua had offered up that late afternoon to her and John Menden. She had turned out the light and scrunched down under the comforter before it came to her, in that brief span of lucidity that leads us into sleep. It was not really passion, she realized with a deep sigh. It was the flip side of passion. What Josh had shown her today was a deep and resounding hatred.

And what she had said to Joshua was, *"he's perfect."*

CHAPTER

THREE

"As you know, Mr. Menden, on March 22, a little over half a year ago, Rebecca Harris was killed in the *Journal* parking lot. She was shot at long range by an assassin. The bullets were intended for her boss, Susan Baum. Whoever fired the shots either didn't know exactly what Susan looks like—unlikely—or couldn't distinguish her at three hundred and fourteen yards from Rebecca. After all, she was wearing a heavy raincoat and hat, and their general coloring, shape and hair color were similar. After all, she was getting into Susan's car. After all, an assassin's heart must be beating awfully hard at that time, wouldn't you guess?"

"I would guess that."

"So, as he let the air out of his lungs to steady his trigger finger, the last thing on his mind was that the woman in his crosshairs might not be the right one. Rebecca died; Susan didn't. It was one of those things that qualify as tragedy, because Rebecca had a tragic flaw that allowed her to die. Her flaw was that she was kind, considerate and attentive. She'd agreed to bring around Ms. Baum's car, and it cost her her life. The fact that Susan Baum suffers from gout and is no triathlete must have made Rebecca's decision easy. None of this, I expect, is news to you."

Menden looked at Weinstein, then sipped again from his beer. "I was a reporter once, but news is always news."

"I couldn't agree more. Now, what I'm about to tell you is what we, the Bureau, have learned in the six months since

Rebecca Harris's death. Some of it you may have read in the papers, but most of it I guarantee you have not. Right now, I need a promise from you, or we can't continue. You're editing the newspaper down here, the *Anza Valley Lamp*. Correct?"

"That's my career."

"I need your word that nothing I'm about to tell you will come out on those pages, or any other, or from your mouth, ever. No matter how many shots and beers you've downed on a Friday night. No matter how dull the Indian you're talking to here on some quiet Sunday afternoon seems to be. No matter how close a lover may come to you."

Menden smiled with a certain obvious condescension, then drank off his shot and waved the waitress for another. Weinstein's insides withered a little.

"Do I have that promise?"

"If it's what you need."

"I wouldn't ask if I didn't." At that point, Weinstein glanced at Dumars, and his expression demanded the same of her, a promise. She began to suspect that his bringing her here under "personal time" and their abrupt exit from the office—no sign-out, no destination, no emergency number other than her pager—was a way of keeping her out of the official loop of Bureau intelligence. She looked away from Weinstein with what she hoped was a conditional yes.

"Right now," Joshua continued, "this is what we have that's solid. The bullets were .30/06 caliber, soft-nosed, factory made at Hornady. They did not come from the cartridge shells left at the scene. You heard about those, I assume."

"Two of them."

"Did you know that they had been engraved?"

Menden shook his head.

"One said, 'When in the course of human events—', and the other said, 'it becomes necessary—' The engraving was professional, or by an expert amateur. The script mimicked that of the Declaration of Independence. Each phrase started at the bottom of the shell, and went toward the neck."

Menden frowned and drank from his glass again. "But they weren't fired?"

"Of course not. That would add to our evidence, and they weren't willing to let us do that. God only knows where the gun itself is right now. The bottom of the Pacific, maybe. They took the real casings with them and left behind two shiny brass shells with their little warning on them. Their patriotic . . . signature."

"Their call for revolution."

Weinstein snorted. "They're not revolutionaries. They're agents of the status quo."

"Like you."

The shot arrived and John arranged it in front of him. The waitress studied Joshua as she made change, then walked away.

"I'll ignore that for now, and address it later. We've got more, but not much. The van, alleged to have been used by the shooter, was found ten miles away from the scene, behind a donut shop in Westminster. It had old plates on it, from a wrecking yard, likely—plates that hadn't been used in a decade, since they graced a Volkswagen bug totalled in 1985. Strictly a disposable vehicle. Nobody saw it drive in; nobody saw who picked up the driver and or passengers. There were fingerprints in it and on it, but very few, and those were all partials. We found traces of talc on the wheel and interior door handles, window knobs, shift lever."

"The old latex glove trick."

"Likely. Hair and Fiber back in Quantico got all the samples we collected and worked them hard—nothing interesting, really, nothing that points a finger. We've got corroborative evidence now—things that don't mean much unless we can match them with a suspect. Nothing primary."

"Hair for DNA?"

"You can't get DNA from hair," snapped Weinstein, "only from the tissue that sticks to it. We've got hair. No skin. We've got sixteen different hair samples. A follicle won't convict like a fingerprint or DNA pattern. Old van, plenty of passengers. Two dogs, a parakeet feather and mouse crap down in the floor carpet. The van had four owners before it was stolen from a repair shop. But the repair shop didn't even notice it was gone because it was fixed, left and never paid for. It collected dust out in the yard for two months. We fired down hard on all the people who owned it, all the people who knew the people who owned it, all the people at the shop, you name it."

Joshua Weinstein perused his beer, and forced another sip.

"And?"

"Something gave. I'll get back to that when I need to. Chronology isn't important here. Questions, so far?"

"Why Susan Baum?"

"Left-wing. A Jew. A woman. A world-class afflicter of the comfortable. A brilliant afflicter. She continues to offend a lot of people, right there on the front page of the *Orange County Journal*, three days a week. Businessmen, Republicans, old-fashioned patriots, churches, hunters, smokers, meat-eaters, drinkers, straights, men, all-boys' Little League teams and boy scouts without gay troop leaders. You know the litany. By some standards, *she's* the revolutionary. She's also an American citizen exercising her constitutional right to free speech. They tried to kill her for it, and they said as much when they engraved those casings for us."

At this, John Menden looked down at his beer glass and tapped its bottom against the table. "You're sure they weren't after the assistant—Ms. . . uh . . . Harris?"

"We worked that possibility," said Weinstein. "And it yielded nothing."

In the moment of silence that followed, even Weinstein seemed to lose his focus. Dumars saw something remote pass across his expression. The memory of Rebecca, she understood, his fiancée, gliding over his mind as quietly as a cloud across the sun. John Menden's face looked mournful, too.

It was Menden who broke the meditation. "Have you had any contact from the shooters? Anyone making a claim to it—a note or a call—anything?"

Weinstein's attention snapped back to the present. "Eighty-six letters, twelve postcards and a hundred and fourteen calls. They surprised me. I knew Orange County was conservative, but I didn't know there was that much hatred, just under the surface. Hatred and fear. Exactly one letter seemed credible to us, the rest were unconnected—we're pretty sure. We've followed up most of them as best we can—most of them aren't signed. The one we take seriously is from some people calling themselves 'The Freedom Ring.' It was computer-generated, on a nice sheet of twenty-five percent cotton bond paper. Here's a photocopy."

Weinstein removed a folded sheet of paper from his pocket. John Menden downed the fresh shot, then pushed his beer and shot glasses out of the way. He flattened the paper against the table.

Rebecca was a mistake and we are sorry. Baum is the tumor we tried to remove. What happened to Miss Harris can

*happen to anyone who seeks to abridge our rights. We will
not have the foundations of America torn down by people
who prosper under our system, only to disrespect it.*
                                    —The Freedom Ring

Menden handed the sheet back to Joshua, who folded it into
his coat pocket. "Well, Mr. Weinstein, do you have a suspect, or
don't you?"

"We do."

Weinstein looked at Sharon Dumars as he said this, and registered with some satisfaction the astonishment on her face. She
ingested the news like a bad taste, then shook back her dark wavy
hair with a toss of her head and lifted the beer glass to her mouth
with extreme knowingness. She is learning, he thought, but right
now her galvanics would send a polygraph into fits.

"But I can't know who it is," said Menden.

Weinstein looked at John, then centered his beer glass before
him.

"No," he said. "You can't know that . . . yet."

Menden shrugged and sat back. "Then why are you here?"

"I'm here, Mr. Menden, because you want to listen to me."

Menden raised his eyebrows in mock exasperation, then let
them down again. "Why do I want to listen to you? With this
whole world full of people with their stories to tell and their axes
to grind, why do I need to hear yours?"

His tone of voice and his eyes were so placid now that
Sharon Dumars couldn't tell if Menden was cunning, innocent,
or possibly, just plain stupid. The alcohol seemed to fortify his
mask.

"Because you were in love with Rebecca, you smug sonofabitch."

Sharon Dumars emitted a tiny breath, then coughed to cover
it. She couldn't take her eyes off of Weinstein. His ears—those
wonderful Ichabod Crane ears of his—were a molten red now.
The poor man was as tumultuous inside as a volcano. And his
thirsty dark eyes fixed onto John's face and didn't let go. They
seemed to be trying to locate something almost invisibly small.
Yet Menden returned the long assessment with a gaze of utter
calm. Weinstein was the active, Menden the passive; Weinstein
the river, and Menden the rock against which it raged.

"I," Josh continued, "was *engaged* to her, as you read in the papers. And while I was, you were courting her at the *Journal* offices, where you both worked. You talked to her, you lunched with her, and later, you entertained her in your home on Sun Valley Drive in Laguna Canyon. You felt something for her that you believed you had never felt for a woman before. You did love her, didn't you? I don't see how you couldn't. It was the easiest thing I ever did in my whole life. It was easier than breathing. I'm not wrong, am I?"

When Dumars managed to look across to John Menden, his expression had not changed. She looked hard at him, but for all her training and perspicacity, for all of the reverberating context that she now understood, she could not read any reaction at all. It was almost unbelievable. Was he a sociopath? A psychotic? Was Joshua quite simply wrong?

"Don't answer," said Weinstein. "What you answer doesn't matter to me, because I know what happened and I know the truth. The truth, Mr. John Menden, is that Rebecca was in love with you, too. Surprised? Then certainly it's a pleasant surprise. Remember the picture they ran, of Rebecca in the rain by the planter? Of course you do. You were in it, though you weren't recognizable. Didn't you wonder why her left hand was naked, why the ring she'd worn for eight months was suddenly gone? I'll tell you. She took it off that morning and gave it back to me. She said she couldn't, there was someone else. She cried. She didn't just cry, she raged. She stormed. That night, the night after she died, I went to her apartment and found two letters she'd written. Here's yours."

Weinstein produced a smallish envelope, pink with a faint floral pattern, and set it on the table. It was sealed. On top of the envelope, he set something small that shined warmly even in the dim light of Olie's Saloon.

Joshua Weinstein's voice had taken on a profound bitterness. "Take the ring, too. Touch it. Smell it. Think of the perfect finger that used to wear it. Think of the times you spent together. Return it to me when you're finished. It's mine. It cost me a lot, and I'm not talking about money."

Again, Dumars's attention went to Menden. He looked for a long moment at the envelope and ring. He blinked twice, glanced at his empty shot glass, then lifted his eyes to Joshua Weinstein. They were just a fraction brighter than before.

Around the edges showed a moisture that had not been there just a second or two ago. And his ruddy face was even darker now, more deeply lined around the mouth and eyes. *There it is,* she thought, *his confession!*

Then, Josh stood. "Rebecca loved you," he said. "They shot out her heart and she died alone in a fucking parking lot in the rain. That's why you want to listen to me. Thanks for your time."

He tossed a few bills on the table and was already through the saloon door by the time Dumars slung her purse over her shoulder, took one look into the pained gray eyes of John Menden, and followed Weinstein out.

CHAPTER
FOUR

In the fall of 1971, John's father and mother bought an airplane. John was nine and he sat with his parents in the Martin Aviation office at Orange County Airport while his father signed the papers. The salesman was a slender, tanned, soft-spoken gentleman who John felt was welcoming his father and mother, even himself, to an elite club of aviators. The office had pictures of the salesman in various airplanes, some featuring a celebrity with him. From outside, the roar of passenger jets rattled the picture frames against the wall, and the buzzing tenors of the private planes cut through the air as they took off and landed. The salesman gave John a styrofoam glider with a weighted nose and short, sharp futuristic wings, which sat on his lap as he listened.

John understood that it was a small plane, a rather old one, but in superb condition and reasonably priced—the perfect starter craft for a middle-aged aerospace engineer bitten by the fly bug early in life and now able to assume the debt of curing what some people called "the disease."

"The only good disease a man can get," said the salesman, glancing at John's mother. "Or a woman. This little craft will open up a world to you that you only suspected was there. Every minute in the air is like dreaming for an hour."

"Well put," agreed his father, rapidly signing away at the purchase agreement. "I wonder if we could dream our way into another six months of service?"

"I'll ask Herb, Mr. Menden."

"Appreciated, Lew."

His mother just laughed in the way that John had come to understand meant that she was humoring someone. In private moments, she had confided to John that her husband needed the airplane far worse than she did. John liked it when she laughed, the way her big teeth suddenly appeared and her rather stern face brightened up like the sun. His father was handsome, tall and exuded a majestic ego made charming by his cheerful good manners. Men always deferred to him, and John's schoolmates instinctively feared him. John liked the way his father and mother looked together.

He stood in the shade of the Martin building and watched his father taxi to the runway. The little Piper was painted bright yellow with red trim, and John's mother had opted for a tastefully theatrical costume—red silk scarf, aviator shades and a leather bomber's jacket—in which to make their maiden, craft-owning flight. John wondered why they couldn't have gotten a three-seater instead of a two, but he was used to the fact that his parents admitted him into their presence as a kind of formal offering. It was a warm formality, and John often sensed love in it. But it was never the kind of thing you just barged into.

His mother waved after she settled into the cockpit, and Lew helped them latch down. The propellor was a yellow, red-tipped blur. Accelerating down the runway, the little Piper emitted a determined, rising moan. It finally wobbled off the ground, looking to John as if it was lifting all the weight of the world.

For the hour they were gone, John threw his glider out on the tarmac, wondering if with just the right conditions it could rise high, ease into the slipstream of the Piper, and follow it wherever it might go. He decided the idea was dumb. It was hard enough just to get the foam ailerons to stay adjusted from one flight to the next.

So he sat on a bench and waited for the plane to return. He saw it when it was just a bright speck in the western sky, tilting its way down. After it landed he positioned himself on the tarmac and waved it in with the curt, martial motions of the ground-crews he much admired. His father smiled at him through the little side window, radio set still clamped to his head. The Piper rolled to a stop.

His mother climbed out, helped by Lew, and gave John a hug. Her face was warm against his and the silk scarf puffed

lightly against his cheek. She smelled as always like her perfume—Chanel No. 5—and the leather of her jacket. She stood
back as Lew helped John into the cockpit, where his father was
assiduously making flight notes in a small book. His father extended his hand and John shook it.

"Off we go, son."

"Into the wild blue yonder."

"Get that shoulder strap nice and tight. Don't want my co-
pilot falling out."

The radio burped non-stop static which his father, amaz-
ingly, seemed to understand.

Five minutes later they were lifting up into the sky. John was
surprised how the airplane moved not only up and down and
went left and right, but kind of twisted, too, as if pivoting on its
belly. The engine worked hard, he thought, and the view was not
as good as it could be because the windows were a little high up.

Looking down on Orange County, John noted that all of the
tracts and lots and groves seemed a lot more organized than they
did from the ground. From above, they were all part of a grand
design. He saw a kidney-shaped swimming pool and wondered if
you jumped and managed to land in the deep end of the pool—
feet first, body stiff, arms to the side—would you live or not.

His father guided the plane out over the Pacific. John was
sure that if you jumped and did all the right things you could
land in *that* and live. He looked down and saw the two jetties at
Balboa, and the Wedge, where he had spent hours watching the
bodysurfers ride the neck-snapping waves that build and lurch
off the jetty rocks.

For a few moments he studied nothing but his father's forearms—one of John's favorite parts—and admired once again the
stout arm emerging from the rolled-up shirt sleeve, the abundant
hair that grew all the way down to where the wrist began, then
reappeared behind the first knuckle of each of his father's fingers.
Did it grow *under* the skin for a ways? He watched the wrist
tendons flex when his father adjusted their course back around
to the east. He casually ran a hand over his own wrist, assessing
the wispy golden fuzz.

"What do you think, Johnny?"

"It's fine. Would you live if you landed in one of those swimming pools, but feet first and stayed real stiff?"

"I wouldn't want to try."

"The wind would blow you onto a roof or something, probably."

"Probably. Look down on that county, son. It's yours. That's a nice thought, isn't it?"

"It's not really mine, dad."

"No. It is. It belongs to whoever puts down his roots there. Your mother and I have. You will. When you look down on it from up here, you see that it's not really such a big place at all. It's like a back yard. It's yours to play in and live on and take care of. Look at that ocean. Look at the mountains. It's a good place, John—you're lucky to grow up here."

"I'll bet you could live if you landed in the ocean."

"Maybe you could. Just maybe."

John sat back, felt the drone of the engine and looked out at the sky. He listened to his father talking with ground control on the radio. He felt good being up here with his father, sitting beside him, a part of his world. A father was someone who controls things, he thought: a plane, a county, the sky.

John looked down at his thin dark legs, his feet, his shorts. Then he looked at his dad. He saw all the changes he would have to go through to become like his father, but he couldn't imagine them taking place soon enough. Everything grew so slowly, just a few inches a year. He tried to imagine himself as big as his father, with all the hair and the rough chin and the way air opens up easier around you when you're bigger. For a while he pretended he was his father's age, his father's brother, in fact. He relaxed into the seat with one knee lifted and his arm draped casually over that knee.

"Yeah," he said. "This county is mine."

"Take your foot off the seat, John."

On the way back to the airport, John convinced himself that they were going to land for just a few minutes to pick up his mother, then the three of them would fly away together for a long vacation in a dangerous place, but a place that had baseball. He loved this reverie and it was believable until he looked back and realized that the plane had only two small seats. He thought, that was really dumb of dad to get a plane that doesn't have enough room for all of us. And he wondered if maybe his father did it on purpose.

CHAPTER
FIVE

Two days after the meeting in Olie's, Weinstein and Dumars were waiting for John outside his trailer when he got home. It was just after six, and the generous September daylight bloomed from a red sun in a blue sky.

John saw the helicopter resting on a flat piece of desert not far from the trailer, heat waves wavering up from the engine compartment.

The two agents, dressed in suits, stood in the shade of the trailer awning, trying to be comfortable and inconspicuous here at the High Desert Rod & Gun Club, which they certainly were not. John glanced up the dirt road toward the club house, where the property caretaker, Tim, was sweeping off the steps as an excuse to look down on the visitors and their gleaming chopper.

"The secret agents," he said with a small smile.

"The city editor," said Weinstein without one.

Boomer smelled shoes as John unstacked three plastic lawn chairs he'd bought to entertain guests, but never used. Bonnie watched from beneath the trailer, with black Belle already asleep beside her. John dusted off the seats with his hand, and offered them to Weinstein and Dumars. He opened up the trailer windows and returned to the deck with beers.

He opened the bottles, gave one to each of his visitors, and sat.

"Nice trailer," said Weinstein, without looking back at it. He looked instead at John's flat-soled moccasin boots, his worn duster, brown vest and the eternal fedora.

"Thanks," said Menden.

"I can tell by your face that you read the letter."

John said nothing. He had in fact read the letter ten times, each reading bringing him closer to her, each reading taking her farther away. It was a sublime torture. To see actual words written by her hand, words revealing her love for him, her heartache over Joshua Weinstein, her confusion and her fear, was something that John never thought would happen. All of the distance he had put between Rebecca and himself closed again, in a rush, when he read that letter. Almost closed, because no matter how hard John imagined her as he lay in the trailer bed that night, his eyes locked shut and all his powers focused on the task of summoning her back to the present—if only long enough for the good-bye he never got to say—the final distance could never be closed. She was beyond him, and during all his days on earth, he knew, she would stay that way. She had dabbed her scent on the paper.

"You only stayed in Orange County a few weeks after the shooting. You gave up a pretty plum job, cashed out your retirement, closed up your house in Laguna. Why?"

John took a drink of the beer and decided that even if, according to the ways men should live, he had wronged Joshua Weinstein, he still didn't much like him.

"You're the spy, Mr. Weinstein. You're the gatherer. You know a lot more about me than I know about you. Why don't you tell me why?"

Weinstein had set his beer on the deck and loosened the knot of his necktie. His nine-to-five pallor was luminous in the sunlight filtered by the awning.

He looked across with an expression John took to indicate sympathy, but read as little more than a bureaucrat's professional interest.

Joshua said, "My mother used to tell me that to be happy in life, you need three things: something to do, someone to love, and something to look forward to. You had them all. Then you lost Rebecca and tossed the other two away. You traveled some, then came out here to lick your wounds—"

Rebecca. The sound of the name takes John Menden back to her. As clearly as if it was yesterday, no, as clearly as if she were there right now, he feels the warm October sunlight on his skin the evening they sit on the balcony of the old Laguna Can-

yon house and he actually touches her for the first time. She has
a scar that runs from the base of her right thumb across to the
center of her palm, and that clean thin line of tissue—a line he
has seen and contemplated so many times before—is soft beneath
his finger as he traces its length across her hand, then back to the
thumb again. She says a gypsy told her it cut across her lifeline
but not to worry because all wounds are superficial compared to
fate. She looks at him in a way that is both innocent and knowing, both assured and inquisitive. Rebecca's hair is golden in this
autumn light. Her skin is fair and her eyes are blue. Her nose is
longer and sharper than the popular notion of beauty. Her face
is slender. Her mouth is wide, full-lipped, healthy. She wears a
frank red lipstick that frames, when she smiles, her very white
and even teeth. She is vain enough, and practical enough, to
know that her smile is her best feature. She also assumes that she
is not particularly beautiful. He knows that she is not beautiful,
though his eyes have made her perfect.

John has always believed that he can judge a person's character by their face, that no amount of acting or cosmetic alter-
ation can change the truth of a face. In the case of Rebecca, he
had seen it all very clearly the moment he met her in the *Journal*
lobby. She was bright, curious, forgiving, optimistic and possessed a hopeful soul in spite of the darkness she tried to hide.
Rebecca Harris, he immediately saw, was the kind of woman he
wanted to spend his life with. He saw her ring, too, and realized
he would not.

And later, sitting on his balcony after touching her scar, then
looking away at the arid hillsides of Laguna Canyon, John Menden felt a true sense of honor at having touched her.

You shouldn't have done that, she says.

*I'm sorry. I've wanted to touch you for a long time. Now
you're here. I never imagined you here. It's throwing me a bit.*

*I've imagined me here. Too many times. Maybe that was a
mistake, but I couldn't help myself. Everything starts there, in
the imagination, don't you think?*

*No, it starts in the eyes, and then the imagination kidnaps
it.*

To where?

To the heart, I guess. Then the heart makes it real.

"—to forget, to start over." Weinstein's voice severed the

reverie like a sword. "So you come here, to nowhere, looking for the next avenue out."

John looked at his dogs, asleep in the dirt beneath the trailer. Rebecca's face fades away. "You've boxed me neatly, Mr. Weinstein."

Sharon shifted uneasily in her plastic chair. "Mr. Menden," she asked, "have you thought over what we talked about last time?"

"Of course I have." In fact, he had thought about almost nothing else. He understood that he was being vetted and auditioned—for what he could only guess. With the words of Rebecca's letter still whispering in his mind, it was difficult to hear much else.

"What are your feelings?" Sharon asked.

"I want to know more," said John.

Joshua nodded and stood, setting his half-empty beer on the chair. "We can't bring the facts to you, so we'll bring you to the facts. Get the chopper ready again, Sharon."

John was ushered through a back entrance of the Orange County FBI office, Dumars on one side of him and Weinstein on the other. They went down a long hallway covered with a pale green industrial carpet, then turned right and passed down another corridor. No one passed them in either. The building was quiet. After hours, thought John—the Feds are home with their little Fedettes. Joshua unlocked a heavy wood-veneer door and let them in.

It was a small room, set up like a theater. Joshua flipped on the lights, bright overhead fluorescents that bathed the air in a chilly, efficient glow. A large television monitor sat on a stand near a wall, and ten feet in front of it were three seats.

"Sit," said Weinstein. "I'm about to show you some things that very few people have seen. Sharon has seen them and my supervisor here. Select people in Washington—two to be exact. All three others know what Sharon and I are doing, but I've managed to get almost a sole proprietorship of this operation. As sole as anyone gets in a bureaucracy like ours. I was lucky. The President cut loose federal funds as part of his crime package and Orange County got some of it. That's where the money comes from. Like any other organization, in the Bureau, everyone wants to know where the money is coming from. Right now, I've got a clean supply. It isn't a lot, and it isn't inexhaustible, and it doesn't flow without scrutiny from Washington. But for now, it's mine. Who knows, Mr. Menden, maybe it will be *ours*. May I call you John?"

"Fine."

Weinstein smiled then, which John took to indicate a new bonhomie. Then, like a dead leaf, it fell away.

"I'm going to ask you to relax now, John, just sit back, look at the screen and listen to a story. I'll narrate. You'll have questions, I'm sure, but wait on them—if you can. Of course, if you're missing what you think is an urgent piece of information, just speak up."

Again, Weinstein smiled. It looked like something rationed, by his soul perhaps, leaving him only so many to spend in a day. His teeth were small and even, but his lips parted around them only momentarily, and with reluctance. It gave John a small shudder. The larynx wrestled beneath his skin. And Weinstein's voice now, so, well . . . welcoming. It sounded to John like something calling out from the first rung of hell.

CHAPTER
SIX

A man's face appeared on the screen. The image was a still photograph, in color. He looked to be in his early fifties, with short silver-gray hair combed back, a heavily lined and sun-darkened face, a wide jaw that spoke of resolve, and gray, level eyes much the color of John's own. He was wearing a white knit shirt, unbuttoned. The overall impression he made on John Menden—the self-professed analyst of faces—was of bearing, competence, experience and intelligence.

"Let's call him Puma, for right now," said Weinstein. "He's a family man. See? He's married, with a twenty-two-year-old son just graduating from Stanford, and an eighteen-year-old daughter at the University of California, in Irvine. There they are, up in Palo Alto for the commencement."

On screen, the photographic portrait gave way to what looked like home-video footage of Puma with his wife and children. They are outside. The son is dressed in gown and mortarboard for a graduation. The daughter wears a white dress. The wife is in pink, smiling widely, and Puma himself has his arms around all three of them, scrunching them in toward him, his tan, lined face smiling and quite obviously proud. He tips the mortarboard down onto his son's face, and his wife rearranges it, revealing the young man's grin.

"Call the son Patrick," said Weinstein. "The daughter Valerie, the mother Carolyn."

John watched. Some of it was video tape, some were stills.

The family on the steps of the Mormon Temple in Salt Lake City. The family—years earlier—at the beach. Patrick fast-breaking down the Stanford court. Valerie graduating from what must have been high school. Carolyn giving baths to a litter of wriggling puppies in a back yard toddler's pool. Puma kneeling alone on a vast white boulder, the body of a ram before him and the ram's head and enormous horns resting on his lap. Patrick, Valerie and Puma walking a gully in what looked to John like the Sand Hills of Nebraska, shotguns in their arms and a pair of springers working out in front of them. The pheasants come up; the camera jostles to frame them; the pops of guns send two of the cock pheasants plummeting to the ground. Then a sequence in which the daughter commands a springer during a field-trial retrieve—hand signals only—directing the eager dog into a river, across it, then left into a dense stand of cattails from which the dog emerges with a pigeon. Then Valerie kneeling beside her dog and a trophy.

"Now," said Weinstein. "August, five years ago. The day it all changed."

The video now showed what could only be police footage. The scene is outside a fast food restaurant and the atmosphere is one of disaster. There is a perimeter of tape set up, and beside it dozens of people, mostly youths, mostly Latino in appearance, stare in glum acceptance toward the restaurant. When the scene shifts inside, two bodies are heaped beneath a table next to a window pocked with holes.

"August fourth," said Weinstein. "These are the facts. Patrick was shot dead. Twenty-two years old, just out of Stanford with a degree in history, engaged to be married in the Salt Lake City Temple the following spring. His mother, Carolyn, was injured, shot in the head. The bullet went through her son first, likely because he saw what was going down and tried to cover her. She lived, sort of. She's been paralyzed from the waist down for five years, bedridden and brain-damaged. She talks, though not well. Collateral damage was three wounded, one seriously. Depending on your beliefs, one of two things happened. One version is that an innocent person was murdered in cold blood and another paralyzed for life by a racist punk, simply for being white, and for being where they shouldn't have been. A hate crime, with all the special penalties hate crimes carry. That's what the DA tried to go with, at first. The other version was that a decent young Latino boy had defended his aunt from a man who had raped and beaten her the week before and who he feared had come back to do it again. That's what he was doing when he took out Patrick through the window of the fast food place. Carolyn, in this scenario, was a tragic accident. That the boy's aunt had been beaten and likely raped was established—bruises, cuts, vaginal abrasions. But she didn't report it until after her son had shot Patrick. She was afraid of being deported. The public defender struggled to establish that Patrick had committed the rape, but couldn't get far—no fluids, no blood—nothing but Teresa Descanso's word and a dead accused. During the trial, in this land of orange blossoms, rolling surf and Mickey Mouse, you defined your soul by what version you believed. You wanted the shooter's blood, or you thought he was a hero. It was ugly and divisive and unnecessary. But then, a lot of life is, it seems."

"I read about it," said Menden.

Next were still shots of the funeral, several showing the demolished countenance of Puma, his hair unkempt and his eyes swollen. Valerie's face looked like that of someone who had seen something she would never be able to unsee again.

The video ended. Weinstein used the remote to hit rewind. Silence filled the little room.

Weinstein took a hearty sip of water. His big Adam's apple bobbed with the swallow. "The alleged shooter was a boy of fifteen—good student, no gang involvement—a minor Latino activist of sorts. He'd written some rather . . . what, Sharon, *vehement* articles?"

"Childish articles."

"No, they were better than childish, but they were naive and strident. Anyway, he'd done some articles about *La Raza* and *Aztlán* for a class at his high school. You know, the stuff about the Mexicans reclaiming California for their race. Naive stuff, like I said, but it came up in court. He admitted the shooting, on the strength of his aunt's identification of Patrick, governed by fear for her safety and life. The jury finally hung on murder two, so he went back to jail. For reasons championed by the media and press, and finally agreed to by the DA, he wasn't tried again for Patrick. He got four years for mayhem on Carolyn, walked after two, moved to Mexico, they say. A controversial decision, to say the least. Maybe it was supposed to keep the lid on the pressure cooker. Maybe it was supposed to be a concession to an emotionally charged county minority that truly believed the kid was defending his family. This was before your time at the paper. You were in Key West, *fishing*, I believe."

John felt, not for the first time, that his skin had been peeled back by Joshua and his people, affording them a full view of everything inside.

"I read about the trial," he said. "It wasn't big in the papers back there."

"It was big here. On the heels of O.J. and Prop. 187. God, what a summer that was."

Weinstein sighed deeply, removed his glasses and massaged the sides of his nose. "How'd you do down in Key West, fish-wise?"

"Does it matter?"

"It couldn't possibly matter less."

"Then get on with it."

"Yeah, that's the spirit."

The glasses back on now, Joshua contemplated John with his voracious eyes. "Cut now to Puma. You need to know something about him. He came from a wealthy family that had been in the county since the early eighteen hundreds. A very wealthy family—bought land grants on the cheap, made a go with cattle and crops, sent sons into the assembly and Congress and watched the land value go out of sight after World War II. Puma was working at the time, that dreary August when he lost his son and most of his wife. He quit his job. He sold his house in Tustin and moved onto family land—a couple of thousand acres down in the south part of the county. The land is hilly and dry, but it overlooks the coast. It backs up against Pendleton Marine Base. It's got a lake. It's got oak savanna, coastal scrub, two hundred acres of orange trees. There was only one road into it, and Puma kept it that way. He built an eight-foot fence around it and wired it full of voltage. There's a guard house where the road comes into his property. He could have afforded electricity, gas and water, but he installed generators, propane and wells instead. He rebuilt the old mission-era house, which ran him almost a half a million dollars. When it was ready, he moved in with his paralyzed wife and his daughter. He began a business that is now thriving. And since then, no one sees him. He's there, of course—I don't mean he's disappeared—but he rarely leaves the place. Oh yes, it has a name. Liberty Ridge."

Liberty, thought John. He liked the sound of the word, though it wasn't a word you heard much anymore. And he knew the land that Weinstein was talking about. It was gorgeous land, tough land, filled with wildlife, nourished by the lake, with a commanding view from its peak. As a kid, John had hiked it, camped it, scavenged it for fossils and rocks and reptiles a hundred times.

John looked around the room, at the bare walls, the blank television monitor, the pale green carpet. For a moment, Puma's paralyzed wife and Liberty Ridge were just blips on the screen of his awareness. But then they grew in size, and he remembered why his stomach had tightened and his heart was now beating so loudly inside his rib cage. Puma was behind Rebecca.

Rebecca.

"Now," said Weinstein, "we need to look forward, to the van used in the . . . assassination. Rather, to the repair shop from which the van was lifted. Sharon? You're on."

With this, Sharon Dumars rose and began pacing. At first she went back and forth in front of the screen, then extended her run to include the entire perimeter of the room. She looked for all the world, thought John, like a female version of Joshua.

"The shop is owned by someone whose name you don't need to know," she began. John detected the relish of power in her voice, the pride of one who commands. "This man has a brother-in-law. Brother-in-law works for Puma. Coincidence? Maybe, or maybe not. Let's say it is. Puma, we learn, is a competent amateur engraver. He actually earned money during college working for a trophy company, even though his family was rich. Coincidence that the bullet casings left behind for us were engraved? Let's say that's a coincidence, too. Then, there's this—Puma loves to hunt big game, and big game hunters use big rifles, sometimes a .30/06 caliber because it's powerful and accurate. Puma—and the men he hunts with—have taken and made four hundred and eighty yard shots. We know this because he's listed in the Boone & Crockett record books, and in the Safari Club International record books. Coincidence again? Yes, let's call it all coincidence, again. We can afford to be generous."

With this, Dumars stopped at the table and drained the rest of her water. John noted the sheen of sweat on her forehead and the way her hair stuck at the temples.

"Then," she continued, "there's the fact, too, that Susan

Baum broke the story about Teresa Descanso—the shooter's aunt—accusing Patrick of rape. It was explosive. The accused murderer dumped the public defender because he couldn't get results on Patrick, and let Glory Redmond take the case *pro bono*. You can imagine the circus she made of it. She didn't even try to link Patrick to Descanso with physical evidence, which was smart. What better could they do—Redmond argued—than an eyewitness? All the while, Baum crusaded in print, with a series of articles in which Descanso, then another woman, accused Patrick not only of the rape, but of solicitations for prostitution, public drunkenness and aggravated assault. Baum argued to her readers what Redmond was arguing to her jury, that a white-male-establishment-Orange County DA was ignoring the facts while prosecuting a fifteen-year old scholar for defending his family. Orange County is supposed to be the hotbed of conservatism, the Republican citadel, the land of the John Birch Society, right? Redmond and Baum set out to challenge that assumption. And the question of Patrick's supposed exploits in the barrio— dramatized by Baum's articles—probably helped deadlock the jury. The shooter's name, by the way, was Jimmy Ruiz."

"I remember now," said John. "Justice please. Justice please. Free the hero, Jimmy Ruiz."

"You weren't so out of touch down in Key West, were you?" asked Dumars with a smile.

"Stick to the story, Sharon," snapped Weinstein.

Dumars's smile faded. She looked at Joshua briefly, then back to John.

"All right. To add insult to injury, Baum wrote an unflattering column about Puma two years after the trial was over. She implied that Puma had become a loose cannon, a profiteer, a racist, a nuisance. Why? Because when Puma moved out to Liberty Ridge, he had opened a private investigation and security firm that catered to the rich and, she tried to prove, refused business from minorities of any color. Baum chose off Puma in print, because Puma had donated generously, very generously, to certain organizations that Ms. Baum dislikes. Organizations such as the California Association of Peace Officers, the NRA, the Freedom Foundation, the John Birch Society, Ducks Unlimited and the California Republican Committee. Her slant was something like, 'here's a man so embittered by the death of his son that he's become infected with hatred.' Ms. Baum seemed to have a point, as Puma had given money only to the Mormon church before Patrick was murdered. Since then, not a penny. I feel that the article was overly aggressive and a violation of Puma's privacy, though—"

"—Sharon, don't—"

"—*Josh, let me continue* . . . I agree completely with Baum's conclusions. But what I feel doesn't matter. So, back to our line of logic, is it coincidence again, that Susan Baum was the intended target? Okay, we can call it coincidence again."

Sharon made another run on the water machine, filling up her third cup. Then she pulled out one of the chairs and sat. John watched her coat close back over the gun.

"When Puma went into his new business after Patrick's death, someone had to file a fictitious business statement, like any lawful company. We took a look at it. The statement ran in a little weekly paper down in San Juan Capistrano, which isn't far from Liberty Ridge. Everything was fine, done by the book, no problem. Trouble is, the original name chosen for his new company, we assume by Puma, was The Freedom Ring. They filed it on statements two consecutive weeks, but on the third week, no DBA was filed at all. Instead, a new name for what we can only assume was the same company—with the fictitious name of Liberty Operations. Some simple research of the newspaper's classified files showed us that The Freedom Ring and Liberty Operations DBA costs were covered by checks from the same account. That account belongs to one of Puma's inner circle—*his* head of security, if you will. Coincidence? No. Hell no. When enough coincidence piles up, it isn't coincidence anymore. The Freedom Ring claimed responsibility for Rebecca. Puma believed the name The Freedom Ring never really existed on record anywhere, and he was right—except for in the dusty files of a little mom and pop paper down in San Juan."

"Have you questioned him?" John asked.

Weinstein stood now and glanced at Dumars. "Thank you, Sharon. No, we've chosen not to. All we would really do is tip him that we're on. He'd have an alibi, and there sure wouldn't be any evidence of a crime left in plain sight around at Liberty Ridge. We're better off letting him believe we're not even looking his way, until we've got enough to justify a search. Questioning him now would be like . . ."

"—Scaring up the bird while it's still out of range," said Dumars.

"Exactly," said Weinstein. He smiled again—that smile so unmirthful, so produced. "John, there's a final element you should know about. Come."

Dumars stayed behind as John followed Joshua out of the room and back down the hallway, then around a corner and into an office. The room was small, lined with bookshelves and bathed by the same chilling, fluorescent light as the conference room. On the wall behind the desk was the Bureau's seal. A chair sat squared to the desk, empty. Joshua shut the door.

"We used to give school children tours of the building," said Weinstein. "Back before we had to check them for weapons. They always wanted to see a real agent. See a real agent's gun. Sit in a real agent's chair. So, have a seat right there, John."

"I'll stand."

Joshua studied him, then walked around the desk and took the chair himself. "I've got a cubicle. If I advance to Senior Special Agent, I'll get an office like this. Maybe this exact one . . . who knows?"

Weinstein was quiet for a long while and John could feel the agent's black, rapacious eyes on him. Always measuring, John thought, always taking, always judging.

"I came here ten years ago. It was a good assignment but I grew up in New York and I thought, California, God, land of fruits and nuts, the self-worshipping and the self-ignorant. Even worse, Orange County. I thought the place would bore me to death in a month. But it didn't bore me at all. It had everything from slick investment hustles up in Newport Center to serial killers running up double digit stats. Orange County had a nice, eclectic criminal menu, and superb weather."

Weinstein offered his dismal little smile again. John leaned against a wall and considered the FBI seal behind the agent.

"For instance," Weinstein went on, "there was a publisher in Little Saigon who got set on fire for suggesting we open relations with Hanoi, same time as Fluor Corporation out in Irvine was jockeying to be the first American behemoth into Vietnam, when Clinton opened it up. Then, there was this bright barrio kid who went to Harvard on scholarship and robbed banks here

during his semester breaks—said you can't take the barrio out of
the boy. There were hookers marching the stretch down Harbor,
bikers and gangs and cutthroats and junkies. Everything. *Everything.*"

Weinstein chuckled. To John, the agent actually looked relaxed now, leaning back in the chair behind the desk. An odd
tone of reverie had come into his voice.

"But what made Orange County most interesting was Vann
Holt. This was his office. He was a legend here—he'd gotten almost every commendation, award, citation and pay raise the Bureau has to offer—and he was still fairly young. I was very young
then—twenty-six—I never really spent much time around him. I
can't even tell you if he knew I was here. But I admired him
because this guy—I'm telling you, John, this guy was absolutely
possessed with the idea of crushing bad guys. He breathed it. He
took a bombing case all the way from Santa Ana to the Gaza
strip and back—and he identified the three bombers who took
out an Arab gentleman right here in Santa Ana. Vann gutted a
white supremacist cell that had serious plans to murder Coretta
King. He just mashed the local operations of the Aryan Brother-
hood, Kahane, the White Alliance—anybody with a race or holy
war to wage. He found something here at the Bureau that very
few people ever find—autonomy. Somehow, he rose above the
sheer bureaucracy we operate under. He didn't break the rules so
much as just, well, levitate above them. His results justified it,
and his sense of personal honor enabled it. He was a mystery to
everyone—and that is one very difficult thing to maintain in a
Federal world. Vann Holt did it by holding the Bureau up to his
standards. Back in eighty-six, he got the highest award the Bureau can bestow—the Director's Distinguished Service medal. It
didn't seem to mean much to him."

Weinstein went quiet and looked away, allowing himself a
pause for introspection.

John wondered if Weinstein had learned his intensity and his
humorlessness from Vann Holt. He looked at Weinstein's profile
and noted the clench of jaw, the hungry eyes, and the morose
lines around his mouth.

And suddenly, John understood.

It appeared to him all at once, seemingly from nothing, like
an oncoming vehicle through rain. The names, the stories and the
setting all coalesced, and he knew.

"Puma," he said.

Joshua didn't react. He just swallowed and continued to stare at the wall. Finally, he looked back at John.

"I thought you might appreciate Holt's situation. You both lost someone very close to you to violence. A murdered son, a murdered lover. You holed up in the desert and tried to forget, he holed up in Liberty Ridge. You two have a lot in common. What you don't have in common is this: Puma did something. He tried to kill an enemy. You've done nothing but withdraw."

"And what have you done?"

Joshua raised his hands expansively. "Why, this, John. This. My work. I've spent a thousand hours trying to solve Rebecca's murder. It practically took a papal dispensation to get assigned to it. But I prevailed. After all, I was not married to the victim. After all, they saw I wouldn't stop, no matter what they did. So they gave me a charge number and cut me loose."

"Why am I here?"

Joshua ignored the question. He leaned forward in the chair now, rested his forearms on the desk before him, and again aimed his unforgiving gaze at John. "You've begun to understand the power of loss, haven't you?"

"I believe so."

"And the hatred that fills a heart when love is removed?"

"That, too."

"Loss and hatred don't just go away, you know. They fester and curdle and grow and they will eat you alive if you let them. The cure is the act. You must do something about them."

"I know that."

"But you don't know what to do, do you? You can't drink your life away in Anza fucking Valley, now can you? No. So, now what?"

"I don't know, yet."

"But you feel . . . willing, don't you? *Inspired*? All suited up for the big game, if you could just find the court?"

"Yeah, Weinstein, that's how I feel."

"Funny feeling. I know. I spent a lot of time like that—it was called training."

"Why am I here?"

The pale agent smiled his death mask of a smile. "Vann Holt murdered the woman I loved and wanted to marry, and I want you to help me take him down. For me. For Rebecca. And for yourself."

"How?"

"You would have to learn how, John. You would have to learn to act and to think. You would have to learn to take steps. One step, then another. I can open the book for you. I can help. And finally, what you learn will be tested, and tested very hard. When it's over, no matter how it ends, you will never be the same again. That's the only promise that I can make."

CHAPTER
SEVEN

John Menden's secret education begins two days after his visit to the Bureau office in Orange County. They use his trailer and the open desert around it for basic instruction in self-defense, small arms skills, micro-camera photography, mnemonic memory assistance and lock-picking.

The long evenings of autumn give them over two hours of sunlight after John's work day at the *Anza Valley Lamp*. It is hard to picture a better place for this kind of training. It is out of the way, accessible only by one road that is rarely traveled, and the kind of area where gunshots, hand-to-hand drills and endless roadwork wouldn't turn a head. Any air surveillance would be immediately apparent. Most importantly, it allows John to continue his work at the paper, which he knows is an important factor in the operation, though he doesn't know why. Weinstein has installed a small trailer—purchased under billing code, "Wayfarer"—alongside John's for the nights when he or Sharon Dumars are simply too tired to drive back to Orange County.

Under the soothing evening sunlight, John shoots pistols and revolvers, puncturing human silhouette targets with tight groups at ten feet, good groups at twenty, fair ones—still all in the black—at fifty.

He spars with Weinstein and Dumars, learning close-in self-defense.

He listens carefully to their guidance regarding the array of micro-cameras they supply for training.

He concentrates on the lockpicking, but is not particularly adept.

He retains the memory boosters and mnemonic devices.

He runs, and he runs, and he runs.

Seven miles a night now, on the punishing, hilly dirt road leading into the High Desert Rod and Gun Club, he runs along a barbed wire fence, watching the deadwood fence posts reel past, huffing to himself with the thudding of his shoes, *Re-bec-ca pause, Re-bec-ca pause, Re-bec-ca pause.*

Re-bec-ca.

Her name is the punctuation of his thoughts, the increments of his clock. It is his blueprint, his refrain, his true north. Her memory is his atmosphere and his sustenance. Her justice is his reason.

Weinstein is pleased to see that John is a natural. He is already better with a sidearm than either he or Dumars, which proves a little embarrassing. Weinstein vows to improve his skills at the indoor range when he can get the time. John's short-term memory, even considering the effect of the alcohol he continues to consume, is excellent. The micro-camera photography goes easily, because all the student has to learn is to shoot documents at a consistent range—the camera is best inside three feet—and to grid off the subject in such a way that nothing will be lost along the borders. A child could do it, Joshua reminds him. Lockpicking is a little tougher, but it is something that Weinstein believes will be of lesser importance. Besides, the real problem with locks these days are the alarm systems keyed into them. So far as the hand-to-hand self defense goes, Joshua believes it stupid to teach in the first place, but he does so anyway due to Bureau protocol. Weinstein notes that John is fast and strong enough to land effective blows to the well-padded Dumars, but even his good reflexes can't keep him from receiving them in turn. John is tough up to a point, Weinstein is happy to see, but he is also happy to see that John knows when to give up and when to play possum. After one particularly fierce battle, his nose bloodied and his eyes glazed, he simply went to his knees in the dust and, groaning, told Dumars, "finish me off." Then he caught her padded foot just in front of his face, and twisted her down to the dirt. Joshua sees to it that John develops a working knowledge of the choke-hold used to render an enemy unconscious. Joshua teaches both the throat blow and throat pull, which puncture the trachea by splintering the delicate bones beneath the jaw, killing fairly quickly. Weinstein has John practice on a dummy they name Amon.

They run. They shoot. They run. They fight.

For Weinstein, the road work is hellish, all three of them jogging down and sprinting up the hard, dusty trail. They start at three miles a day and work up from there. Even for a nonsmoker, Menden's endurance is very good, though the first thing he does after finishing is light up a cigarette and open a beer. Weinstein hears John's rhythmic grunts begin after mile two, and on the third day he realizes that they are the syllables of Rebecca's name.

Most of the training is, in Joshua Weinstein's mind, silly. Silly because, should John need to employ any of this side arm or combat training, he will most likely get killed for his efforts. Bureau experience has proven that. And certainly, whether John Menden runs a six- or a seven-minute mile wasn't going to matter a bit if things went wrong. You can't outrun a bullet. In truth, the training is intended more for John's mental fitness than his physical prowess; it is always to the good if an informant goes in feeling strong. Invincible, no, but strong.

During the first week, Weinstein watches particularly closely for indicators of John Menden's mental state. Weinstein plays the devil's advocate, looking hard for a reason to call the whole thing off. That is an option he—or Washington—can exercise any time until John gets close to Wayfarer, if he gets close to Wayfarer.

They run. They shoot. They run. They fight.

Weinstein observes. He looks for fatigue, doubt, carelessness, and most importantly, any sign that John Menden finds what is happening amusing. The second his student hints that his education or his mission is anything but a matter of the deepest gravity, the whole thing is dead in the water. And although Weinstein does his best to discover something insincere in his student, he does not.

On the dark cool nights he chooses to sleep over in the desert, Joshua lies on his back and looks out the uncurtained window to the big clear stars in the desert sky. He hates the emptiness of it all, the huge spaces between things. He worries, tosses, grunts, curses, dozes. Everything worries him.

What worries Joshua most is that his own feelings toward Rebecca might blind him to Menden's weaknesses—we all have them, he knows. But Weinstein rationalizes that if he could sell this operation to his superiors in Washington—surely the most difficult thing he had ever done—then his vision must have been very clear. It is a matter now of seeing well, of remaining objective and effective.

But staring up from the narrow trailer bed at night, he often wonders: how can I be objective about you, Rebecca, you love, you betrayer. How can I possibly do that? Because you died in the rain and I loved you. I owe you everything, but all I can give you is vengeance.

John keeps his own counsel and allows his easy politeness and placid gray eyes to mask the emotional storm brewing inside him. He is still almost amazed that this—whatever it might turn out to be—is actually happening. He has wanted it for so long. He has tried to imagine it so many times. He has prayed for it so often. And he has believed that someday it would come. It is happening.

So he runs. He shoots. He runs. He fights.

But none of this is really new. In fact, John began his training nearly three months ago, when he moved out to the club property. At the time he had not known what it might be for, only that he must do it, he must be ready, he must prepare himself for . . . something. It was an article of faith that he be fit for the task, whatever the task might entail.

So, by the time Weinstein and Dumars begin to drill him with a pistol he has already shot so many rounds through his own .357 Smith and Wesson that he is fast, accurate and comfortable. He has developed callouses where his hands—he shoots using both—touch the grip and stainless steel frame. By the time they start him on roadwork, he is already running six miles each morning. The three miles a day they start him with is, for John, a gesture. He had even been practicing on a heavy bag and a speed bag up near the club house. For hours on the weekends he had exhausted himself against the canvas and leather, his hands protected by gloves, literally pounding the anger and sadness out of his body. Tim, the silent groundskeeper of the High Desert Rod and Gun Club, had shuffled by occasionally, trying to act uninterested.

With Rebecca's death, John has lost almost all that is valuable inside. He is like a home gutted by fire. Ashes have covered his interior, while his outside remains, to most observers, unharmed.

There was no one he can talk to about her, because he had only been her secret lover. He could not explain to his friends or family why his spirit for living drained away, why he felt a tremendous weight upon him, why the former joys of earning a living, having a drink with friends, making little improvements on his old Laguna Canyon house became unbearable. He was not invited to the private funeral or memorial service. No one offered him condolence.

A man who feels invisible will in fact become invisible. So John simply vanished, one heartbeat at a time, to reappear here, in this vast unforgiving desert, faced with the job of putting himself right. Here, he was free to sort amidst the rubble. Here, he had begun preparing himself for the task of rebuilding. An occasional flicker of hope was the only mortar he had to use.

But the hope became larger when Joshua Weinstein and Sharon Dumars not-so-casually sidled into his life one afternoon in Olie's Saloon. Since that day, John has felt all his evasive, mystifying dreams beginning to come true.

He runs. He shoots. He runs. He fights.

CHAPTER
EIGHT

On the third Saturday of his training, John was to meet Evan. Evan was critical to their purpose, Weinstein said, and Evan had to be reassured by what he saw. This was all that Weinstein said, but John easily gathered that Evan was a superior, perhaps one of those difficult Washington bureaucrats that Joshua had had to convince in order to get a green light for what they were doing. For three days before the meeting with Evan, Joshua was even more humorless than usual, rigidly focused, withdrawn. Dumars was, too.

They drove up to Orange County early that Saturday morning in Dumars' Bureau Ford. It was the first time in three months that John had been in the place where he was born and raised. To enter the county from neighboring Riverside was no great transition—just an older freeway guard rail and the gradual disappearance of the car pool lane. But even this undramatic border was loaded with meaning for John. The second they passed the Orange County sign he saw Rebecca again and heard, quite clearly, her voice and his own:

"I want to tell him. I need to tell him. It's a sin not to tell him. John, I'm having trouble telling him."

"It will happen in time."

"There's been time. I feel like I'm torturing the poor man. He's so . . . so . . . he understands. I know he knows. But he won't make the first move. He's leaving it to me."

"He's hoping you'll change your mind."

"Any fool can change her mind. But I can't change my heart. This hurts me, too, John. Oh, hold me for a minute, just hold me."

And he holds her, there in the kitchen of his Laguna Canyon home, with the blinds drawn and the stew heating on the stove. He strokes her golden, wavy hair. He runs his open hand down the length of her back, then up again to the bunched and shuddering shoulders. Her tears smell like rain and John feels the dampness on his shirt.

Sitting in the cramped rear seat of the Bureau sedan, John looked at the profile of the man Rebecca needed to tell, the man to whom she had engaged herself, the man who knew but out of pride, or perhaps consideration, would not speak first. John studied Joshua Weinstein's features, the tight mouth and proud nose, the slightly large ears, the black wavy hair and the acute understanding in his dark eyes. Yes, John thought, Joshua would have known. Joshua knew. Joshua knows.

They took the freeway down to Irvine Boulevard in Tustin and made a right. John assumed they were heading to downtown Santa Ana and the FBI office again, but Sharon turned left onto a side street, then made another left. They were in a forties suburban tract, notable for its lack of notability. The neighborhood was neat and quiet, and the street was lined with liquidambar trees riotous with dying red leaves. Four doors down, an older gentleman pushed a lawn mower on a wavering course.

"You'll have to wear this for just a minute," said Joshua. He had been rummaging in his briefcase, but now turned and handed John a small cloth item.

Menden unfolded it. It was a hood made of heavy material, with a loose drawstring around the open end.

"Put it on and lie down on the seat. Procedure."

"Up yours," said John.

"Put it on," said Joshua.

John lay on the warm upholstery and felt the car making more turns. To the best of his figuring they had backtracked, and Sharon Dumars was now setting a fresh course from the boulevard. A few minutes was all it took. Then he felt the bump of the car passing into a driveway, followed by a coolness. The garage, he thought. After the car engine was shut off, he heard the garage door clunking into place behind him.

"Rise and shine," said Joshua.

Evan was large and heavy, but when he rose from the table to shake hands, John noted he was not fat. His hand was fleshy and strong. He looked sixty. His hair was straight, gray and cut short. His complexion was gray also, as was his suit. His blue eyes had a mirthless patina, echoed by deep frown lines that ran down from the sides of his mouth and joined those creasing upward from the knot of his chin. A forty-year, two-pack a day cigarette eater, John guessed. But the dour face contradicted itself with a wide and reassuring smile featuring two rows of stunningly white false teeth. He looked to John Menden like a veteran of quiet, unrecorded wars.

They sat around an oval oak table with a dull finish, vintage 1970. There were six plastic placemats depicting floral arrangements, and dust on the surface of the table between them. Four of the places were set with flatware and paper napkins. Beside Evan's fork was a green plastic ashtray, used. The dining room was wallpapered light brown, and a rococo chandelier hung over the center of the table. In the connecting kitchen a young Latino woman poured the contents of a large saucepan into a steaming skillet and regarded John with a profoundly uninterested expression. The house smelled of cilantro and meat.

"What kind of trailer do you have?" Evan asked. His voice was rough and had a very slight Texas drawl.

"It's a Holiday Rambler twenty-nine," said John. "Built in seventy-three."

"Got the power jacks?"

"Yeah. Dual propane tanks and an air conditioner that still works."

Evan's throat rumbled a little and his big smile flashed. "Had a coach myself—a little Airstream—back when I was young. Hunted all over Texas with it—quail, dove, turkey, deer. You name it. I hear you hunt."

"Lots of quail out where I live."

"But you don't use pointers?"

"Flushing dogs, three labs."

"The bobwhite in Texas lock down pretty hard. Need a pointer to show you the way."

"The ones out here like to run. They won't hold for a point except for opening day, maybe."

Evan nodded. He looked at John, then at Sharon, then at the cook in the kitchen. "I miss those days. Young and carefree and the whole of Texas to play in. Me and my brother. You have a brother?"

"No family."

Evan seemed to think about this, nodding absently. "You all grew up right here, didn't you?"

"With my uncle. Just a few miles away."

"How come you've never been married?"

"Never met the right woman."

Evan said nothing, but locked a long evaluating stare onto John Menden's face. "Ever knock one up? Send her to the clinic?"

"Once. High school."

"How'd you feel about that?"

"Sick."

"Not as sick as she felt, though."

"It was bad."

"You a carnivore?"

"Yes, I am."

"Good. We've got some *carnitas* here for lunch."

The cook emerged with three plates balanced on her left arm and one in her right hand. She served Evan first, then Sharon. While she set out the plates, Evan stared at the dusty table top. She returned a moment later with a small plastic tortilla warmer for each of them.

"Bless this food, amen," Evan mumbled, then stuffed the paper napkin into his shirt collar. "Believe in God, John?"

"Yes." John thought a moment. "But I don't claim that He believes in me."

Evan liked this. He laughed from deep down in his chest, and the dead patina over his eyes turned moist and vibrant. "That's good. Last time I checked, He wasn't convinced of my being, either. Busy old bastard, I would think. Spends most of his time worrying about babies and the devil."

Mild laughter.

"To Wayfarer," said Weinstein, holding out his freshly filled glass of iced tea. "Since you mentioned the devil."

John and Dumars clicked glasses with him. Evan rattled the ice in his, but didn't extend it. He set it down without drinking, then plucked a tortilla from his warmer and spooned some pork into it.

"I like to serve pork to Joshua," said Evan. "He won't eat it unless I order him to. Of course, he loves the stuff."

Weinstein smiled rather sourly, but loaded some of the steaming *carnitas* into a tortilla. "Evan loves to find a sore spot, then heal it," he said. "Then rip it open again, then heal it. He's a sadist with a Christ complex, or a Christ with a sadistic side—I haven't figured out which. One of the comforts of my life is that he lives and works on the other side of the continent."

Dumars laughed. "You'd join him in a heartbeat in Washington, if you could."

"No," said Weinstein with his customary gravity. "Wayfarer first. Everything else can wait."

Dumars did one of those downspiraling little chuckles meant to clear the stage.

"You a drinking man, John?" asked Evan.

"When I feel like it."

"Feel like it often?"

"Pretty much so."

"I do, too. Skipped all our wars, didn't you?"

"I was too young for Vietnam."

"Ever feel like you missed out?"

"I had a friend in Grenada. One in the Gulf. They wrote and we talked. I felt like I'd missed little wars and wasn't the worse for it. They did a good enough job without me."

"Would you have gone, in a draft?"

"Sure. They did."

"How come you never registered?"

"I actually forgot. No action when I was eighteen. No draft. No point in it."

"You committed a felony by not seeing the point in it."

"You could arrest me," said John.

"No. That helps us. That's okay. When this is all over and it's become a fiasco, you—an alcoholic, draft-dodging, abortion-happy, meat-hunting woman stealer—will be lots easier to discredit."

"The hood I wore will help, too."

Weinstein almost choked on his tea. "Why do you talk like that, Evan?"

"I'm paid to talk like that. I'm the tire-kicker, John, the guy with fingers in the carb. You're lucky, though, because you don't have to deal with me. Young Joshua here does. The Bureau is *annealing* him in my still strong but fading flame. My task here is to make sure we aren't going into an operation with a complete idiot—I'm speaking now of you. My task is to make sure the Bureau gets what it wants and that you don't get dead. We're dealing with assassins. Anybody who'd shoot a woman from three hundred yards would shoot you in the face from two. So if I'm a little blunt, consider it a thorough check under the hood."

"Check away."

"Why do you want to do this?" Evan asked.

John didn't answer immediately. Joshua had told him that this question would come, and that his answer must be right. The right answer, Joshua had said, was *to avenge the death of Rebecca Harris*. John could not indicate that the arrest of Wayfarer would complete some personal cycle for him, could not imply great personal hatred of Wayfarer, could not suggest that he, John, was after any form of redemption. His desire was to be nothing other than a temporary tool for the execution of justice. *You are just doing your duty—like voting*. But John had never cottoned to Joshua's instruction on this point.

"Because I hate the bastard who shot Rebecca, and I'd like to see him rot in jail. It would make me feel better."

Weinstein's face reddened, so he directed it down toward his plate. Dumars just looked at John, then at Evan.

Evan blinked, then smiled. "Tugging at the collar a little early, aren't you? Joshua will make you pay for that little outburst. That kind of heated honesty might, under the coming circumstances, get you killed."

"You need to know," said John. "You already know. If you didn't, I wouldn't be here. Wayfarer doesn't."

"Christ in heaven let's hope not."

Weinstein was shaking his head toward his plate, as if the *carnitas* had misbehaved.

"But seriously, John, we have no proof at all that Wayfarer even knows who Rebecca Harris was. He's an innocent man. And God knows, he's lethal. That, my friend, is a dangerous combination."

"I take one step at a time. That's all. One little step at a time. I trust these two people."

Weinstein sighed and finally looked up.

Evan took a long moment to study John, then commenced building another pork taco.

"I'm curious," he said finally. "I'm curious about how it felt to be poking Rebecca Harris while she made plans to marry someone else. Can you help me out a little here?"

"No, I can't. That's none of your business."

"Oh, it's most definitely my business."

"Then use your imagination, or go to a library, or call a radio shrink and ask. I won't talk to you about her. She's not a part of this. If that means the whole thing is over, then the whole thing is absolutely over. Don't say her name again. I don't like the way it comes out of your mouth."

Evan stared at John. His eyes were dry, unblinking. "I'll tell you this, Mr. Menden—if you worked for me and said that, I'd slap the living shit out of your head and get you assigned to Alaska."

John shrugged. "Guess I wasn't cut out for Bureau work."

"No. You're the kind of smart guy who likes to stay solo, make his own mistakes, achieve martyrdom. I don't. Joshua doesn't. Sharon doesn't. We're team players. We're real Feds. What we like to do is win."

"I can stand winning."

"You better be ready to. I'll do almost anything to win."

They finished the meal. When it was over and the cook had cleared the dishes, Evan dropped his briefcase onto the table, opened it and removed a stack of paper.

"Loosen up your trigger finger, John," he said. "You've got about a hundred forms to sign. They remove us from any liability for you. They protect us from just about anything you might say to a court of inquiry. They prevent you from going public with anything you do or learn while working with us, whether for private profit, or the catharsis of a guilty conscience, or simply getting back at the bastards who used you. The forms are all standard. I wouldn't even bother trying to read them if I were you. Basically, you're giving away the ranch, and that's the way we like it."

He passed the stack to Dumars, who laid it beside John's elbow.

John didn't look down at the papers. "I need to know what the plan is. I need to know what I'm going to be asked to do."

"You need to what?" asked Evan. "To *know*?"

Evan's deep laugh issued forth again, his shoulders heaving and a pink rush of blood coming to his otherwise gray face. His false teeth shone. Then Weinstein grinned—something Menden had never seen—followed by a giggle from Sharon Dumars. It was all just too much for them. The cook cast a quick glance at him from the kitchen, accompanied by a smirk.

"He needs to *know*," said Evan, stifling his laughter, looking at Joshua. "God, this is some really funny material here."

Weinstein's grin dissipated and he drew a deep breath. "You will learn, John. That's all I can tell you now."

"Comforting, isn't it?" asked Evan, looking down at his watch. "Sign those papers, will you? I've got to see a man about a dog."

Dog or not, Norton *nee* Evan dismissed Dumars and John after John signed the papers. He glanced through them quickly, paying no attention whatsoever to Joshua Weinstein, who sat quietly in his chair. Norton slapped the last sheet over, stuffed the documents back into his briefcase and snapped it shut.

"He's uppity," Norton finally declared.

"We need his spirits high."

"Don't tell me what we need, Joshua. Is this honesty of his a chronic thing or just what he trots out when he's surprised by something?"

Norton now spoke without a trace of Texas accent.

"I haven't seen him surprised by anything yet. Menden reverts to candor when he's not sure what lie to tell."

"Certainly you'd warned him about the revenge and hatred speech."

"Well, yes. You have to understand, Norton, it's his high level of emotion that might make this thing sustainable."

"Stop quoting me." He sighed, hefting the briefcase off the table and onto the floor.

At this point the Latina cook came in, wearing a business suit. Her thick black hair was tied back and she was stuffing her apron into a duffel bag. She nodded at Joshua, then set her pistol on the counter and started putting away the clean dishes.

"Monica?" asked Norton, without looking at her.

"He's just confident enough to get into trouble," she said. "He needs to believe more in us. He needs to depend on us."

"He'll come to do that," said Weinstein. "We're trying to build a relationship with him, not offer a one-night stand."

"I don't trust pretty men," said Norton. "They lack character, period."

"He's passed every phase of his training perfectly. It's not his fault he's got a pretty face. That's what got us all here, isn't it?"

Norton nodded, acknowledging this reference to Rebecca. "How does he react to pressure?"

"The most pressure we've put him through was today, your questions about Rebecca."

"Based on that, I'd say he's liable to become pissed off."

"I think he can keep his head."

"Does he sprint at the end of his runs?"

"Always. Why?"

"He looks like a quick-comer to me. He might need endurance, Joshua. If he saves enough mustard for a sprint after seven miles, all the better. Has he shown any interest in Sharon?"

"A little. Not much. I could be wrong, though."

"Hmm. I'd sure like to have more pull with him than just you."

"Rebecca's the pull, Norton. Not me, or Sharon, or anyone else. He's single-minded."

"No use trying to change that, I suppose."

"Let's use it while it's there."

Norton and Weinstein stood and shook hands. Monica took a chair at the table.

"Things in Washington are okay," said Norton "Frazee is still too interested in Wayfarer, but I don't know how to correct that. And the more I try to shade him away, the more control he wants. He's like a kid with toys. I hate bureaucrats. Of course he's worried sick about the Hate Crimes money we got from the White House—worried about it going away. He's always whining about no money. So he's determined to keep this operation small and deniable. No show of force from us. No Ruby Ridge. No Waco."

"We've all got our crosses to bear," said Monica. "You're Joshua's, and Frazee is yours."

"Whose are you?"

"My husband's, I hope."

Weinstein remained standing when Norton sat back down. Joshua's stomach was trembling a little, and he felt uncertain in his knees. "Well?" he asked.

"Nice work," said Norton. "Move ahead."

CHAPTER
NINE

They dropped John in front of a little house on Sun Valley Drive, a small street off of Laguna Canyon Road, then headed for town to pick up some groceries for their celebration.

He stood there for a while, noting the fresh asphalt under his feet, the ivy choking the Chinese elm in his front yard, the wooden fence he'd built to contain the dogs, the old brick chimney and the forlorn face of the house he had once happily called home. Mrs. Gorman from across the street waved at him uncertainly, focusing on him with her weak eyes as if he were someone returned from the dead. He nodded, walked down the driveway and let himself in through the squeaking gate for the first time in almost five months.

The yard was overgrown, in shambles. Luckily, it was hidden from the neighbors by the ivy-covered fence. The lawn furniture seemed to have sunk into an abyss of weeds. The vegetable garden was profuse with zucchini, and pocked by gopher mounds. A ground squirrel, squash in mouth, hurried away toward the woodpile by the side of the house. The needles of a bristlecone pine lay deep beneath the tree, lashed loosely together by a silk skein of spiderwebs and funnels that shone dustily in the afternoon sun.

John sees Rebecca there, under that tree, sitting in a beach chair with a book open on her lap and her long pale legs stretched into a patch of late December sun.

"Wine?" *he asks.*

"You," she answers.

John worked the key in a lock gone stubborn with disuse. Finally it turned. Then the familiar clunk of the heavy door sucking inward, and the ambience—aged by absence but intact—reaching out to greet him as he stepped inside. Dust. Heavy air. The smell of loss. Shapes of things still firm in their places, matching perfectly the shapes and places in his memory. Sunlight diffused through the dirt of windowpanes. A potent silence. Home.

"Oh," he muttered.

He gathered up the sheets he'd placed over the couch and chairs, the television and stereo, the coffee table and hearth. The covers were heavy with dust, and so were the things beneath them. John had not known until now that motes were smaller than the weave of cotton. He took the sheets outside and tossed them into the weeds.

He walked back inside, leaving the door open, then went into the kitchen. He opened the blinds and windows. The refrigerator still hummed quietly and John was pleased that he had kept the utilities on. Five months, he thought. In the dining alcove off the kitchen he removed the sheets from the table and chairs, then slid open the glass door that faced the canyon drainage creek and dropped them to the patio. The bricks were buried by the bright orange bracts of an enormous bougainvillea growing beside the house. When the sheets hit, some of the bracts lifted up, then floated down in alternating sideways dips, like tiny magic carpets. And he sees her again on that patio, wrapped in a heavy blue robe he has bought for her visits here, with the rain pouring off the roof shingles on three sides of her, and she smiles at him over a cup of coffee as the steam issues up past her eyes and John thinks, yes, those are the eyes I've waited a lifetime to know.

He straightened the downstairs bathroom a little. The toilet bowl was stained, so he brushed it out with some liquid bleach, flushing twice. For Sharon, he thought.

Then he approached the bedroom. He didn't walk right in, but rather hesitated at the threshold and, leaning over it like an inquiring butler, scanned the room for its familiarities, its memories and heartaches. They were dense in there, too packed and coiled and alive for John Menden to confront just now. He kept seeing Rebecca by the planter in the rain.

"Oh," he muttered again. "Oh."

He sat alone on the upstairs deck and looked over the canyon. Vultures and redtail hawks cruised in the updrafts. From isolated stands of scrub oak, heat waves shimmered up against the dry hills.

He thought about when he had hiked and camped in these arroyos as a boy, when he had found shards of Gabrieleno pottery, arrowheads and a revolver made in 1844. He still clearly remembered the mountain lion he had seen in 1960. He recalled with minor pride the tiny night snake he had captured, which local biologists assured him was not found in the region. He wondered if his boxes of 35mm slides down in the garage were still good.

John stared off toward the hills, but in his mind's eye he saw only Rebecca. It was important to be here now, he thought, to touch the same places she had touched, to breathe the air she had once shared.

Just before sunset John uncovered the barbecue, arranged it out by the railing overlooking the street, and lit the charcoal.

Joshua came up with his second gin and tonic, watching closely as John started up the fire. "Want that bottle of tequila now?" he asked.

"Later," said John.

"You almost sunk us with that crack to Evan about hating Wayfarer's guts."

"It worked out okay, Joshua. At least they were my words, not something you put in my mouth."

"True. My words would have been about the same."

Joshua pulled deeply on his drink.

Downstairs, Sharon boiled water for rice and made a salad. John could hear her knife strokes on the cutting board. He had always liked the sounds of a woman in his house, and he remembered the ones he had been with in his thirty-four years. It was odd, he thought, that you could love someone but not be able to imagine yourself with her for very long. The harder you look ahead, the more your vision blurs.

But when he had met Rebecca Harris, engaged though she was, he easily foresaw her presence in his life. She had simply arrived. Up to that point, John had not believed that destiny was anything more than what you decided to do, but the connection he felt to Rebecca made him reconsider. Rebecca wasn't so much a discovery as a recognition.

He had puzzled over this for many nights, wondering if the circumstances of a man's life could conspire to lead him to the one woman destined to join him. It was a corny idea, or was it? Either way, it had happened.

But how could he possibly explain to this woman what he had found, what he knew? It was like having an album of the world's most beautiful music, and nothing to play it on.

Weinstein shuttled between the kitchen and the deck. As John put the chicken on the grill, Weinstein arrived holding his third cocktail, already half gone, John's bottle of Herradura and a handful of limes. He set the bottle and the limes on the railing, then took a seat toward the sunset and drank from his glass.

"I don't usually drink this much," he said.

"You seem to be enjoying it."

"We've got so much to do," Weinstein said thoughtfully. "But no, I don't want to talk about that right now. I want to talk about Rebecca."

John looked at him, then returned his attention to the sizzling hens. Through the smoke, he was aware of Weinstein's eyes upon him.

Joshua drank deeply. "Did her letter surprise you? Had you intuited that she was about to leave me for you?"

John opened the bottle and took a sip of the Herradura. It was warm and sweet in his mouth, and tasted like the desert and the maguey it was made out of. "I knew she had to decide. The time for that had come. I thought she'd stay with you."

Weinstein grunted. "I knew she was leaving. I watched her do it, minute by minute, day by day, month by month. I didn't know who it was. I didn't ask. My father died of cancer when I was twenty-two. It was similar. A slow march, but you understand where it will end. Don't say you're sorry. You can say anything you want about Rebecca, but don't say you're sorry."

John said nothing, but repositioned the chicken on the grill. He took another sip of tequila.

"How come you don't drink that stuff with limes and salt?" Weinstein asked.

"It ruins the taste."

"Is it really hallucinogenic, like they say?"

"No, not for me."

"Does it make you mean?"

"No. It's a green, feminine spirit. It's calming compared to, say, Scotch or gin. Not so angular."

"A feminine spirit," repeated Weinstein. "You fucked Rebecca for the first time on January the ninth, didn't you?"

"That's right."

"I could tell from the look on her face when I saw her that night. Here, was it?"

"Downstairs."

"Bedroom?"

"You really want to know these things, Josh?"

"Yes, John. I want to know them. I have my ways of tending her memory, just like you have yours. What did she do when you finished?"

"She cried."

"Did you cry, too?"

"No."

"How did you feel?"

John sipped again from the bottle as a fresh billow of smoke emerged from the coals. "I felt like I'd finally come home, after a long time away."

Weinstein smiled unhappily. "Did you tell her that?"

John nodded.

"You're a real smoothie," said Weinstein. "I never really had that gift myself."

"What gift is that?"

"Telling women the right thing. The thing they want to hear, even if they don't believe it."

"Well, I don't know, Josh."

"That's what you are, John—a smooth-talking Romeo."

John took another sip of the Herradura. It was apparent to him that Joshua Weinstein was spoiling for a fight, or at least for a way to define John lowly, and believe the definition. Part of tending the memory, he thought. It didn't seem right to resist, really, but you couldn't just stand there in your own house, let some fellow serve you a plate of shit and pretend to enjoy it.

"An hour ago, it was my stupid honesty with Evan you were complaining about," he said. "Now I talk smoothly. Whatever I had that Rebecca liked, you must have had some of, too."

Weinstein took another big gulp of his drink. A visible shudder traveled down his neck. "That's wrong. I've concluded that we are opposites. That, in fact, the reasons she went to you were to acquire what I couldn't supply. Smooth talk was one thing. And cool another. I'm not cool, John. I'm a hot little New York Jew, and nothing can change that. She loved that about me. But what you are, she loved more. You've got the tongue, Menden. You've got the look and the cool. You've got the qualities promoted on cold-filtered beer commercials and ads for sports cars. You've got a touch of something few women can really resist. It's part Hollywood, part myth."

"Don't undermine her," said John.

"Accuracy before sentiment. The truth may not get us far, but lies get us nothing but lost."

"The truth is she loved us both, and for the time it took her to write that letter at least, she thought she loved me more."

"She wasn't fickle. That letter was her heart."

"Well, Joshua, you can decide she left you for a better ape, or that she left you for an ass. The truth is probably somewhere in between. If you want me to take a convenient role and play it out, forget it. I'd just mess up my lines and the whole thing would be a waste of breath."

Dumars entered then, bearing a pitcher of what Weinstein was drinking. She moved through the silence and filled his outreached glass. She glanced at John with a look of concerned inquisition.

"God, you'd need a blowtorch to cut the vibes up here," she noted. "Remember, boys, we're supposed to be celebrating, sort of?" Then she retreated from the deck without another look at either of them.

"Sharon is aware that she needs a man, and the awareness embarrasses her," said Weinstein. "She's of our generation, the first in this republic to be raised with the notion that love can be found with a housecat, and that men are just enemies waiting to screw women over. Even women younger than Sharon have realized how unworkable that is. But there she remains, on the cutting edge of the ridiculous. Do you find her attractive?"

"Yes. She's got a better sense of humor than you give her credit for."

"There you go again, saying what they want to hear, even when they're not around to hear it. You're a smoothie, Menden."

"Yeah, yeah—you've covered that already, Josh."

"There was a time, and I'm not sure if it's passed, when I wanted to challenge you. On any and every thing a man is supposed to be. I knew I couldn't beat you at being tall. But at everything else, I believed I'd kick your ass. I still believe I would. I'm a better man than you, by almost any standard of measure. If ever you want to contest that, just name your game and I'll be there. I've speculated on the most satisfying way of trouncing you. Really smashing the living shit out of you."

"And?"

"It changes."

"Well, I hope dangling me in front of Wayfarer then dropping me in hasn't entered your mind."

Weinstein stared at John for a long moment, then shook his head. "That's business. You couldn't find a more conscientious master than me. What I'm talking now is strictly pleasure. And don't forget—I hate Wayfarer more than I hate you."

"That's comforting, Joshua."

Weinstein finished half his drink in one gulp, set down the glass and pulled the automatic from his shoulder holster. He looked at it for a long moment, as if searching for some new feature he'd overlooked. It was a 9mm Smith with a blued finish and dark walnut grips. He flipped the safety off, then on again.

"Could be an old-fashioned gunfight," he said.

"Could," said John.

Joshua set the gun on the deck, then picked up his drink again. "That scare you—a drunk man with a gun?"

"It sure does. Aren't you breaking some FBI rule?"

"You sound like a faggot, whining about rules. Rebecca liked it on the top with me. You, too?"

"How do you like your chicken?"

"That's a dumb question. When's the last time somebody told you they like their chicken rare?"

Weinstein picked up the gun again, aimed it at John, flipped the safety off, then on.

John studied him through the smoke. The idea crossed his mind to kick the barbecue over at Joshua's feet and watch him scramble to keep his wingtips from blistering. John knew that Weinstein wouldn't shoot him on purpose, but he was worried that his "master" was revealing himself to be a genuine hazard.

Booze and guns were an even worse combination than booze and cars.

Joshua holstered the pistol, sighed, and drank again. "I'm just blowing off a little steam," he said.

"Good to know," said John. "Just that light little trigger between three highballs and a bullet in my heart."

And that was all it took—one mention of a bullet and a heart—to send them both plummeting back down to earth, back down to the tree-shaded deck on which their dinner was cooking, back down to the house which had heard the laughter of the woman they had both loved.

"I'm a lot more sober than I look. And there's one thing I want to get straight, John. It doesn't have to do with competition. It's just a simple fact that you're going to have to accept. It's a fact that I need to remember. This is the fact—I loved Rebecca more than you did. *I loved her more than you ever could.*"

John watched Weinstein as he said this, noting the blood rushing into Josh's ears, the bob of his big Adam's apple, the insatiable glow of his eyes behind the lenses. This whole thing, he thought, is a crying shame. Every second of every day since Rebecca died in the cold March rain, just a crying fucking shame.

"Yes, you did," he said, looking down through the smoke, his eyes burning with more than the smoke.

"Thank you."

After dinner they turned off the houselights, sat on the patio chairs and watched the stars come out. The night was clear and the moon rose full and white over the hilltop. It was so bright John could read his watch face without pushing on the light. He looked out into the canyon and thought of the nights he'd slept back there, nights just like this with the moon radiant and the ground warm enough for a lightweight sleeping bag. He remembered the puma he'd seen out here, in the first light of a summer morning, lying on a rock outcropping only a hundred feet away, calmly eyeing him. Puma, he thought. Wayfarer.

John wondered if Joshua was reading his thoughts.

"Wayfarer," said Joshua. "You know, we still get to make the code names. Most Fed agencies went computer a long time ago. Wayfarer. I chose it. I'm glad we weren't stuck with barnyard, or crackerjack or evergreen or something. He's fared way beyond the limits, way up river."

"He's our Kurtz," said Dumars. "And you, John, are our Marlow."

Joshua looked at her in the darkness, then out to the hills. "There's luck in this business, like in anything else," he said. "Luck was what brought me to you, John. I spent five months after Rebecca's death, putting together my file on Wayfarer. At first, it seemed a distant possibility, but then it became not distant at all. I weighed the circumstantial evidence against what I knew of him, and I saw how it could happen. All of this, and still nothing solid, still nothing that could convict. Sure, I could have questioned him anytime. One shot. One time. And if he was lucky, which he is, and smart, which he also is—we'd have come away with less than nothing. Less, because he would be alerted— impossible to surprise."

Joshua had by now graduated from highballs to black coffee. He sipped it, then poured more from the thermos he'd brought up to the deck. "Yes, I looked at you. My curiosity was not connected to Wayfarer at all. It was a way of understanding what had happened to me and Rebecca. I just wanted to see what she had chosen. What I lacked. Your name on the envelope helped quite a bit, so far as ID went. I tracked your grief, your resignation from the *Journal*, your little sailing trip down in the South Pacific, your purchase of the trailer and your move out to Anza Valley. I observed you at Olie's more than once before our meeting, as you pointed out. So what did I have, except a suspect I couldn't arrest, and a mourning suitor who was disengaging himself from the world? Nothing. Nothing until the luck came in. Then, I had something to work with."

"What was the luck?"

"Oh, it was you, John. But that wasn't apparent at first. It wasn't apparent until I was poring over some Wayfarer intelligence late one night, nothing hot, just the usual kinds of things we collect about people who might prove dangerous. And there I saw the connection. The luck hit. My ears got warm and my lips quivered and I began to see the design of things. There *is* a design of things, John—it is up to us to discern it."

"And you discerned."

"Oh, did I ever. There it was, right in front of me, finally. A little window. I'm reading about Wayfarer. His habits and hobbies. His patterns. Wayfarer sails the Newport to Ensenada yacht race every year. Wayfarer spends every New Year's Eve at a party in Washington, D.C. Wayfarer makes a trophy hunting expedition every spring with two of his friends from the Boone and Crockett record book. Wayfarer flyfishes the Metolius River in Oregon every summer. Then, this oddment: Wayfarer hunts the quail opener every year down in the desert with his friends and daughter. He used to take his wife and son, of course, but no longer. They fly the company helicopter into the Lake Riverside airstrip. He brings his dogs. Dog, dogs, dogs—made me think of you and yours—dogs everywhere I looked. He's got a little home there in Lake Riverside Estates—thirty-five hundred square feet, right on the water. They spend the night, then set out in his Land Rover just after sunup. They hunt the morning, head into town for lunch and a beer at two, then go back out for the afternoon shoot. Every year for ten straight seasons. No variation. Like a clock. On goes my little light. What town do they go to? Anza Valley. John Menden's ground. Oh my, I think—oh *my*! Is John my luck? Is John my man? My miracle?"

"I've been called a lot of things, but never a miracle," said John.

Dumars laughed along with him, but Joshua did not.

"So I start thinking of you two together, in a way I never had before. You and Wayfarer on the same ground at the same time. Synergy. Lots of synergy. I know by then that you're, well . . . at loose ends. I wonder if you might need some vengeance for Rebecca. I wonder if he might like you, might have a use for you if you earned it. You two have very similar backgrounds, you know. You two are frighteningly alike, in some ways. So I see that if I could just get you two together—you and Wayfarer—it might be the start of a beautiful friendship. And here he is, scheduled to invade your desert on October fifteenth. That is when I came to you, John. To see if you were cut from the material I needed. You are. So here we sit, approved from on high, waiting to move. October fifteenth is less than two weeks away."

Joshua drank again from his coffee cup, then set it on the ground beside him. He stretched his legs and looked up into the night sky.

"You are going to be Wayfarer's hero," he said. "But you are going to be my Trojan Horse. My eyes, my ears. I'll get you close enough to Holt for you to smell him."

John took another long drink of the Herradura. It was beginning to make him feel that all things were possible, which he knew by experience was a dangerous way to feel. He had begun to feel that way with Rebecca, just before she died. He had felt that way before his mother and father lifted off in their little Piper for the last time.

He felt the deep rumble of satisfaction moving inside himself. He sensed the action that he had so longed for, becoming clear. Looking ahead of him, he saw the challenge of justice for Rebecca, the one thing he could offer her.

Looking backward, though, he had the sense that something terrible was gaining on him.

"Wayfarer will be ours," said Joshua.

"And I'll be his," said John.

"I'd like the ring back now."

John brought it from his pocket, the modest diamond that Rebecca had worn in honor of her pledge to Joshua.

CHAPTER

TEN

The next day, Sharon Dumars met Susan Baum for lunch at Romeo's Cucina in Laguna Beach. Baum had been calling the Bureau office for almost four months now, trying to corner someone into a meeting. Sharon had politely dodged her at first, not wanting to destroy a possibly friendly media contact. Then suddenly, Norton's green light pending, Josh realized how much they needed her. He gave her back to Sharon.

Baum was much harder to reel in than Dumars expected. The columnist agreed to meet with her, although Dumars was not technically the agent-in-charge. Baum refused to settle on a place for the meeting until half-an-hour before it was to take place. She ran Dumars through three changes of venue before settling on Romeo's. On the phone, Baum's voice was terse and hushed, as if she was being listened to.

The restaurant was large and very bright, with windows that focused the October sunlight onto oil paintings that Dumars found pleasant because of all the yellows. The interior woodwork was curvaceous and smooth—not one hard angle—and Dumars found this pleasant too, though she wondered how they made the sweeping, dramatic cuts. The lamps were fashioned from paper stitched together with thick string, which Dumars didn't like because they made her think of skin. So much pretty in the world, she thought, and so much ugly. Amazing that people did not know the difference. She slid her briefcase under the table.

The waiter was tall, dark and ponytailed, and eyed her with

a tip-upping mix of respect and desire. She wanted to find him annoying but she could not.

"May I offer you the Chardonnay today?"

"Iced tea, thank you."

The columnist entered. She marched across the floor toward the table with her signature limp, which did nothing to diminish the sense of pure determination she exuded. She was dressed in a long, flowing, dark blue and green geometrically patterned dress that appeared to be made from complex layers of silk. It was gathered at the waist by a gold lame sash, and as Baum cut across the floor her oversize cuffs billowed. She wore round, costume earrings bedecked by what had to be *faux* jewels, and which looked to Sharon like something from the Arabian Nights. Her shoes were bright white athletic high-tops with a fancy black zig zag across the ankle; her hair a salon-tortured halo of dry gold. Susan Baum, Sharon decided, was her own entourage.

"Thanks for coming," she said breathlessly, dropping a large and apparently heavy leather bag onto the chair beside Sharon and sitting across from her. She cast a look back toward the doorway. "God, I had to park eighty blocks away. Iced tea, please."

"Special Agent Sharon Dumars—I'm happy to finally meet you, Ms. Baum."

"Call me Susan, Special Agent. But please, could we possibly change places?" Her voice was brittle and she looked again at the door. "I've got a full-blown phobia of doors now. I need to be able to see them."

"Of course."

They traded seats. A palpable air of reassurance radiated from Baum now, but her voice was still reedy and tight. "Food here any good?"

"I've never eaten here. It was your pick."

"I pick for safety."

"You'll be safe here, Ms. Baum."

Baum removed her immense white-framed sunglasses and looked into the menu. "Trendy, I hear. Strange how all these new Italian places refuse to make spaghetti and meatballs. What'll you bet it isn't on the menu?"

Sharon, who had perused the menu, confirmed.

"I lived on canned spaghetti and meatballs when I was a cub reporter. I wasn't much of a home economist. Still am not. First time I heated up Chef Boyardee in college I spooned some noodles, sauce and all, onto the kitchen wall because I'd heard that's how you tell if it's ready. My mother never let me forget that one."

Sharon laughed, looked into Baum's green eyes, then away again. "Maybe they'll make some up for you."

"I suppose. This is on me, by the way. On the *Journal*, actually."

"It's a little easier for me if we just pay separately. You know how gifts to the government are looked at these days."

"Well, then *you* tell that ponytailed hunk of a boy you want separate checks. He thinks you're pretty, you know."

Dumars wondered how such a distracted, frightened whirlwind of a woman could notice so much without seeming to notice anything. "It's his stock expression."

Baum studied the man, who was leaning over a nearby table. "I'm really so glad I'm not young again. I've been married for thirty years, and I can't say it's been all beer and skittles, but to be put out in the world again, looking for a date, or a mate? *God.* You're single, I take it."

"Yes."

"What's it like?"

"Like being single."

"Never been married?"

"No. You're not profiling Special Agent Single Sharon for the *Journal*, are you?"

"No, not at all, though I'd love to someday. I apologize. I'm just so overwhelmingly nosey. And I know so many young, eligible, very attractive men. Jewish mother, Jewish mother—I know."

Sharon couldn't help but laugh again, half from Baum's self-deprecation, half from the relief at being let off the hook. "Then what *are* you doing, Ms. Baum?"

"Susan."

Baum smiled. Sharon noted the nice whiteness of her teeth and the overall pleasantness of her face.

"I've come for an explanation."

Involuntarily, Sharon blinked. "Of what?"

"Of what you've found out, of course."

"You cut right to the chase, don't you?"

"I detest bullshit. Always have."

"Then lose the Special Agent stuff. Sharon's fine."

"Sharon. I've always loved that name."

Dumars looked directly into Baum's face, riled at being flattered, baited and probed. One of the things that had drawn her to the Bureau was that you could comfortingly vanish into the correct side of the law. She had worked too hard for privacy and dignity to put up with this kind of crude intrusion. She was not paid to be on display. She gratefully noted the din of the lunch hour in this restaurant, thankful that no one around could possibly follow their conversation.

"Look, Sharon, I'm willing to get off on any foot you want here. I'm the supplicant. I'm the one in the dark. I'm the one who almost got my guts shot out."

"Maybe you should just go ahead and ask your questions, then."

Let her shoot her wad, Joshua had said.

"Good idea. Would you go with the ravioli or penne?"

"The ravioli."

They ordered, gave the waiter their menus and simultaneously reached for their glasses of tea.

Baum looked at her unabashedly. "It's been six months. No arrest. No suspect. Precious little communication with me for the last five. What gives?"

"What gives?"

"Bluntly, what have you found out?"

"I can tell you that the investigation is ongoing. That we're interviewing, reviewing and collecting information. You should know that it's never been Bureau policy to go public with things until we really think it will yield results."

"Well, with all respect, your flak could have told me the same thing. In fact, he has—several times."

"Every word of it is true."

"So, after half-a-year, you have no suspect?"

"I'm not prepared to say that."

"Then you *do* have a suspect?"

"I'm not prepared to say that, either."

Baum leaned back. "You people. You government people. Honestly. And you say the media is leading this country down the suckhole. You're not prepared to say anything about anything. Fine. Then let me tell you what *I've* found out, just so we have something to talk about while we eat. Okay?"

Sharon waited, picking through the seafood in her bowl of pasta.

Baum's expression seemed to lose some of its vigor then, and a fretful grayness replaced the rosiness of her cheeks. She looked back at the door again. For a moment she looked very old. "The first two months were terrible for us. I felt afraid, anxious, furious, helpless, idiotic. Poor Rob—that's my husband—he was even worse. The *Journal* provided twenty-four hour security, but only for a month. After that, I took a two-month leave of absence in New York. When I came back it was just escorts to and from my car, which I pull right up to the lobby entrance now anyway. Not the same car, of course—I could never touch the old Town Car after what happened. Now, I get a different one every week. Anyway. By then I wasn't really scared any more—I was numb. I was angry. At the people who killed Rebecca, at you people for freezing me out of the loop, at the world. Still, we went through two home security systems that made us feel like prisoners, car alarms that screamed at all hours when they weren't supposed to, even a couple of Doberman pinschers that bit Rob. We've got two apartments now, plus our home, and we shuttle between them like roaches. Not once in that time, Sharon, not *once* in six months have you called me and said 'look out, Baum—we think he'll try it again,' or 'don't worry, Susan, he's not going to try it twice,' or anything at all." She glanced back at the door again. "On the contrary, you barely returned my calls until last month. I'm sitting out at the edge of your investigation like a half-used target. It doesn't seem beyond reason for me to wonder what you've found out—if anything."

Dumars felt a little ashamed but, as with any bureaucrat, procedure was God and procedure was on her side. "Well, Susan, we told you back in March to stay aware, vary your routine, not expose yourself unnecessarily. We told you to be cautious and alert."

"That was sure a lot of help. Is *varying* my routine leaving at a different time every morning, or is it moving to Chicago? Is being *aware* the same as not sleeping for three straight days? Is it *necessary* to actually leave my home? *Cautious?* Well, is going out to dinner cautious or is it not? It took me months to arrange this simple meeting with you. A lunch. I sit here in public. I'm exposed, aren't I?"

Sharon straightened in her chair and inhaled audibly.

"No, really, Sharon. Please answer me. I'm just as exposed right here as I was that afternoon in the parking lot, aren't I? I mean, I'm no less . . . obvious."

"Yes, yes, Susan," Dumars answered quietly. "You are exposed here. And I see your point—if someone is determined to kill you, you're exposed almost everywhere you turn."

"It's a cliche but it's true, Sharon, that if they can shoot the President, nobody else is safe. Just ask Rebecca Harris."

Dumars ate slowly, letting a long silence fall over the table.

"So anyway," continued Baum. "I got mad. And when I get mad I go to work. And when I work I find things out. I'm real good at finding things out. I do the same thing you do, Special Agent, but I make stories and you make arrests. It will come as no shock at this point, I suppose, but *I've* got a suspect."

"Oh, the—"

Co-opt her. Contain her. Anticipate her. Remember, we have been ahead, not behind.

"—Holt idea, Ms. Baum. I've heard it."

"News travels fast."

"You can hardly make inquiries about someone like Vann Holt to the Costa Mesa Police, the Orange County Sheriff and the FBI in Washington without word getting around law enforcement."

"So, you're not interested in that idea either?"

"Like Josh told you on the phone. Like our public relations agent told you—we took your idea very seriously. And we've looked at Mr. Holt very hard and at some length. We came up empty. Although your theory has a certain logic to it, we couldn't find one piece of substantive evidence that incriminated him."

"Not even the articles I wrote about his son? About him?"

"With all due respect, Ms. Baum, those articles only incriminated you."

"Oh, my. One bureaucrat standing up for another. I'm not in much shock."

Dumars set down her iced tea and locked her gaze onto Susan Baum's green eyes. Sharon could feel the heat rising into her cheeks. Her calves felt tight.

"Ms. Baum, if you're implying some kind of kinship between your suspect and the agency he *used* to work for, you are being overly suspicious and naive."

The columnist stared back.

"Do you honestly believe we wouldn't investigate him because of his former employment with us?"

Baum touched her napkin to her lips, then spread it onto her lap. "I don't know what to believe."

"Then I'll tell you. Believe in us."

Baum leaned forward, her voice a hiss and her eyes luminous with the inward light of emotion. "*Then talk to me!*"

Sharon sat back and again stared hard into Susan Baum's eyes. She tried to look pitying, respectful and admiring all at once.

She'll do anything to get inside. She'll lap up our truth like one of John's dogs.

"We have something," Sharon said finally. "That's one of the reasons it took some time to meet with you. We had to make some connections, gather some more facts. We're sorry for what must seem like an incredible delay. But we've been busy, I can assure you. In fact, Susan, right now you could safely say that we're hot."

Baum said nothing, but kept her brilliant green eyes on Dumars.

"We have a suspect. And we're ready to go public with it."

Baum's face turned an excited pink and her eyes seemed to grow even brighter. "*Who?*"

"I think we should talk about this somewhere else. Let's finish up and take a walk. Okay?"

"Oh, I'm finished."

CHAPTER
ELEVEN

They strolled down the boardwalk at Laguna's Main Beach, but Sharon knew Baum could not go far. It was Josh's idea to "pre-fatigue" her, loosen her up for gullibility as a picador would loosen up a bull for the sword. The poor columnist was sweating hard and limping badly before they'd gone a hundred yards. She'd pulled a hat from her bag and jammed it down over her hair, and slipped on a big white windbreaker. She kept looking behind them.

"I don't like looking the same for more than about one hour," Baum stated. "But it's hard on the wardrobe."

"It's okay, Susan. You're okay here with me."

They sat on two multicolored ceramic seats with a multicolored ceramic stand and chessboard between them. Sharon looked out at the autumn Pacific—waveless, breeze-brushed, silver.

Along the boardwalk tourists wandered, taking pictures. Locals smashed volleyballs back and forth in the sand while further down the beach two basketball courts teemed with jerking, jumping bodies. Offshore stood two jagged black rocks topped with birds that didn't so much as flutter when the swell heaved up around them. Sharon could even see Catalina Island, twenty miles away, a low shape separating the metallic sea from a pale blue sky. She liked this town. She had lived here her junior year in college with her boyfriend. The city and its beaches always brought back memories of her love, his betrayal, the way they went from being happy to being over. Donny. That was almost a decade ago.

"His name is Mark Foster," Sharon said. "He's twenty-four, a drifter, a criminal. At the time of Rebecca's death he was living in Huntington Beach, hanging out at a White Supremacist compound in Newport."

"Alamo West," said Baum. "I wrote about it."

"We think you might have touched an even bigger nerve than you usually do," said Sharon, flatteringly.

"I tried to be nice to those skinhead Nazi morons. It was my chance to be forgiving. But the man who runs the place—that reverend?—he actually made me nauseous. I do remember that Mark Foster was less of a swine than the others, or seemed to be. Funny though, I've forgotten which one he was."

"This might help."

Sharon removed from her briefcase the file supplied by Norton. On top was one photograph of Foster—a mug shot taken by Gainesville Police back in 1988. There were two others: one a mug taken by police in Eaton, Colorado, 1992; the other a snapshot of Foster and friends at a neo-Nazi skinhead rally in Huntington Beach, 1994. His face wasn't very clear in this nighttime shot because Mark and his friends were gathered around a bonfire, some holding torches, some holding beers, and the photographer was obviously an amateur.

"The *Journal* ran this picture with my column," said Baum.

"Right. We've got a rap sheet on him, too. Burglary, assault, assault with a deadly weapon, public drunkenness, public disturbance. To be honest, Susan, it took the Bureau some time after Rebecca's death to start poking around Alamo West. I mean, we had quite a list of people you'd attacked in the *Journal*."

"I didn't attack anyone at Alamo West."

"That's why we didn't scrutinize them at first. But you did *condescend* to them. To some people, that's worse than a full offensive."

"Well, I was a little . . . maybe, pitying."

"Maybe Jewish women shouldn't condescend to neo-Nazi men, Susan."

Dumars wondered if she was laying it on a little thick. She had the psychological equivalent of a choke-hold right now, and years of law enforcement training had taught her to never, *ever* surrender an advantage. Still, she flinched inwardly at her own feigned superiority. To hide this, she took a deep breath and looked knowingly at the columnist.

Baum nodded as Dumars continued.

"The man you suspected, by the way—Vann Holt—was someone we looked hard at, early. He cleared. So congratulations on your instincts, Susan. Maybe you've got a career with the Bureau if you ever get tired of newspaper work. Anyway, Holt isn't and never was our man. But by the time we started focusing in on Alamo West, Mark Foster was gone."

"And?"

"Remains so. We've gotten unverified reports that he headed up into the Pacific Northwest. If he shows his snout, we'll hook it."

"Wonderful language. Can I quote you?"

"Absolutely." Dumars smiled then, but it felt strange to be smiling and lying at the same time. She wondered if the columnist could sense her duplicity. Sharon had never considered herself an even passable deceiver, but Joshua had told her it was time to learn the craft. To deceive successfully, he said, began with belief in one's self. Like a religion, it required faith. If you had that, it was as easy as falling into bed.

"I can give you this file copy, if you'd like. I ran it on our best machine, but it's still a little blurred. The photos are really pretty decent."

Baum accepted the file, her eyes dancing with curiosity and pleasure. "What led you to Foster?"

"First, we matched all the people you'd written about negatively against their potential as killers. You'd hit the Boy Scouts pretty hard for opposing gay troop leaders and insisting on mentioning God in their pledge, but we didn't think the Boy Scouts of America would target you for assassination. You had a field day with the tobacco lobbyist who summers in Newport Beach, the GI Joe designer who lived in Fullerton and the Christian recording label out in Irvine, but are they killers? No. So, once we cast our net wide enough, we came up with Alamo West. A different story. We'd heard rumors that some members had planned violence against a local synagogue, and were targeting an Orange County group called One Hundred Black Men. We weren't convinced they had the, uh, the . . ."

"Balls?"

". . . Well, resources for that, but we try to keep an eye on those kinds of people as a matter of course. Maybe, if Foster had just stuck around to answer our questions we might not have latched onto him so fast. You can imagine how skittish these types are, after Oklahoma City. But he didn't stick around. No doubt the reverend tipped him to our interest, and that was enough. In Mark's sudden absence we managed to turn up, at his last residence, a box of .30/06 ammunition similar to that used on Ms. Harris. There were two cartridges missing from the box. We also found copies of your column on Alamo West. The clincher was a letter addressed to you that we assume he never mailed. It was in a safe deposit box that took some time to get into. In it, he implied that he would love to kill you because you were a Jew and a traitor to America and a fool."

"Oh, my."

After you've hooked her, enlist her.

Dumars set a hand on Baum's. "I ask you not to mention that. Say nothing about what we found in his place. It would encourage him to destroy evidence, and evidence is the only thing that will convict Rebecca's killer. Please."

"Understood. I would have come forth with that letter, if I'd gotten it."

"I know. There's a copy of it in the file for you."

"Did you find the gun?"

"No gun. Yet."

"Have you gotten an arrest warrant?"

"No. We want him only for questioning. It's important you say that in your article. There's no reason to put the fear of God in him if there's even a slight chance he'll come forward. It's possible he didn't do it. It's also probable that he didn't do it alone. So we want to give him the opportunity to include his friends at Alamo West, if that's how it went down. A suspect wanted for questioning—not for arrest."

"I understand. God, this is . . . I feel so conflicted right now."

"There's no conflict in busting creeps."

Baum removed the largest of the photographs of Foster and stared at it. "He was the most decent one of them. Or so I thought."

"He's a fringe character, Susan. They all are at Alamo West."

"And you've got nothing on any of the others?"

"Not so far."

Baum continued to regard the picture. "Now that the killer

has a face, I feel . . . it's like . . . this *boy* was capable of that? He looks so innocent."

"So did Ted Bundy."

"Oh, my." Baum flipped through the rap sheets. "A violent man. Of all the people I regularly insult in print, this boy . . . wanted to kill me. You know, I wondered when I wrote that piece on the skinheads if one of them—just one—might read it and, well, learn something from me. Be illuminated. Change. That was naive."

"Optimistic, but naive."

Baum's bright green eyes held Sharon's. "And I'm not a naive person. Not after covering the news for thirty years. And here, I was so sure Vann Holt was behind it."

"Wishful thinking, Susan?"

"I hit him hard a few times in print. All his right-wing this and right-wing that. All those secret men he trains. I exposed his son as a probable sex offender during the Ruiz trial. I was sure he had decided to get me. He seemed like a perfect assassin. A pig with a gun. Though on some level, I felt sorry for him."

"It's a long journey from Republican to assassin."

"I know."

Sharon watched a flock of seagulls scatter as a puppy ran toward it. The birds cried, cawed, circled and gathered further down the beach, landing on feet as orange and bright as plastic.

"The Bureau thought, given the circumstances, that you should get this information first. We'll have a news conference tomorrow up at county, to fill in the other media. They'll get most of what you got."

"Thank you. Sharon, do you think there's a chance that Foster will try again?"

"No. But keep a weather eye."

Baum nodded thoughtfully.

Sharon left the interview with an uneasy conscience. She was a woman most comfortable with black and white, wrong and right, and she had willingly promoted a falsehood here. Yes, it was a lie designed to put Wayfarer's mind at rest, to further draw him away from any suspicion of John. A white lie. It was important that the Bureau be seen as working hard on the wrong suspect.

Of course, the longer Foster remained at large the better, and the Bureau would help him stay that way.

Unsettled as she was by her subterfuge, Sharon was thrilled by the power of it, too. What a feeling, to sway and influence the media. Deceit ruled. She consulted the rearview mirror to see if dishonesty had changed her face. No, Sharon decided: it was the same 34-year old biological-clock-ticking-away face she'd left home with that morning. She wondered about Retin-A.

She drove by the old apartment she had shared with Donny, at the base of Third Street hill. It was still there, though freshly painted. A new Honda sat in the place her old Chevy Malibu once occupied. The apartment had new curtains. She parked in the driveway for a moment. She remembered the life she had then, all the books and part-time jobs and sharing every expense with Donny, all the lovemaking and fighting and tears and long Sunday morning hours in bed with the newspaper strewn across the covers and cups of coffee growing cool on the nightstands. Those were the best times, she thought, those Sunday mornings.

She thought about Josh Weinstein and John Menden—the men in her life now—and how close they could be to her heart, yet so far from it. Maybe that was the price you paid for a career like hers. Men all around you, really, but what did they amount to except teammates, competitors, flirts, maybe friends at best?

A woman could do worse, she thought.

CHAPTER
TWELVE

October the fourteenth hovers gently upon Liberty Ridge. It is an autumn evening scrubbed by breeze, cloudless and dry, ripe with the promise of change.

If seen from above, the dominant feature of Liberty Ridge is the blue oval of lake in its center. In the middle of the lake is a small round island, densely wooded and dark. The lake seems to stare upward at you, like an eye, with its calm black pupil of an island taking you in.

To the north are two hundred acres of orange grove, a perfect rectangle bordered by a windbreak of eucalyptus. Early each morning the irrigation rows fill with water and glisten like stripes of poured silver. Holt has gone to enormous expense to bring his citrus up to certified organic standards, though never applying for the final papers because his operation is not commercial and he detests inspectors of any kind on Liberty Ridge. Without the use of chemical herbicides to control weeds, or chemical insecticides to kill pests, the two hundred acres are labor intensive. Holt's ranch workers are relatively small in number and well paid. Behind the lake, to the south, lie four hundred acres of Southern California coastal scrub and savanna. Because this natural habitat is part of a greater belt of undeveloped land, it is impossible to tell, from above, where the southern boundary of Liberty Ridge lies. Only from the ground can you see the actual border—an eight foot chain link fence topped by another two feet of acutely angled barbed wire, all charged with 24,000 volts of current. The electricity to the fence is turned off and on at arbitrary hours during the day, but it is always on at night. The charge is strong enough to send a deer spasming hoof-over-ear back into the brush, or to knock a man completely senseless. One of Holt's independent springers roamed far from the pack last summer, urinated on the fence and snapped its own spine in a howling recoil. The animal scratched back to the compound a day later using only his front paws, setting off a dispute between Holt and his daughter, Valerie, that Valerie, as usual, won. She demanded surgery for the pup. The dog was operated on that day, but expired during the ordeal.

East of the lake, inland, lie soft foothills of oak and sage, grasslands, and Interstate 5, which marks the edge of the property. From a frontage road used mostly by surfers and the Marines of nearby Camp Pendleton, a private asphalt ribbon lined with date palms winds west toward the house and outbuildings, the lake, and groves. There is a gate near the frontage road—just out of sight around the first bend—which is manned round-the-clock by Liberty Ridge Security, a team of five men supervised by Vann Holt's ubiquitous protector, hunting companion, drinking buddy and personal assistant, Lane Fargo.

To the west is the Pacific. The property line ends almost half a mile before the beach, which is fine with Vann Holt because beach access in California is nearly impossible to restrict anymore, and because a long, narrow, brackish slough runs parallel with the coast on the western edge of Liberty Ridge, making electric fences, guarded gates or even routine security patrols all but unneccessary. In light moments he jokes about stocking the slough with crocodiles. It would be nice to have a beach, but when a strong south swell powers up from Mexico and Holt wants to surf, he and Valerie and Fargo just drive to the dirt parking patch like everyone else, then paddle out and fight for the waves. As a boy he'd belonged to a private surf club there, but privacy in current day Orange County—Holt once pointed out to a client visiting from South Africa—has gone the way of the mastodon, the full-service gas station and apartheid.

The compound itself is built around what Holt calls the Big House—a little joke on himself, a retired Federal crime buster. This house is made primarily of restored adobe over cinderblock and steel I-beam. This expensive combination of materials makes for very good insulation against heat and cold, and of course provides the Big House's old-time California Mission flavor. Holt often points out to guests that it is bulletproof, apropos of little but his desire to raise eyebrows. It is an imposing structure with three stories that seem to just wander on forever once you're inside. Holt designed the re-model himself, which captures the Mission ambience but has contemporary touches such as oversized double-paned windows and twelve-foot ceilings that gather plenty of sunlight. Some of the rooms are furnished with genuine Mission-era appointments, others feature pale gray walls hung with the somewhat sentimental *plein-air* landscapes of the early twentieth century that Holt admires.

There is a separate residence for Lane Fargo. Fargo's home is actually a portion of the restored orange-packing house that sits between the Big House and the lake. It has the functional tin facing and cavernous interior of the original. Holt has kept a great deal of the old packing equipment in tact: the conveyors and hoppers, the processing tables, the two roll-up doors large enough for a truck to drive through. But Fargo keeps the doors locked and the windows shut on all but the hottest days, giving the old plant an air of rusty malignity. The dogs kill an occasional rat along the decking that runs around the perimeter of the packing house.

There is one more home for the two other members of Holt's inner-inner circle: Laura and Thurmond Messinger. This is the adobe church that has stood on the grounds since 1853, topped by a wooden cross to tell travelers they would be treated with Christian respect here. Holt gutted the old interior when he moved onto Liberty Ridge, in keeping with his desire to provide the Messingers with a convenient place to live, and with his profoundly bitter loss of faith in the church after the shooting of his wife and son. Much remains of the old religious ambience inside. Because, as Holt discovered, a church is always mainly a church no matter what you do to it. This is fine with Laura Messinger, a Catholic, and Thurmond, a lapsed Presbyterian.

Nearby, in a loose archipelago that borders a rolling central landscape verdant with grass and trees and flowers, stand four spacious cottages where the cadets of Liberty Operations are trained. One building is for classroom sessions. One is for martial-arts work. The third is an indoor pistol range and the fourth a library stocked with books that are handpicked by Holt and required reading for any cadet hoping to graduate into Liberty

Operations. These volumes include the Old Testament, *The Riverside Shakespeare, The Man-eaters of Kumaon,* the Magna Carta, the Constitution of the United States and Holt's own self-published rumination, *Conscience and Character.* Beyond these are the recreation building, two bungalows for the live-in help, two generous guest flats; and several outbuildings for the vehicles, the helicopter, propane, generators, water supply and storage. The helipad and tennis courts are hidden in a hollow on the other side the main house, as are the swimming pool, whirlpool, rock garden and aviary. Down by the grove are four sizeable cabins for the citrus workers. Beside the lake sit the boathouse, another guest cottage, the kennels for Holt's army of springers, the marina and the drydock. Beside the drydock is a large cinderblock structure, windowless and cheerless as a coffin. Inside is the notorious "Holt Alley," a walk-through small-arms range featuring a city block with 25 bad guy mannequins that can pop out at you from just about anywhere, and 15 innocents who scuttle about their daily lives. No one has ever shot a perfect score in less than three minutes and fifteen seconds.

On the south end of the lake is the beach, cabanas, and the rifle and pistol range. Next to the rifle benches is a modified sporting clays course where, since the beginning of August, Vann Holt has spent many hours getting ready for quail season.

As the sun loosens its orange into the western sky, Holt stands here, on the sporting clays range, at the last station. Behind him is the tower, with its mechanical throwers, stacks of targets, platforms and railings. Holt is in a small wooden cage shaped like a portable toilet stall, with the front and back panels cut away but the two side panels up, to make his shots more difficult. He is a large man, thick-limbed and suntanned. His straight silver hair is neatly trimmed on the sides and back, but in front it juts outward over his forehead like a youngster's. His face is slender, clean shaven and deeply lined; his mouth is taut but unexpressive; his eyes, though pale gray, are now a kind of translucent blue behind the yellow lenses of his shooting glasses. He is dressed in khakis, chukkas and a blue oxford shirt, and has a shell pouch around his waist. He raises the shotgun to his shoulder and calls *"pull."* It is not the sharp *pull!* of the aggressive shooter, not the interrogative *pull?* of the hesitant shooter, but an unhurried, relaxed command that somehow sounds like a prefix. *Puuull* . . . His voice is deep and clear. The clay bird hurls from his blinded left side, streaks in front of him, rising, then disappears in a cracking little cloud of black dust. Holt steps back and reloads, staring down at his gun in the way a tennis player might ponder the strings of his racquet. There is a distinct air about him. Seen from any angle, Vann Holt is a man who emanates assurance, engagement and capability.

Behind the station, Lane Fargo rests his gun across the crook of one elbow and watches.

Holt steps forward into the box again and calls for the second bird. It comes from his left again, but flies lower, faster, and more directly away from him. There is a quick pop, a short follow-through of barrel, and the disc jumps ahead, nicked but still flying.

"The magic pellet," says Lane Fargo. "Pick up your double now, Boss."

Holt appears not to hear. He steps back, breaks open his Browning over-and-under, puts the spent shell into his pouch, then pushes two thin green .28 gauge loads into his gun and snaps it shut. He enters the station house again, positions his feet and raises the stock to his shoulder. Everything he does seems deliberate, experienced. He calls for the bird in his usual way, *puuull* . . ., the way that seems to presage an automatic bursting of his target. The first bird whizzes away, untouched, through the report of Holt's gun. Then the second, faster and further out, escapes too, streaking across the clay-blackened range and settling out of sight behind a hillock.

For a moment Holt stands there, looking out as if he can see them again, each missed bird. He raises the gun again and makes the shots in his imagination. Then he backs out of the station, breaks open his weapon, removes the shells and joins his partner.

"Well, that's an eighty-four," says Fargo. "Put you in A's almost any club in the world."

"Behind them again."

"Yep."

Lane Fargo goes into the station, knocks down both singles and the double. He's shooting a .12 gauge with a heavy load, and the report of his gun booms across the range. He returns to Holt with a cautious look, but apparently pleased.

"Ninety," he says.

"That's good shooting, Lane. You'll slay them tomorrow."

They case their guns and lay them in the bed of a little pickup truck.

"You're not picking them up as soon, Boss," says Fargo.

"The eyes."

"I'm not happy about that."

"I'm less."

"Give you one of my own if I could."

"Hang on to what's yours, Lane."

"Stay out ahead of 'em tomorrow, and you'll limit by ten, Vann."

"Nine-thirty, Lane," says Holt with a warm, genuine, and somewhat impish smile.

Holt is quiet as they drive back toward the Big House. He has, in his law enforcement years, confronted his own mortality enough to be familiar with it, but this new enemy, which introduced itself during a yearly physical eight months ago, is more unnerving than any creep with a gun. What demoralizes him most is not the fact that the disease is inoperable, nor the slow sapping of his strength, but rather the inexorable diminishment of his eyesight. Fifty-five years of 20/10 vision and now some of the clay birds are just a blur.

Much to do, he thinks, while there's still daylight inside.

"Lane, we'll cast off at five tomorrow."

"I'm ready. You want to me to take care of the guns and dogs?"

Holt, of course, has taken care of the guns and dogs for the last thirty-five opening days of his life. He shakes his head and tells Fargo he'll handle it. Fargo is the only one he has told about the blood, and he regrets it. Nothing on earth is more irritating to Vann Holt than condescension. Lane Fargo means well and that is what makes it so disgusting.

"Got those covered, Lane."

"Yes, sir."

Later that night, after dinner and a brief discussion with his daughter about which dogs to take in the morning, Holt roams the main house. Still dressed as he was at the range but without the shell pouch, he has a tumbler of scotch and water in his hand rather than the Browning. He has replaced his shooting glasses with heavy bifocals.

It is late—almost midnight—and he is done with the work of the day. He has talked to the caretaker down at the Lake Riverside Estates place; he has confirmed times and weightloads with his helicopter pilot; he has spent almost an hour on the phone with a close personal friend who is in the middle of a messy divorce. He has talked briefly with Carolyn, his wife.

Now, unsaddled by obligation, Holt is free to tour the enormous house. He has still not gotten used to its beauty and size, its varied atmospheres and internal climates. Lately, he's been particularly drawn to the library, which faces west, is cool in the mornings, sun-dazzled in the evenings, and oddly hushed and handsome after dark. It is on the third floor of the house and provides an overview of Liberty Ridge and the rest of Orange County to the north.

He sits on one of the leather library sofas, with a reading lamp over his shoulder and the day's newspapers set out on a coffee table before him. Holt always reads his papers at night, because his mornings are hurried. He scans the *Los Angeles Times*, the *New York Times*, the *Wall Street Journal*, the *Washington Post*, and of course, the *Orange County Journal*.

He sips his scotch. Holt finds it increasingly difficult to read the mainstream American press. He does not believe that what he is reading is actually the pertinent news of the day. He thinks that large news organizations have an agenda to follow, and that they choose which stories to print and which to ignore, accordingly. He thinks that papers were better three decades ago, when the reporters were less righteous and egotistical, less obsessed with biographic, crowd-pleasing dirt. Still, he reads them, and they inform, amuse, and infuriate him. Here, he notes, is the dread Susan Baum again, in the *Orange County Journal*, bleating on about the "first annual" Gay Pride Festival last weekend in Laguna Beach: "The feeling of empowerment I sensed there was strong. There was a life-affirming scent in the air, as surely as the scent of eucalyptus. I saw the love between a lesbian couple and their two-year old, adopted son. I saw the uncloseted faces of young gay males, stepping into the straight world, without shame, for perhaps the first time. Yes, the American family has changed, and now includes these divergent lifestyles. To deny this is to deny the truth, but to see it, is to glimpse America's future."

Holt himself had toured Laguna during the Gay Pride Festival—Liberty Operations was hired by certain individuals to provide security—and thought that the town had been transformed into one big happy gay bar, a sanctioned street-hustle under the PC banner, a mindless cluster-fuck of the naive by the depraved. God knew how many viruses were passed and caught that weekend. Baum failed to mention that. It makes Holt feel sick and angry. He wonders if the moral sickness of the *Journal* has somehow gotten into his own blood and turned it against him.

And here, another article of the sort that infuriates Holt, this time about the NRA: "considered by some to be a greater threat to public health than the Tobacco Institute."

One lie always leads to another, he thinks: Must send Wayne another five grand.

There is a computer station in the library. In fact, there is a computer station in every room of the house except the bathrooms and kitchen. The computers are linked to practically every other room of every other building on Liberty Ridge, connecting the people on the huge estate like nerves connect parts of the body. There is a computer in the boathouse, a computer in each of the Liberty Operations buildings, a computer in each of the citrus workers' cottages, in each of the guest flats and even a computer in the entryway to Holt Alley. All are linked.

Holt signs on, finds his own mailbox and makes the note to send Wayne LaPierre, the NRA President, $5,000 to blow as he sees fit. Holt knows that Wayne takes extreme positions at times, but believes they are the only things that will work in times of extremity. In times, for instance, when the Attorney General has publicly admitted she wished the citizenry of her country was completely disarmed.

He signs off, sighs, refills his glass from a crystal decanter on the table before him, then walks out to the observation deck off of the library's west windows. From here he can see the Pacific, his perfect orange groves, Liberty Lake, a slice of I-5, then to the north the lighted sprawl of the suburbs—Mission Viejo into Lake Forest into Irvine into Tustin into Santa Ana and stretching beyond, like a huge and sparkling welcome mat, all the way to the door of Los Angeles itself. The breeze-cleansed October night is clear. Holt stands at the railing and trains the telescope west at the ocean. He can see a bait boat squidding under halogen lamps miles off the coast. He trains the telescope north, toward central Orange County, home—he thinks—to whores and junkies, home to thieves and liars, child molesters, rapists, killers. Home to *La*

Raza and *Aztlán* and other aberrations of the mind. Home to the kind of gun-toting racists who shot down Patrick and Carolyn simply because of the color of their skin. Home to the *Orange County Journal*, which claims that the American future is two dykes and their adopted boy.

Holt finally backs away from the telescope, letting it hang by its swivel. Even on a night like this, so clear and clean, what he sees quickly begins to shift, blur and fade. He thinks back to his score of eighty-four on the sporting clays course, to the fact that last year he shot an eighty-seven the day before the quail opener, and the year before that an eighty-nine. The blood, he thinks. "Visual deterioration in majority of cases." And there's nothing anyone can do about it.

Rage on.

This is the haunted hour in Carolyn's room. Just before one a.m., Holt quietly enters. It is a large room, but dark now, illuminated only by the nurse's small reading lamp. The nurse sits at a desk far from the hospital bed, but Holt can see its chromed railings in the minor light, its thick power cable running from motor to wall socket. The night nurse—Joni—looks up at Holt and as always, smiles. She sits at the computer station, as always, scanning through CD ROMs of rock bands. Then she whispers a summary: *Good, Mr. Holt.*

Good, Mr. Holt. Bad, Mr. Holt. Far away, Mr. Holt. Quiet tonight, Mr. Holt.

As always, Holt nods, then goes to the bedside and sits down on a recliner that Joni has moved into position for him. Carolyn stirs when he sits down, shifts position, yawns deeply. Then Holt hands her the bed control unit and the head of the mattress moves up, motor grinding, so that Carolyn can look at her husband. She takes stock before speaking. Her hair is cut short around her face, which is plump, pink and round. Her brown eyes sparkle in the weak light. She wears a nightshirt bottoned clear up because she is, she has told her husband, embarrassed by the girth of her neck and arms.

"I love that coat," she says.

Holt looks down at his oxford shirt, his bare forearms. "Picked it out just for you."

"I'm sleeping well tonight."

"I'd sure let you sleep straight through, if—"

"—I'd much rather talk to you."

"I like this time, too."

In fact, Vann Holt hates this time more than any during his day. He has privately nicknamed it "The Children's Hour," because it is the time that Carolyn slides into one of her many ruts of bullet-induced damage and wants to talk about the children. Not that she doesn't talk about them during his several visits during the day and night, but at one a.m. it is almost always the children. Whose children would not be altogether clear to the outsider, because Carolyn's encyclopedia of names is a shifting, dynamic book. But Holt has realized over the years that no matter what name his wife attaches to what person, she is referring to her own. He is long past correction, past the many months of trying to reeducate Carolyn to the fact that she has only one living child and her name is Valerie, no son. Holt hates this hour because he realizes how much of Carolyn is gone, how Patrick is fully departed, and how deep is his own collusion in his wife's dementia. He hates this hour because he has to look at what the world did to her, witness the half-paralyzed, steroid-bloated, psychotic mess of a woman they turned her into. At times he wishes she was dead, so his memory could select good moments and stanch the flow of the bad, cutting them down to a manageable trickle. It is difficult to remember the good because she remains in the here and now, actual and undeniable as a mountain, a living testimony to her own ruin. In Holt, a fury is always building.

"Where did you get the new jacket?"

"Nordstrom, hon."

"It seems a little small."

"I'm probably gaining weight."

"Did Susan help you pick it out?"

"Yes."

"What color did Nicky get?"

"Same as mine," says Holt dispiritedly. "Blue."

Holt has concluded that "The Children's Hour" is a kind of derivative from the years when Carolyn was a healthy, beautiful woman, and she was always waiting for him in their bed when he came to it, always at one a.m. That was when Holt's workday was finished. He was tired but rarely too tired to make love to her, and she was always eager. They had at least one unbreakable date each day, and that was at one a.m.—work done, children asleep, a nightcap glass of wine for Vann, Carolyn half dreamy and toasty warm, the smell of sleep on her breath, her thighs so unbelievably smooth and soft, her center deep and slick. Whatever was holy about that time, Holt has decided, got translated into this: talk of the children.

"Did he call today?"

"No call. Busy with studies, I guess."

"I hope the Catholics don't get to him."

"?" He just looks at her, mouth open.

"Nothing worse than a lapsed Catholic."

"Oh, well, that's true, honey."

The fact that Holt and Carolyn were married in the Mormon Temple in Los Angeles does not even strike him as odd.

Carolyn's insistence on a living, college-age son—be it Patrick, Randy, Nicky, Steve—has worn Holt down over the years. The fact that she hasn't seen this son since the day they were both shot and he died on the floor of a fast food place in Santa Ana does not affect the march of Carolyn Holt's one a.m.'s. During "The Children's Hour," Patrick is alive and doing well at a good Eastern college—now apparently Catholic—though during the day, Carolyn might weep over his death. Or she might not.

She'll want another postcard soon, Holt thinks, and I'll have to mock one up.

"Terri's lips all healed?"

"Quite nicely."

"Those braces hurt her. I wonder if Dr. Dale could loosen them a little."

"I'll talk to him about it."

"Would you?"

"Of course. We're going bird hunting in the morning."

"You and Terri?"

"Yes. You know, down in Anza. We'll be back the day after, sometime around noon. She wants to bring Lewis and Clark, from this year's litter."

"Terri picks out cute names."

"I agree. And they're fine dogs. She's been working them for nine months."

"What about Sally?"

"Oh, I'll hunt with Sally, don't worry about that."

"I miss those days."

Times like this hurt Vann Holt most, times when Carolyn is lucid and real, when he can communicate with the genuine Carolyn for a few sentences and taste something of what has been, realizing that she is still sometimes very present and very alive. The doctors explained her burned and broken brain matter as something akin to bare electrical wires clotted by wax—sometimes the signals will get through, and sometimes they won't. With a gunshot to the head, they had prophesied, anything can happen.

They talk until almost two, when Carolyn smiles and stretches the upper half of her body, then lowers the head of her bed back into sleeping position. Joni and Holt help turn her so the bedsores on her back—those perennial, agonizing plagues—can heal up and start again.

He kisses her goodnight—once on the lips and once on the forehead—then goes to his room, undresses and gets into the huge empty bed. He feels his heart beating hard in his side, and hears it clanging against his eardrums. It is the rhythm of rage.

He is soon lost to dreams, the same dreams he has had on October the fourteenth since he was twelve and hunted his first season with his father, dreams of birds rising in a blur of feathers and of pulling the trigger of a gun and watching as the birds—every one of them—fly untouched into the sky and disappear over a ridge ablaze with morning sun.

CHAPTER
THIRTEEN

By six a.m. on October the fifteenth Vann Holt felt like a new man, clipping along ten thousand feet above the California desert.

The Hughes 500 was set up for five passengers and cruised at a quiet 130 mph. Holt had included five in his hunting party, which he believes is two too many for safe and good shooting. His fourth was Juma Titisi, a Development Ministry Official from Uganda who is interested in hiring security consultants—a team of them, in fact. The fifth was an old friend of Holt's from his college days, Rich Randell, now in charge of Liberty Op's overseas paramilitary accounts.

Lane Fargo sat beside the pilot, lost in a conversation about grazing rights on BLM land, acres of which slipped past them ten thousand feet below.

Next to Holt was Valerie, at the window, her hair partially stuffed up under the red Irish cycling cap she wears to hunt birds. She listened politely to the Harvard-educated Titisi, holding forth on the destructiveness of tribal rivalries in his nation.

Holt listened also, or appeared to, but his attention was on his daughter, of whom he is often in quiet awe. He nodded along, looking at her from just over a foot away, pleased at the confidence he has cultivated in her, amazed at the breadth of her knowledge after taking a degree in English Literature at the University of California, Irvine. How could she possibly be familiar with the policies of Buganda province's fickle *kabaka*, or the hydroelectric plant near Jinja?

"I've always wanted to visit the college at Kampala," she said. "All the different African religions fascinate me."

Smiling, the tall and noble-faced Titisi invited her to stay with his family and visit the school. "You might be disappointed in its size and architecture, but the programs are rich in heritage and many of the classes are conducted in English."

"See, Dad?" asked Valerie, turning to her father. "*That's* why I studied English."

"It's all clear to me now."

"Dad lobbied heavily for engineering or maybe a pre-med program, but how could I let all those good books go unread?"

"And now that you've read your Shakespeare and Joyce," said Titisi, "you can think about doing something to help your country, your world."

"I've got vet school applications out."

"Overcrowded and competitive," said Randell. "Much less than a 3.85 and you're out of the running. I know because my son tried."

"I got a four-o, about two million assisting hours, and two field champion springers bred, trained and handled."

Vann Holt loved the way a young person could say the most self-aggrandizing things without sounding that way at all.

"I don't think I can help my country," Valerie continued, "but I could help some sick animals. Though here I am, going out to kill little innocent birdies and eat them for dinner. Maybe I should go into poultry ranching, more in keeping with my carnivorous lifestyle."

"Maybe you should help me run Liberty Operations," said Holt. This was an old refrain, but he had seen her interest rise in the last year. In fact, he was already luring her into the world of private security and privatized law enforcement with an odd job here and there.

Titisi and Randell laughed, and Valerie grinned at her father. Fargo looked back with his usual dour face, one thick black eyebrow raised like a gust of wind was about to blow it off.

"Have you shot quail in California?" she asked the Ugandan.

"Never."

"There's nothing like it," she said. "Although I'm sure the lions you took in the plains were pretty exciting."

Titisi looked at her a little uncertainly, not sure if this young

California brat was chiding him for shooting large cats for "sport"—though he had only done it once—or approving the primal ritual of a young Ugandan killing a lion.

"Oh, I did take one, once. Do you disapprove?"

"Yes," said Valerie. "I don't think I could kill unless I was going to eat. But I'm American and you're African, so a difference of opinion is pretty likely. I wouldn't tell a Honduran to leave his rainforest in place either, though personally I'd rather have the forest than a mahogany coffee table. Plus, we don't have lions here, so I can't be tempted. They are pure magnificence, though—at least in parks."

"Miss Holt, they are more magnificent than you can imagine, running free on the Ugandan plains. And consider that there is a certain significance—for some peoples, at least—in killing an animal that could easily kill *you*."

Valerie went quiet. Her father watched her deep chocolate colored eyes, exactly the color of her mother's. Her hair too, those pale golden curls so undisciplined and joyful—pure Carolyn, he thought. Carolyn.

"Well, the quail aren't bad either, and they barbecue up real nice!" said Valerie.

She and Titisi smiled at each other.

Holt, for the thousandth time, was proud of his daughter's uncommon common sense. "It would please her father immensely if she would take over the reigns of Liberty Operations when he goes to the happy hunting grounds."

"Oh, Dad," she said. "You're going to live to be ninety and we both know it."

She climbed over him and squeezed her way to the rear of the copter, where the dogs stood bracing their front paws on the kennel screen, tails blurred at Valerie's arrival.

Two hours later they were near the Anza Valley meadow that Holt had hunted for the last thirty years. The morning was cool, no breeze. The short golden grasses of the meadow stretched across five hundred rolling acres punctuated by clumps of red manzanita, dark oak and sprawling green ghettos of prickly pear cactus. Around the perimeter of the meadow stood the old-growth manzanita and madrone, twenty feet high and too dense for anything but a determined dog to get through. Here, at nearly 4,000 feet and far from any city, the air was clean and the colors and shapes of the flora were unambiguous and rich as paint.

Holt's white Land Rover bounced along a winding dirt trail and came to a stop amidst the high cover of the meadow's edge. Holt told everyone not to slam the doors, then got out. Another rig, red and driven by Lane Fargo, followed just a few yards behind. Holt had already briefed his party on how they would hunt this morning: park the trucks on the west perimeter of the field, drop down into the low grass where the quail should be feeding this time of day, push them outward into the meadow, try to keep them from getting to the far side, where the deep cover would make them impossible to hunt.

The party spread out and formed a loose front—thirty yards between each of them—to work the field. Holt and Sally, his ten-year old bitch, took the far right end. Next came Randell, then Titisi, around whom Holt was feeling slightly unsafe because he had never hunted with the Ugandan before. To Titisi's left, thirty yards down, came Valerie, with Lewis and Clark, just ten months old. They were already working out in front of her, cutting left and right, scrambling back within shotgun range with every sharp chirp of Valerie's whistle. Lane Fargo had the far left end, putting at least forty confident yards between himself and Valerie.

Holt had organized his party like this not only to spread out the dogs and share them, but because he liked to watch his daughter without her knowing. He fell back just a little so he could see her. There she was, just eighty or ninety yards away, taking long deliberate steps through the grass, a tall, healthy woman, with her khakis tucked into her boots, a 20 gauge side-by-side cradled in her arms, a whistle between her lips and the red cycler's cap stuffed down over her pale bouncing curls. She stopped, canted an ear toward a big patch of cactus in front of her and called the dogs over and to the right. Holt never knew when it might hit him, but sometimes, all it took was a look at Valerie to send his heart into a sweet, swelling tumble of sadness and joy. The joy came from beholding her life, her spirit, her being. The sadness came from beholding the fact that she was practically all he had left, all that would outlive him, at any rate, so long as nothing happened to her. And always on the edge of Holt's consciousness was the blip, the reminder, that in the world today, anything can happen. Anything. At moments like that, when his heart was pounding hard with the alternating current of joy and dread, he wanted to hold her tight to his chest; he wanted to surround her with an invisible shield impermeable by any form of harm; he wanted to lock her away and preserve her, forever.

None of those thoughts came to Vann Holt as he stepped quietly through the low grass and watched Sally work a gourd patch. Instead, next to the pride he felt watching Valerie, what he felt most strongly now was his focused anticipation of the birds that would soon be rising. He could hear them, chirping alarmedly out there in front of Sally. He could feel the perfect balance of the Remington in his hands. He noticed the heightened perception of his eyes, though he knew that they were failing him. Even his sense of smell was acute now, the astringent perfume of sagebrush and desert scrub, the dankly human odor of the gourds, passing straight up through his nostrils and into his brain. Like nothing else in the world, hunting made Vann Holt feel alive.

Then, the ground before him seemed to bunch and gather, and the air above it exploded with dark shapes as the covey rose with the wooden knock of wings. Holt's heart jumped into his throat, the same way it had for the three decades he'd hunted here, no diminishment of the rush at all, a charge of purest adrenaline streaking through his body. There were ninety of them, he guessed, bringing up the gun and flicking off the safety. He picked out a large male and shot it, then another, then another. Sally jumped to the first bird while Holt stood and watched the covey bend away in front of him and toward the others, fingering three more shells into his magazine without having to look at them, getting them pointed in the right direction by feeling for the brass base. Shotguns popped to his left now, as the birds accelerated across the meadow. He saw Titisi blasting away into the covey, hitting nothing. Then Randell picked up a single as the birds sped toward Valerie. Holt watched her drop two, then saw her loyal little springers—Lewis and Clark—nosing their way toward the first bird. God, she's great! On the far side, Lane Fargo shot a double at about sixty yards. When Holt stepped toward his dog, two stragglers came up, wings whirring, necks straining, together. He shot the male first, then rode out the hen and knocked her down just as she started her turn. He stood, marking their falls and sliding two new shells into his gun. Sally dropped the first bird at his feet, pivoted and bolted back toward the second.

The covey disappeared, almost as quickly as it had risen. Holt watched them put down mid-meadow, happy that they were still naive enough to allow a second jump. By noon, he knew, they'd be skittish, and in one week so spooked you'd have to get them the first time because there would be no second. That was when the hunting was a true challenge.

To his left, Titisi cursed and examined a handful of shells as if they were responsible for the fact that he had missed. Randell found his bird on the outskirts of a cactus patch. Lewis and Clark managed to come up with Valerie's first quail, but proceeded to fight over it, which brought Valerie bounding forth to land a boot squarely on the butt of each dog. Lane Fargo just stood there and watched, having already collected his kill. Sally, methodical as always, followed Holt's hand signals and easily found all four of his other quail. Holt picked up each one as she dropped it on his boots, felt their warmth and heft, admired the handsome plumage of the cocks and the more subtle beauty of the hens, then slipped them one at a time into the game pouch on his vest. Five birds in the first jump, he thought: it's going to be a good day.

After Holt pocketed his last bird he reached down and gave Sally a hearty "attagirl," rubbing behind her ears with his hand. She sat and looked up at him, her little stump of tail vibrating in the dirt. Before he even straightened, Sally was off again, nose down, zigging and zagging her way thirty yards ahead of him— never more—looking back every few seconds to make sure her master was paying attention.

Holt shot a single that had stayed behind only to burst into the air almost at his feet. Lane Fargo did likewise, out to Holt's far left. Randell and Titisi unloaded on a pair of stragglers, hitting nothing but air. Lewis and Clark started to sprint after the flying birds, but responded nicely when Valerie called them back with her whistle. Tough to call a young dog off a bird, Holt thought, that's why a good shooter makes a good trainer. With pride he watched Valerie praise her dogs as they returned; she slipped a little something to each of them from her pocket. Holt never used food reinforcement for his dogs, but Valerie always did, and her results, he thought, were superb. He looked out to the rising sun, and breathed deeply the fine clean air of the desert. The birds in his vest were warm and heavy against his back. Sally, he thought, is probably the best dog I've ever had. Fleetingly, he remembered Patrick—how beautiful he was out here with his own dog, how gentle he was with her, and how he didn't really care if he shot ten birds or none. But he let Patrick's image flutter on past, like a quail, going out of sight. Sometimes, he reminded himself, you have to remember to forget.

By 9:30, Holt had his limit of ten quail. Valerie had nine and Lane Fargo had thirteen. They all hunted until almost eleven, giving Titisi and Randell a chance to knock a few down—which they did.

By 11:30 they had cleaned the birds, put them on ice, and loaded into the two Land Rovers for the drive into town. Holt was hungry now, and he could almost smell those burgers on the grill. Best in the desert, he thought.

"My treat at Olie's," he said, happy for the moment, glad to be thinking about nothing but birds and burgers and Valerie, who sat in the passenger seat beside him, holding his hand on her lap.

FOURTEEN

Olie's is dark and cool and quiet when they walk in from the parking lot. It is a few minutes after noon and the last of the lunch rush—a young couple with a two-year old—comes through the swinging saloon door while Titisi holds it open. The young mother thanks him, but looks at him askance.

Holt takes a look at the long, picnic-style table near the jukebox, the same one he's used for the last thirty years. He is the kind of man who likes to do things the same way, time and time again, if that way works. But as he looks at the table—certainly no different than it was a year ago—a little voice begins to stir inside him. Vann Holt is also a man who listens to his voices. The voice says nothing, just a little infantlike whine, a protest or complaint of some minor nature.

"Let's sit over there," he says, motioning to a table on the other side of the room. "That looks good."

"We always sit *here*, Dad."

"Now we're sitting *there*, Valerie."

So they sit there.

Holt takes a seat with his back to the wall, which is festooned with an ancient promotional beer sign that features an ersatz running waterfall with bears playing in it. Valerie sits to his left, and Lane Fargo to his right. Across from them are Titisi and Randell, and Holt is pleased to see they are now talking about the security consultants Titisi wants to employ in Kampala.

"Number of ways to go about it," says Randell, nodding.

"Competent, responsible men," says the Ugandan, somewhat obligingly, as he looks at Holt, then back to Randell. "The kind of men who can organize, train, lead. Men like you."

Holt hands out the plastic-covered menus, feigning disinterest in the business. Consultants, he thinks: young armed men willing to take risks for money, willing to kill for it. Mercenaries, or the trainers of mercenaries—what was the difference?

Of course, Randell knows this, and Titisi knows he knows it, but there is a certain latitude regarding definitions that must be offered at this stage. It is a courtesy. There is always the chance—very remote here, but possible just the same—that Titisi has been spun by the Federals, and his real mission is to offer Liberty Operations an opportunity to hang itself. Holt has had those opportunities before, and he is expert at keeping his company on the legitimate side of international law as it applies to security, investigations and military consultation. But gray areas do exist. Holt knows he can smell a rat from about ten miles away, though Titisi has thus far emitted a reassuring air of greed and menace, good indicators of honest intentions and trustworthiness. It always amazes Holt how cruel governments can be to their own people, in the name of helping them. On the other hand, Holt knows that Titisi can be thinking the same thing: that Vann Holt, ex-Federal, may have finally been manipulated into blowing the whistle on certain clients. It is little comfort to Titisi that he and his nation are the smallest of potatoes. At this stage, the Holy Trinity is vagueness, optimism, courtesy.

The burgers arrive and are great. Valerie, who does not like red meat, gets a grilled fish sandwich and a big salad loaded with thousand island. Lunch goes along perfectly.

Until, from outside, comes the rumble of motorcycle engines, the deep, throaty, unmistakable rasp of America's finest, the Harley-Davidson. Dust rises up in the sunlight beyond the swinging doors. The engines are gunned, then killed. To Holt it sounds like a half-dozen of them. When the doors blast open and the boots hit the wooden floor and the men barge into the quiet of Olie's Saloon, Holt sees that he is off by two. There are four men, two of them large, one skinny and tall, one simply gigantic. These are not the kind of people Vann Holt prefers as lunch guests. He looks briefly at them, then turns to his daughter and asks about Lewis and Clark.

The bikers are still taking a table when a voice carries through the disturbed atmosphere of the saloon.

"That one looks good enough to eat."

Holt ignores it, though his pulse has risen and he feels a coolness crawl across his scalp. Valerie glances at the men, then quickly back to her father. She's trying to explain how Lewis and—

"I said, hey cupcake, you look good enough to *eat!*"

It is impossible to ignore him now. Holt sees that it's the tall skinny one, sitting already, while his huge minions shuffle and bang around the table. Skinny has red hair, a darker red beard and a blue bandana wrapped around his head. His eyes are bulging and blue, and look ready to burst from their sockets. His arms are taut as wires, coming through the holes of the stained denim vest. They are covered with tattoos. He looks at Valerie with the dullest of smiles. His cohorts all look at Valerie, too.

She stares back at them. "Try it, and I'll blow your fucking lungs out," she says in a voice so cold it completely startles Holt.

All four of the bikers break into serious laughter, a guttural roar not unlike the sound of their machines.

Then Holt has to laugh too—does my little girl really talk like that?—and Titisi and Lane Fargo, and finally even dour Rich Randell are laughing along, though Fargo's hand slides inside his jacket to certify the readiness of whatever he is carrying in there.

After the laughter trails off, the sounds of the talking bikers fill the room and the incident appears to be forgotten, just another colorful little postcard in the lives of minor outlaws.

Holt's stomach relaxes some and he continues to eat. The pressure he feels in his head when angry, abates. He glances over at the bikers to find them deep in beer and roaring talk, blatantly insulting the waitress, arguing over what should go on the pizzas. With a little discipline and a little education, he thinks, those pigs might amount to something. Big. Strong. They might even make good Liberty Men someday. Perfect for Titisi. Maybe not so dumb as they act. Degeneration of the race, pure and simple.

Titisi finishes his second cheeseburger and focuses his attention on the double order of fries. He leans to Randell, whispers something, and they both chuckle knowingly. Lane Fargo, upright and attentive as always, has that glazed look that Holt recognizes: it means Fargo's attention is everywhere at once.

Valerie has gone quiet. Holt understands that her heated little outburst embarrassed her, and now she's trying to regain composure. He knows from raising her from infancy that Valerie is not a natural combatant, but rather thrives on harmony, accomplishment and love. Patrick was the same way. Yes, Carolyn's clear-eyed, even temperament dominates Valerie over Holt's own reactive and heated disposition.

Suddenly the bikers stand and the giant yells back toward the kitchen: "Stuff your fuckin' pizza."

This brings another roar of moronic laughter from the rest of them, who bang through the flimsy wooden chairs and cram through the swinging doors back out into the parking lot. Skinny is last out, after tossing some bills on the table and looking at Valerie again. In a gesture of purest vulgarity, he smiles at her, runs his wet red tongue over his sharp, widely spaced yellow teeth, then sticks it straight out—it's astonishingly long—and wiggles the tip at her.

Valerie blushes and looks away.

Holt is about to speak, but Skinny is on his way now, barging past the doors with a phlegmy chuckle.

"Let's get out of here," says Valerie.

"Sit tight," says Lane Fargo, his eyes trained on the swinging doors. "Let them go."

The motorcycle engines boom to life with that slapping mechanical flatulence of the Harley. One, two . . . three. Holt can see the exhaust rising from the lot outside. The last bike kicks over and joins the chorus; the engines are gunned to a deafening pitch. Then the clutches release and the bikes scream out of the parking lot, headed south on Highway 371. Holt follows their diminishing sound.

He counts some money onto the table, then slides back his chair. "Well? Shall we try to find some more birds? Something other than vultures? Lane, have a look out there, will you?"

"Love to."

Fargo eases across the floor—he's a big man, six-three, two-twenty but his gait is even and quiet. He slips outside. Holt can see his boots and the bottom of his pants beneath the door.

Then he's back. "They're swarming down the road, at the hoagie place. We may as well just head out, Boss."

They spill into the fierce afternoon sunshine of Anza Valley. Holt looks across the lot to the two Land Rovers parked in the shade, windows down halfway for the dogs. Sally eyes him from the rear kennel of the white one. He has just put his arm around his daughter's shoulder when the low grumble of the bikes suddenly rises in pitch again, and he is only a few steps toward the trucks when the four machines—popping and farting chaotically—roll back into the lot and stop between Holt and his vehicles. Fargo is closest to the Land Rovers, so the Giant jumps his Harley between Lane and the others. Skinny makes a wide, dust-throwing semi-circle and comes to rest closest to Holt and Valerie. One of the others pops his clutch and runs his huge bike toward the group, sending Titisi and Randell one way; Holt and Valerie the other. Skinny guns his hog straight at them, laughing loudly, and Holt can see no alternative but to push her out of his path. He does this, wishing he could get to his shotgun, but he's clearly too far from the truck. Skinny is off his bike in a flash, flipping down the kickstand in a quick, fluid motion. He smiles as he approaches Valerie, who squares off and kicks at him. His own long leg shoots out and Valerie goes down in the dust of the lot, then quickly jumps back up again. She is wobbling; her hat has fallen and her cornsilk hair is firmly wadded in Skinny's left hand, while his right snugs a monstrous Bowie knife against her throat.

"Feel good, smart cunt? You fight me and I'll cut you a new windpipe. Let's go back inside the diner, smart cunt—right like this."

Holt takes a step forward, then stops. Past Skinny's bike he sees Lane Fargo backed against the red Land Rover, his hands up, Giant looming over him with what looks like a toy pistol aimed at Lane's head. The two other bikers are blocking his path anyway, one of them leveling a sawed-off shotgun at him. He looks quickly to his right, only to see Titisi and Randell backing up at the approach of Biker #4 who is whipping a short chain round and round in a blurring circle.

Holt hasn't felt so helpless since he got the call from the Sheriff's Department those five long years ago, telling him that his son was dead and his wife critically wounded. The rage just covers him like a hot blanket, and he has trouble seeing now—everything seems to be taking place in a fractured, sped-up version of reality, like film with hunks of action edited out.

Skinny begins dragging Valerie toward the front doors of Olie's Saloon. Lane Fargo is frozen against the red Land Rover, hands still up as if they might be forever. Titisi bellows and charges into a whip of the chain that thuds into his belly and sends him, jackknifed, to the ground. Valerie draws a pained breath and whimpers. Then, motion catches Vann Holt's disbelieving eyes, a motion not part of this film, an intrusion, a disruption. Into the parking lot lumbers a pickup truck, which moves past Fargo and the Giant before the driver can sense that something is very wrong here. It stops right in the middle of the lot, tires angled toward a parking space, unable to move forward past the Shotgun Biker, who still holds his weapon aimed at Holt but turns now with a prodigious scowl to confront this pain-in-the-ass innocent bystander in the pickup. Holt looks at the truck's driver—just a regular guy wearing a gray hat tilted back on his head and a rather calm—perhaps uncomprehending—expression on his face. There are a couple of big dogs in the cab with him. Holt turns to his daughter and Skinny, as if his vision might pull along the truck driver's vision with it, and reveal to him the immediate danger unfolding here. For some reason, Holt believes that now is the time to speak.

"Let her go, young man. This isn't worth it. Somebody's going to get killed."

"Fuck off, old fart. Lenny, keep that prick's hands up over there. Keep it cool out here for a minute—that's all I need with this bitch."

"Let her go," says Holt again. "Just let her go and ride away and we'll ride away, too. No reports, no cops, no nothing. Just a little misunderstanding between men. You want money, I've got enough to make it worth your while. There's a thousand easy, right here in my wallet."

"Ah, shutup you old woman," snaps Skinny.

Titisi vomits. Randell has taken a knee beside him and has a hand on the big man's shoulder, but he stands back up and hops away a step as the puke jets into the gravel.

The man in the truck seems frozen.

Holt takes another desperate look toward Lane Fargo, who doesn't seem to have moved one inch.

He hears Valerie whimper again, and turns to see her struggling with Skinny, then Skinny yanking her to face Holt, the wide shining blade of the knife up high now, where the throat meets the chin. Then Holt realizes that Valerie's tormentor isn't brandishing her for him at all, but for the stupefied young man in the pickup.

"Drive the *fuck* out of here! This is just a little family dispute. Get out, faggot!" yells Skinny.

To Holt's absolute astonishment, the truck driver nods agreeably, shifts his truck into reverse and looks over his shoulder to back out. An irrational surge of hatred fills Holt as his last potential savior—Valerie's last potential savior—begins to ease his truck backward. In fact, the driver is so shaken he pops the clutch and stalls the engine.

What happens next occurs so quickly and chaotically that Vann Holt does little but watch.

CHAPTER
FIFTEEN

The driver's door of the stalled truck burst open and one of the dogs, a very large German shepherd, shot from the cab into the dust of the parking lot. Next came the cowardly Samaritan himself, still wearing the hat, his body cloaked in a long duster jacket. He landed deliberately, then walked around the front of his vehicle, as if going to lift the hood. Instead, he pulled from inside his coat a bright stainless steel revolver and very casually took a two-hand shooter's stance, aiming the gun at Skinny and Valerie.

"These bullets are a lot faster than that blade," he said. "Let her go."

Shotgun Biker swiveled his sawed-off away from Holt and toward the Hat Man, but Holt registered a far more urgent motion, something swift and brutal and decisive. The dog was a blur already, just teeth and mouth, airborne toward Shotgun Biker, who hip-pivoted his weapon and blasted twice before the torn and shredded dog even hit the ground. The sharp burned smell of gunpowder filled the air and a red mist lowered in the breeze. Then Hat Man fired. Holt spun to see Valerie falling one way and Skinny the other, knife mid-air and about eye level, the top of his shoulder ripped apart in a jagged explosion of vest denim, t-shirt and blood. Shotgun Biker was fumbling with his spent double-barrel as Hat Man pistol-whipped him to his knees, grabbed the tumbled shotgun and hurled it onto the saloon roof. Holt swirled instinctively to Valerie, who was fleeing into the cafe; then he turned to see Lane Fargo. Fargo was still backed against the truck with his hands up, but Giant was on his bike again, backing it away with his feet, pistol still trained on helpless Fargo, who had squatted, knees bent and ready for whatever it was he wanted to do. Giant fired two rounds just past Lane's side, pocking the red Land Rover with flat, metallic bangs, sending Fargo back against the truck hard, his eyes fierce and wide. Hat Man spun to his left and took aim at the biker with the chain, who was frantically trying to kick his Harley back to life. For a second it looked as if he would belly-shoot the grunting biker, but instead Hat Man took four long strides to Skinny and jammed the barrel of the revolver into his face, forcing him to his knees. He kicked away the big bowie knife. The dog hadn't moved but the pool of blood around it seeped leisurely into the sand. Suddenly, Giant boomed across the lot on his bike, one hand on the throttle and his other—without a firearm now—lifted in a placating gesture at Hat Man. Hat Man aimed his revolver at the Giant, then back at Skinny. "Enough, man—you got it," growled Giant. Hat Man gave him a curt nod but kept the gun pointed at him, letting him pass by and stop next to Skinny, who, clutching his shoulder and climbing onto the back of Giant's Harley, cast Hat Man a look of purest hatred. "You'll see me again, fancy faggot," he hissed, glancing down at the dog. "Enjoy dinner." Then, in a booming symphony, the three hogs and their drivers and one pale, bleeding passenger bounced onto the highway and accelerated away with a low-pitched moan of horsepower, fury and defeat.

The man knelt over his dog, running a hand along its lifeless flank. He had set his hat on the ground, and placed his revolver in the crown.

Vann Holt ran past the Olie's waitress, standing on the wooden deck of the restaurant, then disappeared through the swinging doors.

Valerie stood just a few feet away, looking through a dusty window, with a huge kitchen knife in her hand. The color had drained from her face, which was splattered with Skinny's blood. To Holt, it looked like ink on snow. Her hair was drenched in sweat.

"Oh, God, honey," said Holt, wrapping his big arms around her. "Are you all right?"

"I'm okay, Daddy. I'm okay." The knife hit the floor.

"Are you sure you're all right?"

"Who is he?"

"You're sure, absolutely sure you're not hurt?"

"The second I pushed that pig away, he shot him."

"Let's go outside. Can you walk outside?"

"I told you I'm okay, Daddy. I just feel kind of . . . sticky."

The cook emerged from the kitchen with a .30/06 rifle and a wild look on his face. He was a fat man with a rim of gray hair around his face and head, florid cheeks, and a clean white apron. "What the hell?"

"It's over," said Holt. "Put the gun down."

"I'll call the Sheriffs."

"We already did—the CB," Holt lied. It was a given for him that the police would confuse rather than clarify things.

"Ambulance?"

"Nobody's hurt."

"She's not hurt? She's bleeding, you know."

Holt gave the chef a withering look. All of his native authority, not to mention his frustration, fear and anger, came rushing back now, and he saw by the cook's eager nod that he had no intention of calling an ambulance.

He eased Valerie back into the bright October sunlight, where he ordered the waitress, forcefully, to get some coffee ready for the sherrifs. Only now did he register the frantic yapping from the Land Rovers—three springers vaulted into excitement by the gunshots.

Titisi and Randell had gathered themselves to stare, somewhat bewildered, at the man and his dog.

Lane Fargo stood midway between the fallen hero and the restaurant, his pistol drawn. A consuming self-consciousness emanated from him: his face was bright red, his eyes uncertain. He watched Holt and Valerie descend the steps to the parking lot, unwilling to look either his boss or his boss's daughter in the eye as they approached.

"Mr. Holt, I think we could run them down in the Rovers."

"No."

"There's not much out there but clean highway."

"No. Settle the dogs down, Lane. See if those bullets wrecked my gas tank."

"I'm thinking we should get off stage before the cops come."

"Check the dogs and trucks, Lane."

"Yes, sir."

Valerie left her father's side to approach the man still kneeling in the dust beside his dog.

"Can I help you put him in your truck?"

He didn't look at her. "Sure. Thanks."

"Thank *you*. Oh, Jesus in heaven—thank you."

Holt approached, somehow larger now than he was a few moments earlier, and offered his hand to the kneeling man. "My name is Vann Holt."

The man finally rose, slipping his revolver into the pocket of his duster and slapping the hat against his leg, but still looking down at the dead shepherd. He shook Holt's hand without enthusiasm.

"John," he said, looking down again at the dog. "That was Rusty."

Holt contemplated John's slender, stunned face. He saw a trustworthy but uncertain face, a face hollowed with fear and revulsion, the face of a man who has acted and now must live with the consequences. For just a brief moment, the eyes reminded Holt of his own. "You all right, son?"

"Pretty much."

"This is my daughter, Valerie."

John looked at her while he shook her offered hand, his eyes lingering on her face, perhaps on the blood that flecked it.

"I've never seen anything quite like that," said Holt.

"I haven't either, to tell you the truth, Mr. Holt."

"You know those guys?"

"Seen them around. I live out here."

"They know where?"

"I don't see how they could."

Valerie looked down at Rusty. "You train that dog?"

John looked down at Rusty, too, and Holt saw on his face an expression of tragic surprise. "To sit and stay. When he saw that guy choking you, he started growling like I'd never heard. He was just a stray when I got him, so he must have learned from someone else. He was a real good dog. Shit, now he's dead."

"I'd like to give you another one," said Valerie.

"Well . . ." said John. "Uh . . . I need to use the sandbox. Excuse me."

Holt gathered with his party while John went to the bathroom in Olie's. Titisi examined the red inflammation across his stomach and felt for broken ribs, then pronounced himself unhurt. Fargo was still checking the trucks, down under the red one for a look at the gas tank. Randell sat in the shade with Holt and Valerie and the Ugandan.

Ten minutes passed before John returned. To Holt's eye, his face had become more ruddy, his movements were no longer quite so slow, there was a quickness in his glance. He went to his truck, removed the revolver and appeared to stash it under the seat. Then he started up the reluctant old Ford and pulled it into the shade of a pepper tree. Holt could see a big chocolate labrador licking John's face as he reached across to roll the window down a little more.

When John approached, he held his hat in his hand. "What, exactly, was happening here?" he asked.

"That's a story we might want to tell somewhere else," said Holt. "Let me ask you something, John—are you clean with the law?"

"So far."

"Because we'd like to get out of here without filing any statements. Those bikers won't be talking—no reason we should, either. Unless you want to explain that revolver in your coat."

"Yeah . . . I mean, no. You're right."

"Can we take you home?"

"I've got the truck."

"I mean, can we escort you home? We all need somewhere to settle our nerves. You close to here?"

"Just a few miles. But really, I—"

"I insist," said Holt. "It's the right thing to do."

"Well, okay, then."

Holt threw a set of truck keys to Randell, then helped Valerie and John lift the big dog into the bed of John's old pickup. It lay there will all the innocence of the dead, a helpless mass held together by skin. The labrador watched through the rear cab window, puzzled.

"Lead the way," Holt said. "We'll follow."

A few miles out Highway 371, Holt noticed that John's pickup truck was accelerating, fast. The Land Rover kept up easily, although doing seventy miles an hour on the narrow, winding two-lane seemed foolhardy. He checked the rearview to find Lane Fargo right on his tail, a senselessly aggressive act wholly indicative of Lane's shame at being overcome by lowly motorcycle thugs. Holt lowered his window and waved Fargo off.

He didn't even notice it until rounding a gentle bend, where John's right-turn signal began to flash. Holt saw the brake lights, the abrupt slowing of the Ford, the turnoff to a dirt road leading back into the hills, and, only then, the column of deep black smoke rising from somewhere in the middle distance.

"No," he said.

Keeping up with John on the rutted dirt road wasn't easy. The Ford threw up clouds of dust as it skidded around the turns and braked heavily before the drops. Lewis, Clark and Sally bounced savagely in the back of the Rover—at one point Holt glanced back to see all three of them suspended between floor and roof, twelve legs scrambling for a purchase that wasn't there. The road snaked on, twist upon turn, cutback upon rise upon dip. Then it widened into a straight-away that banked into a steep climb. The Ford's back end slid left and right as it raced up the hill and disappeared over the crest. Holt laid back a little, then punched the Rover up and over the ridge, where before him lay a gentle meadow marked with a few trailers, a cinderblock building, and what must have been a house trailer, far on the perimeter of the place, flaring up like a struck match, gushing black smoke into the blue desert sky.

A short heavyset man stood about thirty yards from the inferno, a water hose in both hands. The arc of water feebly vanished into the flames. The Ford skidded to a stop beside him and John jumped out, followed by the dog. Holt braked early and pulled in behind the Ford. He yanked his fire extinguisher free of the floorboard by the seat, but he could see that it was already too late: the trailer looked like a box of fireworks set on fire. The propane tank already had blown, judging by the gaping hole at one end. He saw the heavyset man nodding violently, taking one hand off the hose to point down the road.

"Those *pigs*," hissed Valerie. "Those absolute human swine."

Then, as Holt watched, John returned to his truck, threw forward the seat and pulled out a cloth case, from which he extracted what looked like a 12 gauge Remington automatic. He hurled the case back behind the seat and slammed it back. From somewhere in the cab he took a box of shells, pried open the top and grabbed three, which he loaded into the gun. Then he was back in the truck and the labrador had jumped in with him and the Ford fishtailed in a wide, gravel-throwing turn that threw up a cloud of dust as John gunned it back down hill toward the dirt road.

"Stay with him, Dad."

"I'm staying with him, Val. Hold on tight."

John must have known every foot of the miserable dirt road, because he took it at an astonishing velocity. A mile from the trailers he shot up a wide, well-tended drive to a ranch house set in a meadow of grazing horses. By the time Holt caught up, John was talking with two men by a corral, then he jumped back into his truck and skidded back out in Holt's direction. John nodded at him as he flew past. Lane Fargo, Randell and Titisi had to swerve to miss him. Then another stop a half mile further down. Again John was conferring with neighbors as Holt finally arrived, and again the young man was in his truck and blasting back to the road by the time the dust cleared and Holt could make sense of what was going on. Another half mile down, the Ford skidded to a stop beside a run-down little batch of trailers. Three women sat in the shade, drinking beers and smoking. This time, Holt saw that John took his shotgun with him as he walked past the women and threw open the door of the largest trailer, a sun-faded slum of a unit, slouching off-center and unshaded by a very large and very dead tree. John disappeared inside, then came out and pushed past the women, who appeared to be cussing him mightily. John snapped something back at them, but Holt was too far away to hear it. Beside him, Valerie was scanning the desert with her dark brown eyes. "He'll never find them out here. They're miles away by now."

"He needs to play this out."

Two more miles of anguishing dirt road, three more fruitless stops, all transpiring under the growing desert heat. Finally the Ford slowed and grunted to a stop where the dirt road met the highway again, and the door flew open and John got out, slammed it hard, took three steps to the wooden fence running alongside the road and kicked one of the dry twisted posts, his boot shattering it and the three strands of rusted barbed wire shivering with the impact. He walked back to the truck and looked down into the bed. Then he opened the driver's side door, pulled out the gun and a small, six-pack sized cooler. He walked to the edge of the dirt road and hurled the cooler into the air, then raised the gun and blasted it three times before it landed, each shot reducing the thing to smaller pieces that threw off wobbling jets of dark liquid until the mangled former box landed in the sagebrush, bounced, and rolled off into the sand. John pitched his gun back into the truck cab, looked at Holt, then turned his back to them, shook his head, and lowered it.

"Righteous anger," said Holt. "It's the best thing he can have right now."

"Besides a home and a live dog."

"Well put."

"Poor man. It's my fault. It's all my fault. I'll make it up to him."

"We'll make it up to him, Valerie."

Then she looked at her father with an expression he had come to both love and fear. He loved the way it came so directly from Carolyn and himself, passed on like a gift, the way her pupils dilated and her wide lips formed a slight frown and the vertical lines between her eyebrows furrowed—all of her conviction gathering force, being brought to bear. He feared it because Valerie was intractable when she looked like this, ferociously stubborn. And he knew how that ungovernable determination had led to the best things in his life, and the worst. It was the Holt energy, passed from generation to generation, powerful as a runaway big-rig, and as difficult to stop.

So he simply waited for his daughter to speak.

"We're taking him home," she said.

Holt's heart sank a little. "That's not a good idea for anyone," he said. "But maybe he could spend a few weeks here at the lake house—time to get a new trailer."

Valerie continued to look at him, disbelief mounting in her dark brown eyes. Holt wondered how a twenty-two-year old woman could turn his logic to mush, make him feel idiotic.

"So they can find him, and burn up our house, too?" she asked. "No. He needs a home, a base to operate from. He needs safety and time to regroup. He saved my life. He's coming to Liberty Ridge, Dad."

"Maybe he doesn't want to come to Liberty Ridge."

"He does. Look, Dad, what did you say about thirty seconds ago?"

"I said righteous anger—"

"—You said 'we'll make it up to him.' So, this is how we make it up to him. Simple!"

She reached across the truck with both hands, grabbed her father's face and kissed him once on each cheek, then once on his forehead.

Then, with all assumptions made but not another word, she got out of the truck and walked toward John, the man who had, at great price, saved her life. Vann Holt watched her approach him, his heart pounding not only from the punishment of the chase, but from colliding emotions of gratitude, impotence, jealousy and shame. He watched her place her hand on John's arm.

"Not like that, we won't," he said. "Not like that, girl of mine."

CHAPTER
SIXTEEN

Josh Weinstein and Sharon Dumars watched the scene unfold from the privacy of a 1986 Dodge van parked across the highway at a feed and tack store. The van featured one-way windows, an antenna tuned to the transmission frequency of a beeper-cum-radio attached to John's belt, a parabolic microphone mounted on top, a reel-to-reel tape recorder, and large magnetic signs on each side that said "Empire Cable Services." Anyone calling that number would find it disconnected and no longer in use.

They sat on two stools in the oven-like heat, peering through the windows with binoculars.

When Rusty met his double-barreled end, Sharon gasped and tightened, and though Weinstein found himself profoundly shaken by the sight of a perfectly good Bureau dog blown to smithereens by Bureau part-timers, he told himself that Rusty did not die in vain.

The stunt-packs of blood had gone off perfectly, assuaging Weinstein's second-biggest worry. They'd worked hard on the choreography, but he knew that a lucky, unanticipated move from Valerie could dislodge the wiring duct-taped to Sam's shoulder beneath the t-shirt and denim vest. They'd been thorough enough to use a half pint of Sam's own blood, on the off chance that a suspicious Holt, or, more likely, Lane Fargo, might try to run some lab work on what would surely splatter all over Valerie's body and clothes. Weinstein's greatest fear, though—that some genuine innocent bystander would come by and skew the whole delicate charade—never materialized. The Riverside County Sheriff was a worry, too. So Weinstein, Dumars and all four of their teammates had flooded the Indio Sheriff's Substation with calls just before noon. Posing as property owners, they reported hunters trespassing onto posted property many miles from Anza Valley—a common enough occurrence in many parts of the desert on any October 15. Not a deputy was seen.

Watching through the binoculars while the sweat ran down his back, hearing the soundtrack projected wonderfully by John's transmitter, Weinstein had been anguished at how slowly the whole thing seemed to take place. But later when he checked the time it was almost exactly as they'd planned: one minute and thirty-three seconds from the bikers' surprise encore to their final departure. Josh had taken a deep breath as he watched the war party roar away, and noticed the high-pitched, anxious smell of his own body.

Weinstein could only hope that Mickey—the giant—and Sam would make it to John's trailer undelayed, open the propane valves and toss in the flare without interference from Tim, the groundskeeper at the High Desert Rod and Gun Club. If necessary, Mickey would engage the groundskeeper. But twenty minutes after he'd set the fire, Mickey called on the cellular phone—stashed in the tool box of his Harley—to say that all had gone well. He reported that Tim had looked on from a few hundred yards away as the two bikers did their biker thing on John Menden's helpless domicile. The four men and three bikes had zoomed up the lowered ramp and into the back of a "State-to-State" moving trailer waiting at a turnout on Highway 371, which is where Mickey had placed the call.

Of course, the best laid plans didn't amount to much without luck, and luck was what Weinstein had been praying for ever since Norton had green-lighted him after lunch that afternoon in Santa Ana. They could lead Wayfarer to water, but they couldn't make him drink. And all John could do was save the day, be polite and a little recalcitrant, and use his native likeability to sway Wayfarer toward meaningful gestures. Josh had told John to "aw-shucks the sonofabitch to death."

An invitation to stay at the Lake Riverside Estates home would be the best they could reasonably hope for. If Holt went even this far, however, there was at least a small chance that John's generous refusal ("They'd find me here pretty easy, Mr.

Holt—then we'd both be out of a home.") could lead to the ultimate goal: Liberty Ridge. It was the kind of common sense pessimism that would appeal to Vann Holt.

The backup plan, if Holt offered John no sanctuary whatsoever, was to let John appeal directly to Wayfarer—at some point—for work, shelter, perhaps a little start-up loan to get a new trailer. Burning down the trailer was John's idea, and Weinstein was impressed by his informant's sense of follow-through. Weinstein also saw that John was profoundly moved by the thought of losing the trailer, nasty little piece of aluminum that it was.

Things were out of Joshua's hands now, and luck was what he needed. He had always been a lucky man, except with Rebecca Harris, and, by extension, John Menden. Guiding the van from the feed and tack parking lot after the pickup and Land Rovers had caravanned away, Josh Weinstein could not deny the faint nausea he felt at so brazenly tempting the Fates.

But one hour later, after John's mock chase of his tormentors through the Anza Valley desert, Josh's nausea was banished by pure elation. Josh parked the van two houses away from Holt's Riverside Estates home, assuming that, after the fire, this would be the logical place for Holt and his party to take John. He watched as the two Land Rovers pulled into the wide, semi-circle of a driveway, and John's Ford lumbered up behind them. Weinstein's ears roared with blood.

"God, I'm good, he whispered to Sharon.

"Yes, I am."

"We're good. We're just too damn good, Sharon. We get done with this, they'll want us to run the whole country."

"You're really not worried about that radio on his belt?"

"He's a newspaper editor, and the only full-time reporter. He's always on call. If Wayfarer has an allergic reaction to a beeper at this point, we're sunk. But we're not sunk. What we are is damned good."

The transmission came through clearly, even when John and his benefactors disappeared into the large ranch-style home.

HOLT: Get comfortable everybody, make calls if you want. There's bathrooms all over this damned place.

TITISI: Not what I expected for a hunting lodge.

VALERIE: We've got everything to drink. John?

JOHN: Not for me, thanks.

VALERIE: Some cold water at least?

JOHN: That might hit the spot.

"Listen to him," said Weinstein, actually rubbing his long-fingered hands together in a parody of enthusiasm. "My Joe. My man. My secret agent. My handsome little goy-boy nobody can resist."

"I think he's scared," said Sharon.

"I hope so."

The transmitted conversation followed John, of course, and for ten minutes amounted to little more than polite mundanities. At one point Titisi said that he could use a few hundred men like John in Uganda. The reel-to-reel took it all. Then the moment of revelation that Weinstein had been careful not to expect, was thrown at him like a firecracker:

HOLT: I was thinking we could put you up at my home in Orange County for the night. It's comfortable. I realize it would be a long commute out here to work, but I don't see any sense in stranding you here with those scum on the prowl.

JOHN: That's really nice of you to offer, but it wouldn't sit well with me.

HOLT: Relatives around here? Friends?

JOHN: Well, not exactly. I've only been in Anza Valley for a few months.

VALERIE: Then what doesn't sit well?

JOHN: Well, it's an imposition for one thing.

VALERIE: You ought to see Dad's house. He's got enough room for Juma's army, then some. Really, it could work out just fine. It would give you a chance to let the trouble blow over, then set up a new trailer. If you plan on staying out here, that is.

HOLT: He saved your life, Valerie, that doesn't mean you can run his.

JOHN: (laughter) You know, that's really a generous offer, but I don't know. It's—

HOLT: It's our way of saying thank you. A small way. Please, let us be generous. What you did today was beyond generosity. It still hasn't really sunk in.

VALERIE: Please?

JOHN: Well, I really would be grateful for a place to stay tonight.

HOLT: Then it's settled. You'll be comfortable with us for a night, John. We've got plenty of comfort on Liberty Ridge.

JOHN: Liberty Bridge?

VALERIE: *Ridge*. Dad names everything. Can't even have a house without making it a proper noun. You'll like it, though—and of course your dog is welcome. I've got fourteen springers and Dad's got another six, so there's plenty of kennel run.

JOHN: Well, there might be a problem there, because I've got two more out on the property. I left them with the groundskeeper when I went hunting this morning.

VALERIE: Are you kidding? Three more dogs won't even be noticed.

HOLT: She's right.

JOHN: At some point I need to go back to the trailer and see if anything's left. I mean, I don't want to burden you with that.

HOLT: Understood. We'll do it before we leave, give you a hand if you want.

JOHN: I'd like to bury Rusty out there, too.

HOLT: With honors.

JOHN: That would be great.

"That would be just one-hundred percent totally fucking great," Weinstein whispered. "I'd scream right now, but I'm afraid they'd hear me."

"You can bellow all the way back to Orange County."

"Maybe I will."

But he didn't. Instead, while Dumars drove, Josh called Norton in Washington and told him that Wayfarer was now the proud owner of Owl, Joshua's chosen code name for John.

"All the Hollywood stuff go down okay?" Norton asked.

"One take."

"How'd it look?"

"Rated X for violence."

"You didn't get the live rounds and blanks mixed up? The girl didn't rip Sammy's blood bag off his shoulder?"

"It was perfect."

"Rusty die nobly?"

"Yeah, he was great."

"Fast?"

"Instantly."

"You know that dog cost us seven thousand, four hundred

dollars? That's room, board and training for three years. Club and Fang actually let us amortize him because we wouldn't be sending him back. Those wags."

"Club and Fang sent us one perfect dog."

"True. Things here are odd, Josh. Frazee can't get enough of Wayfarer and Owl. He's old enough to confuse one with the other half the time—you know how Crazy could never keep the code names straight? Anyway, he's riding this one like a jockey. He's good for the money, so long as I let him feel involved. It's like having a banker involved in your remodel. You need the loan but you wish he wouldn't hang around the job site."

"How bad could he jam us?"

"He holds the Hate Crimes purse. You know that."

"I also know he goes all the way back to Quantico with Wayfarer. Student and professor, by way of The Church of Jesus Christ of Latter-Day Saints."

"He believes his ongoing interest is atonement for Wayfarer's lapse. Frazee is atoning vigorously. He actually mentioned ATF—some crack about letting them storm the walls of Liberty Ridge once and for all. A joke, of course. But I think it's obvious he doesn't just want to bust Wayfarer—he wants to humiliate the living shit out of him too."

"If Alcohol, Tobacco and Firearms gets within one mile of this case you'll have my resignation."

"What could that possibly matter to Walker Frazee?"

"*Christ, Norton, we can't let ATF into this! It's*—"

"—We're not letting ATF into this, we're just letting Crazy Frazee pass gas. Now, next we put Owl's toys in place, right?"

"*Goddamn*, Norton. Don't say things like that to me."

"It doesn't hurt for you to know where the wind's blowing back here."

"From a windbag. I just can't believe he'd even joke about—"

"—Hush, son. I said I'd take care of Walker and I'll take care of Walker. Now, do we put Owl's toys in place?"

"Yeah, if Frazee keeps the Bat Boys off the walls long enough to—"

"—Joshua, comport yourself professionally, please."

"*Yes*, we deliver the toys. And we start to leak news of our prime suspect."

"Blow the smoke, young man."

"Sharon will actually do the blowing, sir."

"Well, tell her I could say something that would get me disciplined as a sexual predator."

Weinstein told her.

"You're a dirty old lech," Dumars piped across the car toward the phone, smiling but her face quite red.

"Tell her thank you, Joshua."

He told her.

Back in the Tech Services yard, Weinstein collected his tape and binoculars and checked the van with the services clerk. The billet was already stamped with a direct Washington charge number, the Bureau version of a credit line. The clerk nodded reverently to Joshua as he accepted the keys, and Weinstein nodded back at him.

Then he did something he had never done before. Without stating a business-related reason, without pulling rank, without even asking her to do the driving, Joshua asked Sharon Dumars to an early dinner—his treat.

Sharon noted his flushed face, the tightened bobbing of his Adam's apple.

"I wish I could, Josh, but I've got plans tonight. Another time?"

He blushed even more deeply, but smiled. It was the non-smile of Joshua's, she saw—mirthless, forced and false.

"Sure," he said. "Whatever."

SEVENTEEN

Early the winter when John was nine, his parents flew their new plane to visit friends in Oregon.

John stood beside the dinner table one evening as his father traced their itinerary on a map—air route in red, ground stops shown by black circles. He listened to them talk about the flight; he helped them pack.

A few weeks before their departure, he made an amulet from a fossilized sea shell, three redtailed hawk feathers, a dried thistle pod and a strip of wild gourd tendril he gathered with some forethought in a local wilderness now called Liberty Ridge. John prayed that God would instill the amulet with protective properties and not come apart.

He and his uncle Stan watched the little Piper lift off from the Martin Aviation strip and groan into the air. John could smell his mother's perfume, still on his cheek from her lengthy parting kisses. She had worn the amulet around her neck, holding it to her breast as she knelt to kiss him to keep it from getting crushed. He could still see his father's ramrod straight back as he walked across the tarmac in his silk flight jacket, heading for the plane. The weather was cool and clear. They would be gone one week.

That night, Stan and his wife, Dorrie, were expansive, gracious, amusing. But Stan took a phone call midway through dinner, and when he came back to the table he was preoccupied and subdued. Later, John watched some television and saw them in the kitchen, talking intently. Dorrie's face was resolutely tragic.

Stan seemed to be trying to talk her out of something, imploring her, palms up, head shaking, ending his plea with a thumb hooked out toward John. Then Stan joined him in the den with a massive amber cocktail.

The next day around noon, Stan and Dorrie broke the news: John's parents had lost radio contact late the afternoon before, and had not been seen or heard from since. It could mean a hundred things, Stan told him. Most likely, his impulsive father simply set down early to wait out the storm. Yes, a fairly good sized storm had blown down from Alaska. With all the interference, radio contact is first to go, anyway. Just a matter of sitting tight and waiting to hear. You know how your father can be.

The plane was listed as missing and presumed down. Search and rescue aircraft couldn't penetrate the storm front, which was all the way south to Fresno by then. That evening, as the first gale-driven drops of rain roared against Uncle Stan's roof, John stood at a window and realized—with a huge wave of relief—that no amount of raindrops could foul his father's plans. He hadn't called because the phone lines were down, too. It was reassuring, almost amusing, to watch Stan and Dorrie fret like hens. John had seen the truth already. He could clearly imagine the yellow Piper emerging through a black wall of clouds, guided by the amulet.

For the next eight weeks, through the heart of winter, storms pounded the state. Even the local mountains were buried in snow. John was treated with all the privilege and dignity of the bereaved. He met with relatives he'd hardly known. He was asked about plans. Everything fine with Stan and Dorrie? You are courageous and we're proud of you.

His schoolmates, as if all coached by the same powerful figure, offered a sort of quiet respect to John. They kept away from him. One day on the playground when a little plane flew over, John stopped to watch it and the noon-duty supervisor, unbidden, wrapped a huge perfumed arm around his shoulders and started to weep. He told the woman "hold your mud"—a favorite expression of his father's—then walked off to the far corner of the school yard to get away from all these lugubrious, presuming fools.

By late June the snowpack had melted back enough to reveal the yellow Piper.

Stan and Dorrie drove him up to the Siskiyou County

morgue, to identify and claim the bodies. It was a long ride from Orange County, punctuated by Dorrie's breakdowns. John bought a pair of "Jackelope" postcards from a diner up on 395, addressing one each to his mother and father and writing out a brief message: "Be home soon."

There was some unutterable problem at the morgue. Stan and Dorrie consulted with the Sheriff-Coroner's deputy until Dorrie retreated to the lobby sofa, blubbering incoherently. Stan disappeared with another deputy, then returned to the lobby, sheet-white.

"I just can't say, for sure," Stan confessed.

"I can," said John. "They're my parents."

The deputy would have none of it. John was too young—both legally and emotionally—to make a valid identification. The Sheriff himself stepped in and called the party of three back to his office. His deputy explained the circumstance. The Sheriff was a big man with a bored but honest face, and John appreciated that the Sheriff did not look at him like a dying patient.

"You're willing to do this, young man?"

"I've said so several times, sir."

The identification room was small and official. It had four chairs along one wall, a sink and a faucet. Two large boxes of tissue sat on a counter, beside an arrangement of plastic flowers in a gray vase.

A morgue tech entered through a large sliding door on the opposite side of the chairs, pulling a wheeled gurney behind him. He looked at John and the Sheriff, then excused himself and returned shortly with another.

"They were exposed to fire, then the elements for some time," he said.

"He knows," said the Sheriff.

The first body was unquestionably not that of his father. John knew it less by what was left than by what was gone. It was easy to extrapolate. Add some flesh here. Muscle there. The flight jacket. Eyes. Hair. No—it wouldn't add up to Dad.

He nodded but said nothing.

Likewise for the body they thought was his mother's. Definitely not her, John thought. Everything is just wrong. He looked at the Sheriff.

"These are not my parents."

The big bored face was plainly startled. It blushed. For a

moment the Sheriff's ice-blue eyes held John's, then the Sheriff waved away the tech. The tech pulled both gurneys from the room and the sliding doors met silently.

"You sure, young man?"

"I'm sure, Sheriff."

"Well, then there we have it."

He shook John's hand and they went back to his office. Stan and Dorrie were there, prim and ghastly. The Sheriff explained that the bodies did not belong to John's parents, and John just had to sign the papers to make it official. John signed in six places. The Sheriff leafed through the little stack, then placed it on the table in front of him. From his desk drawer he removed a small plastic bag and handed it to John.

"You may as well keep these."

John pressed the plastic tight and looked at the two wedding bands inside. Even through the plastic he recognized the engraving and the inscription inside each—"Love, Cherish and Honor." A fossilized sea shell rested in one corner of the bag.

"I understand," John said.

"Good man," said the Sheriff.

A moment of pregnant silence passed, then all three adults as if on cue skidded back their chairs.

On the long drive back home, John stared out the window and wondered where, exactly, his parents had gone.

The earth is a small place, but there is sky everywhere, and it never ends. All you need is a little piece of earth to stand on. From there, you can look up and wonder, and find the things out there that are yours.

CHAPTER

EIGHTEEN

John awoke at eight on Liberty Ridge. He had just showered, shaved and dressed in yesterday's clothes when he heard a knock. Looking down from the loft he saw Valerie through the glass inset of the door. When he called out the door opened and the dogs, damp and spiky from the lake, burst in ahead of her. She followed and looked toward the kitchen inquisitively. Her hair was pulled back in a ponytail. She had on a white sleeveless blouse tucked into a pair of khaki shorts, white socks folded to the tops of the heavy suede hiking boots favored by so many young women that year. Her skin was brown, but not overly so, a natural shade produced by activity out of doors rather than hours basting on a beach.

"There's coffee on," he said.

She looked up and he noted the deep brown of her eyes and the arched, interrogatory brows. "Good morning," she said.

"Good morning."

"Beautiful morning, in fact. Fall's my favorite time of year." She looked away, glancing at one of the ubiquitous Liberty Ridge computers, which in this case was stationed on one corner of the dining room table. "What's yours?"

"Spring."

"The labs sure like the water."

"They don't get much, out in Anza."

"Hey, I got to thinking we should go get you some clothes."

"Not a bad idea. Yesterday's wardrobe feels a skosh used."

"We can take my Jeep. It's a good day to have the top off."

They stopped at the Big House so John could call his boss at
the paper. Valerie led him down the cool, vast foyer, which was
framed in massive rough-cut timbers that looked a century old
but were in fact older. The walls were hung with Indian blankets
and baskets, each lovingly specified by a recessed light. A series
of wrought-iron candelabra hung down from the cavernous ceiling on thick black chains. John looked into the huge living room
as he walked by, noting the quiet fire in the tremendous fireplace.
It looked almost distant. Then the kitchen, which was roughly
the size of the house he'd grown up in. There was no sign of Holt
and his guests, nor the Liberty Ridge staff, nor any of the dozen
Liberty Ops insiders with whom Joshua Weinstein had made
John familiar. He committed what he saw to memory. Valerie
poked a few preliminary digits on the phone, saying that the system was a bit complicated here—"basic security." The phone was
a cordless with an automatic channel search. The numbers to call
out—this day's, at least—were 3-9-9.

John started to explain what had happened, but Bruno—his
garrulous and unlikely publisher—was full of questions: Did
John shoot three or four of them; how many trailers did they
burn out at the High Desert Rod and Gun Club; did the rape
actually occur inside Olie's or in the lot itself; and since when did
John travel with a pack of attack dogs? The publisher told him
that the entire city—all 2,450 citizens of Anza Valley—was talking about the incident, and that some people feared the bikers
might return for some kind of retribution. Riverside County
Sheriffs wanted to talk to him. And of course, a first-person account in the *Anza Valley News* would draw advertisers, "fly off
the stands," and was due before four p.m. the next day. A special
section was a possibility for the week after. Did anyone take pictures?

John said he'd be in at the regular time tomorrow, pressed
"off," and listened for any sound of a recording being made. He
heard none, then put the phone back in its cradle.

"So, will there be a hero's welcome for you back in Anza
Valley?"

"A ticker-tape parade, major media, key to the city."

"You deserve it."

"Sheriffs, too."

"That bother you?"

"Better than bikers."

They drove up the freeway to South Coast Plaza, a mall nationally known for its size, crowds and variety of stores. The Jeep—a bright red Wrangler—bounced along on its parsimonious shocks, the roll cage rattling happily, the warm October air blasting through the cockpit. There was no real point in talking. Valerie drove the Jeep fast but with concentration—hands at ten and two, her eyes often on the mirrors, the radio turned up high enough that its static almost matched the roar of the road.

John sat back and watched Orange County go by. Nothing much had changed in the last six months along the freeway here. It was coveted real estate that had been built up decades ago. The new airport gleamed off to his left while a silver 737 wavered toward the landing strip. Traffic was bad, especially around the mall parking lot, but it was always bad. Almost any time of day, any season of the year, this retail metropolis would be crammed with people buying and eating things. The place had seemed to give rise to an entire class of people—the shopping class—though John realized that the mall didn't create them, but simply gave them a place to gather.

He looked over at Valerie several times, indulging the simple-minded pleasure of admiring her. She looked back at him once, then, smiling, returned her gaze to the road.

By the time they parked, her hair was a bird's nest of tangles that she attempted to organize in the mirror, then matter-offactly gave up on.

"Let's go consume," she said. "Be good little wheels in the capitalist machine."

"I'll bet your dad cringes when you talk like that."

"He loathes consumer society. I think he'd bomb this place if he had a chance."

"No offense meant."

"None taken. I'm going to buy you something for what you did yesterday."

"I can't live off my reputation forever," he said. "How about I buy my own clothes?"

"Fine. Then I'll accessorize you."

"No, really—"

"—Put a lid on it, Mr. Menden. You saved me from a rape

and maybe more, and it cost you a dog and a home. So I can buy you some stuff if I want to. End of argument, White Knight."

She bought him three pairs of pants, three shirts and three pairs of shoes at a store billing itself as an "outfitter." He gravitated to the sale items but Valerie seemed unfazed by price. At a department store he stocked up on socks and underwear while Valerie wandered off, only to return bearing a light jacket, a sweater and three neckties. She insisted on a cream linen summerweight suit, with a shirt that matched and a shirt that complemented it, countering his protests with threats to buy more. At a drug emporium he got toiletries and some personal things. At a pet store so overpriced he could hardly believe it, John got a forty-pound bag of food for his batallion.

They stopped for lunch in Laguna Beach. The cafe was little more than a few plastic tables and chairs strung along a clifftop overlooking the ocean. They sat at the far end. The breeze was stiff from the water, crumbling the little waves onto the beach and trying to blow away their menus. Valerie's lifted off but she caught it mid-air.

"Nice grab."

"The softball years."

While Valerie ordered, John took the opportunity to study her. He knew from Josh that she was twenty-two. He guessed her height at five feet eight, but was never any good at women's weights because they always seemed to weigh less than he thought they would. Average, he decided, maybe average plus a few, because Valerie Holt had a full but shapely body that seemed somehow to have retained just a hint of girlish fat. This gave her limbs a taut smoothness, as opposed to the weight-room definition of movie stars and models. Her wrists were slender, her fingers long and beautifully shaped, though the nails were cut short for her hunting and field work with the dogs. Her face was full, with a smattering of freckles on each cheek. Other than the freckles her complexion was flawless and had that kind of moist glow that speaks of health, youth, a body working well. Her mouth was wide and her lips quite pink without lipstick, and when she smiled her teeth were large and even, the kind of teeth no orthodontist could improve. Her nose was small. Her eyes were a dark chocolate brown in the strident October light. To John, her most delicate features were her brows, which arched finely to an inquisitive peak then angled down to frame her calm, steady eyes.

This arch made her look almost uncertain at times, skeptical, perhaps, giving her face an expression of intelligence and doubt. Her forehead was high and round, suggesting a youth belied by her twenty-two years. It was the kind of head, John mused, that would still look good when Valerie Holt was eighty years old. Her hair at this point was still pulled away from her face in a wind-blown tail of gold and light copper. Valerie was by any standards a beautiful young woman, a woman still growing and still unfinished.

She can be a useful tool, an unwitting voice, a conduit. You can know her only to use her.

"Well," she asked, glancing up from the breeze-bent menu, "Did I pass my physical?"

"Sorry. Yes."

"You're forgiven. You are a writer, after all."

"Always studying."

"Like what you see?"

He looked down at his own menu, shrugging. "The chicken sandwich sounds good."

She laughed. "You big oaf. That's what you are—a big sweet oaf. An accidental hero. A mystery man with a quick gun and a long coat and a shy streak. What am I?"

He looked at her, summoning distance. "A beautiful young woman with a whole life in front of her."

"Not just a girl with a brain the size of a table grape and way more money than she needs?"

"Naw."

"Good, because you'll be sitting next to me tonight at the grad dinner. It's going to be quite the affair, and you have to be there because you are a guest of honor."

"Grad dinner?"

"Dad gives a bash for his new Holt Men every six months when they finish training."

"He calls them Holt Men?"

"That's what they are," she said cheerfully. "They're just glorified security guards, even though Dad educates the hell out of them. But you're the guest everyone's dying to meet."

"Hmmm."

"Hmmm nothing. It's a perfect time to wear your new suit."

"Okay, mom."

Valerie smiled then, a wide-mouthed, honest, forthright

smile. It was just a little more open on one side, which revealed some back teeth and gave it a shade of mischief. She looked down at her menu again, with an odd expression of satisfaction on her face. The wind blew a strand of golden brown hair over her round girlish forehead and she caught it without looking up then fingered it back behind her ear.

John felt an odd shifting inside, and a very slight, very clear ringing in his ears.

He spent the rest of the afternoon writing his account of the incident at Olie's Saloon for the *Anza Valley News*. He used the computer on the dining room table. It ran a brief fifty-five lines. John concentrated on dispelling rumors: the woman was not raped or even hurt; his trailer was the only one burned out; he had in fact shot only once, giving the woman's assailant a minor flesh wound that made her escape possible. He refused to give any names because they had asked him not to. He hoped the whole incident would be forgotten soon and that the citizens of Anza Valley would not worry about a vengeful motorcycle gang overrunning their town. He asked anyone with information about the bikers to call the Sheriff's substation in Indio. He also admitted that the single worst thing about the whole affair was the loss of Rusty—the day's true hero.

That evening he walked along the lake with his dogs. He stopped to look at the marina and boathouse, the lovely Hatteras, *Carolyn,* docked there, the little covey of Boston Whalers tarped against the sun. He could see the beach on the island in the center of the lake and the dark oaks and conifers beyond. On the far shore he made out a row of small cabanas and scaffolding of what looked like a sporting clays tower. He thought back twenty-odd years to the summer days he and his friends would sneak past the "No Trespassing" signs, hike to the lake and spend the day swimming, fishing, hiking and looking for animals. They had outlegged the sheriffs more than once. He had even spent the night in the cave on the island, for which he was thoroughly thrashed by his father upon returning home late the next afternoon. John was struck that the place was more beautiful now than then—the foliage thicker and the trees more mature and the water level of the lake higher—no doubt due to Vann Holt's attentions. A flock of mallards veed out across the blue water in no hurry whatsoever, a chevron of ripples widening behind them. He wished Rebecca could have seen this. He thought about the dream he'd had early that morning, the way she had seemed so present and actual. And tonight, he thought, I'll be having dinner with the man who blew her heart out of her chest.

The foyer of the big house is as brightly lit as a movie set when John walks in, led by a ravishingly beautiful brunette who has introduced herself as Laura Messinger. John has already recognized her. She takes him by the arm, saying she always wanted to touch a hero. She leads him into the expansive kitchen, at the far end of which is a bar. A waiter approaches and she dismisses him. She asks John his pleasure and gives the bow-tied barman the order. He can smell venison and elk on the stove-top grill, and a wild, cilantro-based aroma coming from four huge saucepans.

"Are you a friend of Mr. Holt?" he asks.

"His attorney and techno-weenie, actually. A friend, too. Cheers."

She hands him the scotch-and-soda and raises her own cocktail glass very sightly, not touching his, then brings it to her thick bright red lips. Her eyes are an astonishing blue that John decides can only be realized by colored lenses. Her breasts are large and tastefully displayed. She could be thirty, but John knows from Weinstein that she is forty-two.

Laura and husband Thurmond are the high-end foreign team for Liberty Operations. You need a hundred capable men to settle unrest on the diamond coast in Namibia? Talk to Laura. Need some small arms know-how in Sierra Leone? Thurmond can help. He's a lapsed Northrup veep who never got his peace dividend and she was third in her law class at Harvard. They aren't salaried—noboby at the Ops is salaried except for Lane Fargo. Last year their take was a little over four-hundred thousand, counting bonuses.

With her arm again on John's, Laura Messinger leads him into the living room. "Oyez, oyez," she calls in a mellifluous voice, "John Menden."

Heads turn: two dozen of them, men in dinner jackets and women in dresses, tanned healthy faces, mostly middle-aged but some old and some young, expressions of polite assessment, mild approval, curiosity. The newly minted Holt Men stand out conspicuously, clustered together a little nervously near the fireplace. They are late twenties to late thirties, fit, alert and dressed alike in black slacks and white dinner jackets. They have the bearing of West Point cadets. John regards the guests with his native taciturnity, feeling embarrassed and underdressed. He scans the room quickly for Valerie, resting his glance occasionally on a still-beholding guest. They are clapping.

"Don't embarrass the poor boy too much," says Laura, smiling at John. "We don't want to spoil his appetite."

Then she takes John to the first little group of people, releases his arm and is gone. He can feel the warm spot where her hand was, cooling through the fabric of his linen coat.

"Hey, I've missed your articles in the *Journal*," says the first man to shake his hand.

John recognizes him from one of Joshua's endless briefings—Adam Sexton—young, ambitious, married into one of the county's largest landholding families and currently Vice President of Domestic Development for Liberty Operations.

"Thanks. Nice to be back in the county."

Sexton brings in the genuine dollars for Liberty Ops. Domestic takes in triple what foreign does, prosaic as the work might sound. Home security. Plant Security. Store security. Personal security. Private Investigations. Sexton married straight into the Orange County movers and shakers, waved a vague Manhattan pedigree in front of them, convinced them he was one up on them. Easy to do to Californians, of course. His timing was perfect. When crime started grabbing the headlines a few years back, everybody was worried. Everybody was scared. Nobody could remember it being this bad. Afraid to leave the mansion. Who do we trust? Who do we hire? The cops can't help us. Who can really blast away on our behalf when the gook home invaders from Little Saigon show up, or the gangbangers from Santa Ana come scaling our gated-community walls? Sexton was ready with his sophistication-and-a-touch-of-streetsmarts routine, New York style. Thanks to him they all prefer to use Holt Men—excuse me, Liberty Men now. It's as much a status symbol to have Liberty Ops patrolling your bayfront house in Newport as it is to drive the right car or wear the right clothes. Even more so. You own more than just a home or a private plane—you own a man. A Liberty Man. There was a joke going around last year. Question: Why is a Holt Man better than a dildo? Answer: A dildo can't show itself to the door. You know you've entered a profitable vernacular when rich women joke about the penis size of your employees. Well, thank Sexton for the entrée.

"Are you back to stay, John?" Sexton asked.

"No. I've got work down in Anza Valley."

"People down there can actually read?"

"They light their caves with candles."

"Candles. That's rich. Hey, *plenty* of work here in the county, if you're interested. All kinds of it."

"Thanks. I like my job."

The dining room basks in the burnished candlelight of an immense, circular candelabra. The table seems to stretch into infinity. Waiters come and go, glancing occasionally at Laura Messinger, who directs them with the silent nodding of her head. Vann Holt has stolen in—exactly when, John has no idea—and now presides at the head of the table. He has not acknowledged his guest of honor. John sees that his host looks alert, fit and leonine, with his thick gray hair, stout neck and shoulders and an easy physical grace. Holt is also conspicuously underdressed in a black suit with a black polo shirt buttoned to the top. But John senses that Holt is the kind of man who can make everyone else in a room feel pretentiously overstated. Finally, Holt looks his way and stares at him for a moment without expression. Then he lifts his wine glass, nods rather formally, and offers a robust smile. From behind Holt, Lane Fargo stares his way with a look of focused aggression. His widow's peak and mustache are somehow absurd above his tight white dinner jacket. He is drinking a glass of beer.

Holt seats himself and the others follow. John has a seat of honor on Holt's left. They are just settling in when Holt pushes back his chair and stands, brushing up his coatsleeve to look at his watch. Then he bellows in a voice that threatens to rattle the crystal, "*Valerie Anne Holt—you are holding up my dinner party—again!*"

By the unanimous chuckles John understands that this is something of a ritual. Heads turn, and John looks to see Valerie Anne Holt coming up the broad hallway toward the dining room.

Her hair is up and she is wearing a black knit dress with a high neck and that holds her snugly under the chin. There are no sleeves on it and her brown arms sway easily as she walks. The dress ends well above her knees. Her shoes are heeled and black and she makes walking in them appear easy and natural. She claps across the tiled floor and enters the room to a chorus of Hello Valerie; Evening, dear; Worth the wait, young lady; Nice of you to join us; etc. Lane Fargo sustains a piercing whistle that continues for a beat after the general welcome has died down.

"Oh, Lane, put a lid on it," she says, which brings another round of laughter from the guests.

Beaming, Valerie walks the length of the table and kisses her father on both cheeks. Then, helped by a new Holt Man who has popped up to assist her, she settles into the chair on her father's right, across from John. She looks around the table, holding each face for a brief moment. Then, smiling and apparently finished, she sits back and turns her full attention to John.

His ears ring again and he feels uncomfortable, as if the entire world is staring at him.

"Nice suit, Mr. Menden," she says. "It goes perfectly with your blush."

For John, dinner goes by in a pleasant haze. He drinks two cocktails and three glasses of wine. The conversation around him is animated and light. Holt regales him with stories of his Boone & Crockett trophies, most notably a "Grand Slam" sheep hunt during which he nearly froze to death somewhere in Tibet. In fact, one of his guides had been buried in an avalanche. But John hears nothing of the braggart in Holt, none of the macho posturing associated with the rich eccentrics who aspire to the Boone & Crockett "Book" and spend scores of thousands of dollars to acquire that status. John had written about these men in the *Journal*, finding them fascinating, driven almost beyond comprehension, and eerily dispassionate about taking life for sport. Even for a bird hunter such as himself, it was hard to understand their ardor for such gruelling, far-flung expeditions. The articles had brought a cascade of protesting letters from his readers, who chose to believe that merely reporting on these people was endorsing them. But Holt's narratives are self-effacing, almost scientifically objective. He does not use the euphemisms of the contemporary "hunter/conservationist" such as "harvest" or "collect." When Vann Holt tells of killing an animals he uses the verb *kill*, pronouncing it with slightly less volume than the rest of the sentence, in a kind of reverential hush.

Valerie listens to her father, talks with Thurmond Messinger to her right and looks at John from across the table. He can feel her attention on him even when she's looking away, and it worries him that Vann Holt must sense the same thing. But it feels reassuring to know that he is not totally alone here. His eyes are drawn directly to her. They are not willing to look past, through or around her. In the light of the candles above, she radiates a restless, almost ungovernable energy.

You can know her only to use her.

Between his undeniable attention to Valerie, John still notes the face of every guest. Beside him is Mary Randell, a talkative woman in her early fifties with a wizened complexion, the high cheekbones of an Iroquois and a long mane of gray-black hair. Mary is happy to tell John about the interesting characters sitting around the table, spicing her resumé of each with at least one tidbit of the personal. "And next to Laura is Mike O'Keefe, a brilliant motivator but a terrible doubles partner. He *can't* handle pace to his backhand. And Adam Sexton? He brings in piles of money to the company. Cocky kid—the only one around who doesn't worship Vann like a god." She is the wife of Rich, whom John knows is part of the Liberty Ops team trying to draw the business of Juma Titisi.

The Ugandan himself sits at the far end of the table, opposite Holt, expansive in his tux and Oxford English. John collects every nugget of information with some effort, because although his mind is keen and capacious, he's not sure what might be important to Joshua and what might be redundant. He doesn't want to miss a thing. He was told to gather so that Joshua could edit; horde so Josh could winnow. John has always been good at collecting facts—a reporter's first task—so before the evening is over he knows the name, face, occupation and at least one personal item about everyone in the room. Laura Messinger, for instance, has two children from a previous marriage, while Thurmond, twenty years her senior, has none.

The food is incomparably good. Elk and venison, pheasant and chukar, garden greens, basmati rice with slivered almonds, *frijoles* covered with the cilantro sauce, dill-sprinkled rolls, cold asparagus spears with vinaigrette. Holt is unabashedly proud of the dinner, most of which he either grew or shot. He says he killed the elk early last fall while the forage around Jackson Hole was still sweet, and you could taste the berries in the meat. An elk shot deeper into the season would taste of the sparse feed and the stress of winter.

"Do you hunt Anza Valley a lot?" he asks John.

"The last ten seasons, anyway."

"Ever try that meadow out by Copper Saddle, where the old water tank is?"

"There's a nice little covey in there."

"So it's *you* picking over my quail! Funny we've never run into each other."

"Big desert, Mr. Holt. I usually hunt early, then get out."

"Those labradors take the heat okay?"

"Well, they're not designed for it. They go through five gallons of water on a hot morning."

"Why not hunt springers?"

"Labradors have the kind of character I get along with."

Valerie joined in then, with words of warning. "Dad, don't try to convert a dog man. It's more personal than religion or politics—you taught me that."

Holt smiles, reaches out and touches his daughter's cheek. "What were you doing with that heroic German shepherd yesterday? And don't tell me you taught him how to flush quail."

"Well, someone did, sir. He was on them all spring and summer, so I gave him a try opening day."

"I'll be damned. He looked purebred."

"I'd say."

"Who'd let a thousand-dollar dog just wander off?"

"People aren't always bright."

Holt beholds John and sips his wine. "Poor boy."

To conclude dinner Holt stands and offers a toast to the new Holt Men. It is brief and alludes to the fact that Holt considers Holt Men extensions of himself. He then offers a toast to John Menden, "a good shot and a good man and a good stroke of luck. An honorary Holt Man," he says to polite applause.

"Hey Vann," yells Sexton, "Get him a little orange and black costume to wear!"

Uncertain laughter follows.

* * *

After dinner Holt offers John a tour of the Big House. Drinks in hand, they wander the first floor rooms—living, entertainment, den, guest and gun rooms—in which Holt does not seem particularly interested. Then they climb a wide wooden stairway with rough-hewn banisters and leather-capped railings, to the second floor. Here, Holt explains, are the bedroom suites—his wife's, his daughter's, his own and an extra. He hesitates for a moment and John awaits some further elucidation, but Holt merely crosses the tiled landing and continues up the stairs to the third story. Holt shows him the library, a colossal room lined with bookshelves and furnished with very old leather sofas and rawhide chairs. Mission-era trunks serve as tables. Two large French doors open to a balcony and observation deck. Behind a heavy oak door along one wall is Holt's office. He makes them fresh drinks, very strong, from a small bar that swings up from what John thought was a steamer trunk. John looks at the fireplace, a generous cavern overhung by an adobe-and-timber mantle, with nineteenth century wrought iron tools hung from stout dowels protruding from the hearth facade. He notes the smell of leather and fire, cigar smoke and the pages of old books. He thinks that this is the best smelling room he's ever been in.

"I like this room a lot," he says.

"My favorite. Here, let's get an overview."

From the balcony they climb a flight of outdoor stairs to the platform of the observation deck. John can see the northern shore of the lake, the hillsides of Liberty Ridge, the ocean, the chaparral and a distant section of luminous freeway to the east, and the dark carpet of orange trees spreading north toward the heart of the county.

"Try the telescope."

John trains the instrument first on the lake, then on the back of the cottage in which he spent the night, then swings it west to reveal a silver Pacific.

"Do you have strong eyes?" Holt asks.

"I'm lucky that way. Why?"

"Curious. Envious, maybe."

"You've got a lot here to be envious of, Mr. Holt. I've never seen a place like this."

"Have you seen the grounds, the groves?"

"Just from a distance."

"Maybe you'll get a closer look sometime."

"What are all the buildings for?"

"Executives. Staff for the house and grounds. Citrus workers live in the cottages down where the groves start, but you can't see those from here."

"I didn't know you owned Liberty Operations."

Holt nods.

"Are you an investigator, then, a private policeman?"

Holt chuckles. "Of sorts. What I really do is just make people feel safe."

Ever make Rebecca Harris feel safe?

". . . I kind of fell into it. Everyone's afraid these days and they pay me to make it go away. I fell into a bucket of money, too. To be truthful, though, there was already plenty of that in the family."

"Well, you've certainly prospered."

"Liberty Ridge is a pearl of great price. Most things in life come with a price."

John nods and lets the heavy telescope rest on its brass fulcrum.

"How can I reward you for what you did?"

"You already have."

"I'd be grateful if you would let me buy you a new trailer."

"Well, trailers aren't real expensive, you know. What I mean is, with a few weeks pay I'd have enough for a down payment, so it's not going to be a—"

"—What did your last one cost?"

"Just twenty-five hundred. It was almost twenty-years old, but they made them better back then. Some of them."

"Consider it done, then, that your next trailer will be a gift from the Holt family. You will choose it and all the options, of course."

"No, really . . . that doesn't seem right, sir."

"What doesn't seem right? I don't understand you."

John turns to face Holt now, an act of self-confidence and of self-revelation. Holt's eyes, behind the thick glasses, have an unfiltered, unrestrained voraciousness in them. They look insatiable and incapable of pity, simple organs of procurement. John believes that now is the time to—as Joshua put it—bait the hook. *You'll sense the moment to show him what you keep inside, John.*

You'll sense the time to let him glimpse something in you that he possesses, too. When you do, give him a clear whiff of himself.

"Mr. Holt, I just did what I thought was right. To be honest with you, it gave me a chance to be a little hero, which fulfills a nice daydream I've had since I was a boy. Every man's fantasy, to rescue a king and his princess. I got to have a nice dinner and meet some good people. On a less noble note, it gave me a chance to put the fear of God into a bunch of bastards. Felt good. I've wondered a couple of times how it would have felt to just gut-shoot that turd and let him bleed to death beside my dog. Truth is, I'm afraid it would have felt a little too good. And I didn't want to face the paperwork."

Holt is silent for a long moment. Then he laughs. "My, oh my, what lurks in the heart of Menden. I understand."

"Do you?"

"Of course. What thinking man wouldn't?"

"I can think of quite a few."

"So let me ask you—these thinking men you know—would you call them friends, hunt with them, spend time with them, want to know them and their families?"

"I never have."

"Can you respect a man who has no concept of conviction and follow-through?"

Follow-through, thinks John: one of Josh's pet phrases. Did Josh imagine it coming from his secret hero?

"No. I actually can't. And that's why, Mr. Holt, for you to buy me a trailer or make some big gesture would make me feel small. I think I'll just say thank you, no, and leave here tomorrow. I'll take a sense of having done something decent along with me. It's a good feeling to have. I hope I don't seem ungrateful, either. I mean, Valerie must have spent two grand today, just for clothes."

Holt considers. "I understand that a gift might seem demeaning to your intentions, but we also have to be practical sometimes. Look at it this way, too—if you won't take the trailer, you're denying me a chance to be generous."

"I wouldn't want to do that, Mr. Holt," says John, with just a trace of irony in his voice.

Holt hears it and smiles. "Look. What if you think about it for a few days? During that time, stay here with us. There are a few things you might help me out with."

"Like what?"

"Val could use some help with the dogs. Now that she's out of school it's dogs, dogs, dogs. Headed for vet school next fall, probably out of state. So . . . well, anyway, she's still field-training her pups."

John sensed that there was something on Holt's mind left unsaid. He waited, but Holt was silent.

"Nice offer, Mr. Holt, but the paycheck calls."

"Lane talked to Bruno today. As of yesterday you didn't have any vacation time coming, but now you've got a paid week. Lane helped him see the value of your complete convalescence."

"You're bluffing now."

"I don't bluff. Bruno wants the story filed by tomorrow afternoon. Then you're free for a vacation. Don't tell me some R & R on Liberty Ridge would pollute your sense of chivalry, young man."

"Well, it's tempting."

"Settled."

Holt extends his hand and John shakes it. His grip is strong, dry and warm. "I was surprised to learn you used to write for the *Journal*. But when Fargo mentioned it, I remembered your columns. Nice stuff. Very un-*Journal*."

"Thank you."

"Do you know Susan Baum?"

John feels his heart tighten, then speed up.

"Not well."

"In touch with her?"

"Not really."

"Could you be?"

"I hear she's kind of in hiding, since the shooting."

"That's what I've heard. Guess I would be, too."

When John finally returns to his lakeside cottage it is almost midnight. He can see his dogs on the porch, lying next to a chair in which a figure sits, rocking slowly. His heart shifts a little, and the ringing begins in his ears again. Somehow he can remember the smell of Valerie's perfume, a light, feminine scent that he was not even aware of registering.

"So, what did you say?" asks Fargo. "Going to stick around?"

John's heart tightens again and a cool sweat creeps over his scalp. The dogs knock against his legs. "I said I would."

"No big surprise."

"Thanks for the vacation time."

"That was easy."

John steps onto the porch and Lane Fargo stands. In the darkness they face each other.

"So, Valerie bought you some clothes today."

"I guess that's pretty obvious."

"Pretty obvious. You like a little dig now and then, don't you?"

"Hard to pass up, sometimes."

Fargo nods. "You're hard to figure."

"How so?"

"I really don't know yet—you're a puzzle."

"You might be overcomplicating me."

"But I might not be. There's two kinds of people in my world, John-Boy—people I trust and people I hate. On you, the jury's still out."

"Well, thanks for the status report."

"Sleep tight."

For the next three days John stayed on Liberty Ridge, the rewarded Samaritan, the model guest. He shot pistol and shotgun with Holt and Fargo. He enjoyed Holt's tales of African safaris. He endured Fargo's taunts and brooding stares as he outscored Fargo on the sporting clays course.

The three of them shot Holt Alley three times each, the best score going to Holt—32 proper kills, no innocents and a time of 3:25. John came in last with a 28 in 3:30. Walking away from the building there was a silence during which John knew both Holt and Fargo were wondering how a mediocre pistol shot like him had managed to clip a biker's shoulder without clipping the girl next to him.

"Tough course," he admitted.

John felt naked and exposed, like a hermit crab scuttling between shells. He tried to forget his purpose. During the hours he spent with Valerie in the meadow behind the Big House he almost managed to succeed. There, they drilled her dogs with dummies and live birds and lead lines while John's labradors sat enviously in the shade and watched. Boomer just howled sadly.

John went about the hours as if they were his own and he was an actual man doing actual things. The very forbiddenness of Valerie Holt made him all the more comfortable in her company. He enjoyed her talk, he admired her skills with the dogs, he was surprised by her easy intelligence and her sense of control. He silently noted her beauty and relished the covert glances he could steal. He was thankful for his sunglasses. Only once did she catch him, but she blushed deeply and looked away, catching her boot on a rock. She was so bold at times, he thought, and so timid at others, so graceful, then such a clod. He tried to remember back to being that young.

He recognized in himself the simple excitement of attraction. How long since he had felt that for Rebecca, and even then, how impacted and joyless.

For the rest of the afternoon he thought only of Rebecca and the commitment he had made to her, letting the dark aura of her memory enclose his waiting, cunning heart.

CHAPTER
NINETEEN

The first light of the fifth day found John and his three dogs following the west shore of the lake. He carried a big cup of coffee in one hand and in the other a walking stick—a long piece of orangewood he'd found near his cottage. To any observer he would have looked like a man on a morning stroll and nothing more. John had temporarily convinced himself that this was all he was.

He walked along unhurriedly, waiting for the fuzz of the night's Scotch to dissipate with the stern clarity of caffeine. He had been pleased to find the bar of the cottage well stocked. The day was cool, but he could tell from the unclouded sky and the dry offshore breeze that the Santa Ana winds were brewing, and it would be hot before nine. The dogs splashed in and out of the lake, chasing each other like puppies.

He rounded the south shore, then left the lake and struck off down a trail leading into the chaparral. It was already warmer just a hundred yards from the water. On top of a gentle rise, he stopped and looked back toward the lake, then to the training buildings for the Liberty Ops cadets. He could see a pair of them entering the library. Two more, dressed in *gis,* talking outside the martial arts building. Young men, mid-to-late twenties, mostly white, close-shaven, clean-cut, alert. He watched a helicopter rise from the helipad. It was painted in the same unmistakable orange and black of the Liberty Operations patrol cars, and it looked like a big dragonfly moving up into the sky. A moment later another rose and followed. The Liberty Ops lieutenants going out to check their beats, thought John. Holt Men in the sky.

Continuing on, he thought of Valerie Anne Holt and the way she looked to him—and at him—at the big dinner. And though his stomach grew warm inside and he heard that faint ringing in his ears, he forced a rational coolness over them and told himself again that any closeness he had with Valerie would be false. He was, in this fabricated world of Joshua Weinstein, her protector. He thought of Lane Fargo, too, and the unabashed hostility the bodyguard had shown him. It was almost comforting to know that Fargo was after him; it defined the threat. *Fargo is Holt's unleashed paranoia, his pit bull. If he comes at you, hold your ground—if he gives you license, take it.* He wondered too if Fargo's interest in Valerie went beyond the professional. He considered whether Valerie might have deeper affections for Lane, and decided not. She seemed too bright a soul to be drawn to Lane Fargo's dark spirit.

Most of all, he thought of Vann Holt. A surprising man. John had been prepared for Holt's confidence and control, the *aura of capacity* that Josh had described. He had expected the easy command Holt exhibited at Liberty Ridge and the deference of his friends, business partners, guests. He had expected the wealth, the grandness of his home, the extravagance of his table. What John had not been ready for was the simple harmony between Holt and his world. John could see nothing of a master's iron hand, no misshapen power, none of the triumphant strutting of the prosperous. Yes, Vann Holt was the unchallenged king of Liberty Ridge. But his kingdom seemed to project from his imagination, rather than surrender to his ambition. He had dreamed the place, not conquered it; he was its heart, but not its body. They belonged to each other. And while Holt's lavish generosity surprised John, Joshua had predicted it, counted on it. *Once Wayfarer believes he owes you, the sky will be the limit. Decline the sky but accept the Ridge. All we need is your presence at Liberty Ridge. His gratitude will be his Achilles Heel.*

John turned and continued along the trail. For a few hundred yards it was wide and clear, but then the scrub pressed in and choked it down to little more than a game trail winding through brush. It rose steeply and John stopped again at the top, breathing hard, his empty coffee cup dangling from a finger. The dogs snorted up ahead; he could see all three labrador tails—one chocolate, one yellow, one black—protruding from a clump of buckwheat bush. From here, the lake and the buildings of Liberty Ridge were invisible. The first hot gusts of the Santa Ana wind heaved by him, drying the sweat on his temples.

The trail led him down now, past a stand of eucalyptus trees fragrant in the growing heat. He remembered Joshua's map, and that the stand was roughly one-third of the distance from the lake to the electric perimeter fence. His next signpost was a mammoth California oak tree, easily two centuries old, he thought, that stood haunted and solitary atop a knoll to his right. A redtail hawk perched near the top paid him no attention at all as he continued down the trail. The next half mile was laborious and uphill; the final half mile an easy coast down to where the trail ended in a clearing, and the clearing ended in the fence. He checked his watch: 17 minutes, two short stops, a steady pace but not a hurried one.

He called the dogs, walked them across the clearing and made them sit in front of the fence. He took each dog by the collar, pointed at the fence and issued a harsh "No." The puzzled labs then followed him back into the clearing and sat attentively by as John settled onto a stump, pulled out a cigarette and lit up. *When you get to the clearing, take five. See if any shadows fall.*

He smoked and listened to the birds hidden around him. When he was finished he ground the butt into the dirt, rose and commanded his dogs with a firm "stay." He walked across the clearing to a smallish oak tree—no more than twenty feet high—whose branches had been pruned away from the fence. He estimated two yards from the trunk to the fence, then knelt down and began scraping away handfuls of the loose, leaf-covered soil. The box was six inches under. He removed it and opened the lid, then brought out the small flat cellular telephone and slid it into his shirt pocket. He piled the sharp oak leaves around the box before turning to look behind him—just three inquisitive dog faces staring back—then pushing one of the two dial buttons on the face of the little phone. *The buttons are dedicated. You can only call one person on earth and that person is me. Black for business and red for busted. If you're flushed, John, press red. Press red and use the hole. We'll do what we can to help you out but it may take a lot more time than you have.*

John faced the clearing. He felt his heart pounding against

his shirt and the pulse in his forehead. Joshua answered before the second ring.

"I'm here."

"How's the scenery?"

"Superb."

"All your luggage arrive?"

"I think so. No trouble finding it."

"Tell me."

"I've been invited to stay a few days. Whether that's five days, seven or nine hasn't been specified. Wayfarer's insistence. The pit bull has a pant leg already, but no skin inside it. He arranged a week of paid leave with Bruno. These guys move fast if they like you. I met two clients and some of the Liberty Ops people at dinner the second night. Notes to be delivered shortly."

"Can you get some quality time?"

"He's leaving tomorrow. Back on Saturday."

"Beautiful. Is his study still in the main house?"

"Yes. Just like your drawings."

"Then that's your first stop."

"I remember. But I still can't believe he's so lax about his own home."

"Guarded gate, a five-man security team and almost complete isolation do not constitute lax."

"There have to be cameras inside."

"He fashioned Liberty Ridge for the specific purpose of not *needing* cameras inside. Wayfarer had the sloppiest security habits you could imagine on the job. Took it as a personal affront that anyone would open his mail, so to speak. It was a form of challenge. Miscellaneous?"

John thought of Valerie. "He asked if I was in touch with Susan Baum."

Joshua's laughter was low, clear and wicked. "Well, well. He's nibbling already. And?"

"That was all."

"You can be in touch, Owl. At Wayfarer's pleasure."

"I assumed that."

"The world is lovely when things fall into place. Now, the study—papers, notes, files, records. Think Baum. Think what *you* might commit to paper if you were going to cap someone. Anything that has a buzz about it, you shoot. Right?"

"Right."

"After that, we'll branch you out into the firearms and ammunition. How are your nerves?"

"Steady."

"Ten-four, clever Owl."

"Later."

John hung up, his fingers sweating on the slender antenna as he folded it back against the body of the unit. He returned to the box, brushed away the leaves, and set the phone back inside. He looked at the dogs again, then down the trail, listening. Next he took out one of the two micro-cameras mocked up to look like penlights—the beams actually worked—and clipped it to the edge of his pocket. He closed the box, set it back in its shallow hole, and replaced the dirt and brittle oak leaves, turning the dark sides down and the light sides to the sun. A grasshopper landed on his shirt and sent his heart into the sky.

He went back to the stump where the dogs waited, sat down and lit another smoke. He jammed a rock inside the empty pack, crumpled it, then walked to the fence and tossed it over. Joshua's people would retrieve it—notes slipped between the cellophane and the paper—in the darkness of night, just as they would retrieve a used camera and replace it with a loaded one, using the hole to cross the fence. John looked at the ground beneath the fence post nearest the tree and the next post north, and could see nothing that indicated the three-foot by three-foot tunnel Joshua had dug beneath the links. It was only six feet long, running under the fence like a curve of bathroom pipe, with openings on each side of the chain. For a human, it was little more than a tube to wriggle into and out of. But it was a safe way to cross the line. The openings were covered with thin plywood onto which were glued a representative camouflage of dirt, leaves, rocks and sticks. *With a few handfuls of the real stuff thrown on, they'll be invisible. But if someone steps on one, we're in trouble.*

John returned to the stump, ground his cigarette out beside the first one, then put both butts in his pants pocket. The dogs lay in a row, all three with their heads on the ground, but all three eyeing him. He told them "stay" again, then walked around to the oak tree and approached the gnarled brown trunk.

He could hardly believe how loud the leaves under his feet were. Spiderwebs tickled his cheeks. He reached his hand up into the second V of the trunk and, with a sharp click, pulled down from its securing clasp the Colt .45 Joshua had promised. *If you ever need it, you will probably die with it in your hand. It's the last resort, John. Your goal is to never touch it. Your goal is to leave it there to rust in the shade while Wayfarer rusts in a cell. If you say a prayer every night, and I recommend that you do—it should be that you never have to use the Colt.*

He checked the empty chamber and the clip, then rose up on his toes again and wedged the automatic back into its seat. A fence lizard gazed down at him from the upper fork of the V, his eyes curious and alert. The idea crossed John's mind that the lizard was one of Joshua's operatives, keeping tabs on him. Wiping the sweat from his face, he ducked back out from the drooping branches and wiped the dirty webs from his arms and shirt.

A blast of hot wind greeted him as he stepped from the canopy, swirling the leaves up around his legs and roaring against his ears. Then the gust moved on and John stood and listened to it swooshing against the treetops and in the brush.

As always, the sound of the Santa Anas shot him back to his childhood. Now he felt the same way that he felt at age five with the big winds hitting: awestruck, surrounded by a power much larger than his own, immersed in the pure velocity of change. They had always made him think of time, and made him realize how the present passes so quickly into the past, how the present is just a series of future moments marching backward to meet you. He had always loved the way the wind made you feel each of those moments going by. He had always loved the way he could just stand there in that wind and let it blow right past him, flattening the grasses, bending the trees, lifting silver-green spray off the faces of advancing waves. It was like seeing time itself. Seeing himself within time, John had always felt small. But he had felt integral, too. With the wind blowing around him he understood that he was a part of larger things, like the grass, the trees and the waves. He remembered, age ten, jumping off the roof of his uncle's house in a high Santa Ana with bedsheets spread behind his outstretched arms, wanting not so much to fly as to dissolve into the wind and let it take him with it. He was hoping it might carry him to his mother and father.

John stood in the clearing, looking out at the buffeted landscape and feeling his slow reentry into the present. He thought about Rebecca. Here was another day, another moment he wished she could have shared. He listened for her voice in the wind but heard only the wind. He pictured her again on the asphalt in the March rain. Then the Santa Ana turned furious, bellowing up the trail toward him, howling against the oak tree, punishing its branches and hissing into the fence. There it is, he thought: The Fury. The reason I am here. He let it rage into him and he locked it inside, adding the wind's anger to his own. The dogs sat with their backs to the gusts, heads lowered, looking ashamed.

A little after six a.m., he started back down the trail with his walking stick, empty coffee cup and camera.

CHAPTER
TWENTY

Vann Holt was down by the shore in front of his cabin when John got back. A white Range Rover sat next to John's pickup truck. He could see Holt watching him as he came around the edge of the lake, but he had no idea when Holt had first spotted him. The dogs frolicked along, lending an air of innocence to the day. The penlight felt heavy in his pocket and he wondered, who needs a penlight on a morning this bright? He slipped it into his right pant pocket when Holt wasn't looking. Boomer spotted Holt and charged ahead to greet him, barking histrionically and wagging his tail. John waved.

"Hello Mr. Holt!"

Holt lifted his head in acknowledgement but said nothing until John was closer.

"Morning John. Fairly spectacular, isn't it?"

"I love these winds."

"Just like breeze off the ankles of God."

"Who said that?"

"I did."

They shook hands.

"Out for a morning walk?"

"We headed up that trail on the other side there."

"Watch for snakes this time of year. The hatchlings are out and about."

"Saw a few cottontail is all."

Holt studied him for a long moment. "Be a good idea for

you to stay kind of out in the open. Lane's blood pressure rises when he sees something in the bushes. Shoot quick and ask questions never. That's Lane."

"Wouldn't want to give him a stroke." John flicked the last drop of coffee from his mug.

"You don't want to get shot, either. Come on, let's take a drive around the Ridge. I want you to see it."

They took the Land Rover down the road, toward the big house, then veered off north and into a shallow valley. At the top of a rise, John could see the groves stretching before them, perfectly groomed acres of orange trees heavy with fruit. He could smell them, too, not the sweet flowers of late winter and spring, but the oranges themselves, issuing a clean acidic fragrance into the air.

They passed a row of cottages, all neatly kept. Holt waved to a stout red-headed woman who stood in a cottage driveway, having chosen this dusty, blustery hour to wash her car. The stream of water shot from the hose, splashed against a door, then turned to mist. A boy of perhaps three purposefully scrubbed at a hubcab with a large sponge.

"How big are your groves?"

"Two hundred acres. Certified organic, all Valencias. Best for juice. I've got five workers on payroll right now, plus the supervisor. Harvest time, all the cabins are full."

"Do you sell the fruit?"

"Bulk of it. The best I give away. Carolyn—my wife—used to juice them and make preserves, I mean tons of preserves, but she can't do that anymore. No more marmalade from Carolyn. I've got friends all over the world, and getting fresh oranges from Southern California is a real treat for some of them. Floors 'em over in Europe."

"There aren't even any weeds."

"Smooth as a pool table was my goal. No flaws."

"I'd say you accomplished that."

"My supervisor is a duplicitous old prick, but he really gets work out of the workers."

The road was smooth too, though dirt, and the Land Rover slid along the south perimeter of the grove. John looked down the rows as they passed. The sky above them was pale blue, with just a trace of cirrus clouds up high. John watched a silver speck and contrail move slowly from west to east.

"Have you lived here a long time?"

"Five years. It's been in the family for almost eighty. When Mumsey died, the Big House went empty. Five years ago, my wife had some problems and we moved in here. I rebuilt the Big House. Added some of the outbuildings. Pools and tennis. Aviary. Heliport. Fenced the whole shebang."

"It's like a paradise."

"It is paradise." Holt chuckled then. "To me, anyway."

At the far corner of the grove the road forked—one turning to follow the trees and one leading straight. Holt went straight, guiding the truck up a hill, then down the other side. They were in the chaparral now, though it was not as dense as on the other side of the lake. Holt swerved down a narrow dirt road, scraping the truck panels on stiff red fingers of manzanita.

Then the Rover seemed to stand up, and John found himself leaning forward, facing the dashboard, hearing the groan of the differential and the skidding of tires beneath him. The road rose steeply, leveled off, then rose again. Then came a long series of switchbacks, still rising. Finally the road leveled. A few minutes later, they rolled into a wide turn-out, and Holt parked.

"Top of the World," he said.

They climbed another fifty yards to the top. The peak was leveled and graveled. Three large white marble vaults stood in a semi-circle at the far end of the level ground, facing a large stone table and benches. Atop each of the vaults was a statue. But John's eyes were drawn to the doors of the vaults, their rich gold shining in the sun.

"We're at 1,300 feet," said Holt. "Highest part of the Ridge. Best view."

John looked back to the south, in the direction from which they had come, then down to the windswept spectacle of Liberty Ridge. The lake, from this angle, was a deep cobalt blue, the island in its middle a circle of bright green. The hillsides rose above the lake and rolled for miles. The big house was a white box with a reddish roof and windows that threw the sun back at him in blinding silver rectangles. The outbuildings stretched out from it in a diminishing semi-circle. From here, John could see just how large the park-like grounds around the compound were, and how small the tennis courts, helipad and aviary looked. And all of this was bordered by the two hundred acres of Valencia oranges, which from here looked like a green ocean speckled with orange fish.

"Not the same at night. Even from the observation deck."

"No," said John.

"Assessor taxes me on twenty-four mil. If I subdivided and went commercial/residential, you'd be talking a lot more."

"Are you going to do that?"

"Hell no. I'll protect this place 'til the day I die here. Let me show you exactly where I'll be buried. Got it all set up."

They approached the vaults. Patrick's was on the left. His bronze likeness stood casually, with a couple of books in his hand, like a student pausing between classes.

"I'll always remember Pat as a reader," said Holt. "That's Carolyn and I—the sculptor based it on an old wedding picture."

The bronze Holts stood arm-in-arm like wedding-cake-figures, but the sculptor had cast details into their faces that made them seem almost human. "Carolyn's insistence. She is a romantic. Was, anyway."

Valerie's was to the right, flanking her mother and father. She was portrayed mid-step, with a springer spaniel trotting along beside her.

"Nice," said John.

"Just had it done last year," Holt said. "Wanted her to look adult. Val liked it. Said the whole thing up here is ostentatious, and I can't argue that. So a man's proud of his family. Of himself. No harm there. Doors to the crypts are finished in gold. Something, isn't it, the way they catch the sun up here?"

"It's very beautiful."

"Come in. I'll show you Pat's urn."

Holt swung open the heavy door and John stepped inside the cool marble vault.

"You don't lock them?"

"Don't lock much of anything on Liberty Ridge. Don't need to, which is just the way I designed it. There, that urn's got Pat's ashes inside."

It was a stout, low rectangle that looked to John like black marble. Holt stared at it and sighed. "I don't expect it to mean much to you."

"Well, that's not the point of it."

"Sure isn't. God, I do miss that boy. Anyway, that's the inside of Pat's place."

Holt let John pass back out, then pushed the door closed. The gold, stamped with images of birds rising in flight, flashed in the sun.

"Really something," John said.

They walked to the edge of the gravel and looked out. "It's Val's now. I've made enough pesos to see her great-great-grand-children through their lives. It's all paid for. Won't break it up. Ever."

John breathed in the hot dry air. With the Santa Anas blowing from the northeast, the brush on the hillsides shivered stiffly and the lake rippled with uniform wedges. The ocean, far off to the west, looked bright and flat as a sheet of new foil.

John could see the little chain of buildings that housed the Liberty Ops execs. He watched as a platoon of Holt Men—miniature soldiers in their black uniforms—loaded into four orange-and-black patrol vans.

"It'll be gone soon," said Holt.

"I thought it would be here for Valerie's great—"

"—Oh, Liberty Ridge will. But the rest of the county will fester up around it like acne. This is what it was. This is what our berserk and murderous ancestors lived and died for. The West. Manifest Destiny. The California Dream. All those nonspecific words. Well, here's the specificity. Here it is, the soul of what people wanted. Look at it."

John gazed to the north, where the hillsides gave way to the endless housing tracts of Orange County.

"Not that direction," said Holt. "That's the future. Ugly baby, isn't it? Look south or west and look real hard, because what you see won't be there long."

John watched a raven shoot down toward the Big House, then bank up high again on a gust of wind, wings almost vertical, tail angled to catch the air.

"Too bad," said John.

"Brought it on ourselves," said Holt. "People like you and me."

"How so?"

"Didn't reproduce fast enough. Not enough of us. Too busy building cars and cities to get the numbers up. Need a good bench to play in this league. We made too much of everything but ourselves. Just aren't enough of us left. By the time I die, Liberty Ridge will be a little island in an ocean of people who won't understand its value. No concept of the value at all. Price, yes. Any yahoo with a calculator can figure price. But not *value*. Asians, Latins, Blacks, Arabs. You name 'em. Got nothing against those people, but they didn't work for this. Isn't in their blood. Don't understand this land anymore than I could understand theirs. Say, Vietnam or Culiacán or Kathmandu. They can overrun it easy enough. Can buy it up lot by lot. Suck away the fruits. But they won't add to it. Only diminish. Only take. Like vampires. Not their fault, though. Human nature to take what's good."

Holt stood for a moment and looked out toward the ocean. John saw the proud set of his mouth and the hard, prying squint of his eyes.

"Well, I really didn't bring you up here for a lecture."

"Lecture on."

"I'm bored by my own ideas."

"I'm not."

"You've spent ten seconds with them. I've spent six decades."

"No, go on. Explain. Why do these new people have to diminish the land? Isn't that what the Juaneno Indians would say about you?"

"Reasonable question. So far as the Indians go, too bad they couldn't hold on to it. They got it. They understood. Had a totally different slant than us. But they were outnumbered, outpowered, outfoxed and outbred. Same thing that's happening to us. Did we diminish it? Fuck yes, and that'll be the death of it. And us. But *look* at the Ridge. A little gem in the miserable flood of human progress. Beautiful fruit. Habitat for wildlife, plants, human beings. Clean air and a lake jumping with fish. Rich earth. I didn't diminish this, proud to say."

"Then why will the new barbarians diminish it?"

"Already told you. Because they don't understand it. Land makes people. The land shapes people. Forms them to its purpose. So people need to invest in their heritage. Never abandon it. Work their own dirt—it's what gave them life, isn't it? They need to protect and defend it. A land should never be sold. Conquered, maybe, as history proves. What do you think?"

"I think those are words well spoken."

"I didn't ask for a critique of my oratory. I asked you what you believe."

In politics, you should always agree. Wayfarer may couch his pathology in politics, and he may couch his politics in pathology, so you must do the same. Never fawn; and rarely defer. Question his planks; but endorse his platform.

"I believe that what you say is self-evident. What it begs is the smaller personal question of whether to stick it out and watch things rot, or pack it up. I packed it up for Anza three months ago. But I'm not sure it was the right thing to do."

"I can guarantee you it was the wrong one."

"I feel the pull of the land, too, Mr. Holt. I grew up here, you know. I used to poach fish out of the lake, camp out in these hills, surf that ocean. Yeah, it was the wrong decision—to go. I knew that, not long after I'd left."

"Case closed. It's easy to sound like a racist crackpot sometimes. Hell. Maybe I am."

"Not at all. I think you're speaking for the way a lot of people feel but are afraid to admit."

"Probably. But you're wrong about either staying put and watching things rot, or heading out. Third option is the winner. That's to stay put and *do* something. Work. Fight. Create. Resist. Gather. Whatever you want to call it."

"That takes a person of capacity and vision. I'm not sure I have either."

Holt laughed then. "You certainly do. You proved that three days ago when life and death were at stake. Sometimes it takes special pressure to bring one's vision into focus."

"Well, that was an extreme circumstance, sir."

"Without extreme circumstances nothing very interesting gets done."

"You're right."

Holt stared at John then, his pale blue eyes steady behind the thick lenses of his glasses. His look suggested levels of assessment. "What do you want?" he asked.

"Well, sir. I would like to get a trailer set back up for myself."

"*No.* Not right now. The long run. For your life. What's your plan? I've watched you for three days now, and I know you're not stupid. You observe. You consider. You must have some inkling of what you want. How you can get it."

To get a confidence, give a confidence.

"Mr. Holt, I've never thought that way. I've always believed in taking a day at a time, trying to improve a little at the things you do. I started writing when I was a kid and I enjoy it. I'd like to keep at it. But I've developed the unsettling notion that a lot of life is waiting things out between disasters."

"Christ, that's pathetic. It sure can be, if you choose to see it that way. What disaster?"

"A woman I was going to marry."

"So, what happened to her?"

"She was coming over to my place one night and a drunk ran the light. She died and he broke his nose."

Holt nodded slowly, gravely. "What was her name?"

"Jillian."

Jillian is your torch. You can use her to light a path to Wayfarer. She is your Carolyn—the catalyst of your self-pity, the seed of your hate. She is Rebecca.

"Vietnamese?"

"Sir?"

"Was the driver Vietnamese? They can't drive and they can't drink."

"Well, actually, he was."

"And if he'd stayed back in his rice field, you'd be married to Jillian."

"That's correct."

"That's what I mean. Guy should have worked his own dirt. What did you do?"

"Do?"

"Do about the driver."

"He went to prison. I forgave him. I told myself early on that I wouldn't take vengeance. It was a luxury I didn't feel I could afford."

"Regret that?"

"He suffered enough. And no amount of suffering would have brought her back."

"Noble sentiment. I guess. But he's walking around now, living his life while she's dead. He laughs and eats and makes love. She never even moves. That sit comfortably in an alert soul such as your own?"

John looked at Holt then, neither blinking nor wavering his fix on the older man. He thought of Rebecca, of the way she looked sitting at her *Journal* desk, with the phone crooked into her right ear and her hands flying over the keyboard and the big glass of iced tea sweating onto a coaster beside her. The way she had this little smile all the time, as if she was somehow outside herself and amused by herself, as if Rebecca Harris was an interesting animal to observe. The way she looked at him when he'd stop by her desk for a brief hello, the depth of interest, visible to John, at least, beyond the shining convex surface of her eyes.

"I wanted to kill him. I admit that."

"Of course you did. It's natural, and honest. How far did you take your plan?"

John smiled and looked away. "I kept up with his release date. I got the address of his family. I actually sat outside their house one night before he came home, thinking about it."

"And?"

"I scared myself. I quit."

Holt laughed now, a low, understanding chuckle. "A true sense of follow-through is tough to come by. It all comes down to what your heart says. If yours wouldn't let you take him, then you did the right thing not to."

"There's the law, too."

"Always. But it wasn't written for criminals to hide behind. Don't forget it. See an awful lot of that these days. It's the mark of a weak society when pity replaces justice. Everybody gets away with everything."

"That much is true, Mr. Holt."

Holt seemed satisfied that his points had been made. He said nothing for a long while, staring down toward the Big House.

"Well, I wandered again. But back to my original question. What do you want?"

"It would sound kind of silly, compared to all the things you just said."

"Forget what I just said. I love to pontificate. My great-great-uncle was a tent revivalist. Jealous husband shot him. Anyway. I understand his need to preach. Go ahead."

John thought a moment.

"Oh, you know, just a regular life, sir. I'd like to find a love and marry her and make a family someday. I don't aspire to this kind of . . . grandeur, Mr. Holt. I don't need it, although I can sure appreciate its beauties. What I want is to be left alone to do my work and take care of the people I love. Pretty simple stuff, really."

"Not the less meaningful for being simple. I respect your desires. I wish you prosperity."

"Thank you."

"Ever think of trying something different?"

"What do you mean?"

"Willing to approach the quarry from an unexpected direction?"

"That's kind of vague, sir."

Holt smiled. "Yes, it is. Hypothetically, now—would you be willing to try something other than what you've done before, in order to get what you want? Change of venue. Say that you had a chance to try different work—work you didn't know you could do, but turned out to be good at? Say this new work would enable you to find the love that Jillian once was to you. Make you able to begin that family. All by following a path that you didn't know was there."

"I'd have to know where the path ended, where the twists and turns were."

"You would be deliberate, not impulsive."

"Yes, sir. I would."

"Until you lost your temper. Like down on that dirt road, looking for the men who burned you out."

"Well, yes. My patience has its limits."

"It certainly should."

"Do you have something in mind?"

"Yes, I do. It's got to do with a gang of Vietnamese home invaders. I'm going to be waiting where I know they'll be. It's a Liberty Ops job in its purest form. Good guys. Bad guys. Good money. Interested?"

"Interested. Why me?"

Holt studied him again with a formidable concentration. "I want you to meet someone."

John stood outside the bedroom after Holt had gone in and shut the door. He could hear voices, a man's and a woman's. The bedroom was on the second floor of the Big House, and the sunlight poured onto the stairway landing. A moment later a nurse came out, introduced herself as Staci and told John that Mr. Holt said it was okay to go in.

The room was spacious and bathed in light diffused through

the window blinds. It smelled faintly of roses. Holt sat on a stool beside a hospital bed at the far end, motioning John toward an empty stool beside him. John sat down.

"John, I'd like you to meet my wife, Carolyn. Honey, this is the young man I've been telling you about."

"Why, how do you do?" she asked.

"Very well, Mrs. Holt."

She regarded John with a dazed, unselfconscious stare. She seemed both present and absent at the same time. John smiled, returning her gaze, noting her plump pink cheeks, the silver-blond hair cut short around her face, the way the left side of her mouth didn't move as well as the right, the way her left eyelid drooped, just slightly.

Then her deep brown eyes widened and tears welled up into them, spilling onto her cheeks. "Oh dear God," she whispered, still staring at John.

"Honey, John is going to be staying—"

"—Oh dear God—"

"—For a few days anyway, maybe—"

"—It's been so long since—"

"—Just to regroup a little after all the—"

"—I didn't know if I'd ever—"

"—Honey, don't get too—"

But it was too late because Carolyn Holt had pushed her bed control button and the head of the bed was rising and her eyes were still devoted solely to John's face and she reached out with both her arms for him, dropping the control to her lap and leaning forward from her waist.

John glanced at Holt and saw nothing but uncertainty. With little to guide him but his own sense of decency, he stood and leaned forward, so her hands could wrap around his neck, and she pulled him down to her. She was strong. He could smell the rose perfume and fresh bedding and the under-current of sweat that comes from a straining, human body.

"Don't strangle the poor boy, Honey. Remember, he's the one who saved Valerie from—"

"—Oh, thank you. *Thank you.* I've missed you so much, Patrick. Thank you for coming home to me! Oh, Patrick."

"John," said John. "John Menden, Mrs. Holt."

"Oh, Pat. Patty-cake, Pat-man, Pat Hand, Pat-a-tat-tat!"

John unwrapped her clenching hands from behind his neck and eased her back to the pillows.

"Look at me, Mrs. Holt. I'm not Patrick. I'm John. I'm the one who—"

"—You little dickens, you."

She smiled at him, a beaming, consuming smile from which her eyes sparkled as they moved up and down John's body. Then she clenched her fists up under her chin like a little girl, and wiggled.

"We have a lot of catching up to do, Pat. Now you sit back down and start catching me up, all right? First, how are your grades, for heaven's sake? And that cheerleader you were dating? Those priests haven't been rapping your knuckles, have they? I think the best lunch box you ever had was the Disneyland one with the submarine ride on it, but of course the thermos was always—"

"—Carolyn," commanded Holt, "be quiet and listen to me. This man is not your—"

"—You're distracting us, Vanny. Could you maybe get us some root beer? And get your glasses fixed, too. Look who's returned from the college of the dead!"

John looked again to Holt, who had risen from his stool to run his hand over Carolyn's hair and face. In Holt's eyes, John could see the exasperation, the surprise, and the anger. Holt motioned him away.

"Wait for me outside," he said.

"Patrick!"

"He has classes to attend, Honey. Let him go. He'll be back. Don't worry now, Carolyn. He'll be back."

"This is the happiest day of my life."

"It's certainly a . . . happy day, Honey."

John mustered a smile for her, then turned and crossed the expanse of cream-colored carpet. Staci opened the door for him and gave him a pitying look. Carolyn Holt looked past her husband at John, smiling to him as he waved and shut the door.

Holt came out five minutes later. His face was flushed red and the flesh of it looked loose. His hair was mussed. He looked at John with an expression of shame, desperation and seemingly uncontrollable rage. John followed him down the curving marble stairway.

"Fuckin' Mexicans shot her in a fast food place up in Santa

Ana. Fuckin' punks. Killed Patrick because his hair was blond or some such shit. Left a bullet in Carolyn's brain."

Holt stopped halfway down the stairs, turned, and drove a very strong finger into John's chest. "That's what happens when people don't stay where they belong and take care of their own ground. That's what happens when they sneak into this country, breed like fleas and try to steal away what they haven't worked for and don't understand. That's what happens when two innocent people go out for lunch one afternoon in this fucked up melting pot of a republic we've got. And that's why you stay and fight it out. That's why you make a stand on the ground that raised you. That's why you give a fuck. Right, Lane?"

"Right, Mr. Holt."

Fargo was waiting at the bottom of the stairs, a briefcase on the floor beside him. He stared as John descended.

Behind him stood two young men, one with short blond hair, the other with a 1950's flat-top grown long on the sides. They were wedge-shaped and huge. The blond wore a tennis shirt and slacks; Flat-top wore a loose fitting suit. Flat-top had a sharply triangular face, giving him the look of a mantis. They stood with legs apart and hands behind their backs, unmoving. Their eyes were hidden behind identical pairs of dark sunglasses.

"Ready?" asked Holt.

"Ready, sir."

Holt walked across the floor without looking back.

"John, go with Fargo," he ordered into the echoing caverns of the house. "He's got some questions you'll need to answer if I'm going to hire that gun of yours."

CHAPTER
TWENTY-ONE

Fargo walked him along the row of Liberty Ops cottages, the two big men behind them. John felt the heat of the sun on his face as he glanced at the closed doors. In the parking spaces were three Liberty Operations patrol cars and two orange-and-black command vans. There were blinds on the windows of the building, drawn against the fierce sunshine, but through the slats of the martial arts room John saw a man mid-air, heading for the mat. In the library were the shapes of bodies bent over tables. In the classroom he saw Thurmond Messinger lecturing to a group of cadets.

John's nerves were brittle and his heart felt flighty and anxious. *Fargo will be the Grand Inquisitor so Holt can be the generous king. But remember, Fargo is Holt's ears and eyes, his fists. Fargo is Holt, and Holt is Fargo.*

"Here, John," said Fargo. "Up the steps, okay?"

John climbed to the wooden deck surrounding the last Liberty Operations cottage. Fargo pushed open the door and let John in first. He could hear the footfalls of the big boys as he stepped into the air-conditioned cool of the room.

The light was dim because the shades were drawn. The floor was hardwood and there was an industrial desk along one wall, a chair behind and in front of it, and a couch opposite, along the front windows. The desktop was completely empty. John noted a water cooler, two work tables pushed to one wall, and a hallway leading back to what he assumed were restrooms. A surveillance camera hung in one corner. The air conditioner hummed away, though the room was cold.

"Have a seat here in front of the desk, John," said Fargo. "Partch, Snakey, sit on the couch. Oh, John, this is Partch and that's Snakey. Friends."

John turned and nodded. Partch, the blond in the tennis shirt, nodded back; Snakey simply stared at him through his black glasses, his mantis-like head unmoving. When they sat on the couch it seemed to shrink.

Fargo settled behind the desk, unlocked a drawer and removed a manila file folder, which he set before him and opened. Out came a yellow note pad. John could see some writing on the first two pages, which Fargo perused, then flipped behind the backing. Under the notepad lay some loose papers.

Fargo seemed to have a rather sunny glow about him, for Fargo. His black hair was mussed from the wind and his face looked tanned. The mustache was freshly trimmed, though it still drooped. He was back in his standard uniform: black t-shirt and jeans, black boots, black shoulder holster and automatic. A gasket of black hair sprouted up from his lower neck, rimming the collar of his shirt. He smiled, collapsing the humanity of his face into a pointy-toothed mask that suggested to John a deep and abiding sickness of soul.

"Enjoying yourself on Liberty Ridge?" Fargo asked.

"Yeah, it's nice."

"Nice," said Lane. "That's very nice. When Mr. Holt told me you'd be staying a few days, I did my usual—checked you out."

"Hope I passed," said John.

"Mr. Holt has a way of taking people in sometimes. Every once in a while, we get a bad one."

"You can count the silverware out at the cottage."

"We're not talking about silverware."

"What are we talking about?"

"For starters, Rebecca Harris. How close were you with her?"

"Not very," John answered, before he had fully assimilated the question. He now imagined The Lie—that he had scarcely even talked to her. He and Josh had perfected The Lie. To imagine The Lie was to see in his mind a black gray wall, round and tall, like the inside of a well, perhaps, and himself at the bottom of it, staring up. The wall was Rebecca.

"But how close is not very? Elaborate for me here, John-Boy—it sets the right tone and gets this little interview over quicker. If I get the feeling you're holding out, I'll just send you packing."

Your trump card is always your innocence.

"I can start packing now. I'm here because Mr. Holt invited me. I've got no reason to put up with your questions, your crap or your mustache."

Fargo stared at him for a long moment, apparently puzzled. "I think I've just been dissed, Snakey."

"You have."

"Partch?"

"Definitely dissed, sir."

John heard a shuffling behind him. He had just begun turning to look when his right ear seemed to go silent, then explode. He was flat on his back, looking up at Snakey's severe triangle of a face. The ringing in his head was as loud as sirens. He could clearly feel the shape of a jagged lightning bolt crackling through his brain. The next thing he knew he was upright in the chair again, holding on to the seat with both hands, his torso swaying and his equilibrium unfocused and distant as a dream.

"I won't put up with any more jesting from you, John-Boy. I've got my standards of behavior here, rigidly enforced. Clear on that precept now?"

"Clear."

"That's just great. Couple of the *Journal* people said they thought you had the hots for Rebecca Harris."

He saw the blank gray wall. "They were wrong."

"How couldn't you? I've seen pictures of her. She was young, fresh, beautiful. How could you *not* have had the hots for such a thing?"

"Well, there are hots and then there are hots."

His own voice was coming through to him as if from a long-distance line. There was echo, lag, static. The taste of blood filled John's mouth but when he tried to swallow all he could manage was a dry, throat-catching cough.

"And which kind of hot were you, little buddy?"

"I looked at her. I never got a look back. She was engaged."

John turned to look at the big boys, got a grin and a thumbs up from Partch, then swayingly returned his gaze to Lane Fargo.

"She tell you that?"

"Gossip, I think."

"Never talked to her?"

"Coffee machine stuff."

"Ever ask her out?"

"No."

"What?"

"No."

"Then who were you seeing at the time?"

"Nobody in particular."

"Nobody even unparticular, from what I've gathered. How were you managing the urges, Johnny? Just Rosy Palm and her five sisters?"

Suddenly, John's head cleared. The ringing was still there, but he felt his sense of balance return, settling under him like a trusted old horse.

"None of your business."

He swiveled to look back, but Partch and Snakey still sat on the couch, two giants lost in cushions. Fargo was laughing.

"You're right, Johnny—that's not my business. Where'd you get that dog?"

"Dog?"

"Rusty, the hero."

"He showed up at the club one day."

"A purebred, attack-trained German shepherd just wandered up to your trailer one day and asked for a Milk Bone?"

"He was a mess. Half-starved, no collar. My labs came close to killing him."

"When?"

"Last spring."

"So you took him in?"

"That's what I did."

"Funny."

John said nothing. The siren scream in his ear was coming and going now—a piercing whine followed by a pressured silence.

"Funny that nobody in Anza Valley ever saw you with that dog. A truckful of dogs, but no German shepherd."

John shrugged off the unobservant Anza public.

"Maybe you could explain why," said Fargo.

"He liked the trailer. He was territorial and a little mean. He wasn't the best around-town dog."

"But he was a good enough *retriever* to take out hunting on opening day?"

"Yes, he was."

"But how did you know he could hunt, if you hadn't had him out in bird season?"

"He was always after the quail around the trailer. It was easy to see he was birdy. Opening day, I wanted to give him a try, that's all."

"How'd he do?"

"Well."

"How many birds you get?"

"The limit. Ten."

"Why weren't they in your truck at Olie's?"

"I'd gone back home to drop them off."

"So you could shoot ten more."

"Right."

"Kind of a scofflaw for such an upstanding citizen, aren't you?"

"I figure there's guys out there who don't get any birds at all. It works out."

"You could have had fifty birds back in the trailer and we'll never know, since it burned down."

"I had ten."

"Maybe you didn't have any. Maybe you weren't hunting that day at all. You can't really prove it, can you?"

John straightened in his chair and glanced back again at Snakey and Partch.

"You know, Fargo, if you want to get direct answers here, you can ask direct questions. I've got no idea what you suspect me of. But we could save a lot of small talk and popped eardrums if you'd just come out with it. I hardly talked to Rebecca Harris. I took in a stray dog. I got ten quail opening day, helped Mr. Holt out of a bad situation. What in hell do you want?"

Fargo considered.

"I just want to like you, John."

Fargo laughed then, his rodentine teeth flashing behind the thick broom of mustache. "How come you quit your job with the *Journal?* You took a pay cut of sixty percent to move out of

Laguna Beach and into a trailer. That makes no sense to me. Make sense to me, John. Let me like you."

John turned to look at the big boys, then back to Fargo.

When Fargo leans on you, it means that Holt has things to hide. When Fargo leans on you, it might mean Holt has something in mind. But just remember, you are innocent. You have your limits. You are ready, willing and able to simply walk.

"I've had enough," he said.

"Enough of what?" Fargo looked genuinely puzzled.

"Enough of you. I'm going to go back to the cottage, write Mr. Holt a thank you note, get in my truck with my dogs, and drive off. I don't need you, Fargo. I don't need the headbangers sitting behind me. I sure don't need Vann Holt."

"Awww. Have I hurt your feelings? Need mommy?" The smile again, all the latent cruelty showing through.

"Let's go outside and fight."

"You're getting kind of personal now."

John stood, wavered a little, then felt two heavy hands on his shoulders, pressing him back into the chair.

"I'm just trying to do my job, John. Anyone who spends time around Mr. Holt has to be cleared. I'm in the process of clearing you. Lighten up. It's a nice day out. You and Mr. Holt can talk. You can make your mysterious little eyes at Valerie again. The world is good. So just stay the fuck put and give me reasons for Mr. Holt to keep you on Liberty Ridge."

"I don't want to stay on Liberty Ridge."

"What you want isn't up to you. It's up to Mr. Holt. Besides, the keys to your truck are in my safe, along with your wallet, pistol, shotgun ammunition, knife and telephone pager. You can't walk far—there's a gate house on the road with my men in it, and a charged fence around the perimeter of the land."

"Why?"

"Liberty Ridge is kind of a cross between Club Med and Tombstone, Arizona. You check your guns with the Sheriff and you don't need any money because all the fun is free. It's for security. Liberty Ridge *is* security. The name Liberty Operations *means* security. And I'm not about to risk it on some clown driving around with a truckful of guns, now am I?"

* * *

"So, why did you quit the *Journal* job?"

"I was burned out and sick of people."

"Run out of story ideas?"

"Just about."

"Why didn't you rent out the Laguna house?"

"I thought I might go back someday."

"Not avoiding memories there, were you? Memories of a love gone bad? Or maybe a love gone dead, like Ms. Harris?"

He imagined the tall gray blank wall again, curved and surrounding him, the inside of the deep well where nothing ever happened between him and Rebecca.

"Will you please tell me why I'm supposed to have been in love with her?"

"Ever meet Joshua Weinstein?"

John's pulse jumped and he felt his scalp tighten. Joshua had figured very long odds that Holt had linked Rebecca to himself, using the Bureau's influence with the *Journal* to keep his name out of the paper. "No. I never met Joshua Weinstein."

"Heard of him?"

"No."

"Lying to me, Johnny boy?"

"Just the truth for you, Fargo."

"He was Rebecca's fiancé."

"It's beginning to sound to me like *you* were the one in love with her."

Fargo smiled. "Impossible, John. I never even met her. I didn't spend eight hours a day in an office just down a hallway from her. I never was very cute, John-Boy, in that gay kind of way you are. Ever suck dick?"

"Not your business."

"I'm just curious."

"No."

"Ever want to?"

John stood up again, and again a heavy hand pushed him back into the chair.

"Anyway," Fargo continued, "Weinstein's a feebie—Orange County office."

"I never met any of the feebies. I wrote about fishing and hiking."

"Oh, that's right," said Fargo. "That's right. That clears up a lot of things. Know something? The waitress at Olie's said Weinstein looked familiar. I showed her a picture."

"Then maybe he was a regular."

"She said she was pretty sure she saw you talking with him one afternoon. Him and a woman."

"I've talked with plenty of people in there. Joshua Weinstein is definitely not one of them."

"If you'd never met him how would you know?"

"People have things called names."

"Maybe he used someone else's?"

"Why?"

"She couldn't swear, the waitress at Olie's, that is, if it was the guy in the picture or not."

"That's because she never saw me with him."

"Coincidence, I guess. Speaking of pictures, I like this one."

Fargo picked a sheet out of his file and set it, facing John, on the desk top. It was a blown-up version of the photograph taken by the *Journal* photographer in the parking lot: Rebecca by the planter in the rain, with the five newspaper employees approaching in varying attitudes of horror. John was in the center, stepping toward her as if all things could be remedied. The rain spills off his fedora and his leather duster is blown by the wind. He looked at the picture but he saw only the gray wall of The Lie.

"That's you there, isn't it?"

"Yeah."

"Look pretty rattled."

"You would have been, too."

"How'd you get there so fast?"

"I was heading for my car. End of the work day."

"You two have a little rendezvous set up that evening?"

John said nothing for a moment. He just looked at Fargo and thought how satisfying it would be to slam a shotgun butt into his face.

"You're boring me," said John.

"What about Susan Baum? Know her?"

"Not well. Didn't have the hots for her, either, Fargo. She's more your type."

Fargo leaned back and offered his rotting smile. "Keep in touch with her, Baum?"

"No."

"Like her?"

John hesitated. "Not really."

"Too political? Too liberal? Too pushy and self-centered?"

"We finally agree."

"Ever argue with her at work?"

"Nobody at the *Journal* argued with Susan Baum."

"She must have hated your outdoor articles."

"In fact, she did."

"You two never had a big blowout, then one of those reconciliations where you're both so happy you suddenly love each other forever? You know—fight on the playground Monday, best friends Tuesday?"

"We weren't on a playground."

"Haven't kept in touch with her since you left?"

"I don't keep in touch with any of the *Journal* people."

"Well, why not? You worked with some of them for almost three years."

John was silent for a moment. He turned around to look at Snakey and Partch. He could see himself mixing it up with Fargo, but not with either of these two. He wondered if they'd graduated *cum laude* from the Liberty Ops martial arts program.

"People move on, Fargo. You've sure got a rudimentary mind."

"I'm just curious, John-Boy. See, you've been gone six months but you haven't so much as called one of your old drinking buddies? Not *one* of the butts you chased around on Friday evenings after work when you'd all get boozed up? Seems you just dumped them all for no good reason."

"I'm slow to make friends."

"I can see why, John-Boy! What, do you mumble and blush every time someone tries to like you? Or do you act like you're acting now, all defensive?"

"Um-hm."

"Just gave them all up, moved away to tumbleweed city to live in an aluminium box. Just found a trained attack dog that saved little Val's life. Just happened to wander by Olie's that day, like you did in the *Journal* parking lot. Just happened to be packing your piece. Just happened to shoot up a couple of bikers. Funny none of them got a shot off at you. So you go from the skids all the way to Liberty Ridge in one fell swoop, never even losing your hat. You've got good fortune, don't you John-Boy?"

"It seemed better about twenty minutes ago."

"Funny that biker you shot didn't require any medical attention. Looked to me like you blew his ball and socket in half.
No gunshot wounds treated that day in Riverside County—no
shoulder wounds, that is. Your victim must have guzzled whis-
key, bit a bullet and had a redhead named Kitty or Cora Lee pull
out that slug with her teeth."

"If I were him, I'd have dodged the doctors, too."

Fargo put the photograph and legal pad back in the folder
and closed the cover. He looked at John a little gloomily now, his
smile suspended somewhere back in his dark and hostile face.

"Oh, it's all innocent enough, John—I know it is. No, it's
really truly heroic. It all fits. A place for everything and everything in its place. I just worry too much. I imagine things. I always wonder why people arrive and depart, why they do what
they do. Hey, I'm head of security for the head of a security company. So I'm secure. I'm so secure I see a plot every time the
sun comes up. It's just my nature. With Mr. Holt due to leave
tomorrow, I thought it would be prudent to get a fix on you. No
good having a person of low moral character lurking around
here, what with young Valerie so fresh and trusting. Yeah, con-
spiracies everywhere—that's what I'm paid to see. And to be
truthful, it's really kind of a fun way to live."

"Thanks for having my eardrum smashed."

"Just a little pop, John. You won't even remember it twenty
years from now."

"Can I go?"

"Of course you can. I'm sorry if any of this got a little heavy
for you. Hey, can I tell you something in confidence? I mean,
really top secret confidential? A couple of years ago Mr. Holt
hired a supervisor for one of the software companies we guard.
He was a good super—kept his guards happy and alert and honest. But a year later our company got killed on a bid by a compet-
itor using an awfully darn familiar RAM alignment. It took us
almost three months to nail that super for passing the design. But
we did. Oh yes, we did."

Fargo slipped the folder into the desk drawer, shrugging.

"So you're good at what you do," said John.

A little smirk again from Fargo, his eyes deepset but alive
with light. "The point I'm trying to make isn't that we caught the
scumbucket. That's a given. We're not good. We're the best.
We're the best fuckin' private security people on earth and we

know it. Naw, it wasn't that we caught him. We could have caught that greedy dipshit in our sleep. It's how we handled him. That's the part I'll always be proud of."

Fargo locked the desk drawer and stood.

"Well, I give up. How did you handle him?"

"He went somewhere with Snakey, and Snakey came back."

"That's it?"

"For right now. Have a good day, John-Boy. Keep your dick in your pants when Val's around. I think I'm beginning to like you."

TWENTY-TWO

The next day John stands at the front door of the Big House, looking through the glass into the entryway beyond. He opens the door quietly, pushes it an inch or two and leaves it ajar. His heart is pounding against his shirt, wobbling the penlight in his pocket, and his ear throbs slowly from the impact of Snakey's open hand.

"Hello?" he calls tentatively. "Valerie?"

Just one hour ago he saw Holt's Hughes 500 lift into the sky, shivered by the diminishing gusts of the Santa Ana winds. Holt, Fargo and Titisi were on board, and the Messingers.

John can hear the short chips of Valerie's whistle from the meadow down by the lake. He has agreed to meet her there at three o'clock to help train the dogs. It is a quarter to three now. He had gone to the house to see if he might make a quick phone call to Bruno at the *Anza Valley News*, to see if any changes are needed on the article. He had already mentioned to Valerie and Mr. Holt that he wanted to do this.

He pushes open the door, steps inside, and shuts it. The foyer is cool and he can smell the aroma of old wood, candles and adobe. His leather-soled boots are quiet on the tiles as he walks toward the kitchen.

"Valerie? Valerie, are you here?" Then, louder, *"Valerie?"*

He stands in the kitchen and looks at the phone, thinking 3-9-9. He picks up the handset, hears the dial tone, then pushes the "off" button. Holding the phone before him like some kind of insulting household mystery, he walks to the stairs, then climbs quickly up to the third floor.

He enters Holt's library, again calling for Valerie. Outside, the sun is just past its zenith and the tall windows gather the light and hoard it down into the room. He looks up toward the shelves of books and watches the dust motes lifting in the hard, specific light. He takes twelve steps to cross the room and let himself into Vann Holt's inner office. He leaves the door open. He stands before the huge mahogany desk like a man waiting to be asked to sit. Then he takes a deep breath, walks around the desk and settles into the comfortable chair behind it. He puts the phone on the wood, noting the way the finish shines between the mahogany and the plastic unit, separating them like a sheet of glass. He studies the material on the desk top: in and out boxes (both empty); a telephone and fax machine; a blotter (fresh page, clean); a short crystal canister containing ten freshly sharpened pencils (points up); a computer and keyboard; a simple office-issue desk calendar turned to today's date (Wednesday, October 19); a clean crystal ashtray with the image of a flying pheasant etched onto the bottom; a framed picture of the Holt family taken perhaps ten years ago.

Most interesting is the copy of yesterday's *Journal,* featuring the pictures of Mark Foster on the front page, and the story that the FBI is seeking him for questioning in the murder of Rebecca Harris. The edition is folded neatly in the middle, with the masthead and the headline:

FBI PROBES NEO-NAZI GROUP IN JOURNALIST'S MURDER

Joshua's diversion, he thinks: the trail that leads nowhere.

John looks out over Liberty Ridge and pretends that he is Vann Holt, surveying his kingdom, making his plans. Fifteen hundred Holt Men scurry about the county beneath him. Another thousand represent him around the globe. They are trained, loyal, vigilant. They have their own networks of friends, acquaintances and sources. They have their own spheres of influence. And the networks spiral back to a common point, just as the spheres all intersect a common plane. The point and the plane are Vann Holt. And this desk is where Vann Holt sits. So, where would he put the drawings of the *Journal* complex, the notes on Susan Baum? *Nowhere—why keep them?* Where would he put the rifle? *At the bottom of Liberty Lake.* What about the engraving tools used on the cartridges? *Back in the tool kit.* What else does he need to destroy? *Everything that can link him to Susan Baum.*

John turns and looks at the massive stainless steel safe. He stands, takes the penlight from his pocket and shoots four exposures of the box. After each shot, he rotates the penlight head to advance the tiny spool of film inside. On the back of the stainless cabinet he finds the manufacturer's number and takes two pictures of it. Maybe Joshua has a way of getting the combination from the number, he thinks. Wouldn't the manufacturer cooperate with the FBI? Of course they wouldn't. He tries the shining circular handle but it hardly moves. He wipes off the handle with a tissue from his pocket, then sits back down at the desk. He checks his watch—five minutes until three.

The top left drawer of the desk slides open on near silent rollers. Inside are two metal rods running perpendicular to the drawer face, over which rest the metal hooks of perhaps ten green cardboard files. John pulls out the second and third drawers on the left side of the desk, and finds another ten or so cardboard files in each. Every file folder is labeled inside a raised plastic window.

As an agent, Wayfarer committed little to paper, less to disc. He was hyperorganized, exceedingly neat. When I think of his desk, I see a large blotter pad of graph paper with not a single mark on it except for the grids. He kept his tapes and interview transcripts in the Bureau safe.

The labels are perfunctory and uninformative. In the three left-side drawers are a total of only thirty file folders, the first twenty-six labeled A through Z, in alphabetical order. The remaining four are all labeled MISC. Some appear to have substantial contents, some appear empty.

John pulls the C folder and sets it on the empty blotter. It contains a single sheet of good quality, high-rag writing paper, 8½ by 11 inches, and one newspaper clipping. The sheet of paper has a date handwritten near the upper left corner, and below the date only one word, also handwritten:

Anita

Across from the name is what looks like a seven-digit telephone number.

The newspaper article is from the *Journal* and is dated

roughly one year ago. It is a large, "County Section" story about an 18-year old girl found murdered. The girl's mother is named Anita. The family's last name is Carpenter.

John returns the folder and pulls another, then another. Each contains a similar sheet of high quality paper with sparse, handwritten notes, but no news clips. The "S" folder holds ten pages of notes—mostly just first names, and an occasional phrase:

"Hus. Karl capped . . ."

"Locate Sean, son . . . Mex surf?"

"Help in I.D., location and ? of perp."

John closes them and returns them to their rod holders. Sparks, he thinks, just little jump-starters for Wayfarer's closed-system memory. Access codes is what they are, like PIN's for an automated teller. Anything vital is in his head. Anything incriminating. Anything private. Everything secret. He pulls the B file and searches it for any hint of Baum. He replaces it, then scans the H file for some scintilla of information about Rebecca. It is a waste of time and he knows it.

John sets the folders back in place, then looks at his watch. It is three o'clock. He can still hear the muted trills of Valerie's whistle from down in the meadow, between the dull pounding in his ear.

In the right-side drawers he finds more files, but they are brown and more conclusively labeled: Banking, Insurance, Citrus, Guns. Some are fat with material. He pulls the Boone & Crockett folder and scans the club's letter of congratulations to Vann Holt, upon completion of his third "Grand Slam"—ram trophies on four continents. The Kreel file is dedicated Kreel, Dr. Alfred J., whom John sees led the surgical team treating Carolyn's gunshot wound. John looks in vain for a file labeled Baum. He sees none, and knows he will see none.

So John is shocked to find the "Harris" file pregnant with clippings on the death of his secret lover. The infamous picture in which John forms part of the tragic chorus is collected from the *Journal, Time,* the *Wall Street Journal,* and several other papers.

Wayfarer's usual reading list? John wonders.

There are articles about her death, follow-up articles, follow-ups to the follow-up articles; op-ed pieces; magazine features. At least half of the clippings are not about Rebecca at all, but about Susan Baum.

John feels the sweat and the shirt on his back.

The last clip is an entire page of the *Journal*. John looks it over twice before he finds the relevant article, which is a simple notice in the "Listings" calendar under Lectures, which reads:

—November 22, "From John Kennedy to Rebecca Harris— The Assassination of the Spirit," syndicated columnist Susan Baum, presenter.

John photographs it. He spreads a few of the representative clips across the blotter, and shoots them, too. His hands are so tense and sweaty he can hardly grasp the little penlight head well enough to advance the film. He knows he's taking too many exposures, but he doesn't want to lose anything. No accidents.

It seems to take an hour to shoot four pictures. He is wondering if what he has found is good or not as he picks up the cordless phone and leaves the library. He is surprised to be so nervous. He feels a thousand eyes on him as he descends the stairs, puts the handset back in its cradle and walks across the cool foyer toward the front door.

He feels a big breath of relief coming, until, through the glass he sees Valerie stepping onto the porch.

He backs out of her line of sight and eases into the kitchen again, again taking up the phone. He tries to wipe the sweat off his forehead but his palm is sweaty, too. He hears the door open and slam. He hears the soft pad of her boots on the tiles, then he feels the kitchen fill with her presence.

John is standing with the phone in his left hand, his right hand poised above the keypad, a puzzled expression on his face.

He hears her gasp.

"Can you please tell me how to make a simple phone call on this thing?" he asks. His voice sounds thin, starved of truthfulness.

"John. Jesus, you scared me."

"I'm sorry. I knocked and rang and called for you."

"We had a three o'clock date, didn't we?"

"I've spent the last five minutes trying to have thirty seconds of conversation with my editor. Sorry I'm late, but this is the most complex piece of home communication equipment I've ever seen."

She looks at him with an odd expression now, partly suspicious, partly surprised, and partly hurt. She looks like she's just been slapped.

"Well, you do have to be smarter than the phone, John. Try pushing three-nine-nine."

"Is this okay? I mean—"

"—It's okay. Make your call."

"Thank you." He smiles. But his nerves are scalding and his scalp is oozing sweat. At this moment, John loathes himself. It is the first time in his life he has detested his own being so intensely. But he keeps the duplicitous smile in place, like a shield. The penlight in his pants pocket seems to weigh five pounds.

"Well, what do you know—a dial tone."

Five minutes later they are in the meadow. It is flat and carpeted with wild fescue, soft cheat and bluegrass, all nourished by a spring that flows from the center and makes the ground damp under John's feet. The meadow is behind the Big House and Liberty Ops buildings. Beyond it rise the hills and scrub that roll for a mile toward the electric fence. There is just a touch of sweetness in the air because the Santa Anas are almost gone, and the smell of moist earth and grass can now waver up in the heat.

Valerie leads him to the edge of the meadow, where her dogs are still waiting on a "stay" command. Their little springer tails vibrate when they see her. She's wearing khaki shorts, a faded red plaid shirt with the sleeves cut out and a red wool cycling cap under which her hair is loosely bunched and falling out.

"Here," says Valerie, pointing to a burlap bag left in the shade. "Dizzy a bird and hide him over there by that clump of razor grass. I'll keep Lewis and Clark distracted. When I do this alone, they just watch."

"Can do."

Valerie holds open the bag. John looks down at the pigeons waiting in feathered plumpness at the bottom. He lifts one out with both hands and Valerie ties the bag and places it back in the shade. The bird is warm and heavy and looks at John with alert but unfrightened eyes.

"So, are you enjoying your stay?" she asks.

"It's a beautiful place, but I'd like to get back to work soon."

"Dad wants you around for a while longer."

"He's overly generous."

Valerie lifts a little Remington 28 gauge from where it leans against a small oak tree. "I think he might offer you some work."

John tucks the bird against his chest with his arm, like a football, but gently. He strokes its smooth back.

"Something with Vietnamese home invaders."

She looks at him. "Really? What did you say?"

"I said yes. He took me up to meet your mother, then handed me over to Fargo, who grilled the living hell out of me for an hour with two idiot goons by his side. It was weird."

Valerie cradles the gun and looks at John. To him, she seems so odd a sight, this young, bright, beautiful woman standing golden-skinned in a meadow with a shotgun in her arms. He watches her dark eyes watching him, a wholly analytical expression on her face.

"Lane's a . . . riddle. But as for Dad, he's taken a liking to you."

"Well . . . "

"No, really. You remind him of my brother. Did he tell you about Patrick?"

John nods. "Your mother thought I *was* Patrick."

"Oh, I'm sorry."

"No, she was just fine, but . . . well, it's hard to know what to say. I ended up kind of playing along. At least that's what your father seemed to be doing."

"He's been forging letters from Patrick for four years now. Mom just wouldn't accept that he was dead, kept on wanting to believe he's away at college. Dad finally broke down and started feeding that illusion. You should see how happy she is to get a postcard or letter from her . . . son."

"Isn't there anything at all they can do for her?"

Valerie shakes her head and looks away for a moment. "No, there isn't. Okay, go set that bird, John."

John walks across the meadow toward the razor grass. He holds the bird in both hands again, head down, swinging it in a wide circle. As he walks he tightens the circle and accelerates the rotation until the bird's head relaxes and the animal is unconscious. At the razor grass he rights the animal and gives it a moment to recover a little. Dazed now, the pigeon will sit still on the ground until its head is clear—five or ten minutes, maybe—or until something as frightening as a dog scares it into the sky. He sets it behind the clump of grass with a final stroke to its feathers and mutters "good luck."

John sees that Valerie has been diverting Lewis and Clark,

with food treats, making them do simple sits and stays for bits of kibble. When John approaches, she looks at him and smiles. Beneath the dull throbbing in his ear, courtesy of Snakey and Lane Fargo, John hears the ringing again, and he feels that giddy little shiver in his stomach.

You're very beautiful, he thinks, but this settles nothing. He has been around beautiful women many times and only once felt as if his body was receiving a constant, subtle, electrical prod. The first—and last time he felt that way—was with Rebecca. It must be the pressure, he decides. It must be circumstance.

There will be times, John, when you will long for a friend, a confidant, a lover. You will know a loneliness you cannot imagine. The desire to confess will grow inside you. You don't have a friend. You are alone. You must contain yourself—you must stay within your own skin.

I will try, he thinks. For Rebecca.

"What kind of a look is that, Mr. Menden?"

"Admiration," he says, before he can stop himself.

"Of what?"

"Your dog skills,"

"Why thank you. Coming from a dog man, that's nice to hear."

"Pigeon ready," he says with a grin, his ears a banging cacophony now, the throb and ring, surge and flow, rush and eddy of blood.

"You're perspiring, John."

"It's only about eighty-five out."

"Wasn't eighty-five in the house, and you were sweating there, too."

She's still smiling. It is a prying thing, her smile, but not ungentle.

"Sweat is sweat," he says.

"Can I ask you something? Is it only my dog skills you admire?"

"Mainly."

No.

She studies him, then looks toward the bird.

"There's a funny taste in my throat right now," she says.

"Then maybe you should work the dogs."

She takes up her gun again and starts the search with a wave of her arm. She walks into the meadow, dogs ahead of her. She sends them left with two short blasts of her whistle, then right with one. Left again, right again. John is aware of them, but all he can focus on is Valerie as she traverses the green meadow grass. On their first pass by the razor grass, neither dog picks up the scent. But on the second, both get it at once and their bodies snap back toward the clump in unison and their tails blur. Even from so far away, John can see the change in musculature the bird dogs undergo when they're on game—the dogs seem to condense in size and their movements are reduced to pure efficiency. Then the pigeon flutters into the air, unsteady at first, but still rising and gaining speed. It lifts off over the meadow. It is in perfect shotgun range. But Valerie never lifts her gun, she just lets the bird fly, then issues one long loud blast from her whistle. The toughest thing for a young dog to do, thinks John: come back when they've just put up a bird. Neither Lewis nor Clark seem to hear. They bound across the meadow after the diminishing pigeon, yapping skyward, utterly fried with frustration. They disappear into the hillside scrub, still ignoring Valerie's third and most adamant whistle command. The bird is just a fleck in the blue now, bearing south.

A few moments later, Valerie returns with two penitent springers. She has slapped them smartly, then marched them back. John sees no anger in her, no impatience—just a clear and guiding discipline.

"Mission was a failure," she says. "Back to the lead lines."

"Good call. That's always the toughest thing for my dogs. Youth, and all that. Pure energy."

She nods and wipes her forehead, tilting back the cap. John notes, furtively, the darkened plaid of her shirt beneath her armpit where the sweat has soaked in.

For the next hour, both springers come on command, encouraged by long lead lines that John pulls in when the whistle blows. At first the dogs tumble ass-over-teakettle when the lines are drawn, then they get the idea. By the end of the session they're coming back without John's help.

"End of class," Valerie says. "They're tired and I'm hot. How about a jump in the lake?"

"Perfect."

The afternoon continues with the easy, weightless atmosphere of a dream.

They swim in the lake, then sun themselves dry on the

wooden dock. The dogs—John's three plus Lewis and Clark—splash in and out of the water like kids on a hot beach.

They walk the groves in the first cool of the evening, an evening drenched in the smell of oranges.

They leave each other to shower and primp. Valerie says she can meet him on the dock in one hour. She wants to take a boat over to Liberty Island to have a picnic dinner she made up earlier in the day.

John walks to his cabin and tries to put a clamp on the giddy beating of his heart.

CHAPTER
TWENTY-THREE

He stands inside his cabin and looks out the window to the lake. The dogs on the deck stare through the window back at him.

His body starts to buzz inside, a delayed reaction to his first covert mission into Holt's office. He sees the "view messages" light on the computer blinking, and presses command F2, which, as Valerie has told him, will show him what's in his basket. He is confident there is a little note from her.

Two messages appear on the monitor:

STOCKED FRIG WHILE YOU WERE OUT. EAT A CARROT.

*

HOW'S LIFE ON THE RIDGE? JUST KEEPING IN TOUCH—
                                                    A. SEX

John smiles. His nerves are still brittle but he smiles anyway. He wonders if this is some kind of game, so he goes to the frig— freshly stocked, all right—and pulls out the vegetable drawer. He and Rebecca used to play little games on the *Journal* e-mail system, and he has the same anticipatory jitters he had back then, that lifetime ago, reading her innocent messages on the screen at his work station. *Enjoyed flyfishing piece. Never had a barbecued trout. . . . The secret's not to overcook them.* The carrots are in the crisper. But he can see that just beside them is something not vegetable at all.

He looks at it for a long beat, then reaches down, slides away the carrots and lifts up a freezer bag. Through the clear plastic he can see paper, bent over but not firmly folded.

He pulls it open and shakes the papers onto the tile. The pages land face-up, curving slightly from the chilled confinement of the bag. There are two.

The first is a plain white sheet with sketch of the *Journal* buildings and parking lot on it. It is an aerial view. It is not highly detailed, but Susan Baum's parking place is marked by a drawing of the "Baum" sign, with her name lightly penciled upon it. Fairway Boulevard is clearly marked, and the chain link fence that runs along the parking lot is identified as such. In the upper right hand corner is a notation:

> 4 to 5 Mon. Wed.
> 3 to 4 Tue. Thu.
> noon Fri.

Baum's hours of departure from work, John thinks, including her inviolable half-days on Fridays.

John recognizes the neat, forward-slanting print that he saw in the files in Vann Holt's office desk.

The second sheet of paper is a black-and-white aerial photograph of a home somewhere in the foothills. Grease-penciled onto the fat bottom border of white are the words, "B. Residence—Newport Beach—3:15 p.m.—$^1/_{12}$."

Again, it is easy to see that the controlled, almost mechanically perfect printing on the photograph comes from the same hand that kept the notes in Vann Holt's desk files.

John stares down at these things as if they were a burning bush, or a huge nugget of gold. He turns away and goes back to the dining room table, walking with his head down, as if deep in thought, in the hope that no one will see him.

He sits down at the table and stares at his electronic in-basket, now empty, the message consumed by the software.

He feels the cold shudder in the muscles of his back.

He looks out the window to Holt's mission home, to Fargo's orange-packing plant house, to the Messingers' residence, once a church. Falsehood. Facade. Illusion.

John remembers that Joshua had warned him this might happen. That there might come a time when all their planning is not enough, when all their caution is insufficient.

If you're blown, run. If you can't run, deny. When you can't deny, confess. It will either get you out, get you turned or get you killed.

Fargo's voice darkens his mind like a cloud over the sun:

He went somewhere with Snakey and Snakey came back.

He looks out toward the hills, in the direction of his box and his telephone. One hour.

Patience, he tells himself.

Calm.

He takes the sketch and photograph into the bathroom, pulls the penlight from his pocket and shoots three exposures of each document. He uses tissue to handle them. When he's put them inside the bag he wipes down the bag and puts it back where he found it.

He sets out with his dogs again, around the lake, drawn by the cellular umbilical cord to Joshua, sure that every eye in heaven and on earth is watching.

Joshua is silent for a long while, as he digests John's story. He asks John to repeat it all, twice. When he finally speaks his voice is deep and hushed and oddly formal.

"You have been baited. The question is by whom, and what with. Put the penlight in the box now, and get a fresh one. You were thoughtful to leave the package in the vegetable cooler, but I need it by six tomorrow morning, safe in our box of toys with your film. We have two days to analyze it, determine if it's counterfeit, and return it if it is. We know that someone deeply suspects your motives. We don't know who. If it's Holt, you are being tested in his absence. The handwriting will not be his and the photograph will be somehow fraudulent. He'll expect you to take them to him."

"You can tell it's Holt's writing."

"No, Owl, *you* cannot. Forgery is an acquired skill, and plenty of people have it."

"What if it wasn't Holt?"

"If it wasn't, and the material is genuine, then there's another spy on Liberty Ridge."

"Am I going to get killed?"

"Not if you listen, and do everything I say. Continue."

John told him about his trip to Top of the World, Holt's

proposal of "work" with Liberty Ops, the Holt family vaults and statues, the golden doors stamped with birds shining in the sun. "They were unforgettably beautiful," he said.

"And the girl, Valerie. Is she beautiful, also?"

"I don't think you need an answer to that question, Joshua."

"I think I have one."

They meet up again just at sunset, loading the picnic basket that Valerie has made into a little skiff and motoring out to the island in the middle of Liberty Lake. She wears a long loose summer dress of pale gray, with birds of paradise on it, and a pair of rubber thongs. John can smell the lotion she put on after the shower.

The beach on the island is clean and sandy. Valerie points out that her father dumped eighty tons of beach sand to create such a place. The beach is shaded by an immense Norfolk Island pine tree airlifted by helicopter five years ago when Holt began to refurbish the property. They sit on a large bedsheet with the corners held down by rocks. From the sheet John can see the meadow, the top story of the Big House, the backsides of a few of the Liberty Operations buildings, then the expanse of Valencia groves.

They drink wine and eat the cold barbecued quail that Valerie shot on the opener.

"Have you ever been in love?" she asks.

Not this, he thinks. Not now. "Yes," he answers curtly.

She looks nervous, avoiding his eyes. "What happened?"

And because it is his duty, he tells her the story of Jillian. In his heart, he tells her the story of Rebecca. John is more than a little amazed that a lie can contain so much truth. When he is finished all he can hear is the breeze hissing through the needles of the pine tree above, and the buzz in his ears, starting to get louder.

"When did it happen?"

"Twelve years ago."

Valerie says nothing for a long while.

Then, "Never felt the same way again?"

"No."

"Try to?"

"It's not something you create, or even search out. It just happens."

"It arrives."

"Or, it doesn't."

"Things are always in the last place you look for them."

"That's not exactly profound."

"No."

"What about you?"

She looks at him then quickly away.

"Oh, you know, I've had crushes. One time, it was more than that, but he . . . well, didn't fit in very well. That was my first year at UCI. Dad detested him. So for most of college I just read a lot, rode horses and played tennis, but didn't have much luck, boy-wise. I always thought you should feel something special about someone. But I never did. I really *wanted* to. Nice enough boys, I guess, but not special. I didn't experiment with things—men, women, drugs. I'm not the experimenting kind. I'm the kind who waits for the right thing then takes it. Found myself kind of outside things, the Mormon prude, the Federal dweeb. Had a sharp tongue so I got the rep as a ballbuster, even though I wasn't. The guys, they seemed so . . . tiny. Made a few good friends, though. Outsiders, too, I guess."

John nods but says nothing, as if confirming the importance of friends. The smell of Valerie and her lotion sends his stomach into a sweet freefall, the kind he used to get in the family car, going fast over dips in a highway.

He thinks: there she is, talking about college boys while I'm trying to find a way to send her father to prison for the rest of his life.

She knocks over her glass of wine, trying to lift it from the sheet.

"Oh, damn."

"There's more. Here . . ."

He refills her glass and their eyes meet just briefly, before she looks away.

"What are you thinking about?" she asks.

That I will hurt you, he thinks. I hurt Rebecca, and I hurt Joshua, and I am here to hurt your father, and if you touch me I will hurt you too. It's contagious. It's inevitable. It's assured.

"Rusty."

They are sitting cross-legged and side-by-side, but she turns to look at him. She has a plate of food on her lap, her feet buried under the summer dress. Her golden hair is loose, and the breeze lifts a strand onto her forehead. He reaches out to set it back, but hesitates. John knows that to touch her would betray the truth of his desire and the falsehood of his intentions.

"Do it," she says. "Go ahead. Please."

He touches her forehead with his fingertips. It is warm and moist. He moves the lock of hair back into place, and it promptly blows onto her face again. He moves it back once more. His fingers move slowly over her skin because it is damp and no matter how lightly he tries to touch it the tips slow against its soft resistance.

"Just a damned hair," he says.

They finish the wine, then row back to shore by moonlight. Valerie is slow and unsteady as she walks, arm-in-arm with John, up to the door of the big house.

"Like to come in?"

"Sure."

"You can see my room."

Inside, they leave off the lights because the moonlight comes through the high windows and turns everything ice blue. John stands in the semi-darkness of the kitchen and opens another bottle of wine.

"I'm a little tipsy," she says.

"I'll pour you a glass. You can take or leave it."

She takes it and they climb the stairs. Valerie's room is a suite, actually—a huge, high-ceilinged living room, a kitchen with a bar and stools that opens up to a dining area, a bath, and a bedroom into which she leads him. The bedroom has French doors leading to a deck. She still has not turned on the lights so things are both visible and mysterious—sixty percent present.

They drink in the half-light of the bedroom. Valerie's eyes are little pools of light hidden behind her hair. They sit close together on the bed, leaning against each other, her pillows piled against the headboard.

"I've captured you," she says. "You're my trophy."

"Are you going to mount my head on your wall?"

"I like you better breathing. How could I throw away all

those other good parts? Like you hands and your back and your arms?"

"Well, you could do a full-body job. Stand me up in the corner like a polar bear."

"Ugh. Have you see Dad's trophy room?"

"No."

"It's his sanctuary. His ultimate place. With all of the paintings and sculpture everywhere, all the valuables littered around this place, the trophy room is still the only one he locks. He says it's because of the humidifier and air conditioning, but I know it's just because he loves the place so much. *His* place. Nobody else's. His little chapel full of animals. Over a hundred of them. Most of them are real trophies, too—Boone & Crockett, Safari International—true record-book stuff."

"He gave me a house tour, but didn't mention it."

"It's in the basement, actually."

"Your father is a remarkable man."

Valerie sips her wine. "He truly is. He went a little crazy when Patrick died and mom got wounded. I can't blame him. I do feel sorry for him."

"Crazy?"

"Inward. Secretive. Half-there. I mean, he was always secretive about his work—you knew he was FBI for almost thirty years, didn't you? But after Pat and Mom, well . . . he got even more vague. He'd sit for hours with a Scotch in his hand and stare out a window. Wouldn't talk. Wouldn't move. Wouldn't even drink. You *know* something's wrong with Dad when he won't drink. I'd sit down with him and we'd go hours without talking much. It was like sitting with Mom. Pat was killed by that bullet, and Mom was paralyzed by it, but part of it got into Dad, too. Maybe into me, also—I mean, it changed the way I look at things."

"How?"

"It made me love more, and hate more. It made me old. It got into my dreams. It took away two things that were a big part of me, and nothing good can take their place. You have this hole inside, and you've got to protect it, keep the bad things out. I don't know—it's hard to explain."

"I think I understand."

He can feel her looking at him. She drinks more wine. "Yes, you do. When I saw the way you looked at Rusty, I knew you would understand. And when I was sitting across from you at dinner, I knew you'd understand. You're old, too."

"A lot older than you."

"Not years old. Life old. Miles old."

John looks at her bedstand clock: 3:53 a.m. "It's late."

"Who are you?"

He smiles a smile of falsehood. "John."

"Besides that."

"What I told you."

"I'm not fully convinced."

"I'm not who I say I am?"

"No. You're more than that. Much more than that."

"Well," he says, opening the bedroom door. "Let me know when you find out the truth."

At 4:08 a.m. John is back in his cottage, snatching his penlight from the bedstand drawer. A moment later he crouches under the rear bumper of his truck to find the magnetized hide-a-box containing his tension wrench and lockpick.

At 4:16 a.m. he is in Vann Holt's private library office, shooting copies of all of Holt's handwritten notes in the "B" file. Brief and unrevealing as they are, John has wondered if perhaps Baum is being discussed somewhere here, under a code that only Holt knows. He holds the penlight camera to his eye and listens to the faint click of the shutter opening and closing as he rotates the shaft.

At 4:24 he is standing in front of the basement door of what he assumes is the trophy room. It takes him five minutes to get in because the deadbolt has eight springs and he is half drunk and nervous as all get-out crouching here with the penlight in his mouth, the pick clicking in the lock and the sweat running down his neck.

He steps inside and turns on a light.

The room is not what he was expecting. There are no heads on the walls, no antlers, no horns, no ivory, no racks. There are no skins or pelts. There are no flattened bodies with stuffed heads tacked to the wall as decoration.

Instead, there is the natural world. Or something that looks like the natural world.

It is an astonishingly large room, and standing in it John feels like he is in a natural history museum.

Along the eastern wall are dioramas of what appear to be India, China and Nepal. Each stretches from floor to ceiling and is probably forty-feet wide. They are built out from the far wall and literally spill forward into the room. They are separated by massive stanchions of river rock that form a kind of border for each. Opposite, along the western wall, is Africa, the Belizean jungle and the Canadian Rockies. The southern wall offers the Australian bush and the Ecuadoran lowlands. And the middle of the world is an immense North America rising from plains of buffalo and ending high up near the ceiling where a magnificent puma stands alert atop a pile of stones and gazes down toward John.

The dioramas teem with figures that were once alive and now, almost, seem to be living again. Greater Kudu stand alert, on guard for danger, their horns gently tapering and their beards full and pale. A black rhinoceros moves through the veld, one huge foot raised, mid-step. A pride of lions lounges in the savanna, watching a splendid female drag down a fleeing zebra. Hippopotami loiter in a lake while bongo and wildebeest and hartebeest and gnu race past. Water buffalo bathe; tapir drink; a leopard jumps from the jungle, tail trailing up and back, ears back and mouth open, feet extended and claws out, eyes focused on the startled axis deer in front of him. A grizzly bear towers and bares its teeth. A Marco Polo's ram stands at the highest point of Central Asia, his horns curled up, back and out in a spiral more stupendous than any John has ever seen or imagined. Many of the animals are beyond his experience. Tiny red antelope spring through a meadow; spotted, yellow-eyed cats lounge in an Asian treetop; a pure white buck with an eight-point rack peers over his shoulder with an indifferent, patriarchal majesty.

John moves within the world, a tourist. He meanders, walking sometimes forward and sometimes backward, lost in a state of amazement, unwilling to miss anything, eager to see it all at once. Standing in front of the Africa diorama, he begins reading the plaques.

He is even more astonished when the general introduction to Africa blurb instructs him to push the red button on the stand before him when he's finished with this scene. Though unfinished, he pushes the button anyway. His heart jumps as the entire ceiling-high display begins to rotate, smoothly and almost noise-lessly disappearing into the wall as another tableau circles for-ward to take its place.

A bull elephant looms above him, trunk up and tusks hook-ing toward the sky. His ears are extended—each one, John thinks—the size of a bedsheet. He looks ready to charge, because the taxidermist has captured the huge shift of weight to the ani-mals' columnar rear legs, leaving the front legs lighter, their flesh looser, one mammoth knee just now bending and one immense foot almost ready to leave the grass.

John pushes the red button again and the original diorama returns, like an alternate world gliding into place.

He stands there, heart thumping, ears buzzing, amazed. Then he tries more red buttons. He moves through the great shift-ing room, pushing one after another. The world is a kaleido-scope.

Australia becomes Montana.

China becomes Kodiak Island.

A wolfpack tears down an elk.

A Cape Buffalo tilts a Jeep.

And perhaps the most interesting thing of all are the little horizontal platforms beside each information plaque. They are tall and narrow as candleholders. And topping each, like a golden flame, is a rifle cartridge. In the light of the trophy room John can see that the casings contain written information. He leans forward to read the engraved brass that is displayed in front of the Cape Buffalo.

.458
Win.
Mag.
500 gr.
Silver
tip

He notes that the engraving looks very much like the engraving on the shells Joshua showed him, with the cursive script so simi-lar to the Declaration of Independence.

Leaning in with his camera, John shoots several of the gleaming, textual brass casings.

Finished and sweating harder now, he presses the red button again.

But when the last diorama rotates, he's not looking at wild-life at all.

Now, to John's continuing astonishment, he is staring at the front of what might be a pub. In fact, John can see a bar, a long mirror and a row of empty barstools through one of the mullioned windows. The front door is wooden also, with a large window in its center. Green curtains hang on brass rods inside. He thinks of the alcohol he's drunk this night and rubs his eyes. No, the pub remains, and it is inviting.

John steps up to the door and opens it. He feels as lost and curious as Alice herself. The lights go on automatically as he enters. It is indeed a little pub. There are three stools at the burnished bar, and plenty of bottles lined along the opposite wall mirror. There are three thick cardboard coasters on the counter and three clean ashtrays, each with a boxes of matches in it. John leans across the wood of the bar and sees the duckboard behind it, the small refrigerator, the ice bin with a folded hand towel on top of it, the little overhead glass rack. It is all genuine and real. It is neither facade nor mock-up. John feels almost dazed, pulled between the illusion of wildlife—animal and human—"outside" and the reality of the "civilization" in which he now stands. He feels as if he is in some last outpost.

To his right and down a step is a comfortable little room arranged around a big screen television set in a cabinet along the far wall. There are half a dozen chairs set up, all facing the screen. In the midst of the chairs is an electronics control console so the viewer doesn't have to get up to change channel or volume, start or stop tape, etc.

John wonders why Holt has lavished so much attention on his home entertainment system. Somehow it disappoints him. He tries to image Wayfarer sitting around at night watching *Seinfeld*. Suddenly, though, John feels stupid, because he realizes that this pub and its big screen theater are not for commercial entertainment, but rather for something very different. A look at the bookshelves, built eye-high along two walls, confirms his idea.

This is where Vann Holt relives the hunt.

The hunts. Of course. Holt takes trophies, but he also records his hunts.

John stands before one shelf and scans the titles: Afghanistan Ram, 1966; Africa Kudu, 1988; Africa Lion, 1990; Africa Lion,

1977; Alaska Brown Bear 1989; Alaska Elk, Brown Bear, 1974; Alaska Caribou 1993 . . .

John wonders: where would Baum be?

Not under "B", he sees. And not under "S".

Nowhere, he thinks, nowhere I would find it.

He goes to the end of the second shelf and studies the miscellany, but there is no indication on the labels that Holt might have recorded the death of Rebecca Harris in the *Journal* parking lot. He backtracks to "R" and "H", but finds nothing. He tries "C" for columnist; "W" for writer; "J" for *Journal*. Nothing.

He wouldn't label it, John thinks, and he wouldn't leave it here.

Or would he? Where could it call less attention to itself? The needle; the haystack.

He looks at his watch now, and it is 5:20 a.m. Only forty minutes, he thinks, to get all this—and the sketch and photograph in his refrigerator—to the box.

There are drawers under the shelves of video tapes, six to each wall. In the first three he finds predictable odds and ends: blank tapes, spare cases, pens for marking, instruction manuals for the tape player, monitor, speaker system, remotes. There are dozens of photo albums.

Next time in, he thinks.

CHAPTER TWENTY-FOUR

John made his cottage in five minutes. He tried to walk with a casual, up-with-the-sun contentedness, but he could feel his deceit in every step. What he wanted to do was sprint, to outrun the feeling somehow.

He let out the dogs, brewed some coffee, poured a cup, and got his walking stick from the deck outside. With the penlight full of film in his pants pocket and the plastic bag inside his shirt, he set out with his dogs along the lake again. He headed for his box of toys, his tunnel, his reason for being.

As soon as the trail led off into the brush, John broke into a run. A few minutes later he stopped to listen and look, but the morning was quiet—just the songbirds in the bushes, the shuffling of Boomer, Bonnie and Belle out ahead of him and the cadence of Rebecca's name in his head.

Re-bec-ca-pause. Re-bec-ca-pause. Re-bec-ca.

Near the halfway point he stopped again. The sun was creeping over the eastern hilltops, round and bright as a ripe orange. He waited, watched and listened. Just me and the last half to go, he thought. I've got the goods. Everything is going to be all right.

He shot up the narrow trail, gravel loosening under his shoes. He pictured Valerie. But he thought of Rebecca.

Re-bec-ca-pause. Re-bec-ca-pause.

But thoughts of Valerie and Rebecca dissipated as he neared the fence, and all John could think about was what he had found in the trophy room. Joshua would be pleased. They were getting closer.

Re-bec-ca-pause.

He stumbled, then regained his balance. His head felt crowded and his legs heavy. Rebecca in the rain.

A few hundred yards short of the fence, John stopped again and tried to still his pounding heart. He looked down the trail and saw nothing but dense brush. He could feel the warm plastic of the bag against his stomach.

Then he was off again, chased by the images of Rebecca. He sped up, jumping across a deep rut in the trail, pushing harder as he climbed. Outrun the pictures, he thought. Just outrun them all.

Re-bec-ca-pause.

But the pictures stayed with him as he neared the fence. Other sensations entered his memory. He remembered the smell of his mother's jacket on the day of her maiden voyage in the yellow airplane. He remembered the smell of Rebecca the first time they'd made love. He remembered the overwhelming presence of Valerie the night before, the way she looked and felt and the way her skin gave way under the touch of his fingers.

A small smile crossed John's face as an odd feeling began to spill into him. It was a humble feeling, not a loud nor demanding one. He could hear it over the pounding of his shoes on the earth and the thumping of his heart. It said to him: you could love this woman and let her love you back, and have everything a man could want.

Impossible, he thought. Never.

Not after I do what I'm going to do.

He almost laughed at himself.

Was Valerie a way back to Rebecca? Was Rebecca a way toward Valerie?

Who cared?

You have a purpose here, he thought. Fulfill it.

Then he was in the clearing, with the fence nearby and the stump, and the young oak tree pruned away from the electric chain links. He circled the area, breathing hard, dodging the wooden cover of the tunnel. Calm, he thought: be calm now.

When his breathing and heart had slowed, he sat on the stump and lit a smoke. The dogs had sprawled around him, tongues in the dirt, panting rapidly. All three suddenly perked up and looked back down the path as Boomer rose lazily and snapped at a fly. The others lay back down, sides heaving. John listened. Nothing. The cigarette tasted bad so he stamped it out and put the butt in his pocket.

He stood and went to the spot, two yards from the fence, toward the oak tree, and uncovered his box from its leafy grave.

He slipped a fresh penlight into his pocket and set the used one in the box. He unbuttoned his shirt and took out the bag, setting it into the box too.

Then he removed the telephone, stood and was just about to hail Joshua when he heard the dogs scramble upright in the dirt and start to growl.

Snakey stepped from the path, tossed some biscuits toward the dogs, but stared at John. His clothes were covered with thorns and brambles, and sweat dripped from his sharp triangle of a face. He had a little machine pistol in his right hand, with the short black barrel pointed at John's chest. The dogs ate the biscuits and lined up in front of Snakey, tails wagging.

"Drop the phone," he said.

What will the abort button get me, thought John. Answer: an FBI escort to the morgue.

He dropped the phone.

"Open your hands, and lift them."

John put up his hands, fingers out.

"Walk to the tree and stand in front of it. If you run, or if you move quick, or maybe even think about it, I'll kill you. Slow now . . . to the tree. And when you get there, you put your hands way up on that branch and you don't move."

John took an uncertain, leg-heavy step toward the tree. "Mind telling me what in hell you're doing"

"Shut up. Lean against that tree. You keep your hands on that branch or you get this clip. I mean it, Bubba. I'd like to do that. It'd make my whole year."

Think.

He felt Snakey up close behind him now, then cool hard steel between his neck and his skull. A hand crossed his chest, jammed under his arms, moved around his belt and crotch, slapped down each leg.

Think.

"Mr. Holt won't appreciate this," said John.

He heard Snakey retreat through the leaves.

"I don't work for Mr. Holt, cuntlips. I don't want to be a boy scout suckass Holt Man. I work for Lane Fargo and he works for Holt. Press up against that tree now, like you're fuckin' it. Like you wanted to do to Val last night out on the island, and in her room. Yeah, I saw it all. Didn't really get any, did you?"

"Lane didn't tell you?"

"Shut up. You squeak again I might shoot you in the leg just for the fun of it."

John clamped his hands over the big oak branch. Snakey was behind him, maybe twenty feet back. John heard him pick up the box, rummage through the penlights and video tape.

"These little lights got mikes in 'em?"

"To record whoever's been cheating Mr. Holt."

"You're the one's been cheating Mr. Holt."

"You ought to listen to me, Snakey."

"Shut up, Bubba."

John heard footsteps as Snakey headed toward the phone. "Hey little doggies," he said. "How about some more snacks? You dogs are gonna like hangin' with Snakey. This fag you got for a keeper now, he won't be around anymore. There, good dogs . . . there you go. Maybe I'll get you some of them spiked collars, make you look badass. Kinda fuckin' dogs are these, anyway?"

"Labrador retrievers."

"Where's Labrador at?"

"Up north."

John heard the telltale crunch of teeth on biscuits. He turned his head slightly, and could just make out the blurred shape of Snakey kneeling in front of the cellular phone.

"Two buttons," said Snakey. "Who for?"

Think.

"The red one's for Mr. Holt. The black one goes to Lane."

"That's a lie."

"Push one and find out."

Snakey laughed. It was the laugh of someone not quite sure if the joke is for him or on him. "This thing reach all the way to Grand Cayman?"

"Easily."

"Oh, yeah, Bubba. This little piece of shit's gonna reach 'em way out in that ocean?"

"It's linked up by satellite. I could call Mars, if that's where Mr. Holt was going to be."

"Shut up."

"Call him. Ask him if I'm working for him or not."

"We wouldn't have slapped you around if you were working for us. Kinda idiot you think I am?"

Think.

"Lane did it for you two. He and Mr. Holt both know someone's smuggling out docs."

"Docks?"

"Documents. The deal with Titisi. Titisi's lowballing Mr. Holt, but Titisi's desperate, too. It's not adding up."

"Holt thinks someone's spying for that boogie?"

"That's why Lane and I went through that little routine yesterday. So you guys would think I'm under the gun. So if you need another ear, you might try me. Lane thinks one of you might be the leak. You or Partch."

"Me? *Me?* It ain't me, Bubba. You're talking shit again. It's that old fart Messinger if it's anyone."

"Tell that to Mr. Holt and get this thing straightened out. If you don't, he'll blow his stack when he finds out you messed up my job."

"Shut up," said Snakey, quietly.

"Ask Fargo what you should—"

"—*Shut up, Bubba.*"

There was a long silence behind John. Snakey was still in the far periphery of his vision, just an unclear figure now standing where he'd found the phone. John moved his right hand onto the Colt .45 in the crook of the branch.

If you ever need it, you will probably die with it in your hand.

Snakey was moving now. He disappeared from John's field of vision, but his footsteps still registered. He was moving toward the fence, toward the tunnel. John put his finger through the trigger guard of the Colt just as he heard Snakey's shoe hit the tunnel cover. With a gentle prying of his wrist, John unmoored the automatic from its clip.

"The fuck's this?"

"The tunnel he dug."

"The what?"

John's neck was straining as he tried for a sight of Snakey.

"Don't move, man! I'm close to shootin' you. I'm real close.

Just keep screwin' that pine tree with your hands up. Shit, man—look at this hole."

John heard the cover sliding over dry earth, heard the hollow thudding of the wood as Snakey pushed it away from the opening.

"Where's it go?"

"Under the fence, to the other side."

"What for?"

"So he can get in and out if he has to. We're pretty sure it's where he drops the docs, then someone on the other side picks them up."

"You're more jive than a boogie, Bubba."

"It's the truth."

"We'll ask Fargo and Mr. Holt if it's the truth. See, I gotta job to do, and it's keep an eye on you. I got lots to report. You slobber all over his daughter 'til late at night, you pick into the trophy room, you got a bag of paper you took from somewhere and you got a bunch of spy gadgets and a phone hidden in a box in the fuckin' dirt. You're history, man. You're iced."

He's right, thinks John.

Snakey and him went somewhere. Snakey came back.

"You did your job well, Snakey. But you got the wrong guy."

"No. You're you all right. It's pretty simple. I'm gonna collect all this stuff and I'm gonna give it to Lane. Lane the Brain. I'm telling him what you did to Val. I'm telling him the way you snuck out here and tried to use the phone. I'm giving him this picture and drawing here. If it turns out you're working for him then there's no harm in it, right? We all just laugh and you go back to doing whatever you're supposed to be doing. I ain't heard nothin' about no docks and leaks. What I heard from Lane was that you aren't trustworthy. Think I've just about proved it."

John's mind was roiling now, a chaos of fear, confusion and doubt. This was not in any of Joshua's scripts. This was a contingency not covered.

The Colt's safety was already off. There was no round chambered. He would have to cock it. And in the time it would take for him to turn, jack the live round in, find his target and fire, all Snakey had to do was pull a trigger and watch ten bullets go through John's back.

If you're blown, run. If you can't run, deny. When you can't deny, confess. It will either get you out, get you turned or get you killed.

"I'm working for the FBI, Snakey."

"Cool. I'm John Gotti."

"You'll end up in prison like Gotti, if you don't put that gun away."

"You got me shakin' now, Mr. Fart, Burp and Indigestion."

"Listen. Six months ago, Holt tried to kill a writer who'd been after him. She'd bad-mouthed Patrick after he got it up in Santa Ana. She bad-mouthed Holt himself. She made fun of everything he stands for, everything he is, everything he does. She ridiculed his politics. She ridiculed Liberty Ridge. She made it seem like what happened to his son and wife had sent him over the top. She tried to say he was a victim of violence, that it had twisted him out of shape—turned him into a vicious old fool and that he was a sign of the times. She patronized him. She ragged on him, then patted him on the head. But she was more right than she knew. He went crazy over what happened to Patrick and Carolyn and he tried to take it out on someone he hated. They've matched up shells to one of his guns. They've got fingerprints."

Snakey was quiet for a long moment.

"I'd a shot the cunt, too, for writing that."

"Jesus Christ, Snakey, he shot the wrong one! He killed a twenty-four year old woman who'd never written a thing about him. Left her in a parking lot with her heart blown to pieces. She could have been your girl."

"She wasn't."

"I know. She was mine."

Again, Snakey was quiet for a moment.

"Mr. Holt isn't that stupid. And neither am I. You're just piling on the bullshit now, thinking I'm dumb enough to buy it. Nice try, faggot."

"I'm telling the truth now, Snakey. I swear to God, I am. Work with me. Help us take down Holt."

"Can you beat two grand a week?"

"I can't pay you a dime."

"I'm supposed to sell out Mr. Holt for not even a dime?"

"He killed her. If that isn't enough for you, then you better look after yourself. Because when we take him, you're going down with him. And Fargo. And Partch. Remember that supervisor who took a trip with you and didn't come back? They'll nail you on that, too, unless you help. You've got a chance to save our own ass here, and to nail a sick old bastard who killed a girl he didn't even know. You're getting a good deal, man. Think about it for about five seconds if you got brains enough."

"Okay."

Snakey was silent for about five seconds.

"I'm done thinking. You're lying. If you weren't lying, I wouldn't help you anyway. I'm takin' you and all your shit back to show Mr. Holt and Lane. They can figure out what to do with you."

"Listen, Snakey. I'm going to tell you something now. If you help us, you live. If you don't, you die young. It's that simple."

"Pretty funny statement from a guy fuckin' a tree with a Mac pointed at him."

"I'm telling you, Snakey. Let me go. It's the right thing to do. And it's the only chance you've got. I'm begging you, man. I'm begging you."

"Shut up. I hate beggars. Beat one dead back in Jersey one night, just because he smelled so bad. Used gloves on him. Hate those fuckin' stinky homeless bums. Felt his face bones breaking. I was drunk."

John could hear Snakey moving the wooden cover back over the tunnel. He would be kneeling, with one hand on the cover and the other on his gun. John inched his left hand toward his right.

God help me, he thinks.

God forgive me.

"Help me, Snakey."

"Help your fuckin' self, man."

John closed his hand around the automatic then turned and jacked in the shell. He was falling to a crouch while he lined up the front sight with the chest of the still kneeling Snakey.

Snakey had set the Mac beside him to slide back the cover.

He looked at John, then at the gun, then at John again.

John saw a look of determination cross Snakey's face, a look of pure arrogance.

"Don't do it," he said. But Snakey already was going for his gun.

The two shots from the Colt were through him before his hand touched the gun. John saw the little puffs of dirt kick up on the other side of the fence. Snakey hit the ground like a dropped bag of sand, like a bird shot from the sky, like Rebecca after the second shot, a once-living thing now wholly, immediately and forever emptied of life.

John was on his knees, too, his burning eyes still locked on Snakey, whose funny flat-top waved stiffly in the warm morning breeze.

When John reached him, Josh was on his way to the airport to catch a flight to Washington, so the reception was spotty. He and Dumars had been summoned by Evan, post haste. John imagined them in the Bureau Ford, Dumars driving and Joshua fretting, as usual. He longed to be with them. He told him what had happened, and for a long moment, Joshua was silent. Then:

"Talk to me, John. Please talk to me now."

"I've just murdered an innocent man. I got pictures and drawings and notes. I'm coming out, Josh. I've had enough."

"You did what you had to, John. It was not your decision to make. It was Snakey's. He made it."

"I want out. I'm done."

"John, listen to me. I told you this would happen. I told you there would come a time when you would want nothing but out. And I told you where you would be when you felt this way. Tell me now what I said. Tell me where I said you would be."

Dizziness.

Sickness.

Swirling images of blood and bones, teeth and hair. The death waltz. The killing ball.

He puked.

"John," Weinstein commanded, "respond to me now. Where did I say that you would be?"

"In the the darkest hour."

"Was I right?"

"You were right."

Joshua's voice faded, then came back strong.

"But what did I tell you next—when is the darkest hour?"

"Some shit about right before the dawn." He was blubbering now.

"Correct. It was not shit and that is why you are not coming out. You are staying in. If you come out now, you'll always be in that dark hour, John. It will follow you the rest of your life. Right now, you belong to it. But for it to ever go away, it must belong to you."

"I can't do any more."

"Quiet, John. Listen. I'll bring you out the second you're finished. But I can't do it before you're finished, can I? Reason with me now. I need time to analyze the documents you found in your cottage. I need time to get a search warrant, if we can get one at all. We will need more."

"I don't want more."

"Oh, yes you do. You want Holt. That's the agreement, John. Holt. Not Snakey. *Holt.*"

John tried to gather himself, choke back the ugly sobs that kept breaking into his throat. "That poor dumb Snakey. Jesus. Bring me out."

"I need you now, John."

"I don't know what to do."

"You will stay in, John. You will wait until I can vet the documents. If it's good stuff, we'll be close to Wayfarer. Remember, Wayfarer is the only one left on earth who can reassemble your soul. He is the missing part of you. You own him when we take him."

John heard himself breathing, then a blast of static.

Josh's voice again:

"Let me ask you something, John. When your parents were recovered from the airplane, you were asked to identify them, right? You told me so. I've thought about that since then. It's a very tragic thing for a nine-year old to be asked to do, and I am impressed that you could do it. But John, what if you hadn't entered that building? What if you had stayed out, never gone into that cool, disinfected room and had the courage to confront what life had so cruelly dealt to you? I can answer that. If you hadn't, John, you would still be there, still a boy, still terrified and confused and angry. If you had never opened that door, you could never have closed it. But you did, didn't you? And that's why you are the man you are."

John said nothing. His thoughts were underwater. Black, deep water. No up. No down.

"Listen to me, John. Months ago, when Rebecca was alive, I went to her house late one night, after work. She was in the pool. It was cold and there was steam coming off the water. She had been swimming for a long time because her breathing was fast and deep and her strokes were slow, and she wasn't staying in the lane. She was a strong swimmer. I sat down in the dark and watched. Back and forth. Back and forth. Ten more minutes. Twenty. Finally she stopped. She flipped up her goggles and stood in the shallow end a while. Then she climbed out and wrapped herself up in her towel—the red one, you remember, the one with the tropical fish on it. She still didn't know I was there. She hadn't looked my way. She sat on the deck and dangled her feet into the water. She was hunched inside that big towel, just the top of her head showing. And she said something to herself. She said, *You've got to do something. You've got to do something. You've got to do something, and you don't know what it is.*"

John waited through Joshua's silence.

Then:

"She couldn't see a way out, John. She was paralyzed by you. Paralyzed by me. It's the worst feeling on earth, needing to act but not understanding how to act. She never knew what to do, until she wrote those letters. But by then it was too late. She didn't live long enough to send them. You, John, have the path. You are halfway down it. You *know* what to do. Now, you must wait. Learn from what Rebecca didn't do. Let her teach you."

John looked again at Snakey's inert form, the two bloody holes in the back of his shirt.

"For Rebecca," said Joshua.

"For Rebecca," said John.

He could feel his heart begin to steady, and exhaustion settling over him. "Think Snakey left the computer message and the bag in my freezer?"

"No. I don't believe it was Snakey. I believe it was Holt, and that is why I had you bring me the photograph and the sketch, and the notes. We'll have them analyzed in twenty-four hours, God and the Crime Lab willing. They will prove to be a counterfeit of his handwriting and an altered photo. You will present them to him as a token of your trust and loyalty."

John said nothing. He felt like lying down in the dirt and sleeping for a week.

"Leave the bag in the box with your tools. Leave Snakey where he is, God rest him. Get a fresh camera and go back. Repair. Wayfarer is due back day after tomorrow. Let yourself come together again. You are scattered. You are losing focus. Show me that you're the man Rebecca thought you were. Show me she did the right thing by leaving me for you."

The risen sun was a disc of orange now, throwing heat and light into John's face. He imagined floating through the sky with the winds, like he'd tried to do at age ten from his uncle's roof.

"I can't bring her back to you, Joshua. I would if I could."

"I told you to never apologize for that. Never."

"It's not an apology. It's the truth."

A deep, icy chuckle issued from Joshua Weinstein. "I know you wouldn't bring her back to me even if you could, John. You would bring her back and keep her for yourself, now, wouldn't you?"

CHAPTER
TWENTY-FIVE

The first time John Menden ran away from home he was eleven years old. It was not from his parents' home, of course, because they were elsewhere, out in the big wide open, out in the sky somewhere. It was Stan and Dorrie's.

He packed up the neccessities for life on one's own: sleeping bag, a pillow case full of food, pocketknife, all the cash he had—twenty-six dollars, a flashlight and a jacket. It was imperative that he bring his box with him. It was a cedar cigar box his father had given him, and it locked shut with a shiny brass hook. Inside it was the accumulated personal wealth of his eleven years: a silver ring with a big turquoise inlay that his parents brought him from Mexico and that was much too large even for his thumb; a piece of tree turned into a rock from the petrified forest of Arizona; pictures; a wristwatch that no longer worked; some sea shells he collected; two arrowheads he found himself; one shark's tooth he got up in the Mojave Desert and another, black and gigantic, that his mother bought for him; a collection of minerals in separate plastic bags that came with an Audubon Society book on rocks; Stebbins's *Field Guide to Western Reptiles and Amphibians;* and a loose rubble of acorns, tiny sand dollars, crab claws, pertinent stones and snake rattles. His latest addition to the box was the plastic bag the Sheriff had given him with the fossilized sea shell and two gold rings. All of this luggage he strapped to his bicycle with Uncle Stan's duct tape, using the little book rack on his three-speed for the cigar box, sleeping bag and food. He slipped away late one summer morning.

First he went by his old house, which was only half a mile away. He stopped on the opposite sidewalk, leaned his weight onto one leg, and paused there to absorb the atmosphere of the place. The new owners had already painted the outside a dainty yellow with white trim, which John found too girlish. The woman had placed planter boxes under the bedroom windows and spiked them with marigolds and lobelia.

As he watched, two little boys about his age charged from the house and started up a game of stickball against the garage door. John looked on as they proceeded to use the very same strike zone that his father had painted there for him. The tennis ball thudded against the wood. One of the boys looked at him for a moment, then spit into the street. John leaned back onto the bicycle seat, strained his legs full-length to reach the pedals and headed off down the sidewalk.

Down Fourth all he way to the Marine Base, west along the chain link of the military property, past the guard house to the freeway, down the frontage road and old Coast Highway to a gravel path that led through a saltwater slough and into the gentle but wild foothills of the Rancho del Sol and a short three hours later John was on the place that would someday be known as Liberty Ridge.

He pushed his bike as far as he could into the brush, toward the lake. When he couldn't push it any farther he unstrapped his belongings and left it hidden under a lemonadeberry tree. It took him almost an hour to cross the ridge of foothills and reach the lake. He could see the old mission house far on the other side, up on a rise where it commanded a view of the countryside around it. The roof tiles were orange in the summer light and the walls were white. He found the old boat in its usual place, tucked up under a sandstone ledge not far from shore, with bunches of tumbleweeds to hide it. The oars were lying inside the hull.

"Who are you?"

He reeled behind him, toward the voice. A dark-skinned boy stood exactly where John had walked just a moment before. John was impressed that anyone could move that quietly. He was more impressed with the long, slender-bladed knife in the boy's left hand. He was dressed in jeans and a t-shirt and a pair of sandals. He was probably a teenager.

"John."

"That's my boat."

"Okay."

"You stealing it?"

"I want to go to the island."

"That's my island, too."

"Okay."

"I live here. My whole family works for the Holts."

"I rode my bike."

"Then where is it?"

"In the bushes. Way back that way."

"I'm Carlos and this is my lake. I could skin you with this knife and take your bike."

John was trembling and he knew his legs wouldn't get him far. He tried to imagine what his father would say.

"Carlos," he said. "What do you say we go over to the island and bullshit a little?"

The dark boy glared at him, then bent his knife in half and slipped it into his pocket. "I'm gonna row."

It didn't take long to get to the other shore. John helped Carlos drag the boat into the cattails that lined the south edge of the island. The air filled with blue dragonflies and every few seconds he could hear a frog plop into the water.

"Ever seen the cave?" Carlos asked.

"I slept in it."

"Find my magazines?"

"Just bugs and the spring."

"Those are my magazines with the naked pictures."

"'My dad has *Playboy*."

"I got *Playboy* too. You wouldn't believe this one where the girl's in a hammock eating an apple. It's Miss December."

They walked through the brush and into trees growing close together near the center of the island. They went into the cave. It was a big cave, with a mouth wide enough to drive a car through, thought John. As soon as he went in he could hear the warm water gushing up from the earth and echoing off the walls and he remembered how easy it was to sleep with that sound next to you. Carlos lit a lantern.

John set his things on the damp rock cave bottom. He walked to the deepest part and looked down between the rocks at the water coming up. It looked black. It was warm when he touched it and had a soft, silky feel. Carlos showed him the fold-out of the girl in the hammock eating the apple. The seam between the pages was soft and broken in places. John felt that sweet little tickle in his stomach, the same feeling he got once in an elevator with his mother and used to get all the time in the station wagon when his dad drove fast. Stan didn't drive fast enough to make it feel that way.

He and Carlos walked through the woods to the other side of the island. There was a small beach of dark sand just beyond a thick stand of California lilac. They crouched down in the bushes and looked toward the big mission house.

"Don't let 'em see us," said Carlos. "I'm not supposed to be here."

John peered over the bush tops like a spy. He could feel the dampness of the ground seeping into the knees of his jeans. He felt a sudden affection for Carlos.

Then he saw some people walking along the lake on the far shore. At first they weren't there, and then they were. It was a man and a woman and a small boy. When they reached the point opposite him, John could see that the man and woman were about his parents' age. The boy trailed a little behind his mother, holding her hand. The woman trailed a little behind the man, holding his hand. The man had the same stout bearing and erect posture as his father. The woman had bright blond hair and she wore a loose white dress from which her stomach protruded roundly.

"That's the owner's son," said Carlos. "He's in the FBI and he's got a gun. Mrs. Holt looks like Miss March when she isn't pregnant. They come here sometimes, but not very much."

John watched the man and his wife and son walk along the shore. The boy got tired and the man picked him up and carried him.

"That's a good family," said John.

"How do you know?"

"They're like mine."

"What makes yours good?"

John looked at Carlos, then back to the shore. "Just is. We do lots of things together."

"Then why'd you run away?"

"They took a trip for awhile. They're coming back. I'll see if Dad might want to live here someday."

"The rancho isn't yours."

"He could buy it. He bought an airplane."

Back at the cave they sat just outside and ate the cookies and fruit cocktail John had packed. While Carlos looked at his magazines, John lay down in the late afternoon warmth and looked at the sun through his eyelids.

For a brief moment he felt that the sun out there was his sun. He felt that the cool earth under him was his earth. He felt self-sufficient, contained and welcome. He was certain he belonged here in a way he no longer belonged in the old house, or in Stan and Dorrie's. It was the best feeling he knew, this attachment to a place, because a place never went away. But the feeling was over quickly, like the one in his stomach when he looked at Carlos's picture.

Look down on that county, son. It's yours. That's a nice thought, isn't it?

It's not really mine, dad.

No, it is. It belongs to whoever puts down his roots there. Your mother and I have. You will . . .

"I want to live here someday," he said out loud. "Right here on this island. Right in this cave."

"It's not yours."

"It belongs to whoever puts down roots here, Carlos."

"Here's the one that Mrs. Holt looks like."

Carlos brought over the magazine. John steadied the fold-out page in the afternoon breeze. It was Miss March and she was up on her knees, on a bed, wearing a tattered old workshirt that cast her middle in shadow but parted conveniently around her big tan breasts. She had a pretty face and she was smiling. She looked like John's mother, and his stomach dropped and tickled sweetly. She looked like the woman on the shore, too.

That's just exactly what a lady is supposed to look like, he thought. Just like the one that's going to belong to me someday.

TWENTY-SIX

Joshua Weinstein sat in the Quantico conference room and looked out at the sere Virginia landscape. The trees were naked and the ground was tan. It's like Wyeth painted the whole damn world, he thought. A light breeze swayed the branches and moved the leaves in pointless patterns. The central heat huffed on and he looked at Dumars.

"How's your room?" he asked flatly, his red-eye voice.

"The same as yours."

And right next door, he thought—anything to relieve himself of the worry and fear. What could they possible want with him? Did they know about Snakey by now? Impossible, but their job was to discover the impossible.

Right after the call from John, he had ordered Dumars to abort their airport run and speed to the perimeter of Liberty Ridge. There, he had grimly overseen the claiming of Snakey and the package. He heatedly swore his people to secrecy, and arranged for them to book the body at county as a John Doe. He now had two weeks of grace from a deputy, calling in an old favor.

He had flown out John's prizes by courier jet, which landed them in Norton's lap approximately five hours later. Then, making a mock rush for the airport, he had ordered Dumars to stop their car on the shoulder, gotten out, lifted the hood and asked her to locate the fuel line. Joshua couldn't tell the fuel line from a battery cable but Sharon could. He yanked it from the pump, then called Bureau Tech Services to come fix his car.

The next flight out was at eleven.

Now he was here, half a day late, quite literally on the carpet. He looked down at the unearthly shade of green, suitable for a camouflage pattern at best, exactly what you'd expect from the federal government.

Norton entered the room and shook hands. He reeked of after-shave and anxiety. His cheeks were bright pink, marked with the capillary exuberance of forty years of Scotch. His smile looked too jolly; his handshake felt too warm; his tie was too tightly knotted.

All the best appearances, thought Joshua. We're fucked. Even Norton knows it. Did they tell him about Snakey? Norton sat and they made unbearable small talk for five eternal minutes. *What do they want?*

Walker Frazee finally popped in, his bouncing stride enough to send a familiar buzz of horror up Joshua's spine. They all shook hands. Frazee was a short man with a boyish face and a smile so disarming you wanted to hug him. His suit was dark, cheap and years out of fashion, exactly the same color and cut that Joshua had always seen him in. His shoes were polished to absurdity. His hair was an effulgent white, cut with just a little touching the top of his ears. He looked to Joshua like a funeral home counselor, which Josh knew was a wholly inappropriate impression. Because, when the boyishness left Walker Frazee's face and he dropped his ingratiating smile, what was left was the zealous gleam of the true believer. Josh could see it in his eyes, as clear as the beam from a lighthouse on a black sea. It said: *I am the vessel. I carry the word.* Righteousness, and its sad obligation to the sword, was certified by the gleam. He never swore, never drank alcohol or caffeine, never smoked, never missed church, invested shrewdly and—it was rumored—tithed abundantly. His wife was breathtakingly ugly, as portrayed by the photographs in his office. His eight grown children were pillars of Mormon, spread out across the republic like the footings of a foundation. Frazee never stopped talking about his children. Crazy Frazee, went the gossip: One God, one suit, eight wives.

"Good morning," he said, pulling out a chair at the head of the table. "How was your flight?"

"Fine, sir," said Dumars.

"Long," said Joshua.

Frazee held his boyish smile. "Looks like you survived it well."

"The movie was about a plane crash in the Andes," Joshua noted. "I couldn't figure out if it was a bad joke or a good one."

"Oh, I saw that thing," said Norton. "Where they end up eating each other?"

"That's the one."

"Not for the queasy flyer," said Frazee. "Agent Dumars, you're looking very well these days."

"Thank you, sir."

"And you, Joshua?"

"I'm thinking of buying a surfboard."

"Really?"

"No, not really. But the Orange County office is a beehive, I'll say that. There's always too much to do."

"Nice job on the kidnapper buying the Ferrari."

"Dumb shit—oh, I beg your pardon, sir—dumb clod just walked in with the cash. We had people standing around acting like salesmen. I mean, he'd done it before."

"Astonishing, he'd grab a casino owner's daughter."

"Won't last long in the prison population," said Norton. "Dumb sh . . . muck."

"Well, I can't say I'm not a little envious of you two, when I wake up to an October morning and the mercury is right at thirty."

"We don't have weather in California, sir," said Weinstein. "We have nuance."

"I see." Frazee's boyish smile faded as he settled in his chair and looked at Joshua. "And you have Wayfarer?"

"We certainly do," said Norton. "Joshua and Sharon have procured for us documents relating to Baum's home and work."

"I've seen them. Interesting. But no evidence to establish that Wayfarer was at the scene. They're undergoing analysis right now—nothing is certain."

Joshua's heart fell.

"What?" asked Dumars.

"The photograph is of Baum's property," said Norton. "We can establish that. Plus the sketch of the *Journal* grounds."

"Which proves nothing," answered Frazee.

"Then we'll close the loop," said Norton.

"How?"

Joshua thought that he moved in rather nicely. "Owl is digging much better than we thought he might. We've got Liberty Operations docs, and a safe that looks more than promising. We expect a .30/06 caliber hunting rifle next, to work the engraved shells against. Getting the rifle out could be tough. But he's working Liberty Ridge like a gopher."

Frazee's brow furrowed. "I thought we established that the bullets fired at the victim didn't come from the engraved shells."

"Correct, sir," said Joshua. "We're hoping to find that they came from another gun in Wayfarer's arsenal."

Frazee nodded with undisguised irritation. "If Owl hopes to get inside that safe I'd like to know how. Can he bend steel in his bare hands?"

"He's been in just over a week, sir," said Dumars.

"How often do you talk?" he asked Joshua, ignoring Sharon.

"Every other day, sir. It depends on John—Owl—getting to the phone. It's out on the perimeter of the property."

"Why not closer?"

"We assumed Wayfarer would find it."

"I'd say that was a good assumption. Does Wayfarer suspect him, yet?"

The "yet" struck Joshua as condescending and fated, but he held his tongue. "Wayfarer's security man has jumped him through some hoops. He cleared them all, so far as we can tell."

"Fargo?"

"Yes."

"Hmmm," mumbled Frazee. He sat back and looked briefly at Norton, then Joshua. "Hmmm. You know, this Hate Crimes money doesn't come to us for free."

Joshua waited. He had no idea where Frazee was going or why he was going there. An abrupt one-eighty like this was why they called him Crazy. Besides, Joshua believed the Hate Crimes money *did* come for free, more or less, taxed out of a dazed populace and spent by bureaucrats like any other federal funds. It was beyond Joshua's belief that Frazee would have called them back to Washington to talk about money.

"Appropriations feeds us, as you know. As it does Commerce, State Department, etc."

Shit, thought Joshua. My joe kills an innocent thug in the southern California hills, and Frazee's doing Economics 101.

The little dandy droned on.

"We're Justice, of course, so we see our precious dollars shared with such critical programs as the Weed and Seed Fund in General Administration, the Radiation Exposure Compensation Trust Fund, and of course our friends, the Drug Enforcement Administration. The House Committee cut us again this year, as you know. As you also know, the President bailed us out— partially—with the Federal Hate Crimes funding. We were asked by the Attorney General to streamline and cooperate between agencies. The idea was that we could be cost effective. They actually used the phrase 'more bang for the buck.' Well, we've been asked to liase with the other agencies, in order to stretch the Hate Crimes windfall."

"We've been *liasing* all along," said Norton. "What a word. We get our piece of pie, everybody else gets theirs. We always cooperate until everybody gets out of our way."

"That just changed. We're barely past one quarter of the fiscal year, and we—that's not just the Bureau, but all of us inside Justice—have eaten up the Hate Crimes funding like it was candy. C-SPAN aired our foibles before the nation, just last week. Certain Representatives heard from their constituents, and the Inspector-In-Charge heard from the Congressmen. We've decided to joint task some of the operations where we overlap. There's a Joint Task Committee and I am on it."

"Congratulations," muttered Dumars.

"So what are we supposed to do?" asked Weinstein. "Help INS run down aliens?"

Frazee aimed a crisp stare at Joshua. "You are supposed to arrest an assassin."

"We're working effectively toward that end," said Norton.

"Hmmm," Frazee grunted. He sighed and shook his head. "You know, Norton—this isn't the kind of thing I'd have approved, if it had come across my desk to begin with. It's too risky, too time-consuming, too expensive. Joshua, you don't necessarily need to know that, but now you do. Of course, it's beside the point. But the fact that I'm our man on the Joint Task Committee isn't beside he point at all. Are your fingers to the wind now?"

Joshua nodded. "We're wasting money."

"In the eyes of the House, yes. And let's face it, twelve million for Hate Crimes, even divided up by Justice, isn't just change. Would you say?"

"Not at all, sir." said Joshua. "But our total outlay for Owl is less than eighty-five thousand."

"Counting salaries it isn't."

"We're always working on *something*, sir. You can hardly figure that into overhead for Wayfarer." Joshua mustered his best expression of agreeability, but he could feel his Adam's apple bobbing and his ears growing hot.

Though it was hardly the point here, Joshua wanted to ask why the California Feebies always got shortchanged by the Bureau budgeteers. He thought of the Los Angeles office, so strapped for money that the agents actually shared rides on stakeouts. One of them was caught selling Amway products from the trunk of his Bureau Ford, then later busted wide open for selling Government information to his Russian girlfriend. But Josh knew the truth, sad or not: Washington thought California was unworthy of federal dollars the same way New York thought California unworthy of intellectual respect. It was a nasty little prejudice he'd noticed from day one.

"We're playing it as tight as we can," Joshua said.

"You know that and I know that. But Appropriations sees twelve million going out and nothing coming back. If we can't make a cost-effective go of it this year, we'll get nothing from Hate Crimes next time around. I don't have to tell you that. Unfortunately, there's no neat way out of this. That's why I've called you here. You now have a deadline. A short one."

Joshua actually felt his stomach turn. It rotated, then settled back down into a new, less comfortable position. He had tried to isolate his own tiny operation in this labyrinth of finance and politics but that was hopeless. It was just a speck in the federal wind.

There was silence in the room now, all hands aware that Captain Frazee was about to make a major course correction. Joshua's stomach squeezed out a gurgling surge of gas, which he held in with great discomfort.

"And if we can't make a clean arrest of Wayfarer I'm going to have to turn him over to the Bureau of Alcohol, Tobacco and Firearms. Let them finish it."

"*No,*" said Joshua.

"Shut up, Weinstein," said Norton. He stood now, sighing histrionically. Josh saw the fresh rush of blood to his already heated cheeks. He circled the conference room once, like a lion pacing the confines of a cage. "Walker, we can't sit still for that."

"You will if I tell you to."

"*Why?* We've put in the time. We got the money from the Hate Crimes bill. We've worked Wayfarer up one side and down the other, we've got a man inside, just *inches* from pay dirt, and you want the Bat Boys to finish it? On what possible grounds?"

"All grounds," said Frazee, offering his smile, his clear and guileless eyes, his Gleam, his righteousness. "ATF takes Wayfarer off our books, but the dollars stay. We are seen to be Joint Tasking effectively. We use what's left of our Hate Crimes windfall for more achievable goals. We still get our man. Moreover, the nation sees that our fellows in the Bureau of Alcohol, Tobacco and Firearms are not the bumbling murderous fools last spotted in Waco, Texas."

"Oh, God," said Joshua, his stomach churning like a washing machine now, his tongue all but frozen by anger.

"Don't 'oh God' me, Mr. Weinstein," snapped Frazee. "You can sit back in your Bureau seat and call ATF anything you want. You can laugh, scorn, micturate or moan. But that won't change the fact that they're looking for redemption. They're not just looking for it—they're frothing after it. I had lunch with the Attorney General yesterday, and I can tell you that she is absolutely resolute on this point—ATF needs another chance. And, hint, hint: Hate Crimes largesse is much in question for next year. So, if we don't have Wayfarer's head on a platter soon, ATF gets their chance. I've got to give them *something*."

Norton was still standing, his mouth open, a look of incomprehension in his wet, blue eyes. He'd taken a cigarette from his pack but hadn't lit it—federal regulations, of course. For just a moment Joshua saw Norton as ridiculous, a Scotch-soaked old triceratops wandering heavily in a world of smokeless bureaucracies, smug, soulless zealots like Walker Frazee and muscle-headed storm troopers like the Bat Boys. He wondered if Norton would start to fossilize, right before his eyes.

"How soon is soon?" managed Weinstein. His own voice sounded like something released from under pressure. He could hardly form words around his jumping larynx. He saw Sharon Dumars staring at him, which encouraged a fresh jolt of anxiety.

"Six days is the best I could do. Believe me, the Attorney General was *this* close to shutting us down right there, over lunch—redlining about ten of my operations. She pointed out with unfortunate accuracy that the murder of Rebecca Harris—a heterosexual WASP—does not, in fact, even constitute a hate crime."

"We all know who the target was!" yelled Joshua.

"That doesn't change the outcome," said Frazee.

"And if we don't have the arrest in six days?"

"She cannot guarantee us all six days. Six, maximum."

"If we don't have an arrest *in time?*"

"ATF takes over."

"Would you excuse me for just one moment, sir?"

"Of course."

Joshua went into the men's room and vomited. Then he wiped his face with a soaked paper towel, brushed the hair back on his sweating scalp and smashed his foot into the aluminum waste receptacle. He looked down at it: shiny angles now all converging toward the huge pockmark of a center. Round Two, he thought. This fucker will not defeat me.

Back in the conference room, he stood somewhat formally behind his chair, like a party guest waiting to be seated. He buttoned his coat and looked at Walker Frazee, trying to mute the fury from his eyes.

"Sir," he said calmly. "I believe this is the worst decision that can be made at this time. Our informer has performed splendidly, quickly, intelligently. We are on the verge of a clean arrest. I can guarantee you one thing, sir—if ATF storms the walls at Liberty Ridge, Wayfarer will destroy everything that might implicate him in the murder of Rebecca Harris. We will be left with nothing. Nothing. ATF won't even get their ninety-six bodies. It will be an unqualified defeat, and Wayfarer will walk. He'll never offer us another chance again. Ever. You know him, sir. You know I'm right."

It was Frazee's turn to posture. He extricated himself from his chair with meaningful slowness, then walked to the window. He stared out. Then he turned and looked at Joshua. His eyes had that glimmer of conviction in them again.

"I object to your cynicism and irony, Mr. Weinstein. You have been given control. You have had your man inside for nine days. At the most, he will have six more. I can do nothing more for you. And if ATF takes over I'll be happy to see this go. I've never believed in this kind of hugger-mugger, anyway. I believe in bold, broad, decisive action. Take it, or ATF will."

Joshua stared back at Frazee, both drawn to and repelled by the Gleam. It was such a pure, unexamined thing. But when Frazee smiled now, Joshua saw it in a new way. Gone was the boy behind the face, and in his place was the serene sadness of the supplicant. Joshua realized it then: Frazee's onetime friend and ally within the Bureau was now his lamb of atonement. Frazee could not be clean until baptized in the blood of Wayfarer, and blood, Joshua understood, is exactly what Frazee was hoping the Bat Boys would spill for him. For free.

"Sir," said Weinstein. "I guarantee you that we will bring in Wayfarer on a clean arrest. Owl will produce. And I humbly implore you to keep those fucking apes out of my case."

"Go back to California," snapped Frazee.

"We're on our way, Walker!" exclaimed Norton, taking Joshua by the arm and leading him from the room.

They huddled in the far corner of a terminal lounge at Dulles International. Joshua stirred sugar and milk into his third cup of coffee. His ears were still bright red from a bitter confrontation with the airline desk, from which Joshua finally emerged victorious with two tickets for an earlier flight, no extra charge. He had only saved three hours time, but something in his gut told him he would need them.

"Can we shift Owl into overdrive?" asked Norton.

"He's been working as fast as he can," said Joshua. "Now, we'll work him even faster. The Bat Boys will not crash my party, Norton."

Norton nodded without spirit. "Frazee is just a blade of grass in a storm."

"He's a waste of skin."

"It isn't his fault."

"Norton," said Joshua, "that is completely beside the point."

Josh looked at his boss. There was no way he could tell him of Snakey now—it would be certain suicide. Norton would simply enjoy the protection of innocence until someone on Joshua's team leaked the news. Someone would, he knew, but he prayed it wouldn't happen in the next six days. Six days—maybe less.

Knowing Frazee, maybe a whole lot less. If and when Frazee got wind of Snakey, the whole investigation would be completely and forever over. So, he knew, would his career with the FBI. This concept sat inside him without valence, neither positive nor negative, just a stable actuality he had never considered before. With regard to his future, he thought: small business. I've always liked dry cleaning, the way things go in dirty and come out clean.

He turned his thoughts to Liberty Ridge. What a botch, he thought, what a mess. But still, Owl was in there, right where they needed him, and the pearl of great price was in there too, waiting to be discovered. The cellular phone waited on his belt, a silent oracle. The relays and patches and satellites could put Owl through to him almost anywhere in the Western Hemisphere, but there it sat, black and mute on his hip. Ring, bastard, he thought.

"How come you missed the morning flight yesterday?" asked Norton.

"I told you, the Bureau car broke down. It took Tech Services over an hour to get the damn thing to a garage. Too late for the flight, by then."

Norton looked at him with unsatisfied eyes.

"Fuel line," said Joshua.

He felt Norton's big hand brush his shoulder as his boss stood, then plodded through the empty bar toward the exit.

Josh waited until Norton was out of sight before he spoke. "Sharon, I feel betrayed. Six days."

"Better than two."

Josh thought, then gulped down half his coffee. "The sketch of the *Journal* and the photo of Baum's house should be enough. They were in Wayfarer's possession. It is evidence of planning a murder. Why can't Frazee cut us loose with it, at least let a judge decide? We're after a search warrant for God's sake, not the gas chamber. Who in hell made that sketch, took those notes, if it wasn't Wayfarer?"

"That doesn't really worry me, Joshua. What worries me is John. How is he going to take this? He's packed and ready to come out. He's weak and he's vulnerable."

Joshua shook his head. "Fuck him. He's got the training and the ability to find what we sent him in to find."

"He just killed a man to get something to us, and it wasn't enough, Josh."

He looked at Sharon Dumars for a long moment. He could feel the first rush of outrage and adrenaline leaving him, and approaching in its wake the grand fatigue of doubt and waiting.

"Six days," he said again. His voice sounded hollow and ungenuine.

Dumars set a hand over his. When he looked at her, she held his gaze with a look that seemed ready to dissolve, but did not. Her dark eyes expressed the strength and tenderness that Joshua had long thought of as the essence of the feminine. How could they feel both at the same time? He wanted to cry.

"The other day you asked me something, and I answered you with a lie," she said.

He waited. He felt stuffed with information now, overloaded with emotion, and he could hardly believe that Dumars was apparently about to add to his burden. He searched his memory for the conversation in question. Something about the documents? The gun they hadn't found yet? The safe that Owl had photographed?

"You asked me to dinner and I said I had plans. I didn't."

That, he thought. Funny what a good job he'd done of forgetting.

"Oh. Well, that's okay."

Sharon blushed then. It surprised Joshua to see this intrusion onto Sharon's tanned, always composed, always prepared face. Her hand tightened and she smiled.

"Josh, you should have seen the look on Crazy's face when you told him to keep those apes out of your case. It was just to die for."

He allowed himself an uncertain grin.

She grinned, too, looked around, then leaned in closer to him. "I have to tell you, watching you go up against those old farts really made me proud. You're just a babe in their woods, Josh, but you made a sound. You registered. No matter what happens here, you're the future of this Bureau, not Frazee and not Norton. You kicked a little butt in there, partner, and I loved it."

"What, exactly, did Frazee look like when I said that?"

"Like a nun finding a dildo in a Christmas package. Pardon my graphics."

"I missed it, I was so wound up."

"Well, I'll never forget it."

He smiled back at her now, and felt a massive draining of amperage from his nerves. He took a very deep breath.

"Thanks, Sharon."

He felt her hand tighten on his.

"Joshua, for cryin' out loud, will you just ask me to dinner again tonight? What does a girl have to do?"

"Would you?"

"My place. We'll go through Wayfarer files until we can't hold our eyes open any longer. After that, well, we'll just do whatever we need to."

Joshua's smile continued for just a moment, then his eyes took on a look of great reluctance as he reached down to the telephone pulsing against his waist.

CHAPTER
TWENTY-SEVEN

John moves through the Big House like a ghost, past the kitchen and dining room to the stairway where his mocassin boots are all but soundless on the steps. On the second floor he walks purposefully down the hallway to Vann Holt's suite of private rooms and lets himself in. He moves to his right and leans his back against the cool adobe wall. He feels both exposed and invisible.

He wonders what arrogance ever led him to believe that he could accomplish this mission, and questions whether Rebecca would understand what he has done. He knows she would not, and he feels tainted, foolish and cursed.

He looks down at his right hand, still flabbergasted that just a few hours ago it took a human life. He looks at the lines in his palm, then at the tendons on the other side. How could you have done that? he wonders. I am a murderer now. He scrolls through his memory of the Ten Commandments, realizing that, if you count an engaged woman as a married one, he has actually broken every divine order except for the first two. Eight out of ten, he thinks: I'm hellbound.

But he has already begun to embrace his new station. He feels a fraternity with the darker side of his race; he knows sin as a participant rather than a spectator. He senses connection with that great body of offenders, past and present, who have lived with the mark of Cain burned into their souls. He knows their secret, and they know his. He has done something that sets him apart from goodness and light, something that the good and the light might not even see in him. But his brothers, his fellow dark agents, they see and they know. With the Fallen, at least he can be honest. Maybe he can learn from them. Shared burdens make strength.

The entryway opens into a room that is clearly a man's. Its furnishings are functional, with little attention to style or harmony. The blinds and carpet are gray. There are three heavy cowhide sofas set around a very large Kodiak brown bear rug. There are bookshelves along two walls, and one corner of the room is piled high with African drums, weapons and carvings. Facing the window is a long heavy bench set up with Holt's reloading equipment. John can see the long-handled machines of three distinct reloading stations: handgun, rifle, shotgun.

John steps to the table. A covey of stuffed quail make their way from right to left, around the boxes of shells, following a handsome sentry male who hustles along, his head and topknot forward. There are paper boxes at the shotgun station, clear plastic for the rifle cartridges and yellow plastic for handgun loads. Each is labeled with the cartridge gauge or caliber, the shot size or bullet weight and the powder type and charge. John notes again Vann Holt's graceful, forward-leaning draftsman's writing. The table is orderly. John can see that the bulk components are stored underneath. He bends down and pokes a heavy bag of lead shot, then looks into a powder canister to find, unshockingly, powder.

He takes four exposures of the table, following the quail, right to left.

The bedroom is larger than the reloading room but emptier, too. John stands in the double-doorway and views the neatly made bed with a Pendleton blanket for a cover, the nightstand with lamp, small bookcase and stack of magazines on the near side. His eye follows the sunlight to the tall window. There are no blinds here, but a heavy purple curtain that has been tied open on either side of the glass. The curtain strikes John as a sad dramatic flourish in an otherwise forsaken space. Two worn leather recliners sit at opposing sides of the window, facing outward where a perfect tall rectangle of hills and ocean is framed by the glass.

He kneels, pulls open the top drawer of the nightstand and takes out a loose pile of occasion cards. He sees, for the first time,

Valerie's handwriting. It is composed, unadorned and pleasing. There are cards for Father's Day, birthday, Easter and Just Thinking of You. Mixed in with these are cards from Carolyn, whose script is sweet chaos with occasional blurbs of lucidity. Like her mind, John thinks: what does she dream about?

Beneath the cards are four yellow legal pads, all dense with Holt's writing. Unlike the cryptic notes of his business files, the legal pads show a more expansive and personal Holt:

> *Still don't know if Valerie can be persuaded to take over Liberty Operations. Either that, or she'll go on to veterinary school and heal animals all her life. I'll be pleased with either decision, but Liberty Operations could use her and she'd make potfuls of money. I don't want to go outside the organization, but choices seem limited. Laura? She'd lose interest over time. Thurmond? Too old. Lane? He's loyal as a pit bull but I don't think he has the kind of character that builds trust. He'd be bitterly disappointed not to have a shot at it, I know. Must make some decisions before the last good nap.*

> *Can disconnected people be free? When the U.S. Government wanted to solve the 'Indian problem' in the west, they made tribal language, custom and religion illegal. The idea was to destroy the tribes without killing off all of the individuals. Without the tribal connections the Indians were defenseless. In place of the tribe, the white man offered the concepts of private property, agriculture, Christianity and the importance of individual freedoms. Once the unity of the tribes was ruined, so were the individuals within them.*

John flipped back a few pages and read again:

> *More cops make more nuts and more nuts make more cops. No end to the widening spiral until we find a common enemy. Oklahoma City only the iceberg tip.*
> *If I could only have Patrick back I could look into the dark future and see some light. There he would be, my eyes, my seed, my pride and my love going forward into*

the days. When Pat died it was like losing two futures—
his and mine. What to do? Valerie is all that's left, but
will she want Liberty Ridge as her own, or will she need
to separate, follow a husband, and begin her own life
somewhere?

Under the legal pads John finds a small stack of medical bills.
They are all from M.D. Anderson Clinic in Houston, and none
are stamped or cancelled by the Post Office. Carried home personally, John thinks: why? He can't make much sense of the bill-
ings codes or charges, but recognizes the scans: X-Ray, CT, MRI
and PET.

Must make some decisions before the last good nap.

He realizes what nobody seems to know, or at least what
nobody has bothered to tell him: Holt is dying. Yes, he thinks.
Holt brought the bills home himself so Valerie, or Fargo, or
whomever, wouldn't find them in the mail. They don't know.
Josh doesn't know. Does anyone?

He arranges the billing statements, open, in a loose square,
then shoots them with this penlight camera. Then he replaces the
bills, the pads and the cards very carefully, in the same order he
found them. He checks his watch and looks out the window for
a moment.

The bathroom is spare and clean. Hoping for a clue to Holt's
ailment, he opens the medicine cabinet, but finds nothing but
over-the-counter remedies, shave gear and ChapStick.

The last room is a kitchen, which appears only partially
stocked at best. In the frig is some fruit, milk, soda and a full ice-
maker bucket. There is, of course, a container of fresh-squeezed
orange juice. There are crackers and a half-used loaf of bread on
the counter, beside the toaster. The cabinets contain the usual
condiments and spices, and, much to John's surprise a box of
peanut-butter flavored Cap'n Crunch cereal. He can hardly picture Holt sitting down to a breakfast of this kind. A liquor cabinet has two fifths of Scotch and several bottles of old California
wine—Zinfandels, Carignanes, Cabernets.

John stands in the kitchen for a long moment, trying to acquire a sense of the man who, at least on some mornings, begins
his day here. He wonders, given Carolyn's condition, does Holt
make love with her?

*   *   *

Ten minutes later he sits at his own dining table in the cottage, watching through the big picture window as Valerie and her dogs come across the meadow toward him. She is dressed in hiking boots and shorts, a blue button-down shirt with the sleeves rolled up, and her red wool cap. The springers twist with patternless logic out in front of her, noses to the ground for birds. She wears a holster and pistol on her hip, slung down low like a gunfighter. He decides that Valerie Anne Holt is one of the oddest women he's ever met.

John's heart leaps, then plummets. It aches. It aches to soar. It aches for company other than the dead, their murderers and their memories.

There she is, he thinks, a woman I can deny, mislead and betray.

There she is, a tool I can use.

There she is, a beautiful young woman coming to see *me*.

The light of her approach brings out only the darkness in his own killer's soul. He goes out to the shaded cool of the porch to welcome her. He smiles but it feels like a grimace. He watches as Boomer, Bonnie and Belle charge into the meadow and commence an assault upon the springers. Valerie stops to watch, then joins John in the shade. She smiles.

"Dad wants us to have dinner with him tonight."

"He's back?"

"Called from the jet. He'll be here by six."

"Everything okay?"

"He sounds elated. I suspect Titisi has signed on."

"That's good news."

She turns and looks back at the meadow to the dogs. Her hair is stacked up under the cap and coming loose like it always seems to be. "Whatcha been doin'?"

"Making a list of editors to call. I'm thinking I might not want to live out in that desert anymore."

"Be nice to have you closer. Help me with the dogs."

"That would be nice."

"You don't have a crush on me, do you?"

"No."

She tries to smile, but her smile is buried by the sudden redness of her face. "Lane says you do. And that you're trustworthy as a rattlesnake. That's what this revolver here is for—rattlers."

"Thought you were going to say for me."

"Naw. I couldn't shoot the guy who *saved* my virginity. Not until I properly thanked him, anyway."

She pauses and looks at him with a half-grin on her face, the kind where the bottom teeth show just a little and give her a look of mischief. Then she blushes again, washing the smile away.

"Just a little crush, maybe?"

"Maybe."

She takes a deep breath. "I'm going for a walk. Wanna come?"

"Sure."

They start out around the lake. The dogs thunder past them and crash into the water, fighting over a stick. Boomer has it and all the others appear to be tearing him to shreds to get it away. The sun is warm on John's face and for a moment, the cold dead feeling inside him is in abeyance. When they reach the place where he had seen Vann, Carolyn and Pat Holt some twenty-three years ago, he tells her the story of Carlos and the cave and how her mother looked with Valerie inside.

Valerie stops. "Right here?"

"Yeah. About here is where they were. *You* were."

"I'm kind of moved by that."

"It's just a story."

"No. It's more. I think you're *somebody*. Somebody who was sent here for a reason. Sent you then, and sends you now. God, maybe, or the devil."

Her unwitting accuracy corners John into silence. He nods. "She was wearing a white dress."

"Mom always wore white. Did you see the spring in the cave?"

"I slept beside it."

"It's still there, you know. I mean, I haven't been to the cave in years, but the spring's still there or the lake wouldn't be. We should go see it sometimes. How about tomorrow afternoon? I'll pack more food and we'll call it a picnic. Sick of my cooking yet?"

"That quail was world class."

"Settled, then."

They continue on for a while without talking. John feels the jitters leaving his nerves, replaced by the mild happiness of know-ing one's body is alive, of feeling it move, of being in the company of someone it is drawn to.

He notes something shiny on the path before he even sees it. He feels his body draw up tight as he registers the shape, a shape familiar to the deep part of the human mind—a very large rattle-snake stretched out in the dirt ahead. Reflexively he reaches for Valerie but she has already stepped forward, holding her revolver with both hands, glancing quickly back at the dogs. The sound of the gun slams into John's ears, the barrel jumps and the sand explodes red around the snake's head. The serpent retracts into a tight coil, rattle buzzing off, then on, then off again. The dogs blunder toward it and John tries to grab Boomer's collar.

"Don't worry, it's out of commission," says Valerie.

"I'm not so sure."

"I am."

The springers try to converge but Valerie yells them off. John's dogs obey her firm command to sit. Boomer eyes John with the pride of finding an item of such vast importance. Valerie touches the snake with her boot and it strikes, knocking its head-less stump of a neck against her ankle. It rattles again. She slides her toe under it and flips in into the bushes. It twists white in the air, then vanishes out of sight, still buzzing.

"I don't like to do that," she says. "But I lost two pups to rattlers. One died and the other one couldn't move his legs, so we had to put him down. Rattlesnakes aren't welcome on Liberty Ridge anymore."

John looks at her and sees a darkness of mood has pushed the softness from her face. It is a wholly new countenance, one that speaks of regretful obligation, of acts finished only to the soul's remorse. She looks more like her father than herself.

"Well, nice shot," he says.

"Pretty easy, if you graduate from the Liberty Ops pistol school at the age of seventeen."

"Top of the class?"

"Yes. Dogs are family to me. And I'll do anything to protect family."

Back at the cottage, John showered and dressed for dinner. He fed the dogs and had a cigarette on the porch. Just before he left

he saw the message indicator on the computer screen and keyed
into his mailbox with nervous fingers:

THIRD DRAWER DOWN. RIGHT OF REFRIGERATOR, BIG
HOUSE. LIKE YOUR CARROTS, SWEETIE? COULDN'T FIND
THEM ANYWHERE. SEND THEM TO THE FOOD TASTERS?

TWENTY-EIGHT

Holt looked more like a man after a Caribbean cruise than one who had just logged several thousand air miles for the purpose, as he put it to John, of "killing rattlesnakes and putting out fires." He was tanned, trim, expansive. He was sitting with Fargo and Adam Sexton on the porch off the Big House kitchen when John joined them. It was shady under the slat redwood canopy that faced the expanse of lawn and trees. Beyond the lawn John could see the distant haze of the slough and the bright silver plate of the Pacific. The evening breeze was cool and clean and smelled of ocean and sage.

Holt finished a story about Fargo's duel with the Ugandan *turista*, a story told at the expense of Fargo, who looked pale and miserable as he reclined on a chaise lounge in the shade. Fargo glanced back at Holt after the punchline—something about Fargo's bottled water and Holt having eaten everything native he could get his hands on—and cast his boss a doleful look. The look wandered to John, where it turned both bored and hostile. John looked at Adam Sexton, who sipped his drink and shrugged.

"Glad I missed it," he said. "I hate foreign countries. I like right here where I am. Domestic accounts—I'm made for it."

"You wouldn't last a day on the dark continent," said Fargo.

"Roughly, my point," said Sexton. He favored John with a conspiratorial look. "Also my point that ninety percent of the Liberty Ops profit is generated by me, right here in Southern Cal.

So go get sick on an international scale, Fargo. I'll stay here and make dough."

Holt chuckled. "Don't squabble, kids. Let's all just admit it's a good feeling to carry home several hundred grand for a few days' work." He studied John over his tumbler of Scotch and ice. "Does that kind of money interest you?"

"Depends what I'd do for it, Mr. Holt."

"What's the most you ever made in a week?"

"Fifteen hundred."

"And what did you do for that?"

"Wrote some pieces for the *Journal*. And did a freelance job for Western Outdoor *News*."

"Forty hours' worth?"

"Forty-five, I'd guess. Plus the morning of bass fishing for the *News* article. I wrote off the gas and lures."

Sexton chortled. "That's big money."

Holt shot him a glance. "After taxes that left you what, nine hundred and change?"

"I'd say."

Holt drank from the tumbler, the long slow sip of a man who has all the time in the world. "Here's the thing about money, John. A man needs to work. It's what keeps his feet on the ground. Work opens the soul to the idea of heaven. The harder a man works the stronger he gets. I think some of the best moments of my life have been work. I spent eight years tracking down the men who bombed Odeh. You remember, the Arab activist? Those years flew by. Seemed to last about five minutes. By the time I got close to them, I was just getting warmed up. I could have followed those murderous bastards for decades. Never would have gotten tired."

"Then the Jews let 'em go," said Fargo.

"They were detained by Israeli Mossad, but not charged," corrected Holt. "Been watched ever since."

"Some justice for blowing an Arab to bits."

"No shit," added Sexton.

Holt waved his hand. "Beside the point. Outside my purview. I completed my work. Now, the whole point is this, if you're going to work anyway—because it builds the soul—why not get a lot of money for it? You spend the same hours. Burn the same energy. Stay up the same nights. Sacrifice. So why not go for more return? Simple arithmetic."

"Well, the arithmetic is simple, Mr. Holt, but finding work that pays a few hundred grand a week isn't."

Holt shrugged and grinned. "Got to work your way up to that kind of thing. How does two thousand a week sound? That's over a hundred a year."

"It sounds like triple what I'm making now."

"Would that appeal to you?"

"For what I'm doing at the *Anza Valley News*? Sure."

"No, for something different than what you're doing at the paper. For something more . . . actual. More tactile. More . . . hands on."

"That could be embalming. No thanks."

"Embalming," echoed Fargo from his lounge.

Sexton laughed and crossed his ankles: loafers, no socks.

"Embalming," said Holt. "No. No embalming required."

Fargo sat up. "He's not exactly quick on the uptake, boss. Why not ask him what happened to Snakey?"

Holt twirled the ice and liquid. "See Snakey while we were gone, John?"

"No."

"Not even once?"

"Not once. I didn't know he was here."

"See Val?"

"We spent a lot of time together."

"Oh, good. Doing what?"

"Talking. Eating. Working the dogs. We rowed out to the island and had a picnic."

"Killed at least one snake," said Fargo. "That's what Val said."

"Couple hours ago."

"But you never saw Snakey?"

"No, Mr. Holt. What happened to him?"

"He disappeared."

John nodded, looked down at his Scotch. "Well, maybe he found something that pays a few hundred grand a week."

"Real fuckin' funny," said Fargo.

But Holt and Sexton were both grinning. Holt turned to look back at Fargo, then returned his amused gray eyes to John. "Lane isn't—"

"—I heard a couple of gunshots yesterday morning. Maybe John shot him and dumped him in the lake."

With this, Valerie Holt sat down on a lawn chair next to her father. She held a tall glass half full of something clear that edged toward the lip of the glass before she righted it. The most graceful klutz I've seen, John thought.

Fargo, about to speak, let his mouth hang open and stared at John.

Valerie swung around to look at Fargo, her honey blond hair lifting out, then bouncing against the skin of her back. "A joke, Lane. Tee-hee. You look cadaverous. Hi, Sexy."

"Hello, your highness," said Sexton.

"What time were the shots, Val?" Fargo asked.

"I just told you it was a joke, Lane. That means I didn't hear any shots. I didn't see Snakey either, thank God. Dad, give Lane a raise and see if it improves his sense of humor. Or make him work for Adam a few weeks."

"You're spicy this evening, daughter."

"Sugar and spice, Daddy-o."

"Mainly spice. Tabasco, maybe."

"Hello, John," she said, turning to face him. She was scrubbed clean as a new coin, her skin aglow, hair shining, trailing a scent that was dark and unambiguous and slid into John's head like an opiate. She was wearing jeans and a green silk blouse.

"Hello, Valerie," he said.

"What am I interrupting?"

"We're talking about the pleasures of money."

"Dad, you're not showing off again, are you?"

"Just running a little test."

"Of what?"

"John's monetary IQ."

"Well into triple digits, I'd bet."

"I was seeing if a hundred thousand a year might tempt him."

"Into what, Pops?"

"Same thing he asked."

She looked at John and smiled. "Watch out. He'll have you signed on for some boring security work before you know it. I can't see you wearing a black shirt with Liberty Operations written over the pocket, Mr. Menden."

Holt sat back with a contained smile, and a glance for John, then his daughter. "We'll resume that conversation after we visit

Little Saigon tonight. After you see what we can do. Ah—my bride has arrived!"

Through the opened sliding door rolled Carolyn, in her wheelchair, guided by Joni, the night nurse. She was dressed in a baby blue flannel blouse with a high Victorian neck, her legs covered by a blue cotton blanket. Her face and hair were done carefully. They vibrated as her chair wheels passed over the flagstone of the patio. Then her face offered up a big smile when she saw her husband, who was standing now and moving toward her as Joni withdrew to the house.

John watched them embrace. Carolyn's arms were outstretched, wrapping around Holt's neck. Holt leaned down and gathered her close. They kissed each other on the cheeks several times, then once on the lips. They looked to him like mother and son. When Carolyn sat back she arranged her hair with both hands, still smiling at her husband.

"You look wonderful tonight, honey," he said.

"I feel like a million dollars. Oh, Janice!"

"Momma!" Valerie swept over and kissed her mother. "Two million at least, Mom. I love that new blouse."

Fargo had lined up behind Valerie, his posture and expression purely obligatory. With his back to Holt, he stared frankly at Valerie's butt as she bent over her mother, then looked at John. When it was his turn he offered his hand and told Carolyn she lived in a family of skinflints, hiking up her looks to a cool billion.

"She's not being auctioned," said Valerie.

"I call them as I see them," said Fargo.

"Smack your way into the family," said Sexton.

"Patrick! My Patrick!"

Carolyn grabbed her wheels and thrust the chair forward, nearly spilling off the first level of the patio before John caught one tire with his foot. He smiled down uneasily, then glanced at Holt. Holt nodded.

"Hello, Carolyn."

"I got your letter."

"That's good." He looked at Holt again, who held his stare, then at Valerie, who looked away.

"Did you win last week?"

"No game, actually. Had the week off."

"It seems like ages since I've seen you. How long has it been, Pat?"

Sexton's jaw dropped.

John looked over to Holt, who interceded.

"You saw him last week, Honey."

"We went shopping, didn't we?"

"That was it," said Holt, a sudden exhaustion behind his voice. "Val, arrange your mum here. I'm going to make a fresh round of drinks. John, come with me."

Carolyn smiled at John as he walked past her. "He's calling you John, now?"

"Everybody is, Carolyn."

"Kiss your Mumsey?"

He leaned over and kissed her smartly on the cheek.

Holt took his arm as they headed inside to the bar. Holt motioned Joni to join the party on the patio. When she had gone, Holt said, "I'm sorry about this, but play along. By dinnertime she'll think you're Robert Goulet or Sandy Koufax, or a kid named Deke. It doesn't fucking matter what you do."

But after the dinner was over, Carolyn was still calling him Patrick, still bringing up an assortment of memories that, John gathered, were not altogether fabricated. She and Pat at the beach. She and Pat working on multiplication. She and Pat driving to Tijuana one day to see a bullfight, from which young Patrick had stormed out, sickened. He nodded along, a hollow smile plastered to his face, his own memories zig-zagging back and forth from Rebecca to Snakey to Valerie to Joshua Weinstein. With each sip of Scotch the fragments seemed to weld closer together, threatening to become one solid, unpassable gallstone of memory. He looked at Holt and Fargo, smile locked in place, wishing he could just stand up now, beat each to a bloody pulp and call in the cavalry. I didn't hire on to become a crazy lady's dead son, he thought. Poor girl.

"Excuse me," he said, then got up and went into the kitchen. He found a tall glass, pulled out the third drawer right of the fridge with his toe and peered down into it as he held the glass under the ice dispenser. On top of the neatly folded kitchen towels was a video cassette in a plastic case. He glanced outside. Only Valerie was looking in his direction, all other attention was drawn to Carolyn. With the glass still pressed to the noisy ice dispenser, John bent down, whisked the cassette into the pocket of his coat and stood again, nudging shut the drawer. Valerie had turned away. He filled the glass with water and carried it back outside.

After the dessert was served, Carolyn motioned Joni over, then whispered in her ear. Joni looked at her askance, but obeyed Carolyn's dismissing wave. The nurse went upstairs and returned with a cane.

The conversation ended and a silence crept over the dinner table.

"I feel just great tonight," Carolyn announced. "Seeing Patrick makes me feel young again."

"Don't get carried away, hon," said Holt.

"A few small steps for womankind," said Carolyn.

"May I help?" he asked, pushing back his chair.

"You may stay right where you are. I'll walk these four steps to Patrick on my own. Patrick, rise."

"Mrs. Holt," said Fargo, "you haven't walked in six months. Remember last time?"

"Put a lid on it, Lane," snapped Valerie.

Carolyn smiled. "Patrick, *rise*."

John stood.

Holt cast a warning glance at Joni, who nodded and moved up close to the wheelchair. The nurse removed the blanket from Carolyn's lap, locked each tire in place, then knelt down and set Carolyn's apparently lifeless shoes on the pavers. Carolyn scrunched forward on the seat, then set the four rubber-tipped legs of the quad cane down on the patio in front of her. She cleared her throat. Valerie quietly moved behind her.

"Well, I'd say the old feet feel good, but they don't feel at all."

"Get your balance first, Mom."

"I've got that, Val. Ready . . . now . . . okay . . . forward *ho*."

Carolyn Holt's face went red. Her hands—on the cane handle—went white. Her entire body shivered and her dark eyes focused somewhere in space before her. She lifted up, perhaps one inch, then settled back to her seat again with a sigh. She smiled to herself. She was breathing quickly.

"Nice try, Mom. Damn nice try."

"*Whew!* What was it that McMurphy said in *Cuckoo's Nest?* Warming up? Just *warming* up? Well, that's me."

Then she gathered herself to the end of the seat again and her eyes locked into space in front of her and her cheeks exploded with color and her hands whitened against the cane handle again and a hissing exhale escaped her mouth as her body lifted from the seat, then lifted more, and she froze there, bent forward like a swimmer prepared to start, all her weight resting on the four small cane feet that now wobbled greatly upon the patio. Her legs quaked. Her arms trembled. And slowly she unfurled herself, like the stem of a new flower. Her legs swayed, then steadied; her torso swayed, then steadied; her head swayed, then steadied as she lifted the ferocious concentration of her gaze from some private point in space to the speechless face of John Menden.

He was surprised how tall she was. And even with the sedentary months in bed weighing her down, he saw that her frame was once both strong and fine. Composed now, Carolyn looked at him and shook back her hair, as a model might before a stroll down the runway. She exhaled.

Her right foot moved up, forward, then down. An inch maybe, John thought. One whole inch.

Then her left.

Her eyes widened, never leaving John. And in spite of the intensity of her gaze and the rigid determination of her face, the corners of her mouth quivered upward—just slightly—in the most tenuous and fragile of grins.

John was moved by her courage even more than by her damage. Each confronted him from the single spirit of Carolyn Holt, the battling twins of her being. Each was so clear and strong, so contradictory and unmistakable. The courage fought the damage; the damage fought the courage. He had never seen these essential polarities of the living locked in such close contest. With his heart he willed her forward. With his feet he took two steps toward her, matching her own.

Then Carolyn focused her willpower again.

Foot up, out and down. Another inch.

Foot up, out and down. Another.

Four steps.

She smiled at him before collapsing, like a telescope, into herself. Valerie and Joni caught and straightened her, then eased her back into the chair. Through the sweat running down her face and her rapid breathing, her dark eyes still bore into John's.

The applause rang clear and dry against the night. Valerie leaned over and hugged her. Joni hugged her, too. Fargo shook her hand, taking it off her lap himself because Carolyn was too dazed to understand why he was standing there. Then John took the hand, just released by Fargo and still airbound, and kissed the back of it. Carolyn's eyes relaxed as she studied him.

"Welcome home, son."

The only thing he could think of to say was, "Nice to be here."

He glanced at Valerie, who beheld him with an expression he could not decipher.

When John finally turned to Vann Holt, all he saw was an empty chair.

A moment later he heard the loud roar of an engine starting down on the helipad, then the accelerating swoosh of blades moving through air.

Holt appeared, apparition-like in the near darkness of the driveway, waving John toward him. Then he vanished back toward the blurred propellor of the chopper.

"Go," said Valerie. "He wants you."

"Hey, John-Boy," said Fargo, his eyes glittering deep within the twin caves of his dark sockets. "I found Snakey's tape recorder in his room. It's a little log of what he was doing before he disappeared."

John looked from the chopper to Valerie, then Fargo. "Then maybe that's where you ought to be looking."

"Right, John-Boy. Good luck with Holt. Shoot straight. Be impressive."

"Hey John," said Sexton. "I'll give you a call tomorrow. We should talk."

CHAPTER
TWENTY-NINE

Holt, ensconced within the Plexiglas cockpit of the Hughes 500, watched John Menden trot a radius through the helipad circle and climb aboard the craft. A moment later Holt felt the stomach-dropping thrust generated by the powerful engine. He loved it. He stayed low over the hills until he neared the freeway, then hoisted the craft up into an October night of breeze-polished stars.

"Need some milk?" his passenger asked.

Holt was in no mood for laconic humor, John's or anyone else's. He looked over at him, then back to the red ribbon of I-5 taillights winding out below. He banked the chopper hard to the left, very hard, which pushed his shoulders against the seat back, then corrected hard right and down, gunning the throttle almost all the way, which made his head feel like it could float off his neck. The helicopter dove like a hawk. What strong joy it was to fly a chopper when he was high on Scotch. But not too high. He'd had three doubles with plenty of ice, and a big dinner. Just right for a visit to the birthplace of it all, he thought. He looked at John, thought again of his son, then turned away.

"Little Saigon, Mr. Holt?"

"We're making a stop first."

Holt flew the chopper north, over Santa Ana, then descended in a controlled dive so steep that John, to his right, braced one hand on the instrument panel and the other against his window. Holt felt as if his heart had shot through the bottom of the craft to plummet down on its own. Using a triangulation of his usual landmarks—Charles Keating's defunct Lincoln Savings Bank on 17th Street, the darkened campus of Santa Ana Junior College, and a water tower that declared this as the "All American City"—Holt easily spotted the bright yellow logo of the fast food restaurant. Even so, the picture was a little blurred, not what it would have been only a year ago. He refused to think about his eyes. Instead, he thought about the rage he was beginning to feel, and the wonderful clarity he would feel after the rage passed. Yes, he thought, if I can make it through the Red Zone then things will become clear. He eased his fabulous rate of descent and spiraled gently down toward the building. The deceleration brought his heart back on board, returning it to his chest.

"Your gut still with you?" he asked.

"Somewhere in there."

"This is it."

Holt looked inquiringly into John's face. The young man had his usual placid expression, but the pupils of his eyes were big. Over the days, Holt had decided that John's calm was one of intelligence rather than dullness. And he thinks I'm half crazy, thought Holt, maybe more than that.

He found room in the parking lot—easy, this late—and planted the Hughes on the ground. Looking through the cockpit glass and seeing the familiar walkway leading to the entrance, the red handrail, the planter alongside it filled with daisies, the cheery yellows and reds of the building, the dancing burger of the logo, the windows filled with posters of discounted combos, Holt felt all the familiar hatred come rushing back into his soul. Easy now.

He told John to come with him.

He walked up the ramp, pushed open the door and stepped inside. He looked first to his left at the scattered faces in the dining area, the sea of bright yellow tables with swiveling red chairs, and the immense trash cans paired in each corner. He stared directly into the face of anyone who looked at him, but almost no one did. Inside his face, his eyes felt warm—almost hot—and he could feel the heat in them touch every face they settled on. He saw mostly Latinos. The usual.

"Look around you, John. This is our republic. View it."

"Yes."

"The place was full of people that day—the same kind of

people you see here right now. Carolyn and Patrick sat there, by the window."

When Holt pointed, the two girls sitting there looked at him, then down, then back at each other. Holt, through his building fury, was pleased. His eyeballs felt extra warm.

He motioned John to come stand beside him. He spoke with clarity and force.

"The shooter was just a kid, born here. He actually had a brain. Did a year at a local JC, worked on the school paper. Wrote some articles with lots of exclamation points about soft flabby white people occupying a California that rightfully belongs to his people. *La Raza*—The Race. He built a little following. Of losers mostly, as those who follow tend to be. The reason he gunned down my wife and son was because his aunt claimed that Patrick had raped her. That was a preposterous lie, fed and fattened by the media. The murder also lent some credibility to his politics. Politics and hatred, John—bad mix. They were just finishing their lunch. Patrick saw it coming and tried to get between the bullets and his mother. He was successful. The bullet that stopped in Carolyn's brain went through Pat's neck first. It was a mortal bullet, but the other three he took were, too. A .32 slug glances around a little before it goes through. They have a relatively low velocity."

With every sentence of his history, Holt felt his anger heating up, approaching boil. And the anger brought him a little closer to Clarity. But before he felt Clarity, Holt knew he would have to go through the Red Zone.

He watched the few faces that had been confronting him now turn away. A group of girls twittered. Mothers tried to hush their babies, tried to keep their toddlers from eating the wrappers on their food. The girls started putting on makeup.

At times like this he just wanted to take out a good submachine gun and kill them all, but Holt knew the rage would pass into something more rational, and more effective.

In a far corner sat four gangsters, blue bandanas and chinos, dark flannels and black work boots. Holt stared at them for a long beat, guessing their ages: fourteen or fifteen, maybe. He saw three of them conferring—over his presence, likely—while one returned his gaze.

"This way, John."

He walked to the table and stood over it, sliding his right

hand in his coat pocket. It was always good to let these people wonder, he thought. By the time he stopped walking, he had entered the Red Zone, where everybody he looked at was outlined in a visible aura of warm infared. He could actually see it. It was pink more than red, really, and it wasn't bright and solid like a rod of neon but muted and wavering, like a pink mirage surrounding each human shape.

Then he felt the very faint, first inkling of Clarity, an icy, intelligent spot way back in his thoughts. He knew it was still a long distance away. He knew it would come eventually, though, piercing through the Red Zone like a beam of light through fog. He craved Clarity and disliked the anger of the Red Zone. He didn't trust it. Anger was red and it made his heart race and his hands shake, and made him want to do rash things. It made him feel the cells that were reproducing without control inside him. But Clarity brought steadfastness to his vision and his limbs. Clarity allowed his eyes to see and his mind to work. You could ride Clarity, like a good machine, through thickets of confusion and rage, until you came out on the other side, and then you could see—really *see*—what you had to do.

"Look at these things," he said to John, nodding down at the boys.

When Holt looked at him, John's hands were folded before him like a pastor beginning a sermon. His back was straight and his clear gray eyes—so much like Holt's own used to be—beheld unblinkingly the four boys sitting in the booth before them. John was outlined in a warm pink aura.

So were the four young men in the booth. It felt strange to Holt to confront people so powerless yet so harmful. As a boy, he had killed rattlesnakes by cracking them by the tail like whips. He was smart enough to do this only in early spring or late fall, when the reptiles were chilled and slow. It fascinated him that something could be deadly, yet helpless. Later, at the Bureau, the same wonderment came to him when he made his first arrests. With very few exceptions, the crooks were afraid, confused and overmatched. But they could kill you, too. That was what kept your blood warm, your eyes keen and your hand steady. Any one of those nervous little men might be the one to shoot you dead with a cheap little gun. Many years later, when Holt began to lose respect for his quarry, he knew he had become vulnerable. This was what led him to the more sophisticated game—the sub-

versives, the assassins, the terrorists—because they were mani-
festly dangerous and they engaged his fear. As he gazed down at
this tiny gang unit before him, at the clench-jawed little thing
they called a leader, Holt thought: this is deadly vermin. Don't
forget it.

Deadly, pathetic and outlined in red. One option, he thought
again, is just to kill them all and let God sort them out.

Into Holt's mind now flashed the image of his wife laboring
four steps across the patio. He blinked slowly, leaving his eyes
closed for just a moment so that he could see Carolyn without a
red halo on her. And his memory took another leap back, but a
much deeper one this time, and it landed Vann Holt in a darkened bedroom many years ago with his wife up close beside him
and their mouths locked together. He could smell her breath.

Then he opened his eyes and turned to John. "She was perfect for a while."

Holt shook the vision from his head, then focused on the
boys in the booth. There they were, little lapsed Catholics wearing red halos. Truculent bastards, he thought, what do they have,
maybe twenty-five mustache hairs each? Boys.

"Behold," he said. "Uneducated, barely literate. Lazy for the
most part, due to the Indian blood. Given to binge drinking to
replicate the old rites of peyote and mescaline. But a sixer of malt
liquor doesn't give you interesting visions. Just gives you a bad
mood. No future to speak of for these guys. They've never seen
anybody from their streets really make it. What do they have to
go on? Television? Isn't that right, boys?"

"We make it out if we want, man," said the leader. "We got
roots and we got family here. We take care of each other. We die
for each other, if we have to. What're you anyway, whitebread
gringo shitface, a fuckin' philosopher?"

Holt looked at John. Still in a red halo. A little more red in
it, maybe. But he was pleased to see the impassive expression on
John's face, and the alertness of his eyes. He might be getting
this, Holt thought: it actually might get through to him. He's
capable of understanding.

"And that right there, what he just said, is the shame of it
all," continued Holt. "See, John, these guys have the warrior's
spirit inside of them. Most boys do—twelve to twenty-five or so.
They're full of testosterone, bravery, idealism and anger. Perfect
warrior material. He's not kidding—they'll die for each other. Do

it all the time. Parties. Weddings. Funerals. Any event you can drive past in a car and pop some rounds at. But there's the rub. Parties aren't wars and drive-bys are for cowards. No war, no warrior. What you've got is a mean little creep with a flannel shirt. A goddamned blue rag wrapped around his puny head. It's a waste. And it's a shame and it killed my boy and wrecked my wife."

With this, Holt looked down at the boys again. "You remember shooting my wife and boy?"

"We didn't shoot nobody, man. That was Ruiz and Ruiz disappear."

"But there's some Ruiz in all of you. That's the part I'm talking to. I'm in your face right now because that kid was my son and that woman was my woman. Because I don't want you to forget what I look like. I want you to understand something, boys. I'm watching you. My men are watching you. We know you. We're here, even when you don't see us. We would have killed you all a long time ago if I thought it would do any good. But I haven't. It's not because I've forgiven you, or ever will. Not because you don't deserve to die. It's because there are too many of you and I'd have to kill you all. Don't have the time or the bullets for that. If I did, well, you'd be bleeding on that floor right now, like Patrick did after you shot him. Like my wife did. So don't ever think you got away with it. You didn't get away with anything. I've got your numbers. I'll call them in on the day I choose to. I'm all over you. Each and every one of you. I'm in the air, man. I'm the badass gringo ghost and you can't get rid of me. I'm everywhere. This is my turf. My blood is on it."

Holt raised his right hand and aimed his forefinger into the face of one of the boys. The kid had paled.

"Whose turf is this, son?"

"It's yours."

With Holt's finger-barrel aimed between their eyes, the next two agreed.

Holt saved the leader until last. "Whose turf are you on, homie?"

"This here is my fuckin' turf, *pendejo*."

Holt hooked the leader in the nose with two fingers. The boy yelped, then struggled upward out of his seat, scrambled across the table through the junk food and the ketchup, spilling drinks with his heavy shoes, walking on air it seemed as Holt forked his head up high and started across the room. Holt looked like a ventriloquist with his dummy. The boy dangled after him, shoes just barely touching the ground. The kid's piece clattered to the floor as he clawed at Holt's upraised hand, to no effect whatsoever. The blood ran down Holt's arm and dripped off his elbow. At the door Holt let him down, blocked the kid's wild round-house with one hand, then snapped a kick to the chest that sent the leader reeling backwards faster than his heels could go, finally sprawling him over an unoccupied table. Holt kicked away the gun, walked over, yanked off the kid's bandana and wiped his bloody hand and forearm with it.

"Whose turf are you on?" he asked.

"Yours, man. Your fuckin' turf."

"Remember that. The next time someone with blond hair and blue eyes wants to have lunch in here, you remember that."

He looked around the restaurant one last time before turning to leave. An ocean of bright red seats and yellow tables, a few desultory faces staring back at him, the brightly clad employees behind the aluminum counter dully agog—and all of it outlined in pulsing red.

His heart was beating hard and his breathing was fast and shallow.

They don't understand, he thought.

"Do you?"

John's expression was blank. Maybe he isn't the man we need, thought Holt. Maybe it was too much to expect.

"Do I what, sir?"

"*Do you understand?*"

"Yes. Absolutely."

CHAPTER

THIRTY

Holt guided the chopper across the dark blanket of the night. He felt better now that he had seen the place where Pat had died, because he had come through the Red Zone and found Clarity. It was like having an orgasm of fury instead of an orgasm of pleasure.

Now the control stick felt like an extension of his body and his body felt like an extension of his mind. To him the Hughes seemed a tiny solar system under his control.

My control.

"What were you trying to accomplish?" asked John.

Holt looked over at him, pleased by his direct, if naive, questions. Sometimes, John seemed so ready to be guided. Maybe he *is* what I need.

"Clear my head. I live pissed off twenty-four hours a day. The only time I can get through it to the other side is when I'm right there where it happened. Or when I'm planning justice. Like getting back on the horse that's thrown me, when I go to where Pat died. The fury boils over into something else."

"Peace?"

"Oh, Christ no. Lucidity. Clarity. Vision. A clean sightline to what I need to do."

John seemed to think about this. Holt watched him stare out the window, then glance over toward him.

"Are you planning some justice, Mr. Holt?"

"Of course I am. It's my work. I do it every day. You'll see."

"Ever think of vengeance?"

Holt looked at him, pleased again that John was neither as innocent nor obtuse as he could seem.

"Hourly."

Holt could feel the silence forming a question, and he knew what the question was. Once you got John going in a certain direction, he took things all the way. Holt liked that. He liked the way John had tried his best to find the bikers that day in Anza, after they'd torched his home. Follow-through, he thought, one of my favorite qualities in a man.

"No," said Holt. "I did not disappear Ruiz. I never had the chance to. Would have."

"Really?"

"Really. Tried to find him, actually. All of Liberty Ops did. Cops did. Everybody did. No Ruiz. Think he went back to Mexico. I've got some people down there."

"And if you find him?"

"Justice requires his life. So does vengeance. Take your pick."

"What's yours?"

"None needed. Get to the victims of any bad crime, you'll find the same thing. Justice is the law of the state. Vengeance the law of men. Dovetail, sometimes."

"I didn't mean to pry. I just remember the questions you asked me about Jillian."

Holt banked up and away again, watching the lights of the city grow smaller as he climbed up into the darkness. And with every foot he rose in elevation, Holt could feel the Clarity inside, and could enjoy the diminishing strength of his body, could see what he must do. Up here, above the world, was the only place you could really understand. You needed perspective for vision. Patrick was gone. Carolyn was a thousand miles away, it seemed. From here, removed from what had happened to them, untethered to the earth on a clear October night, he could feel the influence of heaven and hell so clearly. He looked over at John Menden—this simple, and in many ways ignorant young man— and felt even more strongly that John was a gift from God. He has been sent to us, thought Holt. A son for Carolyn, a brother for Valerie, a tool for justice. Dropped like manna into the Anza desert.

"So, are you planning justice for what happened to Patrick?

More than what just happened back there? More than letting your people look for Ruiz in Mexico?"

Holt turned and bore into John Menden's eyes with his own. "Justice is larger than Ruiz."

"What can you do, then?"

"Silence, young man. Look. Listen."

They were hovering above the city of Orange now. Holt dipped the chopper down low and hit a search light that threw a wide white beam onto the street. This particular downtown spot always made him just a little sick.

"See the street? Right down there, just in front of that store, that's where they parked to go buy their drugs."

"Who did?"

"The people with the infant in their car, and the pet rat. Of course, the couple got stoned, came back to the car and passed out. They slept it off. Rat ate the baby. Three hundred bites. Bled to death. Didn't hear it crying they were so loaded."

"I remember the stories," said John.

Holt steadied the chopper in place, fastening the light beam to the curbside where the car had been parked.

"That was a perfect story, John. Gave everyone on earth someone to hate. Sentimental. Revolting. Plus the couple was white. Media couldn't have lavished so much horror on a Black couple, Latins, Asians. Important to crucify the whites when they can. Nourishes the mobs they help create."

"Is that what happened to Patrick?"

"God, yes. Ruiz said Patrick raped his aunt. Aunt said so, too, then said she wasn't sure it was Pat, then told Susan Baum that she was positive. I got the Sheriff's transcripts and reports from a friend in the department. Teresa Descanso's the aunt. Said she told Ruiz she *thought* Patrick was the man who'd raped her. Wasn't quite sure it was Pat, really. But it was enough for Ruiz in the heat of the moment. Hates gringos anyway. All tied to his political thinking. Plus his aunt was probably scared shitless, and he's a self-proclaimed reincarnated Aztec warrior or some such thing. Naturally, he's got a gun. Anyway, Teresa Descanso wasn't really sure it was Pat who raped her until Susan Baum got her to say so in the *Journal*. That was during the trial. Made sensational copy. White Mormon son of FBI man, raping poor immigrant women in the barrio. One of Descanso's friends came out and said Pat had raped *her*, too. Baum had a field day with that one, figured in a whole backlist of unsolveds. It was open season on Pat. Ruiz took his life and Baum took his good name."

Holt rotated the chopper over the street, then rose up again over the suburb and bore west.

"I hate Ruiz for what he did, but I respect his action," said Holt. "He acted on faulty information. But he acted honestly. It was a public statement. But I loathe Susan Baum. All she did was tell lies for money. That I do not respect. It's the purest distillation of the cancer that's eating this republic. It's everything that will take us down. Disregard for the truth. Slavish devotion to profit. Manipulation of people less sophisticated for advancement of self. Lie upon falsehood upon deceit. Utter destruction of a man's honor, name and reputation. All for entertainment. All to frighten a people already addled by fear. Fear is what sells now. Even better than sex. It's for every age. Every color, every faith and creed. Make them afraid and you can profit from them. They'll pay you to do it. In a just world, John, Ruiz would die for his acts, and Susan Baum would be forced into a life of community service. Untell all the lies. Correct all the errors. Repay all the profits. Personally speak to every person who ever read one of her articles and admit to them that she deceived them. Shine a light where she let darkness in. Whisper the truth where all her lies have festered and grown and rotted and stunk to highest heaven. No wonder God doesn't walk the earth anymore. Can't stand the smell."

He sped into Santa Ana and dropped down toward a darkened, tree-lined street, then used the spotlight to beam a rather quaint, yellow house. "Two months ago, at a party in that house, the gangs went at it. Three dead—one of them a boy of eleven. Turns out the boy was the third brother in a family that had already lost the other two to gang wars. Now the mother lives alone in that yellow house. Husband ran out two years ago. Mexicans."

He sped to Fullerton and hovered over the back yard of a handsome suburban home, illuminating the grass with the spotlight. "Three high school boys murdered their friend right down there—beat him to death with shovels and suffocated him. Poured bleach down his throat. They buried him about a foot down. The ringleader blamed it on Camus' *The Stranger*, which he'd read not long before the murder. Chinese."

He sped over Westminster, lowered the chopper over Bolsa

and followed the lights of Little Saigon down the avenue. "Down there at the newspaper office they set an editor on fire because they didn't like his politics. Across the street, at the noodle shop, two girls died in a shootout between rival home invaders. Right down there, at the corner where the light's red, an elderly man was beaten to death one evening, but nothing was taken from him. Politics again. That's the name of the game down there in Little Saigon. They're different than us, John. Vietnamese."

He sped south again, staying low into Mission Viejo. "Down on one of those little streets—they all look the same to me—was where the Nightstalker took two of his victims. Raped the woman, shot the man in the head. Ramirez—a Mexican."

Then south and west to San Clemente, hovering near the pier, spotlighting a narrow road leading down to a parking lot. "That's where a tough Mex gang speared a seventeen-year old surfer in the head with a sharpened paint roller. He died in the hospital a little while later."

Holt ran the spotlight across the cars in the lot, looking down from the port window of the Hughes. "I find these places from newspaper articles. I come out to the ones I feel might have resonance for me. Because when you get right down to them, when you put your feet on the ground where these things happened, you understand how ordinary it is. They don't happen in cursed places. They don't happen in certain parts of the country where you expect it. When you stand down in that parking lot and look around you—like I have a half dozen times—you see that things like this can happen anywhere. It's in the fabric now. As I told you before, these interlopers don't understand the value of where they are. They should not be here. But this is our country, our world. My years at the Bureau did nothing to change it—in fact, it got worse. But I refuse to go through my life up on Liberty Ridge and ignore it. I'm not immune. Patrick and Carolyn proved that to me. They're all around us now, John. The killers and the fools, the rapists and the morons, the vicious, the stupid, the ignorant and the murderous, the desperate and the furious. This is our context now. And that is why I started Liberty Operations. I'm trying to stanch the fear. Make people feel safe from each other. Give people the freedom of security. When a family buys protection from Liberty Operations, they get protection. They get consultation on home alarm systems, safes, firearms defense if they want it, tear gas certification, manual self-defense. They get threat assessment. They get mirrors to check their cars for bombs, scanners to check their mail. They can get training for their dogs. They can get scramblers and tape recorders for their phones. They can get training to use any self-defense gadget on earth, and the gadget, too. They get armed response from the Holt Men. They get follow-up investigations if the cops don't make an arrest. They get preemptive action, preventive strikes, protective aggression. They can even get extra-legal satisfaction, once known as vengeance, John. Expensive, but I provide it. They get two-thousand strong, healthy, capable Holt Men on the streets twenty-four hours of every day. Men who observe. Men who protect. Men who are on their side. Holt Men. The new centurions. Guardians of freedom. Best men in the world."

Holt spun the chopper back around to the north and accelerated through the darkness. He was thankful again that the Hughes was strong as ever, because he was not. Fading, he thought, but not faded; going but not gone. The orange and black machine supplied the strength that was draining from his body every hour of every day.

Rage on.

"Reach behind you," he said.

John found the bundle and unwrapped it on his lap.

"Put the vest on under your coat. Don't fire that forty-five unless it's to save your life."

Holt smiled at John's puzzled look.

"Let's go to work," he said.

CHAPTER
THIRTY-ONE

He set the Hughes down in a small vacant field on Bolsa, not far from Little Saigon. It was private property and he knew the owner, knew his chopper would be safe there behind the chain link fence with the concertina wire on top and the patrolling Dobermans the owner would release when they were off the lot.

He saw the two command and control vans—orange and black, clean and waxed to a finish that reflected the streetlights along the avenue—waiting on the street at the far end of the lot. He jogged across the barren dirt, waving John toward the vans. The young man looked perplexed but game. Holt could feel his heart beating evenly in his chest, and a growing affection for his newest apostle, whose lanky body and long coat moved through the darkness behind him.

He saw four of his lieutenants standing outside the vehicles, arms crossed, waiting for him. There stands justice, he thought: Kettering, Stanton, Summers and Alvis. The best of the best. Holt Men. *The Men.* They were in standard patrol uniform—black pants and boots, short-sleeved button-down black shirts over Kevlar vests, bold orange neckties knotted in half-windsors and tucked into the shirts just below the third button. Each wore the sidearm they were licensed to carry on the job, and the hip radio, ammunition belt, flashlight and handcuffs.

Holt's eyes were strong now and Clarity informed every movement of his body, every thought that issued from his mind. He slipped into the Kevlar vest offered by Summers. He cinched the shoulder holster over it, slid out the .45 Colt Gold Cup with which he was certifiably lethal, checked the clip, jacked a round into the chamber, safed it and set it back into the leather.

"What's the word from Terry?" he asked. Terry, the ersatz fence, Terry the mole, Terry the confidant of the Bolsa Cobra Boys who were the mark tonight.

"Terry says we're on," said Alvis. "Sometime after midnight. Six of them."

"How's the family doing?"

"The girls are with friends. Mr. and Mrs. were having dinner when we left. They're scared and they're laughing a lot."

"Good," said Holt. "This is John Menden. Friend of the family. Good guy. May be working with us in the future."

The Men shook hands with John.

"Nice work, what you did out in Anza," offered Stanton.

John thanked him.

Holt could sense that they were mildly surprised, certainly wondering about Fargo, but saw no need to explain. There's plenty of room in the world for good Men, he thought. Someday there was bound to be a changing of the guard.

He climbed into the first van, motioning John to follow. Summers drove and Alvis sat in the back with John. Holt watched the bright lights of Little Saigon pass by on either side, saw the noodle shops and cafes, the empty parking lots littered with flyers, the steel gratings behind the shop windows, the young people still out walking. He turned and spoke to John:

"Our clients are the Vu-Minh family. He's a dentist; she's a lawyer. Been in the country since 1974. Two daughters. Bright and beautiful. The Bolsa Cobras picked them for obvious reasons—nice house, plenty of income. Upper middle class and unsuspecting. We've got a man close to them. Now, we're going to let them move in, start their thing, then kick their fucking butts."

"How many men will you use?"

"Six, including you, inside. Five pursuit vehicles with two men each, and the two vans, which are about to get fresh crews. One helicopter, in case things fall apart. Stay close to me and do what I say. Don't do anything else. Clear?"

"Yes, sir."

They pulled along the curb ten minutes later. The house was in an older suburban neighborhood shaded by jacaranda trees that threw dark profiles against a darker sky. Holt looked up to

the stars beaming in the cloudless night. He walked up the driveway toward the house. He saw two more of his Men coming
from the front door, followed by Mr. and Mrs. Vu-Minh. New
Men, he noted: Rodgers and Mason. He stopped as they approached, but said little more than a short hello to Allen and
Joan Vu-Minh. Stanton had already told them what would happen, and this was no time for elaborate Asian pleasantries.

He stood in the doorway of the home and watched the two
command and control vans slide off toward the avenue. He
closed the door and locked it. He watched Kettering place the
long canvas bag on the carpet and distribute the four semi-auto-
matic shotguns, keeping one for himself. He smelled the sweet
aroma of mint and noted the plate of spring rolls left by Joan Vu-
Minh on the living room coffee table. A pot of tea and six small
cups sat beside them. He noted the lacquer paintings on the
walls—romanticized treatments of pre-war Saigon, pastoral
scenes from the Vietnamese countryside. The furniture was modest and tasteful, with Asian accents incorporated into Western
design.

The home brought contradictory feelings to Holt, a state of
mind with which he was never comfortable. It was obvious that
Vietnam needed people like Allen and Joan Vu-Minh more than
the United States did. The land needed its people and the people
their land. It was also possible that the Vu-Minhs would have
been persecuted—perhaps executed—if they had stayed behind
after the fall. More to the point, they were citizens of the republic
now and they deserved justice.

He dispatched Summers, Stanton, Alvis and Kettering to
their positions: two in one of the girl's bedrooms and two in the
other.

He took John into the living room, made sure the drapes on
the windows were closed, then turned off all the lights except one
in the kitchen. In the faint houselight he motioned John, then
moved down a hallway and into the Vu-Minhs' master bedroom.
He turned on a lamp and moved two chairs against the far wall,
beside the light switch, facing the door. He turned off the lamp
and moved in darkness to the chairs. He sat and flipped the light
switch on and off three times.

"Sit next to me," he ordered John. "Listen. The Bolsa Cobras have a little different routine from other Vietnamese home
invaders. They don't like daylight hours. The last three jobs they

pulled were done around two a.m. They pick a doorlock—usually the front door—let themselves in and catch the victims sleeping. Tie them up at gunpoint. Take them into a bathroom, fill the tub and dunk the woman's head until the man tells them where the cash and jewelry are. If the man won't tell, they dunk him and work the wife. If she won't tell, they ransack the place. They haven't hit families with kids, yet. They like older people, people with savings. You know the Vietnamese don't trust cash and don't trust banks, so they keep lots of Krugerrands and jewelry. Keep it at home. They also don't trust the law. Allen and Joan are known to have money. They do charity work. They drive expensive cars. They make the papers. So the Bolsa Cobras have decided to branch out and try a younger family with kids. They usually work in pairs. They've bulked up to six for this one. They'll be full of adrenaline. Nervy. Quick."

"Will they shoot when they see us instead of a sleeping couple?"

"They won't know what hit them."

Holt sat in the darkness and listened to the blood moving through his body. He tried to feel the bad cells replicating but he could not. His eyes were strong again—they were always strong when he was doing justice—and even in the dark it was easy to become familiar with the room. He could smell Mrs. Vu-Minh's perfume mixed with the fresh odor of soap that moved in from the bath. He thought about those early years with Carolyn, when he'd graduated from law school and entered the Bureau. Just them in the little apartment in McLean, the Bureau training programs, the long Sunday dinners at the Fish Market with some of the other trainees. His favor in the eyes of Walker Frazee, who brought him along and sent him west as soon as he could because Frazee was a Mormon and a family man too and he knew how badly Holt wanted to be back in the land that had bred him. Holt chose not to think of his excommunication when he renounced the church those many years later, when Patrick's death had turned loose all that was furious and secular and ungodly inside him, when he had been unable to sense the presence of God anywhere upon the earth, in any form. Holt did not think of that. Instead, he thought of Patrick's birth and the overwhelming, unforeseeable pride he felt when he first took Pat's little body into his arms. He thought of the way that Carolyn looked when she was feeding their infant son, her hair up and her robe open around her breast and the aura of wisdom that had surrounded her ever since she had become a mother. It was as if she had connected with something inside her that he—and even Carolyn herself—had never known was there. He thought of Pat's first steps, the funny little outfits Carolyn always got for him, the evolution of the boy's smile from gummy toothlessness to the manly assurance of Patrick, age twenty-two, graduating from college. He thought of Valerie's premature birth, the natural debut of her headstrong personality. He pictured her with the little ribbon taped to her head at Patrick's insistence because she was born bald and Pat thought a girl needed a ribbon, hair or not. He remembered the time at the breakfast table one Saturday when Valerie announced that Pat had dreamed the night before about driving a car and she knew this because she had been in the back seat. He could see her shooting her first round of trap at age six—she knocked down four—and how proud he was that she stood like him on the trap range, brought her gun up like he did, called for the bird like he did, held her gun at rest like he did, set her empties back into the ammo pouch like he did. He remembered her coming down the stairs for her junior prom and how she seemed to contain enough life and beauty to animate a dozen young girls all at once. He thought of all these things and marveled that the world had stripped so much away but left him standing. He could feel the great fury that animated him in slumber, resting. He understood that he now had, in John, an avenue to Susan Baum. He could feel things beginning to end.

He looked at John in the darkness. The young man sat erect in the chair, his long coat parted to each side, his fedora placed squarely on his head, no angle, no comment implied. He was taller than Pat, and thinner, but John had the same strong profile and calm eyes of his son. He seemed so far away in his closeness: not blood but something akin to blood. Spirit, he thought? A kindred spirit? He wondered if he was imagining things for John that were foolish to imagine, if he was ascribing an inflated value to hope. He wondered, briefly, if perhaps there was a God who looked over the affairs of men, and had arranged John in his path as a sort of salvation. No, he decided. No.

"Did Jillian come back and talk to you after she died?"

John was quiet for a long beat. He didn't move. "I thought I heard her voice in the wind once, but it was just the wind."

"How did you know it was just the wind?"

"I listened hard."

"I read a lot after Pat died. Voices from the grave. Spirit communication. All that. I tried my best to be open. Keep my senses ready for him. Never really happened. I figured maybe he was talking to Carolyn. I was always tone deaf."

"Those ideas aren't for everybody, Mr. Holt. I don't think it's a measure of your soul, how much you think you hear the dead."

"Ever dream about her?"

"Oh, yes."

"Me too. Sometimes I'd wake up laughing. Or crying. Or screaming. He seemed so real, then."

"Maybe that was his way of talking to you."

"Anything's possible. Though I never took much heart in that banality."

"Me neither. What I wanted most was just one minute to see her again, to say good-bye."

Holt listened to a car pass by on the street outside. "That was a nice thing you did for Carolyn tonight." He shuddered, though, when he thought of her taking the four majestically pathetic steps.

"I'm not sure what to do."

"Let her call you Pat. No harm I can see."

"Just as long as . . . well . . . I don't disappoint her."

"She's never looked better. Since the bullet, I mean."

"Makes me feel dishonest."

"Small price."

"True."

"The thing I like best about these kind of stakeouts is really nailing the sons of bitches. Law enforcement, you can't set up a situation like this. There's no manpower for it. And the courts would murder you."

"How many have you done?"

"Two hundred and four."

Holt felt the telephone throb against his chest. He brought it out and listened. Carfax, one of the Holt Men assigned to the juniper hedge across the street, told him a car had passed once and was now about to pass again. Holt radioed Summers and Alvis.

"I think we're on," he said to John. He nodded to the window, where headlights gently illuminated the blinds in a moving, horizontal line.

He put the phone back in his pocket, took out his .45 and breathed deeply.

"Silence, son."

It was ten minutes later that the Bolsa Cobra Boys came through the front door. Holt could hear the pick inside the lock, the furtive anxiety of the picker, the impatience, then finally the tumble of the steel. When the door opened he could feel the change of pressure in the air. He could hear the shoes—sounding like so many—on the linoleum of the entryway, then the muffled sound of shoes on carpet, then the quickening report on the hallway tiles. Whispers. Answers. Whispers again. Suddenly the beam of a flashlight hit the far wall and they were in the room. Three, four, six. They filed in with a kind of organized hush and as the flashlight beam trailed along the walls toward him Holt stood, hit the light switch and extended his automatic straight toward the hand with the flashlight in it.

"Don't move," he said calmly.

Holt allowed his eyes to scan them all but focus on none. And, just as he thought, at least two of the kids were moving their guns toward him. He shot the hand that held the flashlight and the metal and bone and flesh exploded and the boy screamed. All six of them leaned back toward the door like sea grass swayed by a current but it was too late. Alvis blasted them from behind with two deafening roars from his shotgun—beach sand instead of lead, but painful inside of ten feet—and the whole contingent accordioned in upon itself while Kettering, Summers and Stanton leaped into the collapsing fray like rodeo cowboys. In less than twenty seconds the Holt Men had five pairs of hands wrenched behind five backs and cinched tight with lacerating plastic ties. Holt pulled the revolver off the kid with the splintered hand, then dragged him into the bathroom and lifted him into the tub so he wouldn't bleed on the carpet anymore. He gave the boy a bath towel and told him to wrap it up tight. Back in the bedroom he looked down at the five trussed gangsters and the five guns—a sawed-off shotgun and four automatics—that the Holt Men had kicked against the closet door. He looked at John, who still stood in front of his chair with the .45 dangling from his right hand and a look of bewilderment on his face.

Holt smiled at him. There were few moments more pleasurable in life than seeing the look on the face of someone who had just witnessed a Liberty Ops private interdiction action for the first time.

"Call the police and get an ambulance for the kid in there," he said to Stanton. "John, our part of this procedure is over. Let's go home now. Nice work, men."

He tossed the boy's revolver into the pile of firearms by the closet door and headed out with John behind him.

Ten minutes later they were back in the chopper, levitating through the star-studded early morning sky. Holt watched the lights of Little Saigon dissipate below them, then turned his gaze to John.

He took a long time to assess John Menden—his face and expression, his motives and fears, his capabilities for loyalty and betrayal. His weakness. He waited for these things to manifest. They always did, if you waited and knew how to listen. He could always feel them coming off of people—what kind of heft they had inside, what sense of follow-through they possessed. Whether or not they had bottom. He had always felt it coming off the people he worked with, the creeps he collared, the prosecutors he worked with, the defenders he answered—this silent and inadvertent confession of capacity. It was a glimpse of content.

They screamed south toward Liberty Ridge. "Smitten by my daughter, aren't you?"

John seemed to almost choke. He cleared his throat and looked at Holt with a dazed expression.

"Very much so, sir."

"Most beautiful thing left on earth. Cat got your tongue?"

"Just a little. I've never seen anything quite like that."

"Anza comes to mind."

"That was just a reaction. This was . . . surgical."

"We might have trouble with the kid I shot. Summers will stand in for me on that."

Holt stared for a moment into the eyes that looked so much like his own, so much like Pat's.

"John. Call Susan Baum tomorrow and tell her you want to meet with her. Tell her you're interested in working for the paper again. She's afraid, I hear. Not going out much in public. Moving between her home and an apartment in Santa Ana. Ask her to see you as soon as she can. You're hard up—need the steady paycheck again."

"Why?"

"I want to talk to her on Liberty Ridge."

"But how are you going to talk with her, if she's meeting me somewhere?"

"You will bring her back to the Ridge with you. Simple. You can handle her, can't you?"

John was quiet for a while.

"Sir, after what she did to Pat, and you, why talk to her?"

"Justice, John. Simple justice."

Holt took the Hughes through a sudden shower of meteors falling all around him. The eyes again, he thought: all stars are falling, all lights liquid, all moons melting. He could see the lights of Liberty Ridge below and to the south. They were his destination, his immediate goal.

But so far as his larger desires went, Holt felt for the first time in many months that he could accomplish them. He felt that the whole tragic circle of his life was about to complete itself, become whole. And he now believed that soon, very soon, justice would be done and he could rest.

CHAPTER
THIRTY-TWO

John's dogs rumbled toward him as he walked across the meadow in the generous white moonlight of two a.m. A cool breeze puffed in from the ocean and rippled the lake. He heard the barking of Boomer, Bonnie and Belle, then the heavy pounding of their feet on the ground. Boomer crashed into him as he always did, then jumped up and put his rough paws against John's stomach. He stood there and rubbed the big labrador's ear with one hand and fingered the video tape in his coat pocket with the other.

He let the dogs into the cottage with him. They sniffed around the dining table legs, then looked guiltily at him, not used to the privilege of being inside.

Looking down at the computer screen, he keyed up his mailbox messages and read:

PLAY IT, CUTIE-PIE. PURE OSCAR MATERIAL.

John looked out the picture window at the inhospitable silhouette of Lane Fargo's darkened packing plant of a home. He gazed toward Laura and Thurmond Messinger's church, noting the faint light in the bell tower. In the Big House he saw lights on the second floor—Holt's rooms, Valerie's, Carolyn's? *Who's leading me to Holt,* he wondered. *Which of you would betray him? Or is this only a test?*

He went into the living area and slipped the tape from his

pocket into the video player. He hit rewind but it was already rewound. All three dogs lined up, sat, and watched him.

He pushed the play button and waited.

The screen filled with gray light, then static, then an image—taken from the observation deck of the Big House—of the hillsides and the Pacific being pelted by a steady, heavy rain. The camera panned to record views in all four directions. There was no sound at all, just a mute storm.

Then the camera simply held, facing north, to capture the acres of orange grove beneath the gray and troubled sky. John couldn't tell if it was morning or evening or sometime in between. The orange trees shivered in the wind and the rain heaved down in slanting torrents. It turned the irrigation ditches into flat brown ponds with surfaces that popped and roiled. It looks like March, he thought, the month of all the rain, the month Rebecca died.

Three minutes. Five.

John looked at his watch: 2:12 a.m.

Seven minutes, then eight. A storm that never ends, he thought. He reached down to press the fast forward when the image shifted from the dripping Valencias to a long shot of a building. He took his finger off the button and felt a surge of blood hit his eardrums. The *Journal*.

The camera held on the lobby as a woman wrapped in a raincoat makes her way through the doors. She wears a hat cinched down over her blond hair. She hesitates at the edge of the entryway overhang and looks skyward.

Rebecca, John thought. Rebecca the beautiful. Rebecca the unmistakable. *Rebecca*.

The rain has lessened to a constant drizzle and she jogs out into the asphalt. She chooses a path through the cars, then, holding the hat onto her head with her left hand she accelerates toward the camera. She looks far away. But the camera follows her through the cars, then it swings ahead and zooms in on a new Lincoln Town Car—white. It almost fills the screen. It is parked beside a brick planter that separates the parking slots from the driveway. The camera jiggles slightly, then stops, as if—John thought—the operator has just tightened a tripod nut. A few seconds later Rebecca enters the picture again, stops at the driver's side door of the Town Car, extends her hand toward the doorlock and inserts a key. Her back is to the camera. The picture jumps slightly. Rebecca's arms raise as her body pushes against the car. It looks as if someone has yanked her forward with a hidden wire. Then she rolls away to her left and takes two small, feminine, dance-like steps toward the camera, which jumps again and Rebecca folds to the ground. The camera holds the image for five seconds. There is a red blotch on the Town Car window, chest high. There is no sound. Then the picture fades to black and the black abruptly gives way to gray static.

John simply stood in place, unmoving, and stared at the silent gray screen. He felt the revulsion gathering in his stomach and a frantic anger knotting up in his heart. He imagined setting fire to the cottage, loading his dogs into his truck, driving over to the Big House and lighting it on fire too, shooting Holt in the head when he ran out, then speeding away forever. For a moment he felt like he had entered Hell and was unsure if he would ever get back out. How do you forget what is seen, erase a memory of the real?

Drawn to the horror, feeling that he owed at least this much to Rebecca, he watched the tape again. Every moment of it removed something measurable from his soul.

John loped along in the moonlight with his dogs ahead of him, *Re-bec-ca-pause, Re-bec-ca-pause*, along the lakeshore where he had first seen Vann and Carolyn Holt many years ago, around the western edge of the water and into the scrub hills of Liberty Ridge. He looked down on the island. He imagined being eleven again and hiding there with Carlos in the cave with the spring bubbling up from the rocks and wondered why he had spent a lifetime trying to outrun the snapping jaws of loss.

What he had just seen seemed to him the ultimate profanity; Rebecca's once vibrant body reduced to a lump of lifeless flesh in the rain. But the tape in his pocket was a prize beyond anything Joshua could have dreamed.

He made the clearing, sat on the log and felt his heart thumping in his temples. The dogs sprawled around him. He looked at the place where Snakey had died. The breeze rattled the stiff leaves of the oak tree. What had they done with his body? It all seemed such a waste.

I am here to atone and begin again, he thought.
I am here to put things right.

I am here, like Holt, to do justice.
And I won't leave without his head on a platter.

John had never heard Joshua Weinstein so excited. Not that the special agent was giddy, no. But his voiced dropped a register when he asked John again about the video tape, the message on the computer, the interdiction mission in Little Saigon, and most of all, when he asked John to tell him again *exactly what the tape showed.*

John told him. He told him again. The images slugged away at him until he couldn't describe them anymore.

"Fuckin' *enough*, Joshua!" John listened to the hush on the other end of the line. "Give me something back, goddamnit. What about the notes on Baum? Are they real or not?"

"Affirmative. Documents confirmed it against samples from Wayfarer's Bureau days. It's his writing."

"And the picture of Baum's house?"

"Unretouched. Unaltered. Genuine. His fingerprints on both of them."

"Then he isn't testing me. So who's setting him up for us? Who knows what I'm doing here?"

"The Messingers might be next in line to run Liberty Ops if Holt is up the river. They might have intuited your true mission and decided to give him a push."

"*Might* doesn't get me very goddamned far, Joshua."

"It's a privately held company. We don't know what the by-laws are, if there even are any. It's Holt's show. We can only speculate."

"What about Fargo?"

"He's loyal as a dog."

"So was Cassius. And he's the one who checked me out. He was close, Joshua. He traced us to Olie's together, but couldn't get the proof. He knows you don't hunt quail with a German shepherd. He knows I'm not good with a handgun because we shot together out there. He smells Rebecca all over me. Snakey, too. What if he found more than he's telling Holt?"

"If he did, then he'd blow you wide open. Why betray his master? It doesn't make sense. What's in it for Fargo? Do you think he really likes you?"

"He hates me."

"*Then he's not going to feed you evidence to hang his own*

boss! Jesus, John. Try this: he's not being set up by a traitor, but by a conscience. Someone who knows what he did and hopes you can do something with the evidence. Someone who suspects not that you're a plant, but a man with a strong sense of right and wrong. Someone who knows everyone else is loyal to Holt. Someone who's loyal to Holt too, but not quite enough to let him get away with murdering an innocent young woman."

"Who?"

"His wife. His wife's nurse. His daughter. Thurmond or Laura Messinger. One of the Holt Men who works closely with him. Holt himself. Maybe he's broken down, needs to confess."

John tried to think through the possibilities, but they all sounded wrong. "Joshua, you don't have a clue about what's going on out here. Do you?"

"John, I don't give a damn what's going on out there. We've got five days. We're being fed evidence and I'm going to take it. If it comes from an unexpected source, fine: I'll use any bit of rope I need. When Holt's in lockup we'll sort through the program and identify the players. But as long as it's going like this, then in the name of God in heaven *let's burn his sorry carcass while we can!*"

John listened to Weinstein's clear baritone. He imagined his Adam's apple doing its little jig; he imagined Joshua's black eyes and pale skin and the unshakable focus of his vengeance. And John realized for the first time that he was utterly expendable here, only a tool for Joshua. He was a conduit, a piece of pipe. And no amount of danger or threat would make Joshua waver in his crusade to ruin Vann Holt. What an odd feeling, he thought, to realize you are only valued for what you can do. *I don't care what's going on out there.* What a simpleton he had been.

He said nothing for a long moment. Instead he felt the chill of the wind cutting through his coat, all the way to his bones, and the loneliness of his body here on Liberty Ridge. He felt the solitary nakedness that was his. He felt the border between his own skin and the world outside it, and knew that he could only trust what was within. He shivered and felt cold.

"The tape's in the box, Joshua."

"Very good, Owl. We can hope it's good enough for a warrant, but that's up for a judge to decide. Now, has he asked you to meet with Baum?"

"He made it official tonight. I'm supposed set up a meeting

somewhere, then bring her back to Liberty Ridge. So they can . . . talk."

Joshua was silent. His voice was even lower now, quieter. "It is happening, Dear Owl. Good things are happening for us. It is coming together. *When? When does he want her?*"

"As soon as possible."

"The gods are smiling. Call her this morning at 8:30. You'll find her reluctant to meet, but not suspicious of you. She'll insist that Sunday noon is the soonest, and best she can do."

"You've been busy."

"Always. Once Wayfarer agrees to a time, the clock starts ticking. I'll need to know what he's planning, where on the Ridge he might take her, *anything* you can find out. Sundays, the Liberty Ops training school is down. It's quiet, not a lot of Holt Men around."

"And you'll make the arrest while I'm out retrieving her?"

"Ideally. Now, has Holt frisked you since the first day?"

"Holt didn't. Fargo did."

"Well, has Fargo?"

"No."

"Have your things been disturbed?"

"I told you he took my wallet, shotgun and ammo."

"Have your things been disturbed since?"

"I don't think so."

Josh went quiet again. John heard the wind in the fallen oak leaves, the scratch of needles in darkness.

"Owl, we're down to five days. This, as ordered from mid-level deities you don't need to know about. Sunday will be the third of those five—our last best window. We've played well, but our time is running out. I want you to do something different. I want you to keep your phone with you from now on. Hide it in the cottage. When you've set up the meeting with Baum, and Holt has agreed, call me as soon as it's safe to do so."

"Fargo can check the cottage any time he wants."

"It's time to take acceptable risks."

"You've got the whole sad thing on tape, Joshua. Holt's finished."

"Not yet, he isn't. We'll need a warrant for his arrest. Judges frown on information obtained from covert, untrained, unsworn sources."

"I thought you trained me."

"Don't get precious on me, now. It's a little late in the game for that. We're here to flay Wayfarer alive and let the vultures eat his guts. Aren't we?"

"I've got to be alive to enjoy it."

"I'll keep you alive, Owl. You're indispensable to me. You're my secret agenda. My hidden reason. My invisible passion. Just like you were, to—"

John hung up, slipped the phone into his coat pocket where the video tape of Rebecca had been, and set his box of toys back into the ground.

THIRTY-THREE

John rows toward Liberty Island, watching the shore in front of his cottage graduate into the distance. The dogs prowl the receding beach, ordered to stay and yelping with frustration. Boomer finally dives into the lake and swims a few yards before turning around and paddling back to shore where he shakes himself out in a nose-to-tailtip shiver, then starts barking again. It is morning of the next day and John's heart is sick with memory.

But his senses are attuned to Valerie. She sits astern in the little rowboat, side-saddle on the bench so she can look forward at John, backward to the shore, or to her right, where the western parcels of Liberty Ridge stretch over the hills toward the sea. The picnic basket sits at her feet. She wears a big black straw hat that sweeps up in front to form a white rose-studded wave that tapers dramatically back to a flow of white ribbon and a spray of red gladiola that dangle over the back of the rim. Her dress is loose and sleeveless, white, with lace around the neck and a wide shiny black belt. John suspects it is out-of-date. He suspects she wears sleeveless dresses to complement her smooth brown arms. Beneath the hat, her hair is free and falls over her shoulders. She is barefoot and her ankles cross as she turns and looks back at the dogs. To John she is a riddle of the known and the unknowable, familiar as a sister but exotic as an orchid.

"Where's your six-gun?"

"Hanging on my bed post. Like my dress?"

"It's nice."

"It's the one my mother wore the day you saw her. It took a while, but I found it."

"Why would she keep it?"

"She's always been sentimental about things she wore when she was happy. Has closets full of clothes. A couple of months ago she cut her wedding dress up the back with pinking shears and put it on for dinner. Anyway, I thought you might like to see this one again."

"It's becoming."

The blush again. The smile. "It's becoming difficult to take my eyes off of you, John Menden."

"Then it's good I'm the one rowing. What's for breakfast?"

"A surprise."

"Do you use the computer in your room much?"

She looks at him quizzically, her brown eyes seeming to take in, then release him. "Not since I graduated. I talk to Dad or the Ops guys, if I'm doing work for him. I did my vet school applications on it. Why?"

"I've been getting some odd mail. Little taunts and jabs. Things to let me know I'm being watched. No sender, of course."

"Dad's a prankster, believe it or not."

"Doesn't sound like him."

"Lane would pester you because that's his job and his character. Could be Snakey or Partch—one of Lane's goons. Snakey's supposed to be MIA but I don't believe it."

"What about Sexton?"

"Well, he's linked up. Works from home, mostly. It's not me, if that's what you're asking."

John feels the sand sliding up under the hull, then the abrupt stop. The stern drifts as he climbs out, pulls the rowboat in a little farther and helps Valerie unload the basket, then herself. With one hand she bunches her dress up over her knees and with the other she reaches to John. He leads her through the ankle-deep water to the beach.

"Let's walk around the island," she says. "Work up an appetite. Find a good spot to eat."

She hangs onto his hand—and he hangs onto hers—as they set out around this inner shore. Emerging from the shade of the giant Norfolk Island pine, John feels the thin warm sunlight on his back and smells the rare Orange County aroma of sagebrush and fresh water. John has the basket. The rim of Valerie's hat touches John's neck when they get close, so she takes it off and carries it. She walks closer to him and he can feel the heat and softness of her bare arm as it presses against his own.

"You seem tired."

"Your dad kept me up late."

"How did it go?"

"We cuffed six home invaders in about thirty seconds. Your father blew a kid's hand off, then one of the Men blasted the rest of them with twelve-gauge beach sand. When the lights went on, the Bolsa Cobras looked like gophers caught above ground."

"Do you find that impressive?"

"The kid with no hand did. How involved are you?"

"Well . . . Dad's been trying to get me on board for about a year now. He supported my college, but he's less enthused about me practicing veterinary than helping him run the Ops. He's made no secret of it—he'd like me to run the business when he's too old."

When the final bills come due, John thinks. Sooner than she knows?

"You're not tempted?"

"Tempted, maybe. I'd like to please him. But I can't say that security and privatized law enforcement really turn this girl on. It would be years before he really needed me. I could practice veterinary, think about it. More to the point is, I don't approve of blowing off people's hands."

"There's that."

"And that's why I'm taking my time."

"He must make lots of money."

"It's unbelievable. The Ops is international, you know. We just inked a deal with the Ugandan Development Ministry. What they're developing is a SWAT team to kick tribal butt fast and hard. It's a three-million dollar deal over time. But the foreign stuff is just kind of glamorous. The high-tech industrial accounts we have in Irvine alone account for a million a year. That's not including personal security and investigations."

"He told me that the Ops does vengeance. For money."

Valerie shrugged. John could feel her fingers tighten against his own. "That's not really true. Dad exaggerates."

"He sounded serious."

"There were a couple of creeps let go on legal technicalities. Real flagrant miscarriages. One was a stalker with a former for forcible rape. The other one a thug hired by an ex-hubby. They walked before trial. Both of their victims had contracts with us. Well, the pay-per-mug just plain disappeared. The stalker got squashed in a hit-and-run. I won't say anything more about them because that's all I know. I've heard a few things spoken, but nothing really said, if you get the drift."

They round the western shore. With the Big House and all its subordinate buildings now invisible behind the island, John feels the expansive privacy of a world of nature without men.

"God, it's nice out here," says Valerie. "So, dad sees me as the front-woman for Liberty Ops, and Lane wants to head up day-to-day stuff. I'm not sure if Dad wants Lane in that position. I know he's trying to vett Sexton's worth. Adam's great with people but he doesn't know much about the day-to-day things. Does he want to put you to work, too?"

"I sense that. I, uh . . . participated last night. Tangentially. He gave me a little task for today."

"What?"

"Contact Susan Baum of the *Journal* and set up a meeting with her."

John feels Valerie's hand go stiff now, and the sudden tension in her arm. For a long while she says nothing, but John still feels the strong energy inside her.

"What?" he finally asks.

"I hate that self-righteous cunt. Dad does, too. She crucified Pat for no reason, then went after Dad. Dragged up a bunch of crap that wasn't true, published it to a million-and-a-half Orange Countians. No apologies when Teresa Descanso *finally* couldn't positively identify Patrick. Patrick, with the 'innocent certitude of a Mormon zealot.' Baum never even *met* my brother. Hardly a mention in the *Journal* when Liberty Ops turned over the real rapist to the cops a year later. Not hot. Not news. I can't imagine one reason on earth why he'd want you to contact her now, except maybe to . . ."

"What?"

"Nothing. I was going to say put a bullet between her eyes, but I'm a little peeved. I wouldn't have really meant it."

"Someone already tried that."

"That skinhead dweeb from Alamo West, according to the FBI and the *Journal*."

She looks at him, the smooth skin of her face flushed pink

and her dark brown eyes aglitter. The tensile strength of her grip recedes and she squeezes his hand gently.

"I know. I have a bad temper sometimes. When it comes to the people I love—or hate."

"Do you think he'd really want her dead?"

Valerie looks up at him again as they walk. "No. Not any more."

"He did, once?"

"Sure. I did, too. It's over now. Pat's gone and the rage abates."

"He said he wants to talk to her."

"That might be hard, given that she's paranoid now. Para-lyzed by fear that someone will try her again. By her own profit-able, unparalyzed confession, that is."

"I think that's where I'd come in."

Valerie looks at him, then out at the water, then to the little stand of toyon trees ahead of them. "Here," she says, pulling him along. "Here's where we should eat."

They find a clearing. They each hold two corners of a soft white acrylic blanket and set it on the ground amidst the toyon trees. A little cluster of the red berries falls to the blanket, tiny red apples in ultraminiature.

Valerie reaches into the basket and pulls out a gas lantern.

"For later," she says, setting it aside.

Out come two perfect oranges, a bottle of Zinfandel, a loaf of bread wrapped in foil, a triangle of cheese and a large plastic bag filled with chunks of white meat.

"No wonder that thing was so heavy," says John.

His first long sip of the wine is a communion with Rebecca that ends in a shudder as he pictures her image from the night before. *To you.* His second drink is to the woman beside him.

"Cold?"

"No."

"You shivered."

"The wine."

"That makes no sense."

She moves close to him, one arm against his. "Eat your lunch."

He pulls out a fine-ribbed segment and tries it. It tastes of garlic, mesquite smoke and faintly of flesh. He has never had a firmer, subtler meat. "Catfish from the lake?"

"Not fish at all."

He examines the piece in his fingers, the thick spine and close ribs curved in unison. In his mouth it has the feel of abalone. "Oh. Now that's funny."

She giggles. "Going to be sick?"

"No. It's good."

"Freshness counts."

"You retrieve it after our walk?"

"Straight into the marinade. Ten minutes on a side in the Weber. Not in the little cookbook they give you."

"Well," he says, swallowing and lifting his wine glass. "Here's to shooting the devil before he speaks."

"To the new improved Eve."

"To aspiring vets."

"To safe puppies," she says.

"To wasting not."

"To wanting not."

"Young lady, you seem to have it all," he says.

"I would like to."

Suddenly her eyes are point blank and her nose is against his cheek and her lips are on his. Her breath smells, illogically, of milk. Her fingers on his face feel cool. When she pushes him back her hair falls forward to make a shade that smells like apples. She cradles the back of his head as she might an infant's as he settles onto the blanket and her tongue comes past his teeth. He feels its changing girth, the slickness of its bottom. John places his hands on her face, then her neck and shoulders, then runs them down her arms. She is tense as a bulldog, he thinks, and just as strong. She's trembling. Over him, her weight shifts and he feels the loop of his belt pulled up, then a long strong yank that frees hole from shaft, then strap from buckle. But when she tries to pull it free it sticks from its own friction and she only manages to turn him half onto his side.

"Uh, Val, it's kind of stuck. I can—"

"*No.*"

He feels her weight vanish. Then she's standing over him with a half-stricken expression, smoothing her dress with her hands, her eyes riveted on the ground, face red as a Christmas tree bulb.

"I thought you just . . . I'm awfully sorry. It's my mistake, John. Just forget it."

"Come back."

"Oh, no. Really, it's not . . . I shouldn't be—"

"You don't have to."

"God*damn*it."

He laughs.

"Do not laugh at me."

"You're funny."

"This isn't funny."

"It should be. You almost tore that belt in half, you know."

She still won't look at him. "I'm trying to . . ."

"I know what you're trying to do."

"Ah shit, John, I don't know how you *do* this."

"I know you don't."

Finally she looks at him, just a glance. Then she shakes her head. "I'm such a spaz."

"Come here. You don't have to do everything. You don't have to do anything. Just come here and lie down with me and be quiet. Okay?"

Her face is still ablaze and her eyes are flittering everywhere again, like birds looking for somewhere to land. "You know I'm pretty good at just about everything. I can shoot and cook and think and get into vet—"

"Can you lie down and shut up?"

Eyes still on the ground in front of her, she moves toward the blanket, then lies down. Her back is to him.

"No reason to pout, you know."

She says nothing, so he props up on an elbow and strokes her hair. "It's even worse when you're a guy, because you can feel it being over with before you're even really started."

"Can't you fight it?"

"Not very successfully."

"It's just . . . kind of embarrassing, John."

"Well, don't be embarrassed. It's kind of funny, anyway."

"It is?"

"If you picture what you're doing, or if you watched it on a screen, I think you might find yourself laughing."

"I watched a dirty movie once, and laughed."

"Then there you have it."

"What do we do?"

"Why don't we just wait until it happens?"

"I want it to happen now." She backs her rump and shoulders into him. "Found what I wanted. Had my heart set on it."

When she turns around to face him, her eyes are shiny and the pupils are big and her forehead beaded with sweat.

He moves on top and her legs part around his weight. He lifts them and the dress falls over her brown smooth knees.

"Don't stare." Her eyes are closed.

But he does stare while he sits back to work his pants down because she's naked underneath the dress and he just can't believe how good she looks. He scoots back into position and begins to see himself as a comic figure, not necessarily a good sign, he feels. But she's got him in one hand, stroking him hard, trying to pull him inside herself.

"Uh, easy does it, sweetness," he says.

"All right."

In the next whirling moments John's thoughts explode in rapid succession, like a line of bottles pierced by a single bullet. None stay whole long enough to name. They are shattered, derationalized, lost. He follows her adamant guidance, moving inside until he feels the threadlike sinuous resistance, then the quick gasp of her breath against his ear.

"Thought you were kidding, Val."

"No."

She uses her hands on his flanks to control him. She shudders and withdraws, opens and accepts. The increments of pleasure build and drop in John, whose thoughts careen back and forth between immensities of chaos and hyperfocus. He is a hawk streaking through blue. Does it hurt? He glides beneath a black tonnage of water. Does it actually tear? He is a thousand silver butterflies netted in skin. Are we smashing her hat?

"*Oh!*"

"Sorry."

Her hands draw him deeper.

"*Oooh!*"

"Go slow . . ."

But he knows he is past it. She shivers and tightens around him—all of her—hands and fingers, arms and stomach, legs and mouth. He tries to be still but she forces him hard up inside her and John imagines the wash of dark red blood. Thinks it's imagination anyway. She's still shuddering and holding him tightly and he's aware for the first time of the nails jammed into the twin peaks of his ass and the cool-wet pain around them, of the groans vibrating from her throat into his, of the hissing of her nostrils tight against his face, and of the power of her legs clamped hard at his sides. All he can think to do is just wait, locked here like this. So he waits while her arms close around his shoulders and head, and the inside of her is jerking and he hasn't got clue one whether this is pain or pleasure until he looks down at her wide open eyes and the look of surprise on her face and the little lines at the edges of her mouth that suggest a smile. He tries to hold still but suddenly here comes a wholly unpostponable surge of effervescence that feels like a long fizzing string being drawn out of him. Out it goes. Then the riotous discharge of voltage, all the mixed up thoughts, the sweet shakes.

Time does pass.

"Oh," he finally says.

"Oh."

"Oh."

"Oh, *my!*"

CHAPTER
THIRTY-FOUR

When they wake up it is almost two. During their sleep someone has brought the sides of the blanket over them against the afternoon breeze, but John can't remember doing it and Valerie can't either. John's neck is stiff from the ground. Valerie's hat has blown up on its side against a toyon tree and stayed there. Her dress, which twenty-three years ago protected Carolyn as Carolyn protected her, is now wrinkled everywhere and spotted with blood. She stands in the clearing, twisting the stained part around so she can see it, and looks down at the material. John packs up the basket in a heavy silence that seems to him breakable only by meaningful discourse. But he can't think of anything to say that can approximate his feelings at the moment.

"The spring," Valerie notes. "I'll dip it in the spring to get out the stains."

"Are they bad, Val?"

"They add a primitive cache to the garment. It's a keepsake, after all. Imagine what I can tell *my* daughter about it."

"You all right?"

"I'm great. Don't you think so?"

She looks at him with the same matter-of-factness she looked at the stains with, then a little smile breaks across her mouth, but fades as her eyes well with tears.

"I sure do."

"Let's just walk with our arms around each other. We'll go see the spring in the cave and I'll wash the stains in the water."

"You know you could just take it to a good cleaner."

"I could tear it into gun rags, too."

They emerge from the trees, John with the basket again and Valerie holding her big flowery hat.

"I feel like a teenager who just got away with something," she says.

"Me, too."

"Twenty-two years one way, then you're another. I feel like I'm supposed to think of everything differently now. I don't feel really different, though. There's a pain down there, and some blood on my clothes. I know what it is to have a man inside. I've made the offer and had the taking. But I'm not so sure this is the most revolutionary moment of my life. I mean, I was really crushed when I found out there wasn't a Santa Claus."

"I guess I don't know what you mean."

"Well, you know, just a time when the illusion is gone. Or the change is made. The page is turned. You've thought about it a lot and then it happens and you're still the person you always were. It's good. You're still there."

"I'm glad you're still here."

She turns her face to him and consumes him with the darkness of her eyes. He can tell she's going to ask him how he feels about it and he wishes she wouldn't. Too many gradients of the truth to register. Too much complexity to unite.

But she doesn't ask that, exactly. She looks away, out toward the water and leans her head against his shoulder.

"Does this mean I have to love you?"

He laughs. Then, quietly: "I don't think so."

"Well, I do. So there."

"Then that's a good thing."

John marvels for the millionth time in his life: How can a woman lead you to say something that's true in the way you say it but not true in the way they hear it? Somewhere in between, the meaning changes direction, like a signal bounced off a relay. You both know it, which complicates rather than simplifies.

"Good?" she presses.

"Good."

"Look, I gave my body to you. With it came my soul, my love, my devotion. You took all of me. And I expect all of you back. Every last cell of you. I demand love, affection, sacrifice—

and I demand it forever. I demand that you love, cherish and honor me, 'til death do us part. I expect to be your new religion."

"Sucker," he says.

"Get down on your haunches, raise your paws up to me, and *bark*. Bark your adoration."

"Woof."

She stops and faces him, drops her hat, plants her feet and swings a big arching cross with her right fist. She opens and slows just before it hits his cheek. Her other hand shoots up and both pull his face down to hers.

"I love you anyway. Brute. Simpleton. Oaf. Dope."

"In that case I love you, too."

"There. We both win. I'll be satisfied with that, temporarily."

The opening to the cave is now covered by a massive iron gate. It is connected to an equally stout frame, hinged on one side and fastened on the other by a long chain of forbidding size and heft.

"This wasn't here when I was a kid," he says.

"Is now."

"Who built it?"

"Who do you think? Said he wanted his very own dungeon."

"Quite the party gag."

"Just like everything else on Liberty Ridge—doors but no locks. Dad said if he couldn't build a safe home for his family here, he'd go somewhere he could. The electric fence might have something to do with it."

She pulls out the chain a little, then it slides of its own weight to the ground. John steps away as Valerie uses both hands to pull open the gate. It creaks unmercifully, a long, shrill protest.

"Been a while," she says. "After you."

The sunlight gives way to a partial darkness as John moves into the cool of the cave. He remembers the way the ceiling is low at first so you have to crouch a little, then opens up maybe twenty yards further down to the big cavern with a high ceiling, the smooth dirt floor and at the far end the opening in the rock where the spring bubbles forth in its aromatic, mineral-heavy steam. He remembers that the size of the opening is just big enough to climb into if you want to sit in the hot water, and the rock ledge around the opening is a good place to sit. He can smell the clean, fecund odor of fresh water pooling up from the earth. He remembers that once your eyes adjust in the cavern you can see just well enough to keep from banging into the walls or tripping on the rock ledges surrounding the spring.

"Want to crank up the lantern?" he asks, turning.

"Let's wait until we're in, okay?" Valerie has her hat on. In this minor half-light—just as in the glare of the sun—he finds her absolutely beautiful.

He senses the ceiling rising as he steps into the big cavern. He can't see the top but the echoes of their footsteps have extended resonance. He can make out the pale draft of steam rising from the pool at the far end of the vault. He feels Valerie's body press up against his side, the brim of her hat nudging his neck.

"Let there be light," she whispers.

John sets down the basket. He steps to the other side of it, kneels, lifts the lid. He looks up at her from across the basket, beholding her form in the faint light that has followed her in from the cave mouth behind her. He looks up at her face but he can't see much except for the shine of her eyes. He gets out the lantern and turns the electronic ignition switch, hearing the click-click of the spark and the quiet hiss of the gas coming into the mantles.

"Thank you," he says. "For what you gave me back there."

"You're really very welcome."

"I feel more than welcome. I feel honored and blessed."

"So do I, John."

He smiles.

In the growing light he sees that she is smiling, too. She has knelt to face him across the picnic basket, her expression revealed by the whitening glow from the lantern that rests on top of it.

"You're beautiful," he says.

"You're just flattering me now."

She turns her back to him and John unbuttons the dress. She drops the top and steps out of it in a motion of pure femininity, then walks to the bubbling pool in the rock. He watches her kneel and work the water into the material.

"I knew you'd come here," she says.

"How could you know, when I didn't?"

"From a dream."

"Tell me about it."

"No," she says quietly, looking over her shoulder at him. "We're only as interesting as our secrets."

When they leave the cave the Santa Ana winds have just begun to blow again. They move greatly against John's face as he leads Valerie into the formidable sunlight. John notes the high-desert smell, the dryness of the breeze, the clean outlines of the hillsides against the sky. He has Valerie by the hand. Time passing by, he thinks, the future marching backwards to meet us.

Back at the cottage, John has an e-mail asking him to call Adam Sexton. He e-mails back that he can't—no phone handy. A few moments later, Sexton's reply appears on his screen:

SENSE CHANGES IN VANN. PURELY A HUNCH. IF YOUR NOSE
IS TO THE WIND, PICKING THINGS UP, WOULD MUCH LIKE
TO COMPARE NOTES. ANY LITTLE BIT HELPS. VAL LIKES
YOU. LUCKY GUY—

A. SEX

That night, late, Holt summons John to the Big House. John crosses the meadow in the building wind, his dogs bouncing out ahead of him, hunting birds in the moonlight.

He waits for his host in the living room, looking into the red-orange glow of the fire. When Holt finally comes down he has got a tumbler full of ice and Scotch in each hand. He gives one to John but says nothing, simply motions with his head and leads John down into the basement, the Trophy Room.

When the lights go on, John acts surprised by the wildlife dioramas around him. Even this, his second viewing, fills him with awe, almost a child's sense of wonder. Animals from all over the world—the biggest, the best and the most beautiful. Animals he could never even identify.

"I've never seen anything like this, Mr. Holt."

"You won't. Half of them are illegal to take anymore."

Holt guides him. He tells him about the hunts, the circumstances, the weather, the guides, the shots. He seems most proud of the Kodiak bear. It towers above them, ten feet tall, at least, with a gleam in its eyes that is utterly convincing.

"Biggest flesh eater on land," Holt says. "Fifteen hundred

forty-seven pounds. Took me three weeks on the island to find this one. Another three days to get a shot at him. Thought I was going to lose some toes to frostbite. Didn't care. One shot knocked him ass-over-teakettle. Broke the backbone, clean. Should have heard him. Kind of sound that stays in your dreams for years."

Holt leads the tour. Asia. India. North America. Africa. Central America.

"Talked to Baum?"

"She said Sunday noon would be her best time. Day after tomorrow. Does that fit your schedule?"

Holt ignores John's question, as he often does. Instead of answering he takes a slow drink of his Scotch and continues his tour through the exhibits.

"Where will she meet you?" he asks.

"Newport Harbor Art Museum. She's going to a fundraiser that starts at one o'clock. She said she'd fit me in before."

"Can you get her here with minimal drama?"

"I thought I'd meet her in the parking lot, when she's heading in. It's a good-sized lot, off to the side of the building. I've been there."

Holt nods, perhaps pleased that John has given this errand some forethought. He looks up at the bull elephant, then moves toward Australia. John remains beside him. He notes that Holt's brow furrows briefly then relaxes, as if some problem has been raised and solved.

"Good, John. When you come back in with her, the guard at the gate will wave you through. You won't have to stop. Don't stop at the Big House, either. Just head up past the groves into the hills. Bring her to Top of the World. I'll be there."

"Why Top of the World?"

They arrive back on Kodiak Island. Holt looks up at the bear. "We'll have lunch there, Baum and I. Plan on joining us. Great view of everything. Nice place to talk. Don't you think?"

What John thinks is: a nice place to off someone. No one around to see or hear.

"It's perfect for that."

Holt finishes his drink, still examining the towering bear. "Lane took off the right inside handle of your truck door. If she gets antsy once you two are on the road, too bad."

"Thank you. I gave some thought to her appointment calendar, though. I mean, she probably wrote me in somewhere. It's possible she'll tell her husband or her bosses she's meeting me before the function."

"Don't worry about that—you didn't get to the museum after all. Truck crapped out, starter. You've got me for an alibi. Lane, too. And Val. Getting her here is the important thing. Nobody's going to look for you here because nobody knows where you are."

"That's what I came up with."

Will he kill me when he's done with Baum?, John thinks. Half of him feels gratitude that he and Baum will be miles away from Top of the World when Joshua and his Federales take down Holt. The other half of him wishes he could be there to see it, to see this animal face his hunter.

"So, do I tell her we're coming to see you?"

"I wouldn't. But tell her anything you want. Just get her here."

"Consider it done."

Holt turns and stares at John with his cool gray eyes. A little smile creeps to his mouth. "You're a good man."

John says nothing, returning the stare, hoping he really looks as stupid as he's trying to seem.

"I want you to see something now," Holt says. "I want you to look at it. I don't want you to say a word. I want you to think about it after we leave here. Tomorrow night, if you've changed your mind about this arrangement, you'll have a chance to tell me. Agreed?"

"Agreed."

Holt presses a button on the railing in front of the diorama and the scene in Kodiak gives way to a parking lot. No animals. No rocks. Just asphalt, and one eucalyptus tree with a thick white trunk that rises from a planter filled with Iceland poppies. A new Lincoln Town Car is parked in a space marked "Baum." The backdrop is a blown-up photograph of the *Journal* building.

John feels his breath catch, *hears* it catch. He stares at the tableau. The way it feels to see it now takes him back to the way it felt to be there. He brings in a deep breath and exhales. John wonders if his knees might buckle. And he knows for sure that whatever information his face reveals is being easily recorded by the man in front of him.

Holt's expression is so ordinary that John can't infer even the tiniest meaning from it.

"We'll talk tomorrow night, John. If you feel the need to. Big dinner. Lots of big doings. Got to have everybody whistling the same tune."

"Okay. Sure. All right."

CHAPTER
THIRTY-FIVE

As John Menden watched a young woman wash a stained dress in a spring, Joshua Weinstein stared briefly at Sharon Dumars in the muted light of the County Crime Lab Audio-Visual room. He silently shook his head and resumed his pacing. He could not stop the pacing, only interrupt it for brief, anguished moments of worry. He worried that the Sheriff-Coroner's deputy who had lost Snakey in the county's paperwork would change his mind and blow Joshua's operation to smithereens. He worried that Walker Frazee had found out about Snakey, and was ready to fire him. He worried that everyone knew he had slept with Sharon Dumars. No image of her tanned, strong, beautiful body was enough to dispel the fear that he was about to be exposed as a traitor to Rebecca. It is hell being me, he thought, looking at his watch and shaking his head again, his big Adam's apple traveling up and down his throat like an elevator as he swallowed.

Kenwick, the Bureau's crack AV man, sat stooped beside Sharon, looking into a Fuji editing machine through which was running the VHS format tape of Rebecca Harris meeting her end in the *Journal* parking lot. He was running the frames one-by-one and Joshua had heard nothing but Kenwick's steady, deep breathing for the last five minutes. Kenwick wore headphones to listen to the soundtrack. Cute, thought Joshua, considering there *was* no goddamned soundtrack. Kenwick had been flown in from Washington, accompanied by Walker Frazee. Joshua had felt nothing but disaster brewing since the two got off the Bureau jet.

Why analyze my precious video tape, Joshua thought: what was there to say? If there was ever a case of content over form, this was it. They'd already run it through the infrared scanner for prints. Four thumbs, all perfectly delineated, all John Menden's. Did they enjoy watching Rebecca die over and over again? Only Walker Frazee and his captious lab men could ruin a free lunch. If this wasn't enough to earn a search warrant, what was? Owl had performed, and they had won.

Kenwick finally straightened and removed the padded headphones. He was a big man with the features—Joshua thought—of a bison, right down to the curly brown hair that began just above his forehead as abruptly as a piece of carpet and crept around the expanded bottoms of his heavy earlobes. Watching him come down the jet ramp with Walker Frazee beside him was like watching a vaudeville act. His voice had the resonance of an opera baritone.

"It's not complete," he announced, fastening two black eyes on Joshua. "It's not intact."

"What do you mean, not complete? He didn't shoot the whole tape, if—"

"—That isn't what I mean. I mean, we have the image here. But the soundtrack has not been transferred."

"What happened?"

"No accident. It was re-created this way."

"This isn't the original?"

The big bison head shook a shaggy negative. "This is a dub. Sans soundtrack. Second, perhaps third, generation. Listen. Watch."

Joshua sat down. Kenwick handed him the headset then started the tape in motion. Rain. Oranges. The *Journal*. Then, Rebecca.

Josh watched her pick her way through the parked cars, trying for all she was worth only to make life a little easier on Susan Baum. It amazed Joshua that he could watch this now. It took all the self-control he could muster to watch this tape as dispassionately as he might an evening news clip of college basketball. Rebecca as evidence. Rebecca as a clue. Rebecca as forensic data. But surely as there was no soundtrack to the tape, there was a soundtrack in Joshua's mind and it said: You loved her, she betrayed you, she died. And as Joshua listened to that voice inside him, he wished again that he had something more to give Re-

becca than the bitterness of his rejection and the fury of his revenge. I can only give you what I have, he thought. I can only
give you back what you left me.

He snapped the headset off. "If there's no sound, what am I
listening for?"

"The hiss. The hiss tells us that the original sound strip re-
ceived input. The copy was run with a soundtrack of its own—
silence. Or near silence, except for the hiss."

"You're positive this is not an original tape?"

"Absolutely."

Kenwick looked at Joshua with his big lugubrious bison
eyes. "The sound strip must have contained something that
someone was not supposed to hear."

Joshua sat back and stared at the now-blank editing screen.
"So it exists?"

"What exists?"

"The original movie soundtrack."

"Well, it certainly did at one point. What happened to it
would be purely speculation right now. I'd also speculate why the
filmmaker would let the images remain for posterity, so to speak,
but erase the audio."

Joshua nodded, but didn't look at Kenwick. There would be
no looking into this gift horse's mouth, either, until Wayfarer's
carcass was deep in Federal lockup.

He stood. "Thanks, Wick."

"Good luck, Joshua."

Frazee greeted them at the door of the Bureau conference room.
He seemed even smaller than the last time Joshua had seen him,
though Joshua could not imagine why. He wore his eternal blue
suit and his usual open-faced, boyish expression. He stood aside
to let them in, then appeared seated on the other side of the conference table without seeming to have actually walked there, as
only a small man can do. Down the table sat Norton, red-faced
and inflated as always, as if he had just gotten off the canvas after
a knockdown.

Frazee cleared his throat and leaned forward, which made
Joshua wonder, as always, whether or not Walker's feet were
touching the floor. Joshua was amazed that he could wonder such
a thing while the climax of his operation was being planned.

Frazee's eyes looked dead now, not a glimmer in them. Joshua could not remember anything so akin to sympathy on the little man's face. His stomach dropped.

"The warrant petition has been denied," Frazee said.

Joshua felt the earth shift underneath him and was hit by a sudden decompression he could not fight. His spirit seemed to pour out from his heart, right onto the floor. He felt a darkness closing in and the walls sliding in to surround him. His own voice, when he finally found it, embarrassed him.

"*Why?* he bleated.

"Chain of custody weak. That's Owl, unsworn and unaffiliated. Partial evidence—that's the tape with no sound on it. The fear is 'appearance of impropriety.' I quote the magistrate verbatim now. It's become a given that law enforcement tampers with evidence. We can thank the Los Angeles Police Department for that."

Joshua sat back, allowing the rancorous anger to build inside him. He took off his glasses, rubbed the dark divots on either side of his nose, and looked at his compatriots through the haze of his 20/80 uncorrected vision. He could feel his eyes getting a little misty, so he slipped the glasses back on.

"Can we try another—

"—Already did," said Frazee. "He sided with the first finding. It's the atmosphere of the times, Joshua. You can't change it."

He looked at Sharon, who had actually gone a little pale. "I can't abide by it, either, sir."

"This hurts me, too. I'm left with no other choice than to turn the whole thing over to ATF, as we discussed. Liberty Ridge is a cold potato now. Let them have it. We'll move on to more productive fields. Perhaps they can glean something from Owl that—"

"*Let them run my mole?*"

"Well, if they take over the op, they get the baby and the bath water."

Joshua felt his anger boil over now, this cascade of rage behind his eyes and mouth, burning through his skin. He got up slowly from his chair, pulled it out from the table and kicked it so hard it shot back on its rollers to the wall and flipped over. Frazee's face seemed to behold him from the far end of a long tunnel.

"*I've got three more days. They were promised by you, Walker. They were promised by the Attorney General. They are mine and I own them and I intend to use them to take down Holt. At the end of that time, if I don't have solid enough evidence to arrest him, you can turn Owl over to the Bat Boys and reassign me to El Paso, Texas. But until then, I have an operation here and I am going to finish it.*"

"Sit down, Weinstein."

Josh pulled out the next available chair, and sat.

"You have your three days, as promised. Today is Friday. Monday morning, we'll joint-task this over to ATF. Joshua, all I can say is I'm sorry. You gave it a good run."

Then Frazee rose to his feet—or slid down to let them reach the floor—and the meeting was over.

Josh looked at his cohorts as they made their way from the conference room, realizing that he was about to finish the longest, most bitter journey of his young life. How it would end was anyone's guess.

Joshua studied Norton's Scotch-riddled face. Norton was his mentor and trainer, a man who within the limits of a bureaucracy had been as good, decent and honest with him as a man could be. He could bear Norton no ill will. And when he looked at Frazee's aging but unlined face, his innocent expression and unshakable self-faith, he saw someone not only to fear, but to pity. He couldn't even look at Dumars.

He sat for a while after the others had gone. He could see Sharon lingering in the hallway for him. It took sheer willpower to simply stand up and leave the conference room.

He walked across the parking structure with her—his ears burning, his throat tight. He was trying to figure out how to react, what to do.

"What's your plan, Joshua?"

"I have no plan."

"You're lying."

Ever since their nights together—there had been four of them in the last four days—Joshua had noted an increasingly bold and proprietary air in Sharon. She seemed quick to bore into things that most people would simply leave alone. His defenses were no longer unassailable for her, and Joshua wasn't sure whether he liked it or not.

"God Sharon, I wish I was," he said.

*   *   *

Owl didn't call until late that night, when they were sitting in her living room watching Leno. Sharon's cat, Natalie, was sprawled across Joshua's lap, purring. He was stroking the cat, though he hated cats. He had not touched his dinner. The cell phone was on the coffee table in front of him, but Joshua dreaded the words he would have to say.

And then it was ringing. Two. Three.

Joshua picked up the handset and went outside to the patio. He simply couldn't let Sharon hear his defeat. There was a large enough shred of his pride left to never allow that. John's voice was clear and small, as if coming across the globe rather than the twenty short miles from Liberty Ridge.

John repeated his conversation with Holt and told Joshua about the Baum exhibit. Joshua asked him to repeat it again. He wrote it down in his notepad, as always, as if any of it mattered now. He was furious that they couldn't get an arrest warrant for a man planning to stuff a corpse and put it on display with his elk and lambs and kudu or whatever the fuck they were. Joshua looked up at the sky and wished he were on one of the stars.

Of course, his gears were spinning, no, *shearing*—he could almost see Wayfarer, Baum and Owl sitting up there on Top of the World, finishing off lunch before Holt finished them off. It was almost more than he could take, being able to see it so clearly but knowing it would never happen, that he would never be there.

And then, of course, the inevitable question from his snitch:

"You'll bust Holt while I'm supposed to be getting Baum, right?"

"That is no longer the plan."

"We didn't get the warrant?"

"No."

"Why? What in hell more can I—"

"—I don't know, Owl. I honestly don't know how you could have done better."

Joshua explained the meeting with Frazee, the denial of the warrant petition, the reasons. He couldn't remember ever having to give more shameful news in all his life. It was bad enough being governed by fools without having to speak for them, too.

In the long silence that followed, Joshua truly accepted that his longstanding appointment with fate had been canceled forever.

And then, while he searched his vocabulary for the best terms of surrender, a light flashed inside him.

The light was so bright that Joshua couldn't look directly at it, only to the side, like trying to peek at an eclipse of the sun.

Was this real? Was he seeing it correctly? Or was it just a mirage hovering over a long, hot, lonely highway?

"Wait," he said.

He thought it through one way, then back again. One more time, then another. It *was* there. It *was* real.

"I'm tired of waiting," said Owl.

"I need thirty seconds. Give them to me."

Gentle static. The occasional breathing of his mole. His own accelerating heartbeats thumping in his ears as he flipped back through his little book to the notes of John's second call—after he'd accompanied Holt to Top of the World and seen the statues and the vaults. He backed toward the porch light to see them better. Pay dirt.

"Listen to me. There's a way we can do this. It is possible. You would have to put your head on the chopping block. Right there, directly on it. Then, trust me."

"I'll listen."

"There's nothing for you to listen to, Owl. Just do what Holt tells you. Bring Baum to Liberty Ridge for him. I'll be there when you need me. I promise you that."

Sharon was eyeing him as he returned to the house a few minutes later. He glanced at her, then away, then set the phone back on the coffee table and began pacing the room. Natalie looked at him with eyes that seemed fixed on some other dimension.

"I ordered him out, but he refused. He's going to take Baum back to Liberty Ridge for Holt."

Sharon said nothing and Josh felt the accusing silence. He knew she would unravel his dishonesty in a matter of seconds.

"You asked him to disobey you."

"It was totally his doing. He refuses to come out."

"Joshua—that's perilous. It's stupid and it's . . . homicidal. Holt plans to kill her, and John, too. You know it."

He allowed himself the smallest of smiles. "Therefore, we

have a reasonable assumption that a crime is about to take place. On those grounds, we can be there to prevent it. We'll take him for conspiracy to commit the murder of Susan Baum. We'll add Rebecca later."

Her silence tried to accuse him, but Joshua Weinstein's conscience was beyond reproach. He was beginning to feel invincible now. He felt as if he had banged his head against the wall, and the wall had given.

"John is willing," he said.

"Of course he is. He needs Wayfarer just as bad as you do."

He looked into Sharon's level brown eyes and saw the terrifying evenness of her common sense, the endless flat line of her moral horizon—good above and bad below and nothing in between.

She went to the kitchen and poured herself more coffee. When she came back she sat at the far end of the sofa, away from Joshua and the cat.

Joshua could sense the envelope of tension around her, palpable as the buzz in a prison.

"I don't know what the right thing to do is," she said.

"Welcome to the human race."

"Fuck you and your hatred, Josh."

"It makes a better light than your doubt does."

"I don't like the doubt, either. It makes for weakness and indecision. It's paralyzing. But this is the first time since coming to the Bureau that I haven't felt right about something. Something big, I mean. If this goes wrong, Josh, it goes wrong big."

"Then I'll be looking for work in the private sector. Maybe Holt could use me. I might open my own little dry cleaning business."

"You might be dead."

Thoughts of his own mortality couldn't dent him. The joy of victory, even the *thought* of victory swept the fear from Josh's mind. He looked at Sharon now, at her face behind the rising steam from her coffee cup. She's beautiful, he thought, isn't she? In a different way than Rebecca, but beautiful just the same.

"I'll do it alone, Sharon."

"Do you want me there?"

"Of course I do."

"I'm afraid of doing the wrong thing. Of getting someone innocent killed. Aren't you?"

"No."

"You should be."

"It scares me that I'm not. So I'll do it alone."

"No, you won't. I won't let you. I never considered that, even for a second."

CHAPTER
THIRTY-SIX

John had just ended his conversation with Joshua when he heard the cottage door open and close. He was upstairs in the cottage loft. His hands were jittery as he replaced the cellular unit under the sink cabinet, pressing it down into a box of cleaning products between two sponges of roughly the same size and laying the rubber gloves over them.

"Val?"

"No such luck, Bun-boy."

He heard footsteps across the hardwood floor. He quietly closed the cabinet and went downstairs.

Lane Fargo sat in the living room, an open *Sports Illustrated* draped over a crossed knee and a paper grocery bag beside his leg. He looked at John with his standard expression—meanspirited and noncommittal.

"Come to borrow some Pepto?" John asked. There was something in Lane Fargo so easy to detest.

"Not exactly."

"You still look a little peaked from Uganda. Bed rest, plenty of fluids."

"Feel great, actually. I've made some solid formulations lately."

"A firm stool can't be overpraised."

"Always talkin' shit, aren't you?"

Fargo tossed the magazine to the coffee table, uncrossed his legs and stood, never taking his eyes off of John. He made a fast sighing sound as he turned. John studied Fargo's dark, shadowy face. The vein throbbing in Fargo's neck and the one throbbing in his forehead kept the same cadence. His black widow's peak made him look simian. He had on his black t-shirt again, and the shoulder holster with the automatic jammed up along his rib cage.

"Look, Lane. You couldn't put me with Joshua Whatshisname or Rebecca Harris, so why don't you just cave in and admit you were wrong? I'm clean. I won. Valerie kind of likes me, too. Go home and weep."

"That was the past," he said. "You beat me at it, like you beat me out at Olie's that day." At this, Fargo's dark visage crimped into a mock frown. "I'm more interested in the present, the right-now. Like in what happened to Snakey."

"Not him again."

"The plot's thickened, Bun-boy. I found this little tape recorder in his room, remember? Listened to the tape that was in it last night, after you and Mr. Holt went up to see the sights in Little Saigon. Snake was just using it for an activity log—what you did each day while we were gone. He was watching you. You know, Snakey wasn't a literary giant like you. But he was a good watcher and he loved to talk, though, so he just used the tape. Some awfully revealing notes on that tape, about you and Valerie. Quite a picnic on the island, wasn't it? Meaningful, touching and all that. How'd you keep the sand from sticking to your pecker tracks? Anyway, he's still up the second morning, watching you leave the main house just before sunrise. What a night. Then at 6:20—he says on the tape—you set out around the lake with your dogs, heading up into the hills. Says—this is right on the tape again—he couldn't figure out how anybody could have so much energy after being up all night drinking and necking, so he's going to follow, have a look. Do his job. That was the last thing he had to say to anybody, as far as I can tell. So, where'd you go that morning?"

"I thought you just told me."

"How *far* up the hills did you walk that morning?"

John went to the refrigerator. "Beer, Lane?"

"No thanks. So, how far up?"

John returned to the living room with a cold beer. He sat in a leather chair with his back to the picture window overlooking Liberty Lake. He popped the can and drank.

"Lane, beat it. I'm done."

"Come on, John, humor me. Play along. You play along, I won't tell Mr. Holt about touching his daughter."

"I told him anyway."

"Made a quick father figure out of him, didn't you? I loved the Patrick-act for the Missus, by the way. I can see Holt and Carolyn falling for it, but not Valerie. Mister and Missus, they're so fucked up after Patrick they'd believe anything. She's got a bullet in the brain, but I swear some of it chipped off and got into Mr. Holt, too. Anyway, you told him you touched his kid. Good for you. Humor me anyway. Just cooperate for a minute or two. Show me how futile it would be to go to Mr. Holt and tell him we should bounce your ass off Liberty Ridge. He listens to me, you know. I keep him alive."

John felt tired and surprised. He was not expecting to be playing this game on this field now. But he recognized that he needed to play. Anything on earth was worth forstalling now, until noon Sunday.

"I went a ways up the hill, Fargo."

"To the fence?"

"What fence."

"Perimeter, chain-link, electrically charged."

"No, then."

"Why?"

"Exercise. I couldn't have slept. I knew that, so I took a walk with the dogs. It's an old habit."

"When did you first see Snakey?"

"I didn't."

"You're not observant, are you?"

"Gee, Lane. I guess not."

"Then what happened to him, Bun-boy? He just fell in a hole up on the hillside and we haven't found him yet?"

John shrugged. "I guess. I don't care what happened to him."

"Well he didn't, and you should. I followed his trail and there was no Snakey, no hole. Wasn't very hard, either, because the brush is dense and he was paralleling the path you used. You do take paths on these morning walks, rather than blazing fresh trails as the sun comes up, right?"

"Right." The tree, he thought. The gun. The hole. The box of toys.

"The tracks up on the trail are from your Redwings in the closet up there. Plus, Snakey wore these ugly athletic shoes with the wavy pattern on the bottom. I remember because I told him to get some decent hiking boots if he was going to pay good money anyway. So, there was the Snake's shoe pattern, going the same direction as your path."

John looked at Fargo with all the weary patience he could feign. "Next time you drag out my Redwings, put a little mink oil on them, will you?"

"Two sets of tracks, heading up the same way. One was yours, the other Snakey's. Nobody's seen him since."

"Wow, this drama's so thick you could cut it with a knife. I surrender. Where'd he go, Lane?"

Fargo paced the living room once, his black combat boots thumping soft against the wood floor. "I don't know yet."

"Yet."

"I made it to the property line, mostly by following Snakey's trail. Tracks led me almost to the fence—twenty, thirty yards shy, maybe. And there, they mixed with yours. Yours were everywhere. His were, too. A young oak tree. The fence. Two sets of prints. I sat down on a log and tried to figure it. Snakey could have gone over the fence if the electricity wasn't on, though that's a helluva lot harder than just driving his Toyota away. He could have tunneled *under* the fence, then back-filled the hole. Not likely. He could have been lifted headfirst by God's thumb and index finger, straight up out of there and into heaven. Naw, not Snakey, he was too much of a sinner for that."

John felt a low voltage buzz through his bones. Fargo missed it, he thought. He must have missed the hole. If he had found the hole I'd be a dead informant right now.

"Maybe he did something really wild, like walked back down," he said.

"No prints leading back down."

"None you found. Maybe he prowled around a bit, looking for me, then headed down another way."

"Then you did make it to the fence."

"I didn't see any fence."

"It's only eight feet high and six fuckin' miles long."

John did not stifle his yawn. "I had better things to think about. Besides, I'm unobservant, like you said."

"You sized up those bikers in Anza pretty quick, for being

unobservant. So you don't notice the fence, but how'd you ever miss Snakey? Boot marks everywhere out there, Menden. Yours."

"Pit your hefty IQ against this one, Lane. Marks don't put us there at the same time, do they? I probably got there first, and Snakey probably watched me from a bush or something. That seems about like Snakey's speed—I can see him watching from a bush, hunkered right down in the middle of it like a big tick. When I left—which was after about twenty minutes—he came up and crabbed around and wandered back down the house some other way. There's enough brush and rocks and sandstone up there, he could pick a way down an Apache couldn't track."

John stood up and looked at his watch. "I hate to be rude and imply that you're wasting my time, but you are."

Fargo stared at John, all his reigned menace concentrated in his gleaming, recessive eyes. "I just saw Val on my way over. Looked kind of shook up. Hardly even looked at me. I don't like to see her that way. She'll see through you before very long. She's bright."

"What's she going to see, Lane?"

"I don't know, yet. And it frosts my balls not to know."

"Sorry to keep disappointing you. Keep trying and you'll be able to bust me for something, but it won't be for disappearing Snakey. By the way, I want my wallet, guns and truck keys back."

"Right here," he said, looking at the grocery bag. "Not the gun, though. Won't need it. Mr. Holt's orders."

"He tell you when to pee, too?"

"He'll tell me when I can bust your head."

"Bring help."

Fargo studied John again, his ugly little smile breaking mustache. "I don't think you appreciated that slap on the ear he gave you last week. I think you're just cool enough to pop a man for that if you could get away with it. You're ulterior."

John held out his hand toward the door, palm up. "Must get tiring, being wrong all the time."

"I hardly ever am, about people's characters. You and Adam getting kind of cozy? Touchy-feely through the e-mail?"

"Print them out and read them."

"Have."

"Happy trails, then."

"That's not a bad idea."

The door shut and John cursed himself for the stupid invitation. What if Fargo did go back up the trail and take another look around for Snakey?

He downed the beer and cracked another. He fed the dogs on the deck, then stood there for a while and watched them eat. He watched Fargo disappear into the rough packing plant that was his home. He felt the wind beginning to move in off the desert now, warm, dry and with a hint of the great power behind it.

In the shower his knees felt rickety, his hands shook and he felt again that something terrible was gaining on him.

His dreams were filled Rebecca and Valerie. Both women opened their mouths to talk but he couldn't hear their words. So he just took off, flying over them with a bedsheet stretched between his hands, riding the wind up off the earth and into dark heavens.

CHAPTER
THIRTY-SEVEN

By Saturday night the wind was strong. It folded the blades of meadow grass and exposed their paler sides, washing Liberty Ridge with the astringent smell of the desert. John walked toward the Big House. Holt had invited him to dinner, "big doings." He looked out at the ocean where a yellow sun sank toward bronze water. There were too many things to think about so he picked the most important: Don't rock the boat now. By noon tomorrow, you will be finished.

He was surprised to see the dining table set up on the expanse of lawn that fronted the Big House. A green-and-white striped canopy rocked in the wind, its rounded edges flapping against the poles. Two servers—Liberty Ops trainees, John guessed—moved across the lawn with large chafing dishes on wheeled carts. Behind them came Carolyn in her wheelchair, pushed strenuously across the grass by her evening nurse. He could see Laura and Thurmond Messinger standing at the wet bar with Lane Fargo and an older couple John had never seen before. Adam Sexton waved at him.

He crossed the lawn, stepped under the snapping canvas canopy and onto the parquet flooring, then headed toward the bar. Laura greeted him with a handshake and a peck on the cheek, surrounding John in a brief front of perfume. She had on a pair of jeans, a low-necked white blouse and a black jacket that showed off her ample front and ample suntan. Thurmond nodded to him over the rim of a cocktail glass, and extended his hand when his wife was finished. He was a balding man who wore the oversized black-framed eyeglasses John associated with eccentrics, clothing designers and old-time talent agents.

The wind yanked the cocktail napkin from Thurmond's hand. "Heck of a night for outdoor dining, I'd say."

His wife untangled a strand of long dark hair that had blown into her lipstick. "Damn Vann doesn't have the brains he was born with."

"What makes you think he was born with any?" asked Fargo, his smile putrid as always and his short black hair peaking down over his forehead. He wore a black silk jacket, adorned with images of shrunken heads, over his invariable black t-shirt.

"He is keeping you around," said Laura, solicitously.

"Why wouldn't he?" asked Fargo. He acted affronted at first, then John saw it was not an act at all. Fargo caught him noticing this, then covered up by sipping his beer.

"John," said Laura, taking his arm, "I'd like you to meet Scott and Mary Holt of Salt Lake City. Scott is Vann's older brother."

Scott offered John a grave smile and a gentle handshake. He was a shorter, leaner version of his brother, with the same prying gray eyes, stubborn jaw and abundant gray hair. He looked to be ten years Holt's senior. His wife was broad-faced and handsome and smiled at John as if he had done great things in life. They both held glasses of what looked like sparkling water, with lime wedges afloat on the ice.

"Just in for a visit?" John asked.

"Well, quite frankly, we don't quite know *why* we're here," said Scott.

"Vann practically had to beg him," said Mary.

"That's not true, Mary."

"I mean . . . L.A.'s not our favorite place."

"Pat! Pat!"

John caught the aghast expressions on Scott's and Mary's faces as he listened to Carolyn's voice, hesitated, then turned to greet her.

"Hello, Mrs. Holt."

"Oh, don't you Mrs. Holt me, my clever little prince. Kiss, my son?"

John bent over and kissed her, then stood and awkwardly shook her hand.

She looked up from her wheelchair at Scott and Mary, an expression of confusion on her face. "I'm so sorry, but we haven't met, have we?"

"Scott," said Scott. "We just—"

"—and I'm Mary, Carolyn. Nice to meet you, again."

"Oh, of course. The Ides of March. How could I be so forgetful? You remember my son Patrick, of course? Back from the White House?"

"Well, sure we do," said Scott, casting John a look of profound doubt. "Um-*hm*. The White House?"

"Well, you know," said John.

"Top secret," said Carolyn. "Where on earth has my president gone?"

"He'll be right out, Mrs. Holt," said Joni, putting her hands on Carolyn's shoulders. "Here he comes, right now!"

Grateful for the diversion, John turned to watch. Holt walked across the lawn buttoning his blue blazer, looking out toward the ocean, lifting his nose like a dog to smell the air coming in from miles away. He moved deliberately, like a man willing to learn something with every step. He looked positive and alert, but preoccupied. John could see the worry lines in his forehead and the inward cast of his eyes as he stepped under the canopy, nodded to Fargo and Laura, then came toward the bar.

John moved to the edge of the canopy away from the house and watched the flat-bottomed crescent of a sun evaporate into the ocean. As always he waited for the flash of green; as always it failed to show. He walked out onto the lawn. To the north he could see the Valencia groves shimmering in the wind and the fading light. The western hillsides were autumn yellow with patches of green in the tight, shaded folds. The lake was buffed to a dull silver patina by the wind and the big Norfolk Island pine on the beach swayed with each gust. John imagined the wind whistling through Rebecca's bones, and then he unimagined it.

Adam Sexton walked up with a lovely blond woman he introduced as his wife, Odessa. She offered her hand and John shook it.

"Did you get my message?" Sexton asked.

John nodded. "Not sure what you were after."

Sexton looked at Odessa, then took John's arm and guided him outside the shade of the awning and into the sun. His voice was confidential now with none of his usual swagger.

"All I'm hearing is good things about you from Vann. He's taken. I think his daughter might be, too. I just want you to know that you've got a friend in court. I want you to know I believe you'd be good here. Whatever you're doing, you have my endorsement."

"What do you mean, doing?"

"Everybody's doing something. It's all a game. Everything. That's just a fact of life."

Sexton looked at him with an odd expression, a mixture of acknowledgment and acceptance. "So, whatever your game is, keep it up and play it well. There's room on Liberty Ridge for good people. People like you."

"Thanks, Adam."

"Keep your eye on Fargo, if you aren't already." With that, he clasped John's arm and returned to Odessa.

Valerie was coming across the emerald lawn. He watched her walk on the grass, her red high heels in her right hand. Her red dress with the white polka dots looked fifty years out of date, and unmeasurably beautiful on her. Her hair was up. When she saw him, she raised the hand with her shoes in it in greeting. Then she smiled and ran across the lawn to him, threw her arms around his neck and swung him around, kissing him on the mouth. Everyone under the canopy was watching.

"Hello, Mr. Menden."

"Miss Holt."

"Happy Saturday night."

"Back at you, young lady. Disengage. We're creating a scandal."

"I love a scandal. What's to drink?"

"More than enough to put you on your butt."

She looked at him sternly. "I can hold my liquor, young man. That runs in the family. Shall we join the party?"

John offered his arm in a formal angle and Valerie responded, running the bottom of her forearm against his, touching him very lightly. At the edge of the canopy she steadied herself against him and slipped on her shoes. He felt her weight tilt and her fingers dig hard into his arm.

Fargo was there. "You look really pretty tonight, Val."

"Oh thanks, Laney-Poo. What's that, your shrunken-head jacket?"

"This is it."

"You're a dark man, Lane Fargo, but I like you anyway. Against all my better instincts."

"Get the lady a drink," he said to John.

"What'll it be?"

"Gin and tonic, John. And double up on it, would you?"

When John came back with the cocktails, Fargo had just said something into Valerie's ear and Valerie had just started faking her laugh.

"Lane called you P-Boy," she said. "Because of your coat. Can't tell if you're a private eye or a cowboy."

"Stop it, Lane. I might bust a gut."

"No, really, I mean, what's that coat all about?"

"Warm in the winter, cool in the summer."

"Oh, I'm just teasin', John-Boy." He smiled his small-toothed smile and leaned in close to Valerie. "John's always got his panties in a bunch because I'm following up on him for your Dad. You know, verifying his character. Think he's got something to hide?"

Valerie eyed John playfully. "Everything."

"Me too! See, John-Boy, I'm not alone in suspecting that you're a character of low moral value."

"Oh, now I didn't say that," Valerie offered. "I think he's hiding . . . hiding . . . genius, advanced moral development, and a big . . . heart."

"Doing one hell of a good job of it," said Lane.

"Some people are easy to fool," she said.

"Then I rest my case," said Fargo, kissing Valerie's cheek. "Watch this guy, now. And I'll see you later, gorgeous."

"Okay, Laney."

"You too, P-Boy."

"Fargone Lane," whispered Valerie, as Fargo attached himself to Scott and Mary Holt. "I don't trust him as far as I can throw him. Dad does."

Her dark eyes flashed and a mean little smile came to her lips. "I must learn to forgive and forget. We all should."

"Best advice I've heard lately. By the way, you look absolutely beautiful tonight."

"I like these clothes that are out of style. Don't know why that idea appeals to me so much."

Two hours later they were finished with dinner.

"Everyone have a drink?" Holt asked. "Then lift it to the United States of America and the freedoms that we have left."

Murmured agreements, clinking cocktail glasses.

"Here, here," he continued. "Lend me your kind ears for a bit. I've got some things to say."

John saw the young Holt Men step inside the canopy with dessert trays, then turn back toward the house at the wave of Vann Holt's hand.

"We're eating outside in the wind tonight because this is my favorite weather," he said. "Feels like God's own breath to me, but that's probably just me. Hell on the hair and skin, I know. Wouldn't want it blowing every day but you've got to enjoy it while it's here. One of my themes tonight—enjoy it while it's here."

Another round of mumbled assent, another meeting of glasses and nods. Holt stood.

"I want to start out by welcoming Scott and Mary from Utah. It's been exactly four years, eight months and two weeks since Scott and I have spoken. I know I disappointed you, brother. I was trying my best not to disappoint myself. That God of yours that I turned my back on is none the less supreme for my lapse. Stick with him. I don't expect his forgiveness. Would love to have yours, though. Don't say anything now. I'm not asking anyone for anything tonight. Except to hear me out."

John looked over at Scott and Mary, both statue-still and erect, both crimson in the face. Fargo was staring at him. Carolyn's gaze seemed infinite as the cosmos. Laura Messinger aimed a brittle smile up at Holt while her husband tried to study Scott and Mary as he sipped his drink. Valerie in her polka dot dress looked at John, then back at her father.

"It's important to me that we be together tonight," he continued. "You are my family. Both literal and extended. You are the people I love. You're my life. Carolyn—I love you the most. You were my beginning. You'll be my end. Thanks, girl."

"Oh, Hercules."

The laughter was immeasurably polite and John could feel the anguish behind it. He tried to imagine Carolyn whole. He also saw a darkness pass behind Holt's gray eyes, a darkness that seemed familiar and known, a part of him.

"I had something funny happen down in Texas a few months

back. Didn't tell any of you about it. Wanted to mull it over. Well, it's been mulled. They found a spot on a scan, then a bunch more. No reason to get into detail. Biopsy, all that. The upshot is it's been in there a while, in the system, doing what life does. I'll be pushing up weeds here on Liberty Ridge inside a year, if the doctors are right. Feel pretty good all around, actually."

Carolyn clutched John's arm with surprising strength. He looked at Valerie, whose powerful glow diminished while he watched. Her mouth parted just slightly.

"*No*," Holt said. "Don't say a word. Nobody. We've got months until good-bye and I hate good-byes. You all know that. I'm just getting out the facts. No use hiding them. I don't want tears and I don't want special treatment. Least of all I want is pity. It's insulting. Anybody can't handle this can get up and leave the table now. I mean it."

In the silence that followed John heard the slap of the canvas over them and the hiss from the hills around them. Valerie's face had gone slack, her lips parted in astonishment.

Carolyn smiled, not understanding.

Scott sat with his arms crossed, expressionless.

Thurmond Messinger looked at his plate; Laura had taken his arm in both her hands.

Adam Sexton slouched in his seat, but his eyes were resolutely fixed on Holt.

It was Fargo who surprised him. The dark man in his shrunken-head jacket was scanning the faces around him, as if much more interested in reactions to the news than the news itself. His eyebrows were raised in a thin attempt at alarm. His gaze came to John. It was frank and probing, maybe even a little amused.

And John realized: *Fargo knew.* No surprise in his face, no befuddlement or sadness, not the slightest hint of shock. Fargo knew. John held the curious stare until it moved on.

He felt Valerie's fingers digging into the flesh of his palm.

"Now," said Holt. "Main reason I bother you all with this is that things are going to change. We've got a nice little empire here and I want it run right when I'm gone. I want things understood. I want things clear. One—Valerie, I've been trying to get you into Liberty Ops for a while now. Especially since you got out of school. I'm asking you again, right here and now, to think about it. Think hard. I want you in charge someday soon. Two—

Laura and Thur, Adam, keep on doing what you do best. You're our glitter and our gold. You're the people to answer the world for us. I'm asking you to work with Valerie, when that time comes. Three—Lane, I'd take you to the grave with me but I think you might get cold. You're the best friend a man could have. I'm thanking you for everything you've ever done for me. I needed you for everything on Liberty Ridge. You watched my back. Kicked butt when you needed to. I don't know if anyone here appreciates all we've been through together. I don't know if you'll even want to be here when I'm gone. We have some time to ponder that. But you will be well taken care of, when the time comes. Taken care of very well. I've already started putting some of this organizational stuff in writing. I'll finish it, soon. We'll need some law for this company, just like the country does."

John looked at Fargo again. Things were beginning to make sense: Lane was going to get his walking papers when Holt died. Fargo was nodding with approval, smiling slightly, as if basking in the glow of Holt's praise. But his eyes peered into deep space while the smile just stayed in place, preserved by effort.

"Oh, go Vanny go."

"Be quiet now, honey. There's just a couple of more things I want to say. You all know that Liberty Ridge was built up over the decades. It rose and fell with the times. It was cattle once, then horses, then nothing. Now citrus and security. Tomorrow, who knows? Things will change. We live in an ailing republic. Too many people. Too few values. Too much fear. Too many lies. All the spirit pounded down to mediocrity. My last years have been given over to work and hatred—you all know that. I'm good at those things. I learned to hate everything around me that wasn't you. I hated the people who took Pat. I hated the people who took away his good name. I hated the God that let it happen. We'll still find the kid who pulled the trigger. I'm honor-bound to finish that. I'll still have my day with the woman who smeared him in front of the world. John here is helping me see to her. I can't forgive the unforgivable. I'll see to the final justice for them. I said some things I shouldn't have. Thought some things. Did some things. But, quite frankly, I'm tired of it now. I've got a few months to be here with you people. I've got another winter and another spring. Summer's a maybe. If I could get one more fall to chase those quail and work those dogs, that would be a real good thing. If nothing else I've got you all pinned down here right now, with the Santa Anas blowing the ridge clean and that ocean out there heaving away. So, drink with me again tonight. To here and now. To all of us. Cheers. Boys—haul in the dessert."

The conversation continued—muted, fretful and forced. Valerie was almost silent, but she moved to be as close to her father as she could. She kept drinking. John could see the emptiness in her eyes, and the pain the alcohol couldn't dull. Only Holt was expansive, and soon everyone else was quiet and listening. He was lost to tales of meeting Carolyn, his good days at the Bureau, his first Grand Slam, his best quail shots down in Anza. He drank four Scotch and waters, his voice and delivery unaffected so far as John could see, his big leonine head scanning the guests to let them know he was still here, still alive and powerful, still Holt. The wind blew harder and the canopy shivered. The guests huddled into themselves and still Holt held forth, his voice and the wind taking turns until they seemed to become one force, together breathing life and sound into the tiny universe of Liberty Ridge.

The canopy lifted off and somersaulted across the lawn toward the ocean. Holt stood with his drink in hand, raising it to the sky. Valerie stood with hers; John with his. Then all of them were standing, even Carolyn locked to John's free arm, holding their glasses high while the wind snatched the tablecloth off the table and sent it skidding into the night.

"To vengeance completed and the restoration of soul!"

Then, all:

"To vengeance completed and the restoration of soul!"

They drank.

Then Holt looked at John with all the consuming focus of his character. His gray eyes looked hungry and hard. The wind bent his hair in one direction and lifted one lapel to the side of his neck.

John looked back, feeling reduced to the meager essentials of his falsehood.

"Are you with me?" demanded Holt.

"Yes, sir."

At this, Valerie straightened and lifted her glass. "Dad, I'll run the Ops better than it's ever been run before. I'll make you proud. I promise."

John glanced at the stony face of Lane Fargo while the applause lifted around him.

Then Valerie sat heavily in her chair, her face gone the sudden pale of too much drink, and her eyes focusing on the surface of the table.

"Oh," she whispered.

"John," said Holt. "Take her to your cottage. Tend to her tonight."

"I'll help," said Fargo.

"She won't need you, Lane," said Holt.

John thought: Fargo's future in a nutshell. And that's why he's been funneling the evidence to me. John suddenly understood, too, why the soundtrack to Rebecca's slaughter had been removed before he was led to the tape—because Holt's wasn't the only voice on it.

Holt had shot Rebecca while Fargo shot the video.

CHAPTER
THIRTY-EIGHT

They walked across the lawn then through the trees and hedges until they came to the meadow. Valerie leaned hard into John as they started across. The wind gusted from behind and John could feel it pushing them forward. The grass lay flat in the moonlight. He heard his dogs barking and saw them sitting three abreast in the cone of brightness from the porch light. Boomer lunged into the dark and the others followed. Against his outstretched arm Valerie's back was warm, and beneath his palm the curve of her hip rose and fell with each step she took. He thought: you are beautiful and I could love you and I would give almost anything on earth not to betray you.

He carried her upstairs and laid her on his bed. He opened the windows to let in the cool, wild air. In the bathroom he wet a washcloth, folded the cloth, took it out to Valerie and set it across her forehead. Her face was shiny and pale in the dark and her breathing was fast. He thought about his phone.

"Nice," she whispered.

He brought her the ice water and sat on the bedside. He turned over the washcloth and put the cooler side against her head. He could see the shine of her eyes down against the pillow.

"Think I drank a little too much. Today," she said. Her words seemed to wobble from her mouth and her punctuation was off. "Then drank a little more. Too."

"I think you did."

He ran the backs of his fingers down one clammy cheek. She

began sobbing. He saw the shine of tears on her face and the pools of wet light on her eyes.

"I knew something was wrong with Dad. Sometimes I thought he didn't look. So good. Then a big burst of energy. Like tonight. Then tired or something. When he told us tonight it was like I knew and he was just . . . Confirming. Sometimes I try to picture the world. My world. And all I see is Dad standing there. He's it. He's the world. And I can't think about him gone now. I just can't see him in an urn. Fancy tomb or not. Quiet and cold. My heart's feeling weak and hard right now. Like it's gonna stop. Like when Pat and Mom. Funny feeling. Heart gets sideways in your chest and doesn't have any rhythm left. Throat tickles. Head gets light. Heart just beats anyway. Life keeps pounding away even though you're not interested. Is that a broken heart, John?"

"Yeah."

He took the ice water from her and set it on the nightstand. Then he climbed in beside her and she rolled toward him, putting her face into the crook of his shoulder. He felt her back shaking and the warm liquid of her tears soaking through his shirt.

"In the beginning there was us. Mom 'n' Dad 'n' Pat 'n' me. Then Pat shot. Mom all messed up. But somehow it was still a family. But if Dad goes then it's over. It's just two crazy women and no men left. Bunch of oranges and guys with orange neckties. Bunch of money. Bunch of people. Dad goes, I don't want to run this place. I wanna get on a cruise ship and not come back. I wanna get a penthouse and not come out. I wanna follow the seasons and shoot birds 'til I keel over. From shotgun recoil. I'll be the first girl to die from recoil. Ever."

"Stick around."

"Why?"

"Because you're bright and beautiful and the world needs you."

"You need me?"

"I'll always need you and I'll never forget you."

"Sounds like you're tryin' to. Already. You gonna go like Pat and Dad?"

"I'll be where you want me to be."

"You're a good liar, huh?"

"I don't think so."

He looked at her eyes bright in the darkness. Their knowingness, even in her drunken state, unnerved him.

"You got somethin' about you that's hard to not like. You got this face and this voice. You got this nice paint job. But I think underneath you don't have a you. Underneath it's all moving around, all these John molecules. Don't have a pattern. Don't have a plan. Don't have a place they came from or a place they wanna get back to. I think when Jillian died your compass broke down. The needle stuck. You didn't mind 'cause you needed a rest. Everybody needs a rest. After a loss. But you gotta be careful because if you float too long. If you just wander 'round being tall and cute and telling people what they want to hear, then you turn. You turn into a big bagga shit with a smile on it."

Cogent, he thought. "Drunk and heartbroken, you still get the gist of it, Valerie."

"What was she like?"

"Kind. Pretty. Alive."

"What did you like best about her?"

"Her happiness."

"Dream about her?"

"A lot."

Valerie was quiet for a long moment. John listened to her fast breathing and to the wind outside antagonizing the overhang and window glass. He thought of standing on his uncle's roof with the bedsheet spread.

Valerie took his hand. Her fingers felt hot and damp.

"I had this dream," she said. "Then I had it again. Then I had it a bunch. These two men come to Liberty Ridge. One's dark and handsome. The other's light and handsome. The dark one, he takes Dad away and Dad doesn't ever come back. The light one, he makes love to me over and over again and I can't get enough it feels so. Good. Then the dark one comes back and they're standing there and they blend together into one guy. And Dad's gone and the light guy doesn't look the same anymore. I can tell he's gonna rape me. I try to kill him but he's too strong. After that I'm this dog that runs around here. I watch these guys run the place. They don't know I'm me, and pretty soon I don't, either. Finally I just run away."

"Your dream is telling you to stick around, too."

Her breathing was a little faster now. John could smell the thin sour vapors of liquor coming up from her face. She pressed harder against him.

"And when you came here, John. I wondered, is this the

dark one or the light one? Is this the guy who's gonna make my dad disappear. Or the guy who's gonna love me? Then I realized it's one and the same guy—that's what the dream's about—it's about one thing turning out to be the other. And here it is a few weeks since you arrived and you do what the light guy does and Dad's sure enough gonna die. What the hell am I supposed to make of all this, John?"

"Not sure."

"What's your real name?"

"John Menden."

"Just checkin'."

"Hold me."

"I am."

"I should barf."

"Come on, then."

He helped her off the bed and into the bathroom. Through the closed door he heard the toilet flush, then flush again, then flush once more. Water running, splashing, the sound of a soap bar thudding against the sink. Then the door opened and she came out with an air of minor replenishment.

"Okay?"

"Little better. I still got the spins."

"Lie down."

"Think I'd better sit up straight."

She sat in a big armchair that overlooked the railing and faced the window of the living room. She put her feet up on the wooden staves of the railing. John stayed where he was, on the foot of the bed, still holding the now-warm washcloth.

He stared out the window on which their reflections blended with the darkness outside, with the sycamores by the lake shaking in the wind, with the lake surface rippling left to right in the broad path of light where the moon beamed down. Looking at the glass it was hard for him to tell where one thing ended and another began. He tried to see one image at a time, clearly, because he wanted to feel in his heart one thing at a time, clearly. He did not want confusion, complication or compromise. He did not want to believe that for some questions there are no good answers, for some problems no solutions. So he tried to isolate the outline of a tree against the water. But the thin autumn branches became the ripples and the tree was gone—not lost to the water, really, but joined into it. Same with the reflection of

Valerie. She became the room behind them projected back from the window, then became the water itself, her shining eyes just another pair of silver flickerings on the lake.

This woman can mean nothing to you because Rebecca meant everything.

"Can I get you anything?" he asked her reflection.

She wrapped her arms around herself. He could see her head swaying very slightly. Her hair fell down around the sides of her face and in the window the white polka dots on her dress became the stars.

"A cure for Dad. A declaration of your undying true love for me. Something for my head."

"I'll get some aspirin. You get in bed."

"One outta three. Not bad. I'm sorry."

"For what?"

"For what happened to your girl."

She was under the covers when he came back. Her voice was just a whisper now, fading:

"Thank you for taking care of me."

"It's an honor."

"You always say the right. Thing . . ."

"I mean it."

"Scariest thing. Scariest thing tonight was the way Lane looked at me when I said I'd run the Ops."

"Lane wants it for himself."

"Mine, now."

"He's going to fight you for it."

"Can take him. Easy. Easy . . ."

Soon she was breathing deeply.

Downstairs he checked his messages:

THOUGHT YOU MIGHT LIKE SOME FRIENDLY MAIL. STILL
SHAKING FROM ALL WE DID TOGETHER. MUCH TOO SOON TO
SAY I LOVE YOU BUT I DO SO ALL COMPLICATIONS STEM-
MING THEREFROM ARE YOURS. FEEL A CELEBRATION COM-
ING ON TONIGHT. YOUR EX-VIRGIN QUEEN—

VAH

*   *   *

AM UP AND RUNNING AND FEELING BETTER. STAY IN
TOUCH.

                                        SNAKEY

               *   *   *

LIKE THE MOVIE? KNEW THEY WOULD. WHEN'S IT ALL
GOING DOWN?

He played me well, thought John. Kept me dancing under
pressure when he knew all along. Had he found the toys? The
hole? Had the waitress at Olie's ID'd Joshua somehow, put them
together? It really didn't matter how. It was Fargo's job to know,
and he had done it.

What did matter was that Fargo had landed outside the Bureau's net for now—and if he'd destroyed the soundtrack, he
might stay that way forever. Holt might talk, but it wasn't likely.

That left Valerie. What would be in store for her, alone on
Liberty Ridge with a killer and a traitor? A thousand reasons to
leave control of Liberty Ops to him? Certainly. And those failing,
as they were likely to fail on as stubborn and devoted a daughter
as Valerie, then what? A good, old-fashioned hunting accident?

He walked outside and stood on the deck. Boomer, Bonnie
and Belle looked up from sleep but showed him little interest,
their tails knocking slowly on the wood. He looked out at the
profile of Fargo's darkened packing plant of a home.

That's all I can leave you with, he thought: the name of the
serpent in your paradise.

To this end he wrote her a short letter on his notepad, folded
the sheet neatly and wrote her name on it. He set it on the bar
that separated the kitchen from the living room, under the salt
and pepper shakers, so it wouldn't blow off. There was little in it
about himself or what he had done or why he had done it. Just
what he had learned about Fargo since coming to Liberty Ridge.

In case Holt prevailed tomorrow—rather than Joshua—she
might find it sometime when she was in the cabin, looking for
some clue to where he had gone, wondering why he'd left so
quickly. In that case, of course, she wouldn't believe his words
anyway. Her father would be around to smooth comforting lies
over the truth. And Lane would take the long trip, also, sometime
in the near future, courtesy of the man he had loved, feared and
betrayed.

Just as well, John thought.

He went upstairs and lay down beside her. He wondered if there was any way she could forgive him for what was about to happen, and he knew there was not. He wondered where he would go tomorrow when it was over—back out to the desert, a motel, back to the Laguna Canyon house and the uneasy ghost of Rebecca. Maybe the ghost will be gone. Isn't that what this was all about?

He felt again that he was about to leave a place where he could do some good and go somewhere else, to a place he had never seen or no longer remembered, to a place not his, a place where time might or might not grant him the privilege of casting his own shadow.

CHAPTER
THIRTY-NINE

All Sundays should be so restful, all mornings so clear.

Vann Holt, in khaki pants and safari shirt, stood before one of the Africa dioramas in the trophy room. It was the scene where the bull elephant is caught mid-stride, his trunk raised and mouth open for a sonorous bellow that Holt remembered clearly from that hot April day on which he stood in the grass and let the big animal charge close—fifty yards, it was—before he squeezed the Weatherby .400 magnum load into the bull's forehead, and the elephant didn't even flinch. Holt remembered it all with precision: his methodical retracting of the bolt while the elephant came, the thunderous tremor of the earth under his boots, the way the bull lowered his blood-spattered head as he closed the distance, his big ears folded back and the knotty dome of his skull enlarging over the iron sights of the rifle, the second shot cracking through bone and brain, the stumble and graceful correction, the way one ear fanned out and the mouth dropped askew pouring blood and the tusks stayed aimed straight at him and the third shot that seemed to yank the animal's head forward and down into the grass through which it dozed toward him, rear end still high for just a moment before the whole magnificent creation grunted to a ground-shaking stop ten feet from the barrel of his upraised gun. Holt had urinated.

That was before Carolyn and Patrick, he thought, back when life left time for sport, excitement and challenge. A trophy from days of strength and happiness.

"I thought you'd be in here, Dad."

"Hi, honey."

Valerie slipped her arm around his back and laid her head on his shoulder. "I'm sorry I got so drunk last night."

"It was a night for high emotions."

"I've never felt so foolish, and so sad, and so proud of you. Ah, Dad, why didn't you tell me?"

He snugged his arm around hers. "I told you in plenty of time, hon. There was no profit in doing it sooner."

"Isn't there anything we can do?"

"We can do whatever we want."

"I mean about—"

"—I know. No. It just runs its course like anything else in nature."

"I knew that day would come. I just had it pegged for thirty years from now."

"What's important is to live with grace and dignity, and die that way too. What I don't want, dear girl, is a thousand long good-byes."

She shook her head against his chest and Holt could feel the warmth of her breath through his shirt. "I don't want that, either."

"Atta girl."

"I'll run the Ops when you . . . need me to."

"You've got lots to learn. And lots of time to learn it. I'm feeling good. We will have our hours and our days."

"I love you."

"I love you, Valerie."

She hugged him close then pulled herself away to stand before him, running her fingers down his clean-shaven cheek. Holt looked at the wet trails the tears had left on her face, the tangle of golden hair pinned atop her head with chopsticks, and the deep chocolate richness of her eyes—her mother's eyes. Her lips were tightly pursed but her chin quivered.

"We'll get there, Dad."

"I know we will, dear child. Hey, I'm entertaining some not-very-interesting people for lunch today, around noon. Laura and Thur said they'd like to have you over to their place. I told them you'd be there."

Valerie breathed in deeply, then let it out. Holt hadn't seen such sadness in her eyes since Pat and Mom.

"I was planning to take my lunch over to the island. Just me. I've got some thoughts I'd like to be alone with."

"Then I'll tell them you had a previous engagement."

"Thanks, Dad."

She stepped forward and kissed him. "I want to say just one thing. I want you to know that I never did anything to you, or for you, that wasn't done out of love."

Holt smiled. "I'm trying to remember a time when I doubted that."

"There will be doubt in the days ahead, Dad."

Holt felt that great choke of emotion taking hold of his throat, that big lump that seemed to catch just under his voice box and made his eyes grow tears. He reached out and they hugged again, but Valerie broke it off and backed away with an attempted smile.

"I hear John's running an errand for you later."

"Just bringing the client up for lunch. Rich lady from Newport, thinks her husband is fooling around. Not with his secretary, with her money. Of course."

"Glad to miss that one."

"I thought you would be. When you're alone with your thoughts on the island today, send a pleasant one my way. I'll snag it, and send one back."

"You got it," she said, turning to leave.

"Honey? Send Lane down here, will you?"

Fargo appeared five minutes later, just like Fargo would, Holt thought, not there and no entrance, then suddenly sitting one seat away from you in the theater. Over the years he had become used to Fargo's invisible arrivals and departures. He could see that the dark man's hair was mussed from the steady wind outside and that Lane had hung his sunglasses over the neck of his black t-shirt.

"Sunday morning cartoons, boss?"

"How's everybody seem to be taking it?"

"Pretty good, Mr. Holt. Val was disappointed you didn't tell her first."

"Scott?"

"Can't read a guy like him. He's probably still talking to his God about it. Got them to the airport an hour ago. How are you feeling?"

"Strong."

"How come you're looking at a blank screen?"

But Holt plowed through Fargo's questions, as he did John's and everyone else's. "Val's going to start taking over the Ops. She'll need all the help and support you can give her."

Fargo said nothing for a moment, then: "She'll get it."

"And when I go, she'll be the one in charge."

"I figured it like that."

"Disappointed?"

"Yeah. You and me built the Ops, not her."

"I don't blame you. I've drawn up an agreement with the bank that will put two million in your pocket after I go. It's separate from the estate plan and company by-laws, which I still haven't gotten around to changing. Haven't executed that bank arrangement yet. Obviously, I wanted to hear you out."

Holt could see in Fargo's eyes the ill-concealed disappointment and the flicker of menace. "You always did right by me, Mr. Holt. When it comes down to it, I'd rather run the Ops than cash out, even for that much. I'm firm, there. I think you know that's what I'm about. But if it's Val's show it's Val's show. Maybe I'll take the money and split. I gotta little time to think, don't I?"

Holt studied his factotum and felt stymied—not for the first time—by Lane Fargo's odd amalgam of subservience and ambition.

"I'll need you more than ever these next months, Lane."

"You got me, boss. I don't have to say it, but I will anyway—I didn't just stay here for the money. I stayed here for honest work with a guy who didn't take any shit from the world. I stayed here to build something good with my life—Liberty Ops. Something that lets the little guy stand up to creeps and the government. I've always been proud to stand by you."

Holt reached across the empty theater seat and lay his hand on Fargo's shoulder. He could feel the cool leather of the shoulder strap over the cotton.

"Follow Menden this morning."

"I figured you'd want that."

"Let him know you're there. Don't want him to start thinking for himself."

"He's not capable of it."

"Anyway, when you come back past the Big House, let him bring her up to Top of the World. You park here. Stay around.

Keep your eyes open. Stay mobile. I need to know you're out there, watching my back."

"That's what I do best, boss."

Fargo stood to go, then sat back down.

"I gotta favor to ask you, Mr. Holt. If you can arrange it. I'd like to take care of Menden when it's time. I hate that cute face of his and I know what he's doing with Valerie. It'd be good for me, if it's all the same to you."

Holt nodded and Fargo rose again.

"If it works out that way."

"I'd be grateful, sir."

"Let me ask you something, Fargo. You get the feeling something's about to go down? Besides this thing with Baum?"

Fargo actually raised his face to the air, like a bird-dog might, then crossed his arms over his chest. Holt had seen Fargo do this dozens of times: Lane's way of assessing the moment, of judging the invisible physics of threat.

"No. I'm not getting that."

"Good. Something just seems a little off to me."

"Damned wind gets on my nerves. But you should always listen to your instincts, Mr. Holt."

Holt did in fact sit in the theater after Fargo had gone, staring at the blank big-screen, listening to many things. He heard the wind moaning outside. He heard the cells replicating inside him. He heard Baum's voice—the self-righteous tone of outrage she used on TV—but now she was pleading for her life instead of *a full-scale investigation into Patrick Holt's treatment of women*. He heard Valerie's and Fargo's words. And he heard the quiet voice that always counseled him in times of engagement, now telling him that when he was gone, Fargo would do anything he had to to get the Ops for himself.

John awoke at five a.m. after a dream in which Joshua, a six-gun in each hand, simultaneously blew away Vann Holt and John Menden. He was drenched in sweat. He listened to the sound of the wind rattling the windowpanes of his cottage. Valerie was huddled to the far end of the bed so he reached out and set his hand on her shoulder—so warm, so smooth. And now, he thought, it's time to betray you. In his state of half-consciousness he tried to let his mind find a way to take down Holt without breaking Valerie's heart. But the more he tried to find one, the more he awakened and the more impossible it became to even imagine such a way. It was the deal I made for you, dear woman, he thought, right from the beginning. Now comes the follow-through.

So again his thoughts returned to Joshua, and the perilous course the agent had chosen. He had long understood that Joshua would risk everything he had to avenge Rebecca—this was the motor behind all that had happened in the last months. But not until last night had he realized that Joshua was willing to risk Baum, John himself, and even Sharon, in his unilateral charge of revenge. Everyone else would come second. John realized that on a primal level, Joshua needed to see him dead. John's death would be the purest retribution for what John had done with Rebecca, the purest defeat of a rival. Why not? Love and hate are always beyond control, and Joshua was clearly consumed. It was a gut-tightening idea, and John tried to purge it. But it was there just the same, along with the image of Joshua's face on the deck of his Laguna Canyon house last summer, when the agent pulled his gun and told him that he'd been looking for a way to contest John for Rebecca's long-cold heart.

With everything on the line at noon, John thought, Joshua's loyalties will finally lie with himself.

I'll be there.

But when? How? And to accomplish what?

John thought of Holt, and the possibility that Holt would dispose of him along with Baum, if he should fail in this assignment. What would Holt really like to give him, the keys to his kingdom or a bullet in the head?

With these realities in mind, John rose quietly from the bed, dressed and slipped out the door with his dogs. From the oak tree by the electric fence he retrieved the .45, and stashed it in the center console of his truck. When he got back into bed forty minutes later, Valerie hadn't moved.

CHAPTER
FORTY

John guides his truck up the last steep incline at Top of the World. He's glad to be rid of Fargo, who frisked him twice before letting him through the main gate, then blatantly followed him all the way to Newport Beach and back. Baum sits beside him, dressed in a flowing bright green silk ensemble with a loose vest and oversized cuffs, huge sunglasses, heavy faux-emerald earrings and white high-top athletic shoes. At first, she took John's change of plan—we're going to Liberty Ridge—with a giddy acceptance. She'd silently evaluated the long, palm-lined drive up from the frontage road, the magnificent house and grounds, the windswept hills and Valencia groves. But now, as they climb the last few yards toward the vaults, John can feel her fingers digging into the flesh of his arm.

"He's actually going to be here?"

"Actually."

"And what about Josh? And Sharon?"

John slows the truck, then stops completely. He turns to Baum and lowers her sunglasses so he can look into her pale green eyes. "They'll be there. And Susan, if you much as imagine their names, it will get both of us killed instantly. That's the deal we have. Do you understand?"

"What I *don't* understand is why—"

He reaches out and takes her arm, hard. "—Then shut up and play along. It'll be over with soon."

"Oh, God, as if that's supposed to console me. Who are you really working for, anyway? You're hurting my—"

"—I said shut up and play along. Act pissed off that I tricked you into this. That's all you need to do."

"I really *am* pissed off."

"Run with it."

He leaves the brakes, punches the gas and mounts the crest. His truck levels off and he pulls it over next to one of Holt's Rovers.

"I'll get the door," he says.

Baum gathers up her big leather bag from the floorboard and, of course, starts trying to find the door handle that Fargo removed. John uses this time to retrieve his .45 from the console and slip it into the pocket of his duster. Then he hops out and goes around to the passenger side to let Baum out. She slides out of the big truck, cursing under her breath.

Together they walk across the gravel toward the stone table and benches. John feels loose and alert, but his heart takes a little downward twirl when he sees the wedge-shaped figure of Partch, standing, with his arms crossed, behind the table area. He wears the same golf shirt and slacks that he wore the last time John saw him, the same sunglasses, and a short leather jacket to cover his sidearm.

Holt comes from the table, nodding to John, then smiling at Baum. He offers her his hand.

"I'm Vann Holt."

"You know who I am. Just what in hell is going on here?"

"Lunch. Bring an appetite?"

"Not really."

"I made some special dishes."

"I'm dieting."

"Come over here to the edge with me, will you? I wanted you to see Liberty Ridge from above."

He takes her arm and guides her past the silent Partch, over to the edge of the summit.

"I can stand up on my own," she says.

"It's a simple courtesy. John? Why don't you join us?"

They stand three abreast—Baum in the middle—and look down at the Ridge. The wind is dying down, the bulk of its fury spent during the night, but it gathers now to a steady howl that lasts a few seconds, then dies.

"When did you come to Orange County from New Jersey, Susan?"

"Eight years ago."

"Ever seen anything quite like this?"

"Sure I have. Orange County's all the same unless it's the beach or got streets and houses on it—just hills and vultures and plants that don't get flowers on them. I always thought the houses looked better than oak trees and cactus. I don't see why people like you get in such a snit about other people wanting to live where you do. Or maybe I just answered my own question—you just want it for yourself."

Holt laughs. "I certainly do. It's been in the family three generations now. What you say is exactly what I'd expect from a Jersey Jew."

"Predictably ugly words. I happen to think a vibrant community of people is more interesting than something like this. The rancho days petered out about two decades ago. Haven't you heard?"

"There's more than just nostalgia here. There's the community you mentioned—there's family and blood and business and production. There's shared culture, religion and language. There's regular people trying to live on the land, take something from it and give something back."

"Privileged white people," says Baum. "And their magnificent playthings. A helicopter next to your mansion? Get real. Nobody can afford to live like this any longer."

John inwardly winces at Susan's words; she isn't just standing up to Holt, as Joshua had no doubt coached her, she's right straight in his face. How could they have expected less from her?

"I can," Holt answers. "And I intend to. And I've done it without dragging innocent people through mud. I've done it without slandering people for profit."

Baum looks at Holt now, and sets her sunglasses atop her swirl of hair. "Mr. Holt? Let's cut the bullshit and maybe get to some kind of point. What in hell are we doing here right now?"

"I brought you up here to tell you about Patrick. There was a time I wanted an apology from you. But not now. I just want you to understand."

"Apologize for what? Everything I wrote was true."

"What you didn't write was more true. When the real rapist was caught, you didn't retract a word that you'd written about Pat."

"It was in the paper. On the news side. I can't apologize every time I rub somebody the wrong way."

"I'm no longer expecting one."

"Okay. I'm sorry. There. Make you feel better?"

John watches Holt look down on Baum with an expression of pure bitterness.

"I suppose you want it in the paper?"

Easy, thinks John.

"It's amazing to me how little you know."

"Then what am I supposed to do?"

Holt smiles. "*Understand.* Join me for lunch. This way. Your place is right here. John, you're at the head."

John looks at the fancified table: three settings—two facing each other from each of the long sides of the rectangular stone, and a third at the head of the table, facing the two others and the Holt vaults. There is a linen cloth, a small vase of wildflowers as a centerpiece, place settings, cloth napkins, wine and water glasses and plates at each place. The plates are covered by shiny silver domes. The wind buffets the little flowers.

John sits. Baum is to his left, and beyond her, still fastened in his silence, stands Partch. Holt is on his right, directly across from Baum. He wonders why he is at the head of the table, knowing it's not an accident. For one thing, Partch has a clean line of fire at him.

He looks up at the blue. He wonders how they'll arrive—by land or sky. He pulls the long side of his coat up onto his leg so the .45 rests on his thigh. He unrolls his napkin and scrunches it out of the way between his legs. He feels to make sure the coat pocket slit is up and convenient and the flap is tucked inside.

John watches Baum look up at the figure of Patrick and his books, then to Vann and Carolyn in a wedding-cake pose, then to Valerie with her dog.

"Susan, take off your sunglasses," says Holt.

"It's bright out."

"I want to see your expressions while we talk."

"I choose to leave them on."

Holt leans forward and reaches out to her like an optician, slowly and deliberately, with both hands open. He's smiling. Then he takes her lips between the thumb and forefinger of his right hand and sharply yanks her face toward him. She whinnies, raising both hands helplessly beside her face. She wiggles but her face can't move. With his left hand he pulls off the glasses and sets them next to him.

"Better," he says, letting her go.

"Oh, God," she hisses. "You . . . *you* . . ."

But she doesn't finish the sentence and for the first time all day John can see the fear rising in Susan Baum's lovely green eyes.

"Pat was twenty-two, just out of college," he says, laying his napkin across his lap. He points to Baum's. "Show some manners, lady."

Baum dumps the silverware and snaps the cloth open. John watches her shaking hands take the napkin beneath the table top.

"Religious kid. We started Mormon, but by the time I gave it up, Pat was had. Okay with me. There's worse things than religious convictions. Something to believe in is always better than nothing, long as it lasts. Had a girl he was going to marry after his mission to Africa. Had an A-minus grade average—Economics. Had a nice way with people and animals. Actually, kind of a shy kid. Never really liked to hunt or fish, didn't care for the killing. I respected that about him. Had these real pretty blue eyes, light skin. He was a happy soul. The kind of kid who'd wake up happy, jump into bed with you and smile and say, it's time to get up, Mom. Time to get up, Dad. One of those kind of kids. Rare. Val was always grumpy in the morning. Me, too. Carolyn so-so. But Pat, there he was, first light of day charging in to get you going. This was when he was three."

John watches Holt. Maybe it is the events of the night before, or the cancer inside him, or the memory of his son or the hideousness of the task at hand, but his face—John sees—has lost its usual robust glow and now looks pale and loose. Behind the lenses of his yellow shooting glasses his gray eyes have taken on an ocher, otherworldly cast. He catches John looking at him and John looks away.

"In fact," Holt continues. "One of the reasons it was so easy for you—and those alleged victims of yours—to put Pat down in the barrio was because Pat *was* down in the barrio a lot—doing his domestic mission work. That's what they do before sending them out into the world to convert souls. And you, Ms. Baum, you and your frightened lady friends turned *that* into the possibility of a rape spree. It was so preposterous I'd have laughed if it wasn't my own son. But it wasn't very goddamned funny when I read about it in your columns and there was no Pat left to even fight for his own good name. I'll tell you, Baum—I've been a lot of places in my life and I've done a lot of things. And nothing ever made me as sick as what you wrote. Nothing made the bile jump into my throat and my face sweat and the sweat smell foul. Nothing ever."

Baum looks at John.

Hang in there, he thinks.

"Then you should have called me," says Baum.

"I did. Several times. And not a single return call. Not one."

"I was busy."

"—I was busy, too. Trying to find a good motorized wheelchair for Carolyn. Whom you described in one column as 'the kind of subservient wife and child-bearer Mormons cherish, who had probably never disobeyed her husband in all her life.' You implied rather obviously that those characteristics—untrue, by the way—were what made her *deserve* what had happened to her. 'Perhaps a more independent woman would have refused to accompany her *twenty-two* year old son that day on a Christian crusade into the dear, near barrio to troll for souls less in need of redemption than either of them could have known. Perhaps she had suspected that in the past his sorties into Santa Ana might have been for quite another purpose altogether.' "

Baum looks down at the silver dome covering her lunch. "Overwrought. Maybe."

"Carolyn would have laughed at that if she'd had any sense left to laugh with. I couldn't. Still can't. It's an insult to the finest human being I've run across on earth. You knew nothing about her. You just took the trendy generality and ran with it."

"Then I apologize."

"Too late."

"You want it in print?"

"No. An apology was never the point."

"Then what is it you want me to do?"

"Eat your lunch."

John watches Baum lift the cover of her plate and set it aside.

"What is it?" she asks with a diminished self-assurance.

"Your articles, shredded and topped with fifty cc's of Carolyn's blood and a dash of Pat's ashes. It might need salt and pepper."

She looks at Holt with a glazed expression. John sees the panic building, the tic in her cheek.

Holt lifts the cover on his plate to reveal a snub-nosed revolver, polished and gleaming on the white china. In an act of humor, a sprig of parsley sits beside the cylinder.

"John, see if you like your entrée," he says.

John looks at Holt and tries to assess the intentions in the pale ocher eyes. The eyes seem to hold only conviction, nothing more—no humor, no pity, no latitude. As he looks into those eyes John passes the point where he is sure how to act, sure what is expected and planned. In his mind he sees Joshua and Sharon parachuting down from the heavens but this is only a mirage of hope.

Where are they?

Then, like a prayer answered, he really does see something that makes his pulse race—yes, he's sure it's actual, far out over the Pacific—a small dark object in the sky. Inwardly, he smiles.

The wind howls across the Ridge and John lifts his silver dome to find an identical revolver on his plate. It is pointed toward the tombs, mid-way between Baum on his left and Holt on his right. A similar sprig of parsley shivers in the wind.

Baum looks at John's plate, then at John.

"I'm finished," she says. "I can't do this anymore."

"Too bad," says Holt. "Take a bite. John, when Susan's finished, either one of us can serve the dessert."

We're ready, John thinks. He looks out to the airborne miracle moving in over the ocean now, a helicopter etching an achingly slow line toward them. It is descending.

Holt follows John's gaze. "That chopper coming our way, John?"

"Looks like it, Mr. Holt."

"Well, I wonder who it could be."

"I've got no idea."

"Maybe it's the air cav, come to rescue Susan from having to eat her words."

Baum's head is turned toward the helicopter.

"Eat your lunch, Susan," orders Holt. "There's nobody on earth who can relieve you of your obligations now."

Baum looks at John again, and he can see her panic. He tries to express reassurance with his eyes. *Hang in here,* he thinks.

"Do what he says, Susan."

She takes this as evidence of John's duplicity. Her gaze hardens against his. She looks quickly at Holt, then back at Partch, then up at the chopper lowering toward Top of the World.

"Oh, shit," she says.

John watches too as the black-and-orange machine hovers above them, tilting one way with the wind, then the other. The tail pivots out and the nose drops and the pilot waves down at them. John is aware of Holt waving back. Then the Liberty Ops patrol chopper rises as if strings are cinching it back into the blue.

"Good soldiers," says Holt. "Always looking out for the old man."

John notes the satisfied smile on Holt's face. The sound of the helicopter's engine vanishes in the wind and the mute craft tilts back toward the Pacific.

In the wake of its departure John feels a sickening emptiness in his stomach. He knows that what Baum is feeling is worse. He understands that all roads have led him here, that all moments have converged here, though this understanding leaves him with little but a sense of profound foolishness.

Where are they?

Baum looks at him, crestfallen: "John—I'm finished."

Holt looks hard at him. John can see the gears turning now in Holt's mind, the questions ratcheting by, the answers rotating up to engage them. He knows it will only take another second or two for it all to mesh. Time, he thinks, anything now for time.

So he picks the revolver off his plate with his left hand and holds the barrel out, inches from Baum's head. He slips his right hand into his coat pocket and locks his palm around the butt of the automatic, slipping his finger through the trigger guard. He tries to tilt the muzzle toward Holt, but the hammer is caught in the soft material of the pocket and he can't free it.

His own voice sounds tight and unconvincing: "Shut up and eat, Susan. Trust me now. It's good for all of us. Believe me."

Holt: "Eat your words, you wretched swine."

John sees nothing but terror in Baum's green eyes. Her pupils look like black dimes.

She looks down at her plate, lifts her fork, and picks at the pile of shredded newsprint with the tines.

"Drink some water, Susan," John says. And as he says this, he glances past Baum to Partch, gauging the distance he'll have to swing the revolver in order to shoot past her head and hit the big man. Four inches? Five?

"This gun loaded, Mr. Holt?" he asks, staring down the barrel at Baum.

"What do you think?"

"I think you'd like me to use it."

"It would reveal your weight. Conviction. Follow-through."

"Question is, do you trust me enough to load it?"

"That is the question, John. Million dollar one. What if you lost your nerve? Tried to use it on me? I had to consider that."

"There's Partch."

"Damn straight. Up to you, John. Totally your call. Follow your heart."

Where are they?

John glances at Partch: arms loose at his side now, full attention directed back at him.

When he shifts his gaze to Baum, he sees something different in her eyes. But is it resignation or understanding?

She lifts her water glass and drinks.

She picks up her fork again and pokes at the bloody, ash-strewn paper. Then she looks at Holt.

"Mr. Holt, how was this meal prepared?"

"With tender, hating care."

"No, I mean, did you saute the paper, or brown it in an oven?"

"It's newsprint tartar."

"Well . . . let's see how it . . ."

She gets a little mound of shreds on the forktip and looks at it. She brings it to her nose and takes a quick whiff. The wind blows some of it back down to her plate. She breathes deeply, opens her mouth, closes her lips around the fork and looks to John in complete and utter capitulation.

Then she spits the paper toward Holt and hisses: "You killed Rebecca Harris and I know it. You thought she was me." She whirls to face John, her nose inches from the muzzle of the revolver. "Okay, Mr. Sporting Life. You were in love with her. I could see all the way across the office. What are you going to do about her now? How could you throw in with this . . . *pig?* I hope the FBI busts both your asses wide open."

Holt regards John from behind his yellow glasses. He is smiling, but John sees that he knows. The realization has broken on

Holt like a wave on a fatal shore. Strangely, there is disappointment in the big, handsome face. "Well, John. She can't be telling the truth. Wouldn't know how, would she?"

John knows he's out of options, out of stalls. He understands that Joshua has stranded him here in the high lonesome to fend for himself and for an innocent woman who very well might die. Was that his goal, all along?

His heart is thumping. His stomach feels like it's down around his boots. The revolver has grown heavy in his left hand, but he eases it four inches to the left of Baum's head and aligns the sights on Partch's chest. He still can't free the .45 from his coat pocket. It is snared in a tangle of strings and folds, and he knows that any hint of this problem will be Partch's cue to draw down.

"The truth is I loved her," says John. "And you killed her in the rain."

Holt stares at John for a long moment. When he speaks, his voice is tremulous and soft. "Yes, I did. Forty years of law enforcement and never made a mistake like that one. An accident. Bad one. Forgive me?"

"Never. I'll shoot Partch if he moves. And I'll shoot you by the time your hand reaches that plate. That's my follow-through, Mr. Holt."

But the truth of it is that John is too afraid to move. Things seem to be proceeding in slow motion. Every muscle in his body is locked tight, cold, nullified. In the center of his chest is a hard, frozen anchor that fastens him in place. He has finally worked the automatic in his coat pocket to point, roughly, at Holt, but his fingers are so numb he can hardly feel it.

"I'm real sorry, John. Could have used you. Here on the Ridge. Everywhere. Tricked my girl, didn't you?"

"I guess I did."

"Can't let you get away with that. Scared now? Bad feeling, gun on a man. Real life."

"Yeah, it's a bad feeling."

"I don't think you can fire."

"I will."

Holt looks over to Partch and nods.

It is pure reaction now. John holds on the middle of Partch, silhouetted against the sky, and pulls the trigger. The click is the most final sound he's ever heard in his life.

Then Partch is bending into a shooter's crouch, one hand inside his jacket, just as something shifts on the periphery of John's vision—gold flashing in sunlight. To his left Partch's gun points directly at him. But two phantoms have already materialized from the shadows of the tombs and into the bright day. Two sharp explosions jerk Partch onto his heels and over.

Baum is screaming horrendously and the vibrations of that sound rattle into John's brain. Because for him it's an eternity in a moment as he tries to yank the .45 from his coat pocket. In that second he sees a figure turning a gun toward Holt. And the next thing he knows his whole body is being pulled across the table, his head clamped in Holt's big arm and something hard jamming into his forehead. The world is sideways. Baum is screaming so loud his ears whine. Holt yanks his face into the lunch plate. John feels the arm cutting off his blood and breath while straight in front of his eyes he sees the bullet tips in Holt's revolver, and past them the thick finger locked around the trigger and beyond that the unfocused figures of Joshua Weinstein and Sharon Dumars frozen in sunlight and gold.

Holt's voice reverberates through the arm that chokes him. "My show now, kids. I'll absolutely kill him. Drop the guns. Lie down. Be good boys and girls. *Now.*"

John's hand is still in his pocket and he knows it's still in his pocket but there's nothing getting to his brain or lungs and the world is getting fuzzy, warm and distant. He tries to focus on the agents but can only see the bullets right in front of his eyes. Are they starting to rotate? Then there's a roaring, percussive cluster of blasts and John feels his flesh shudder with the impact, feels the crack and splinter of bone around his face and the sudden splatter of blood into his eyes, and the terrible surge of something weighty and pressurized exploding. John falls thinking, so this is how it feels. You fall. Just like I thought. The next thing he knows he's on his back staring up at a clear blue sky and there's a warm breeze on his face and the air is rushing back into his lungs and someone is screaming *call the ambulance, call thefuckingambulancejosh* while her fingers dig into his neck. He can smell something metallic and wet on his face cooling in the breeze. A lot of it. But he realizes that he still has his hand on the gun. He grabs Sharon's arm with his free hand, climbs to his feet and finally draws it. It doesn't take him long to find what he's after. To get the sonofabitch in his sights. No. Because Holt is right there at

John's feet with a blank look in his eyes and a big black hole between them, just above the frame of his glasses, another one in the middle of his forehead and another one an inch from that. John feels himself swaying. He tries to follow the sight of the automatic passing back and forth across Holt's chest.

"Easy, John," someone is saying. "Easy, John. We got him. You did your job. It's over."

He stands there and for a moment feels above it all, sees himself from above looking down at himself standing over a dead body and pocketing his gun, looking down at a young man sprawled on the gravel with an automatic beside him, at a woman with dark hair and blood on her blouse and a lithe little guy with a pale face and a telephone in his hand, speaking but making no sound.

I'm still alive, he thinks, but I've gone to hell anyway.

A few moments later a red Jeep flies over the rise and skids to a stop. Valerie Holt stares at him from the driver's seat. Fargo sits next to her.

The sight of her brings John back to himself. He strips off his coat and covers Holt. He steps to meet her as she breaks into a run. She pulls up just short of him and glares at Dumars and Joshua. Then she brings her full attention to what lies on the ground.

"Oh," she says. "No? *No.*"

John sees her confusion turn to horror as she raises her eyes and beholds his face. He tries to guide her to the Jeep but she slugs and kicks her way past him. Joshua and Dumars converge, badges flashing. Then Joshua is barking his Bureauspeak while he and Sharon defend their prey. Fargo joins in, helping them drag Valerie back to her vehicle. Her arm trails out, hand open and fingers stretched, reaching back toward her father. As they pass John, Valerie fixes him with an utterly comprehending stare and Fargo adds his own malevolent gaze. "We have a date now, friend," he says.

John stands there, watching them stuff Valerie back into her Jeep. The tablecloth skids across the gravel in the wind. The silver domes and china lie on the ground like old treasures. Susan Baum still sits at the table, silent, shivering and unseeing beneath the monumental bronzes of the Holt family.

Fargo drives the Jeep away.

You did your job.

A while later a helicopter descends toward Top of the World in a lazy spiral and three Bureau sedans trail their way up from the road below.

John is sitting on the stone bench next to Baum when the cars make the summit. Though he has an arm around her shaking body and though he mutters words of comfort to her, John feels nothing but darkness inside. And as he gazes out at the autumn splendor of Liberty Ridge, he sees nothing but darkness there, too.

FORTY-ONE

Late that afternoon he packed up his things and set them on the breakfast counter of the cottage. Not that he had much: his personal effects, the clothes that he and Valerie had bought, half a sack of dog food, his birdgun and a couple boxes of shells. He stood for a while in the little kitchen and looked out at the lake, watching his dogs in the water fighting over a ball. He slipped a shell into the shotgun, let the action snap shut and put on the safety, leaving it on the bar, pointed toward the door. He took the .45 from his coat pocket and set it on the bag of kibbles.

For the third time that day he walked across the meadow to the Big House. But for the first time, Lane Fargo was not there to turn him away at the door. He brushed his way past one of the cooks and walked down the tiled entryway, beneath the big timber beams, past the wrought iron candleholders and the oil paintings of the rancho days.

Valerie was in the living room, sitting before a small fire that flickered in the cavernous fireplace, a blanket wrapped around her shoulders and a cup of something on the rough-hewn table in front of her.

If she saw him come in, she didn't show it.

"May I?" he asked.

She looked at him for a long time, then nodded. He walked far around her and sat on a steerhide sofa on the other side of the table.

"Is there anything I can get you?"

She looked at him again, shook her head, then returned her gaze to the fire. "Mom doesn't comprehend. I tell her, but she doesn't get it. Says, 'oh, no—wait 'til Vanny hears.' "

John sat there for a long while, listening to the pop and hiss of burning wood. He watched Valerie in profile, her unblinking eyes vacantly attuned to the embers.

"Agent Dumars explained it to me," she said, without expression. "Who you are. What Dad did. I didn't understand why. I didn't understand why you did what you did to him."

"Did she tell you about the woman?"

"Jillian?"

"Rebecca."

"She didn't mention a Rebecca."

"She worked for the paper when I did. We were in love. She went to get Baum's car in the rain and your father shot her."

Valerie turned her head slowly to John. "It was your girl he killed, then."

"That's right."

"So you killed him."

"No. Joshua did. I thought . . . we wanted to arrest him. For Rebecca."

"Oh, it all makes sense," she said flatly, turning to the fire again. "All makes sense."

"I don't—" But John didn't finish the sentence. Instead he watched a shadow move way up on the stairway landing of the second floor, just a little motion between the bannister slats reflected on the wall from the fire. Then nothing moved at all. "I don't . . . I know you can't forgive me, ever. But I want to say a few things. Will you listen to me, for just a while?"

She shrugged beneath the blanket, but didn't look at him.

"First, I want you to know it wasn't supposed to happen the way it did. If I'd have known how it would end, I wouldn't have done it."

Valerie half-nodded, her chin lifting just a little, but never coming back down. "Not even for Rebecca?"

"No."

"Why. She was your reason."

"I never set out to get anybody killed. I . . . I worked awfully hard to make sure that wouldn't happen. I worked hard to make sure we had the right man and that they could arrest him. And I never set out to fall in love with you."

Then came the other half of Valerie's nod, a little downturn of her chin. She shivered and pulled the blanket tighter.

"It doesn't change anything," he said. "But I want you to know it."

No response.

"And I have to say this, hopeless as it is—I love you now and I'll do anything on earth for you. I want you whole again. I'm yours. I know you won't have me but that doesn't change the way I feel. I want you to know that before I go."

She looked at him again for a long while. He could see the fire reflected in her eyes. "There's no room left for you, John."

"I realize that."

"All I feel is hate."

John looked at her until she turned her face away again, back to the dying fire. He got up and threw on two more logs. While the wood caught he glanced up to the second story landing where the bannister shadows sharpened on the plaster wall.

"There's something you should know too, about your future here. When I was looking for evidence to arrest your father, someone on Liberty Ridge was helping me get it. Some of the help was subtle. Some of it was obvious. I thought Sexton, then I didn't."

"No," Valerie said dreamily. "Lane. So he could run Liberty Operations."

"Yeah." John looked up to the landing. He almost said something about who shot the video tape of Rebecca, then he told himself again that he'd never have to tell anyone that. "Fargo, you want to add anything?"

A faint shadow moved within the sharper ones of the railing posts and Lane Fargo looked around the edge of the wall against which he was sitting.

"Come down, Lane," said Valerie. "It doesn't matter. I'll shut down the Ops anyway. Never liked it."

Lane moved quietly down the stairs, easing into the living room like a ghost.

"Leave us alone," Valerie said. "Will you, please?"

"He's not telling you the truth, Valerie Anne. I can prove it, if you give me a chance."

"Later, maybe," she said.

Fargo's face was tightened to a smirk as he looked at John and headed out.

"Anything else, John?"

"One thing."

"You're sorry. You love me. Watch out for Lane. What else?"

"Just that I know your father was a good man. The world turned him and he went bad. He lost a lot for no reason and then he lost himself. I wouldn't have done any better in his place. What happened up there on Top of the World proves it. And I was trying to do the same thing he was. I was trying to get back something I'd lost. But I didn't get back anything at all. I just lost you. And your dad never came any closer to Pat. He just got what was coming to him for killing an innocent woman. He'd be the first to admit that. And I'll get what's coming to me, too. That's the way it should be. I'm not real smart. But I know now that hatred isn't enough to live on. It'll kill you and everybody around you. Don't live that way, Valerie. If you're lucky enough to find it, love can fill the emptiness. You've got every bit of mine if you ever need it. Ever."

She turned her head toward him again and John could see nothing in her face but the emptiness of infinite loss.

"Come here," she said.

He rose and walked over to her and put his hands very gently on either side of her head. Something hard clacked to the tile and John could see Val's revolver spinning to a stop. A big teardrop landed beside it. Then the storm hit and all she could do was cry. He held her. He had never thought a person could cry so hard for so long. It was much later when he finally left her asleep on the sofa. He made sure the blanket was snug around her and set three more logs in the fire before he walked out.

Fargo was standing in the driveway, leaning against the red Jeep. His arms were crossed, his right hand snugged under his armpit, inches away from the handle of his automatic.

"Clever guy," said Fargo.

"You're the clever one, Lane. You smelled me out from day one."

"Couldn't believe Mr. Holt didn't."

"That's what he got for trusting you."

"It bothers me that you know."

"It doesn't really matter that I know."

"Does, now that you squawked to Val."

"She's closing the Ops. Or didn't you hear?"

"She's emotional right now. She needs time to think."

"Then give her some. Anything unpleasant happens to her up here on Liberty Ridge, I might tell the man to have a talk with you."

"That won't be possible because you'll be dead."

John shook his head and looked out to the sunset gathering in the west. The sun was smearing a lot of red in the clear autumn sky, the same bright color as the Jeep behind Fargo, the same color as Holt's blood on the stone table.

"I'm not playing that one, Lane. I don't ever want to see a gun pointed at a man again. It just isn't right and there's no goddamned end to it. Haven't you learned a thing?"

"You've got to understand the situation. I got no boss now. I got no money out of my time building the Ops. I got no job. All I got is a dead master, a bad conscience and a lot of frustration built up. Something's gotta give."

"Well, do what you have to, but I'm walking down to the cottage to get my stuff. I'm packing that stuff in the truck. Then I'm getting in and driving away forever. Shoot me in the back if you want. It's all the satisfaction I can offer."

John started off down the drive. He could hear Fargo's boots pivoting behind him, and he could hear the quick whip of steel leaving leather.

"Turn *around*, mother*fuck*!"

John didn't break stride. He lifted a hand and waved, trotting down the embankment and into the meadow with his heart up in his throat.

The dogs charged as he got close to the cottage. Boomer crashed into him while Belle and Bonnie snarled at each other and wagged their tails. They were wet and dirty from the lake, oblivious to the bloodshed of the day. He let them into the cottage anyway and they sniffed around the floor as he picked his clothes off the kitchen counter. He looked through the window toward his truck, and set the clothes back where they were.

Through the meadow, constant as the northern star, Fargo marched toward him. John studied the wide-legged gait, the purposeful swing of the arms, the odd cant of the dark man's head and the automatic in his right hand. John's heart fell and rose again as a cold sheen of sweat broke out on his face.

He clicked off the safety on the birdgun, which was enough, as always, to send his dogs into a frenzy. They careened into the kitchen, sliding on the hardwood floor, yapping. *No bird*, John muttered, double-checking the safety and leaving the gun on the counter, pointed at the open doorway.

"No bird."

The dogs took off into the living room, noses down.

He stood where he was, behind the little chest-high bar, resting his finger on the trigger of the shotgun, not moving. He thought of Fargo shooting the video of Rebecca Harris while she took bullets in the winter rain.

Fargo hopped up the steps and into the cabin. It took him a second to find his target—going from sunlight to the shade. Maybe he was distracted by the dogs. But when he saw John standing there motionless in the kitchen he raised his gun quickly and John blew him back out the door, over the railing and onto the bed of sycamore leaves piled high by the wind.

The dogs raced outside. They leapt off the deck and charged past Fargo's body, looking for the quail. Then Boomer circled back and sniffed the dead man's face, twice, before backing away and looking up at John with a puzzled expression.

FORTY-TWO

It is a quiet restaurant off the tourist path in Laguna Beach, given to candlelight, mismatched flatware and locals. John, the nominal guest of honor, lifts his tequila glass to Joshua and Sharon, who face him from across the booth. Their proximity to each other surprises him.

It is five days after Liberty Ridge. Boomer, Bonnie and Belle are snug in the Laguna Canyon home, a place where John has spent many solitary hours in the last five days, trying to decide if he belongs there or not. He has been looking into rooms a lot, as if someone he cares about might be there, as if anyone ever really was. It feels good to return to a place that is, in some small way, his own.

"To the three of us," says Joshua.

They drink.

It is the second toast of the night, though dinner hasn't arrived yet. The first was to the three of them also, and John can see that Joshua's rum and coke has gone straight to his non-drinker's head.

"What was the worst of it?" asks Sharon.

"Snakey."

Snakey, of course, has been vigorously forgotten by everyone but John. Joshua revealed to Frazee what had happened to Snakey—one Peter Boardman, originally of Trenton, New Jersey—the day after the shooting of Holt, and Frazee managed to insert the official paperwork regarding his death after the fact.

The questionable circumstances of Snakey's arrival at the morgue have been tucked into the larger folds of Federal procedure, vagueness and clout. Snakey, it seems, had lived his life as a criminal, and his memory has been treated like one, too.

The food comes and they eat, but John cannot find his way into a celebratory mood. In fact, the dinner seems more an obligation than anything, a business meal with people you have spent too much of your life with as it is. Still, he describes his days on Liberty Ridge to a surprisingly curious Sharon and Josh. Tonight, the tequila offers an anaesthetic touch to his brain. He looks out the window to Coast Highway, slick with the first rain of the fall. Through the cracked window beside him he can smell the sweet aroma of rainwater and asphalt.

". . . So we're hiking across Liberty Ridge in the dark, on our way to the tombs, and Josh jumps every ten feet because of snakes. He made *me* crawl under the table to attach the microphones, because of bugs."

Sharon smiles and throws back her hair in a way John has never seen her do. He notices that if you traced the arc of Sharon's arm down from her shoulder you would find her hand resting on Joshua's thigh. Her high spirits surprise him, because he has learned that she and Josh shot almost simultaneously at Partch, both hitting him with fatal bullets. He was expecting a more subdued agent.

Joshua looks as he always looked, and just as John always pictured him during those feverish minutes when he was with his box of toys by the young oak tree, calling in: pale, hyperfocused, humorless. Even the alcohol can't dull Joshua's sharp edges, though it does unleash a little sentiment in him. John looks at his black eyes, his thick curly mop of hair, his big Adam's apple traveling up and down his throat. And oddly, he sees that Joshua is ashamed of something, embarrassed. It takes John a moment to realize why: Sharon. Not the woman herself, he knows—she's far too handsome and level and healthy for that—but the idea of a Sharon at all. Joshua, he sees, has finally embarked down the long path away from Rebecca and back into the world. John wonders if Dumars will be able to withstand the test that Joshua will put her through, as he judges whether or not she is worth the journey.

"Good luck," he says.

"With what, John?" Sharon asks.

"Everything."

They ask about Baum and he tells them. She has called him every day since it happened, with a truly transparent mixture of curiosity and sympathy. She simply cannot hear enough about John's time on Liberty Ridge. She is concerned, deeply, with his welfare. He can hear her computer keys clicking as they talk. Her five-part series about Vann Holt's death began just yesterday, and is set to run over the next week. Baum has asked him, confidentially, if he would be interested in consulting with the producer she has chosen, or possibly using her agent. She has also arranged for the *Journal* to begin publishing his "Sporting Life" columns again if he should wish to write them, with the caveat that the *Journal* actually knows not enough people in the country are interested enough in fishing, hunting and camping to justify the space. She explained that the cost of newsprint has gone up sixty percent in six months and Orange County now is, for better or for worse, an urban environment.

"So basically, my articles wouldn't be worth the paper they're printed on," John explains, "Though for me, the *Journal* was willing to waste the paper."

Joshua looks at him blankly and Sharon giggles. "What did you say?" she asks.

"I said yes."

Joshua describes his new status at the Bureau, a status borne of the fact that he came awfully close to an internal investigation for the shooting. In the end, he explains, it was easier to endorse him than to question him, and he's now up a pay grade, with a promotion pending. The fact that he was the agent who took down the once-great Holt has left him with admirers as well as detractors in the Bureau ranks. He explains to John that the ranks are split, of course, by age.

Joshua leans back and sighs, smiling. It still isn't much of a smile by joy standards, thinks John. For every angel at Joshua's side, there's a demon on the other.

Josh leans in close. "By the way, John. My ear inside the DA's office says they're not going to press the Fargo matter. Open-and-shut case of self-defense, is what they're thinking."

"Well, that's what it was."

The silence becomes uneasy. "Tell me, Joshua," John says, "When you had Holt in your sights, and he had his revolver aimed at my brains, what made you shoot?"

Joshua shook his head quickly, either needing no thought to answer, or unwilling to entertain thought. "The knowledge that he'd kill you if I didn't."

"And what if he had?"

"I no longer live in the world of what-ifs. Rebecca taught me that."

Johns thinks: Holt. Snakey. Baum. Cost of newsprint. Pay grades. Some guy named Frazee. Open-and-shut. What-ifs.

Who gives a shit? In the beginning there was Rebecca and now she can begin to fade from our memories. Is that all we were in it for?

"To Rebecca," says Josh.

John again remembers the night on the deck of his canyon house when Josh was drunk and convinced that he had loved her more than John ever could. He remembers conceding this point as a way of offering some small victory that Joshua seemed to need far more than he did. In the same spirit he reluctantly raises his glass and considers a toast that to him demeans her memory as much as anything else they might do.

"I can't say that now."

So he puts down his glass and walks out.

By the time he gets to the Canyon house it is raining, hard. John can't remember ever getting this much rain before Thanksgiving and wonders if a record winter is coming. Good for the quail, he thinks.

Inside he takes off his coat and hat and places them over the couch. He goes straight to his answering machine to check messages. He's gotten a total of nine calls since coming back here—five from Baum, three from Joshua and one stranger asking him to subscribe to the *Journal*.

The message light is on and he wonders if it is a call from Valerie.

He goes back outside and stands in the rain for a long while, letting it get down under his clothes and against his skin, all through his hair. It's softer than tap water, he thinks. Good stuff. The dogs slide around like seals on the wet grass. He thinks of Rebecca in the rain, and then he thinks of only the rain.

Back inside he plays the message. It isn't from Valerie, but someday, he knows, it could be.